EVGENIY

Titles available in this series

Yannis
Anna
Giovanni
Joseph
Christabelle
Saffron
Manolis
Cathy
Nicola
Vasi
Alecos
John
Tassos
Ronnie
Maria
Sofia
Babbis
Stelios
Kyriakos
Monika
Emmanuel
Theo
Phaedra
Evgeniy

Greek Translations

Anna

published by Livanis 2011

EVGENIY

Beryl Darby

ISBN 978-1-9997176-4-3

Printed and bound in the UK by
Print2Demand
1 Newlands Road, Westoning,
Bedfordshire MK45 5LD

First published in the UK in 2019 by

JACH Publishing
92 Upper North Street, Brighton, East Sussex, England BN1 3FJ

website: www.beryldarbybooks.com

Author's Note

At no time, as far as I am aware, have refugees of any nationality been smuggled into Crete. This is a product of my imagination for the purpose of the novel.

Prehistoric bones were found on the land down from the Salt Pans when properties were being constructed in that area. Having been excavated and studied they are now stored in the museum at Agios Nikolaos.

January 2015
Week One – Monday and Tuesday

Vasi answered his mobile 'phone, knowing that it was his father calling.

'What's wrong, Pappa?'

'Nothing. I wanted to know if you had looked at that house in Elounda that Monika mentioned.'

Vasi shook his head. He had completely forgotten. 'I'm sorry, Pappa, I've been rather busy with "The Imperia". I'll go down this afternoon and see if I can find out who owns it.'

'Ask if they are willing to sell.'

'You don't want to commit yourself to anything until you and Cathy have seen it. You could decide that it isn't suitable.'

'It may have to be.'

'What do you mean?'

'I have a prospective buyer for "The Central". If we come to an agreement he wants to buy the apartment in Heraklion as well.'

Vasi whistled through his teeth. 'Has he won the lottery like you did?'

Vasi heard his father chuckle. 'Not that I know of. He's a business man.'

'What business is he in?'

'Shipping.'

'You mean he has a fleet of ships?'

'I don't think so. He said he was a 'middle man' and arranged transport for goods being sent around the world. He's probably talking about shipping by air.'

'Is he Greek?'

'Partly.'

'What's the other part?' asked Vasi suspiciously.

'Russian.'

'Russian! Why are you thinking of selling to a Russian?'

'Now I've made up my mind to sell I want to do so as quickly as possible. "The Central" is a large hotel in a prime position. I want to sell it as a going concern and with the present state of the economy I don't think any Greek could afford it. The banks have clamped down on loans or else the interest rate is extortionate. This man has shown an interest and appears willing to pay me the asking price. He assures me he has the finance available. You go and look at that house. If you can gain access from the owner take Saffron with you and then drive up to Heraklion tomorrow. You can tell me if you think it will be suitable and Saffron can talk to Cathy. Arrange to stay over and you can also meet Mr Kuzmichov.'

Vasi ran a hand over his head. 'I'm opening "The Imperia" next week. I have stock arriving tomorrow. Couldn't I come up in a week or so?'

'I'm sure Yiorgo is capable of dealing with that. You said you plan to make him the manager. If Mr Kuzmichov is seriously interested I want to close this deal as quickly as possible.'

'Does Mr Kuzmichov speak Greek and have you consulted a lawyer? He may have the money available but will he be allowed to transfer it from Russia? There could be all sorts of international restrictions. You don't want to sign the hotel over to him and then find you cannot access the money. I'd like to meet him and discuss this further with you, Pappa, before you make a decision.'

'Then come up tomorrow. We will have the morning to iron out any problems you come up with. I'll arrange for my lawyer to come in the afternoon and I'm sure he'll know the legal position regarding money transfers. I already have an appointment with

Mr Kuzmichov for the following day so you can meet him and we can talk again after he leaves. I'm sure we can solve any of the problems you envisage between us.'

Vasi sighed. His father was not going to accept any excuses.

'Once you're satisfied that the sale to Mr Kuzmichov is feasible, and if you both think the house in Elounda is suitable for Cathy we can drive back with you and have a look for ourselves.'

'I suppose so.'

'You don't sound very happy about the arrangement.

'It will mean changing my plans and also asking Saffron to get the bedroom ready for you. Will Cathy be able to manage the stairs?'

'If she takes it slowly and I help her. Tell Saffron she only needs to make up the bed. We'll see you tomorrow.'

Vasi closed his 'phone and shook his head at Saffron. 'There are times when my father is impossible. I have to go and look at that house today, find the owner and then ask you to come with me to look inside. Then tomorrow he wants us to drive up to Heraklion and stay with them. He has a meeting arranged with his lawyer for the afternoon and the following day he wants me to meet a prospective buyer for "The Central".'

'Why does he want me to go with you?' asked Saffron.

'So you can talk to Cathy about the house in Elounda and he probably thinks you would be company for her whilst we are having business discussions.'

'I'm happy to spend some time with Cathy, but I wouldn't want to make a decision on her behalf about the house. She would need to see it for herself. I know Monika said the front door would be wide enough for a wheelchair but the other doorways inside could be too narrow; even a few centimetres could make access impossible.'

'That's the other thing. My father wants to return to Elounda with us so Cathy can see the house for herself. Are you able to get the bedroom ready for them? He says they'll stay over. I really could do without this. I've already advertised that "The Imperia" will be opening next week.'

'Stop stressing, Vasi. You know Yiorgo will deal with everything there. You contact the owner of that house and arrange when we can visit. Call me and I'll come straight down.'

Saffron went into the spare bedroom and looked around. All she needed to do was place some toiletries in the bathroom area, although knowing Cathy and Vasilis they would probably bring their own. She hoped Cathy would be able to cope with the stairs. They were too wide to allow anyone to hold the hand rails on each side. Provided Vasilis was able to help her and she did not attempt to go up or down alone she should be safe enough.

Before she returned down stairs she collected a small suitcase and placed toiletries, night clothes and clean underwear inside. She debated whether she needed to take a dress or would her usual trousers, blouse and jumper be suitable. She was not expecting to be meeting the Russian and she would prefer to be comfortable. Vasi would probably want a white shirt and a suit and she laid them on the bed, adding a choice of ties.

Her next job was to check the freezer and ensure that she had sufficient food. Although Vasi had said his father and Cathy only intended to stay over they could easily decide to extend their visit if the house they were interested in was suitable and it would not surprise her if Vasilis wanted to be there for the opening of "The Imperia". She would need to buy some fresh salad vegetables and bread on their return from Heraklion but there was plenty of fish and meat available.

Vasi turned into the side street that led to the house that Monika had thought might be suitable. To his surprise the area widened out and there was quite a large square bordered by houses, each with a small front garden. He parked at the end of the road, hoping he was not going to be accused of obstructing someone's parking space, and walked back down to the house. He peered through the dirty windows into the large empty room. He knocked on the door in the vain hope that there would be someone inside whose attention he could attract but there was no response. Frowning in annoyance at his wasted journey Vasi took a last look at the house and turned away.

'Can I help you?' asked a man as he rounded the corner.

'I was hoping to speak to the owner of the property and ask if it was for sale.'

'Giuseppe is in hospital. He knows he will not be able to return here when he is discharged. His original plan was to redecorate and rent out the apartment. The last I heard he was considering going to live with his sister and that may have changed his immediate plans.'

'Is he considering selling?'

The man shrugged. 'Maybe.'

'If he wants to sell I could be interested in buying. Are you able to contact him?'

'I can try.'

'Are there any other houses along here that the owners are planning to sell?'

'Not that I know of. Most of the occupants live here all year round.'

'Well, thank you for your time. Could I leave you my business card and if you are able to speak to the owner I would be grateful if you would call me.'

The man looked at the card. 'I thought you had that big house up on the hill.'

'I have, but my father and his wife want to move back down to Elounda. His wife is a semi-invalid and ideally she needs somewhere on level ground.'

The man slipped the card into his pocket. 'If I hear of anything I'll let you know.' He would call Giuseppe and ask if he was definitely going to sell the apartment and advise him that he had a man interested in making a purchase.

Vasi took out his mobile and 'phoned Saffron. 'I've spoken to a neighbour who says the owner is in hospital. Apparently he has mentioned selling and the neighbour is going to try to contact him and let me know. There's no point in you coming down as we cannot get inside.'

'So,' said Vasi, 'Where do we go next?' He asked as he sipped the coffee Saffron had placed before him.

'Why don't I drive around and see if there are any other apartments that could be suitable for Cathy?'

Vasi nodded. 'That would be a good idea. If you find anywhere that you think is ideal you could call me and I could come down and take a look. Even if you are unable to go inside it could be another possibility for my father to consider. Make sure you take the rule with you so you can measure the width of the entrance and make a note of any 'phone numbers.'

Saffron smiled to herself. If she found any premises that she considered suitable from the exterior she would try to inspect the interior before she contacted Vasi. There was no point in trying to drag Vasi away from "The Imperia" without a good reason and she knew he would want to make an early start to drive to Heraklion the following morning and not spend time viewing apartments.

'I need to call Yiorgo now and ask him to meet me at "The Imperia". He doesn't know that I am going up to Heraklion tomorrow so I'll need to make sure that he can be at "The Imperia" to receive deliveries and check that all the final jobs have been completed whilst I'm away.'

'I'm sure that will be no problem to him. You'll probably be there for the remainder of the day with him. If I find anywhere I think might be suitable I'll call you.'

'If you do find anything I can speak to my father tomorrow and give him my opinion and you talk to Cathy. We can always tell the owner that they want to look at it. That does not commit them to anything. I suppose I'll need to take a suit with me. It's as well to look presentable if I have to attend a business meeting.'

'I've put out your blue suit and a white shirt along with a selection of ties. I'll take a dress and shoes for myself, but I'll probably not need them.'

Saffron drove slowly down to the main square in Elounda. It was difficult to tell whether the various shops were temporarily closed for the winter or were not planning to trade during the coming season. She parked in the car park and walked to one of the three tavernas that were open. It could be worth her while speaking to the owners. They often knew of premises that were becoming available.

From her seat she could see the various shops that lined the main thoroughfare. They would certainly not be suitable for Cathy as each one had a small step up at the entrance and once the season commenced the narrow pavement would be cluttered with goods that the shops displayed outside and tourists forced to walk out in the road. There were a number of side roads that could be worth investigating. Even if there was a step up to the entrance it would be quite simple to make a wooden or concrete ramp.

'Kostas, do you know of any apartments that are for sale in this part of the town?' she asked as her coffee was placed before her.

Kostas shook his head. 'If you have an apartment down here you don't sell. Locals are always looking for somewhere to rent and the owner can make even more money from holiday lets. Are you thinking of moving from that big house where you live now?'

Saffron was not prepared to admit that she and Vasi were also looking for somewhere smaller. It did not do to tell one of the local people your plans. By the end of the day the whole village would be aware of your business.

'I've been asked to find somewhere suitable for a couple who used to live down here. They want to return to the area, but they also need somewhere that has wheelchair access and is close to the town.'

'There are various places that are to let. You might find something suitable in one of the side roads. There's always property available in Kato or Pano but you need to be able to negotiate the hill.'

'That would be out of the question, but thanks for your help. If you do happen to hear of anywhere would you let me know?'

'No problem. Have you looked in Plaka?'

'I think that would be a little far out for what they have in mind, but I can always have a look there.'

'Mr Giovanni would be the man to ask. The family own a number of properties down there. You rent your shop from them, don't you?'

Saffron nodded. 'I'll give Giovanni a call later when I've had a walk around here.'

Her coffee finished Saffron walked across the road and into the first side street. She immediately shook her head and returned to the main road. There were shops on each corner and then the road began to rise with only two houses on each side that would be suitable before the road became too steep to negotiate safely with a wheelchair. She could see Vasi's car parked further up the hill outside "The Imperia" with Yiorgo's scooter behind it.

Saffron spent the next two hours entering the side roads and walking along to the next intersection. The ground was level, but the houses were very small as they were the original village houses and probably inhabited by their owners. She finally reached the road where Vasi had tried to visit the apartment that morning. The houses here were larger, but they all looked occupied, curtains or blinds at the windows and cars parked outside.

With a sigh Saffron returned to the main street. There was only one more possibility and she walked up between closed premises. Blank walls greeted her with windows higher up making it obvious that access to any apartment was up a flight of stairs. At the end of the road she continued to her right knowing that she would end up close to a self catering establishment and opposite the church. The road behind the self catering premises was a delightful surprise. Small, but modern, two storey houses were on both sides, each with a small front area. Two appeared to be empty, but there was no notice in either window to say they were for rent.

Hesitantly she approached the first one and measured the doorway. It would be just about wide enough for Cathy's wheelchair and there were no steps. She measured the width of the door at the second house and it was the same. Feeling pleased, Saffron entered the name of the road onto her notepad. If Vasi thought the area suitable they could make enquiries regarding the owners later.

Saffron crossed over to the church and then walked past the small parade of shops, rounded the corner at the taverna at the end and looked at the houses opposite. There were three that looked quite large with gardens in front of them. She thought they were probably let as apartments although she could only see one entrance door. Unwilling to be asked why she was trespassing she did not open the gate and measure the front door. She would just make a note that they were there, although she was not sure that the location was ideal. There were tavernas and shops on each side of the road and an almost continual stream of traffic would make it noisy and the fumes could be unpleasant.

Taking the turning between the houses and the next parade of shops she saw there were a number of houses that appeared to meet Cathy's requirements and again she made a note of the street name. Feeling that she had done as much as possible she retraced her steps to the car park and climbed into her car. There was no reason to call Vasi and ask him to come down. She would tell him of her findings when he returned from "The Imperia" and provided it was not dark they could always drive down later for him to look.

'You're later than I expected,' observed Saffron when Vasi finally entered the house. 'Good job I decided to make a chicken casserole that could sit in the oven.'

'Various problems had to be agreed upon. I'm still not happy with the chef. He seems to think that he can cope unaided in the kitchen. I don't want customers kept waiting for their food. Bad service soon becomes known.'

'Forget "The Imperia" for this evening. Pour a glass of wine and I'll have our meal on the table within a few minutes. Then I'll tell you how I spent my afternoon.'

'Did you find anywhere suitable?' asked Vasi eagerly as he followed Saffron into the kitchen.

'Not really. I saw some possibilities that I'll tell you about and you can decide if you want to drive down and take a look tomorrow before we drive on to Heraklion.'

'Of course if this business deal with the Russian falls through all this will have been unnecessary.'

'Cathy still wants to return down here to live.'

'I've no argument with that, but these negotiations do not happen overnight. It could be some months before my father actually signs over "The Central" which would give them time to find somewhere suitable.'

'We also need to look for somewhere ourselves if you are still willing to go ahead with using this house for self catering holiday lets.'

'I need "The Imperia" to be successful and have my father and Cathy settled somewhere before I can think about that.'

Saffron nodded. Although she knew Vasi did not like living in the enormous house he had been given by his father, he was reluctant to turn it into self catering accommodation for summer visitors and live elsewhere in Elounda.

Saffron insisted that Vasi drove past the various properties she had noted the previous afternoon. At each one Vasi had shaken his head.

'That is a very pleasant road but there could be a considerable amount of noise from the self catering apartments during the summer.'

'We could ask the neighbours if they are disturbed by any noise.'

Vasi nodded non-committally and drove past the houses with the front gardens that were close to the street. 'I don't think they would like living here. It's impossible to drive down this road in the summer as there is continual traffic. Which other places did you see?'

'Only the houses that were in the same road as the apartment you looked at yesterday. They look like private houses, not apartments and all appear to be occupied.'

Vasi shrugged. 'You did your best yesterday. Property that suits Cathy will not be easy to find.'

Privately Saffron thought that Vasilis could also be difficult to satisfy. He was used to having fairly spacious rooms in a quiet street within a short distance of "The Central". There was nowhere quiet down in the centre of Elounda during the tourist season and many of the original houses consisted of no more than a large living room with a kitchen area at the back and a bathroom that had been added on outside in the yard. The older inhabitants were content to live in the same way as their parents and grandparents, whereas the younger population had refurbished an old property and made an acceptable small apartment for either themselves or for visitors.

Upon arriving in Heraklion they were greeted enthusiastically by Cathy and accepted her offer of coffee. 'I have a light lunch prepared as I know Vasilis needs to visit his lawyer this afternoon. Will you be going with him, Vasi?'

'If that's what Pappa wants. I'm waiting to hear more about this Russian and his proposals. It's possible the lawyer will advise against dealing with him.'

'It will be far better if both of us are there. Bring your coffee through to the lounge and I'll tell you exactly what Kuzmichov has proposed.'

'We'll stay in the kitchen,' Cathy smiled. 'I understand that you and Vasi have been looking for an apartment for us in Elounda. Have you had any success?'

'Not really. Yesterday morning Vasi visited the one that Monika had spotted that had a ramp up to the entrance door, but a neighbour said the owner was in hospital and not planning to return. Vasilis gave him his business card and the neighbour has said he would contact him if he was able to speak to the owner.'

'Did you look anywhere else?'

'I spent the afternoon wandering around Elounda, the side roads and those that run parallel behind the main street. I couldn't see any notices in any of the windows saying they were available to rent or for sale. There is one very pleasant road a short distance away from the church, but there is a self catering hotel close by. That could make an apartment very noisy in the season.

'The only other area that I thought might be a possibility were some houses just on the way out of Elounda towards Plaka. I showed them to Vasi this morning and he seemed to think it would be impractical to consider living there. The road is always congested with traffic.'

Cathy pulled a face. 'I think those houses can definitely be ruled out. If the neighbour Vasi spoke to contacts him and says the owner is willing to sell I'd like to look at that one. The road that you said was near the self catering apartments could be a possibility. After that I think Vasilis and I will just have to drive around and knock on doors.'

Vasi sat with his father in the lounge. 'Tell me more about this Russian. How did he find out the hotel was available to buy?'

'I had mentioned it to some of the other large hoteliers in the area. I hoped they might be willing to expand, but everyone is wary of investing at the moment. Kuzmichov contacted me and asked if we could have a business discussion. I invited him here as I don't really want all the staff at the hotel to know that I am contemplating a sale, but he declined. They might think their jobs are in jeopardy and begin to look for employment elsewhere. He said he was definitely interested in purchasing "The Central" and then he mentioned this apartment. He asked if I would be willing to sell to him if he purchased the hotel as he and his wife would need somewhere local to live.'

'So you haven't met him?'

Vasilis shook his head. 'Not yet. Our respective lawyers have been in touch as he was busy winding up one of his business interests in Russia.'

Vasi frowned. 'Is the sale of the hotel dependent upon him being able to purchase the apartment?'

'I'm not sure if it is dependent, but if he had to look for somewhere else to live he might consider withdrawing. It could take me a long time to find another buyer. I would be reluctant to take the chance. As Cathy has this desire to return to Elounda I am happy to sell the apartment to him now rather than leave it empty and have it on the market for a considerable amount of time.'

'Have you discussed this with your lawyer?'

'Not in any great detail. We have an appointment with him this afternoon. I asked him to find out whatever he could about Mr Kuzmichov and his financial position. I don't want to find I have signed away the hotel and I'm unable to get my hands on the money.' Vasilis ran his hand across his head. 'I feel ready for a quiet life without any business worries. Tell me, did you manage to visit the apartment you mentioned?'

Vasi nodded and proceeded to tell his father about the apartment where he had spoken to the neighbour. 'If you are interested in viewing it I can call him and arrange a meeting, but personally I think it would be a waste of your time. The owner is in hospital at present and could well reconsider letting or selling if he is well enough to return to his home.'

Vasilis shrugged. 'Even if this business deal falls through I would still like to find somewhere in Elounda where Cathy and I could live eventually. If we have to move from our apartment at short notice we can always live at the house for a while, although that is not what Cathy has in mind. I should never have built the house for the view. I should have realised the hill would become a problem.'

'The house served its purpose well. When my grandparents visited us it never seemed too large and they loved being there, but it is isolated from the village and far too big for just a couple to live in. If your hotel deal goes through are you willing to back me in making the house a self catering establishment? Technically you are still the owner and I would be unable to proceed without your agreement.'

'And where would you and Saffron live?'

'Saffron also wants to move down into the village area. In the winter there is no problem, but in the summer her journey home from Plaka can take well over an hour due to the tourists who are driving around.'

'Are you considering moving to Plaka?'

Vasi shook his head. 'That would be convenient for Saffron but not for me having to get to and from the hotel and into Aghios Nikolaos. Whilst we look for an apartment for you and Cathy we can keep an eye out for anything that would suit us.'

Vasilis and Vasi sat in the lawyer's office. Mr Antonides smiled benignly. Mr Iliopolakis was a wealthy man who never questioned the amount he was charged for advice and his latest request had been easy to fulfil.

'I have looked into Mr Kuzmichov's background and could not find any problem. His business accounts, as far as I was able to ascertain, appear scrupulously kept and his taxes paid on time. I think Russia could be more particular about prompt payment than we are.' Mr Antonides smiled thinly. 'He has the necessary permits to both import and export goods across the world, although he seems to favour the Middle Eastern countries with his business. I have checked with the bank and they confirm that there would be no problem transferring the funds to you provided you were willing to accept the transaction in American dollars for conversion to Euros at the rate of exchange on that day. There would obviously be a charge for the conversion.'

Vasilis frowned. 'I would expect any charge the bank made to be covered by the amount I received from Mr Kuzmichov.'

'That would have to be an agreement made between you and him. It could be advisable for you to have a meeting at the bank to ascertain the amount you could be expected to be charged for the transaction. Bear in mind that the rate of exchange can vary from day to day and even having a surcharge agreement could see you out of pocket.'

Vasi nodded. 'What about his private life? Anything unsavoury there?'

'Nothing. He has dual nationality, Russian and Greek. He has been married to the same woman for over thirty years. They have no children. There is no suspicion that he is keeping a mistress, although he is often away from his home for a considerable amount of time. He may, of course, have an arrangement whereby a companion is provided for him on occasions.'

Vasilis looked at his lawyer. 'So, in your opinion, provided we can reach an amicable agreement over the purchase price of "The Central" there is no reason why I should not proceed with the sale?'

'None at all.' Mr Antonides sat back with a benign smile.

'What about the sale of my apartment? I imagine that would also be paid in American dollars.'

'I would assume so. Have you a price in mind?'

'I will need to speak to him again regarding my apartment. If he wishes to purchase the furniture the price will obviously increase.' Vasilis sighed. 'I had hoped to sell the apartment separately at a later date.'

'You are under no obligation to sell the apartment to him.'

'Mr Kuzmichov made it quite clear when he spoke to me that if he bought the hotel he would want my apartment also. I just hope he was not expecting it to be included in my initial asking price for the hotel.'

Mr Antonides spread his hands. 'That again is something you will need to discuss with him. If you are not completely satisfied with the overall transaction arrangements you do not have to agree to them.'

'Having gone this far I would like to complete the sale as quickly as possible. I may have to make some concessions regarding the apartment as I would not want the sale of the hotel to fall through over the purchase of a few pieces of furniture.'

'When do you meet with Mr Kuzmichov?'

'Tomorrow. I will advise you of the outcome.'

'Quite. Where would you like me to send my interim bill?'

'To my apartment as usual, please. Thank you for your time.'

'No problem. It is always a pleasure to do business with you Mr Iliopolakis.' Mr Antonides shook hands with Vasilis and Vasi as he showed them out.

'So are you satisfied?' asked Vasi of his father after they left the lawyers' office.

'I'm satisfied with all Mr Antonides told me, but I obviously need to get some legal papers drawn up regarding the money transfer. I'm not prepared to pay an enormous amount to the bank for converting dollars into Euros. We deal in Euros over here so Mr Kuzmichov should be liable for conversion charges.'

'I agree. You need to make that quite clear to him.'

'He'll probably want to divide the charge between us,' remarked Vasilis morosely.

'Then stand your ground. If he wants the hotel and apartment that badly he'll be willing to pay.'

Vasilis shook his head. 'I don't want to fall out with him so I lose the sale.'

'What's he like?'

'Seemed pleasant enough when we spoke.'

'I meant what does he look like. How old is he?'

Vasilis wrinkled his brow. 'I'm not sure. I've not met him. He has either spoken to me on the telephone or sent questions through his lawyers.'

'Are you intending to wear a suit tomorrow? I asked Saffron to put one in for me.'

Vasilis nodded. 'I think we should. It looks more professional and we're meeting in my office at "The Central" at eleven. Before then I'd like you to help me put some figures on the computer that I can show Mr Kuzmichov. He is bound to want to know our annual turnover.'

'If the man is an astute business man he should already have investigated and have a pretty good idea of your profit margin. I think you should also enumerate the number of employees and their overall wages, along with the utility expenses and general repairs. I'll call Dimitra and ask her to send over copies of all her disks and I'll be able to work out some reasonable figures.'

January 2015
Week One – Wednesday

Cathy kissed Vasilis. 'That's to wish you good luck,' she smiled. 'I haven't put my make-up on yet so I won't have left any tell tale marks on your shirt.'

'I may have to ask Mr Kuzmichov to come back to the apartment later. I'll telephone you to give you a few minutes warning.'

'That's no problem. Saffie and I will make sure everywhere is spotless in case he wants to look around again. We can easily hold lunch back and invite him to stay if you wish. There's bound to be enough. I'll be looking presentable by the time you return.'

'You always look presentable,' Vasilis assured her. 'There's no need for you to dress up as if we were expecting him.' He looked at his watch. 'We ought to go, Vasi. I don't want him arriving before us.'

Vasilis and his son were sitting in the office when the hotel manager tapped discreetly on the door and told them that Mr Kuzmichov had arrived.

'Please show him in and then wait whilst we ask if he would like anything to drink.'

The manager nodded and held the door open wider to allow the Russian to enter. Vasilis and Vasi tried to hide their surprise. They had expected Mr Kuzmichov to be smartly dressed in a suit similar to their attire, but when he removed his jacket they saw he was wearing a pair of ordinary blue trousers and a checked shirt. His hair varied between white and grey and was tied back in a short pony tail. He had at least a three day growth of facial hair that was also partly grey and white. His shrewd blue eyes roamed around the office appreciatively, but he declined the offer of anything to drink other than the water that was already on the desk.

Vasilis waited until the manager had closed the door. 'This is my son, Vasi. He is also my business partner and is aware that you are interested in purchasing "The Central".'

Mr Kuzmichov shook Vasi's hand. 'Please, call me Evgeniy. Although we will be discussing business it is far more friendly if we do so on first name terms.' He looked at Vasilis. 'You say your son is also your partner. Does that mean that he has to agree to the sale of "The Central" before it can go ahead?'

'I would consider any advice he gave me, but the final decision would be mine alone. At one time I signed this hotel over to my son and he became the owner and manager. At a later date he signed it back to me and I handed over control of the hotels that I owned lower down the island to him.'

Mr Kuzmichov nodded. 'I like to know who I am negotiating with.'

'Naturally. I took the precaution of consulting my lawyer yesterday. I wanted an assurance that you were in a financial position to be able to pay the purchase price.'

'He gave you a positive answer I trust.'

Vasilis nodded. 'I was expecting any financial transaction to take place in Euros, but he said you would want to pay in American dollars. That makes things a little more complicated.'

'Not as complicated as if I said I wanted to pay in Russian roubles,' smiled Evgeniy. 'Most of my business is conducted using American dollars. It is a useful international currency. Many of the countries in the Middle East that I deal with would be quite unable to transfer large sums of money in their local currency out of their homeland. There are strict regulations to prevent money laundering, counterfeiting and fraud. Dealing in the American dollar is acceptable to those countries.'

'What exactly is your business, Mr Kuzmichov?' asked Vasi.

'Evgeniy, please. You want it, I supply it. Let us say you are in the business of assembling and selling refrigerators. You need the cooling system. I will search for the company offering them at the most reasonable price, calculate the cost of the shipment to your nearest port and advise you of the total cost.' Mr Kuzmichov sat back with a satisfied smile on his face.

'Apart from refrigerator parts what other items do you supply?'

'I only used refrigerators as an example. Anything a manufacturer wants I am usually able to obtain at a good price. I am known to be reliable. If I say I will ship tomorrow and you will receive the goods in a week I am usually able to keep to that schedule, provided the weather at sea is not unduly bad so that a delay is caused.'

'If you are so successful with your shipping business why are you now interested in this hotel?'

'Shall we say it is an old man's whim? I am planning to gradually wind down my import and export business over the next few years. Although I employ I am still in overall charge and it is time consuming and often stressful when arrangements have to be changed at the last minute. My wife has been very patient and deserves to have more permanent company than I have given her in the past. I would be very bored sitting at home doing nothing, but this hotel would give me another interest and my wife would be able to stay in Heraklion with me. I stayed here for a few days last year and I was impressed. The rooms are comfortable, the service is excellent and the staff are friendly. I then heard that you were considering selling and I thought I would make you an offer before a consortium stepped in and added your hotel to their list of assets and made it look the same as all their others. It never hurts to expand your business interests.'

'Have you ever run a hotel before?' asked Vasilis.

'No. It would be a new challenge for me. I hope your current staff will be willing to stay on and help me to find my feet. I am a quick learner. I would also appreciate your help, Vasilis. Are you able to give me the number of staff who work here, their wages and the number of visitors you expect each year?'

'I will need to look on my computer. Give me a moment. Vasi, you are the expert.'

Vasi turned the computer screen towards Mr Kuzmichov. 'This is the total number of employees as at today's date. During the height of the season we sometimes employ more chambermaids and cleaners on a temporary basis. The staff are obviously paid according to their responsibilities.' Vasi pointed to the amounts listed on the screen. 'You can see that the rate of pay depends upon the amount of responsibility the job entails. The manager is the most highly paid, followed by the assistant managers and the receptionists. The chefs receive the same amount as the assistant managers, the bar tenders earn the same as the receptionists, followed by the waiters and general kitchen staff who are on a lower scale and of course the chambermaids and cleaners are paid less.'

'May I make a note of this?'

'Certainly.' Vasi waited whilst the Russian copied down the figures.

'Before we continue may I ask why you have four assistant managers, three chefs and three bar tenders?'

'Each assistant manager is in charge of the bookings for a single floor. If all his rooms are full then he would pass the request to one of the other assistants. As some visitors arrive late at night or in the early hours they do not wish to be kept waiting before being shown to their room. There is a rota system whereby there are always two assistant managers working between eleven at night and seven in the morning along with a receptionist. During the day there are two assistant managers and four receptionists on duty along with the overall manager.'

Evgeniy Kuzmichov made a further note. 'And the need for three chefs, three bar tenders and a housekeeper?'

'The breakfast hours have to be covered by the kitchen, along with the lunch time and evening service. Breakfast is served between seven and ten. Once that is completed the chef will meet with the dining room manager and confirm that the menu that was agreed the previous week will be available, along with suitable meals for those who have an allergy of any sort. The kitchen staff are then able to have a half an hour break before commencing on the preparations for lunch. Lunch is available from twelve until three. The kitchen staff will then leave and the new rota will arrive at five thirty ready to prepare the evening meal. The evening meal is available from seven until ten. The dining room manager is responsible for arranging the rota for the waiters to ensure there are always sufficient staff on hand to provide an efficient service.

'The bar opens at ten each morning and stays open until the early hours. The men need to have regular breaks without interrupting the service the guests expect. The manager is in charge of organising the work rotas to ensure that the relevant staff have the opportunity to receive the same pay as each other. He receives an account of the stock each week and will place an order with the off licence as necessary.'

'If an employee does not work for any reason do they still receive their pay?'

'Provided they are absent for genuine sickness they receive full pay for a week and then it is gradually reduced depending upon the length of time they are unable to work.'

'And the person who is listed as the Housekeeper? What exactly are her duties?'

'She is in charge of the rota for the chambermaids and cleaners. Should a chambermaid find any damage in a bedroom or a faulty tap or shower be reported to her she would advise the housekeeper who would be responsible for rectifying the problem. Likewise if new towels or bedding are required the housekeeper will request the manager to place an order. She also checks that if one hundred sheets are recorded as going to the laundry then one hundred are returned. All the bedding and towels have the word "Central" machine embroidered so there is no reason why they should not all be returned to us.'

'How often do you send the laundry?'

'The beds and towels are changed every day. Each floor has its own sack and the number deposited inside recorded by the chambermaids. Each week the laundry presents an invoice and provided there are no discrepancies it is paid immediately. I also pay the baker and green grocer on a weekly basis. Groceries are paid for monthly.'

Evgeniy Kuzmichov continued to question the staff payment structure and their duties for a few more minutes and then turned his attention to the overall expenses that were listed. 'I see that you allow rather a large amount for repairs and renewals. Is such a figure necessary?'

'I like to know that I have sufficient money available should the air conditioning or lift break down. Each year I redecorate a number of bedrooms and renew any items that I consider to be sub standard, like carpets, mattresses, curtains and blinds. If there are funds left over at the end of the year I roll them forward to cover the cost of external redecoration and repairs in the following year.'

'Would you have a breakdown of the expenses that you have incurred over the previous two years?'

'I can arrange for you to receive a copy. I do not have the figures on this computer.'

'I see that during the off season you also cater for conferences that take place in Heraklion. The delegates stay here?'

'Some prefer to stay elsewhere, but most of them appreciate being on the premises.'

'Where do these conferences take place? I would not have thought the lounge was an ideal location.'

'On the top floor there are two large rooms with a dividing door. Depending upon the number of people who book to attend we can either accommodate two separate conferences or open the dividing doors and make a far larger area.'

'And these conferences are profitable?'

'Definitely. The organiser is charged a sum for the room and the refreshments provided. If those attending wish to stay in the hotel they are charged the same rate as all the other paying guests and any meals they take in the dining room are extra, of course. My manager would be able to help you further regarding the booking system for the guests and the conferences.'

'You appear to have very little to do with the running of your hotel. How do you know that you are not being exploited by your staff?'

Vasilis smiled. 'I do call in at the hotel unexpectedly two or three days each week and if necessary ask to look at the current computer programme. Each day the assistant managers send details of the rooms they have booked and those that have been vacated to Dimitra. She will check these against those from the previous day and query any discrepancy. Likewise the chef will send her copies of his orders from the local suppliers. If she should see that five hundred kilos of sausages have been ordered she would immediately ask the chef the reason. In that eventuality it is usually a typing error and it would be rectified. All the staff rotas also go to Dimitra to be checked and when she is satisfied that all is in order she then sends a copy of everything to me which I also check. If the manager thinks there is a problem he will send me a confidential report and I will come in to discuss the situation with him.'

'There is one thing I do not understand. Who is this Dimitra person?'

Vasi looked at his father who nodded. 'Dimitra was instrumental originally in setting up the computer system. Unfortunately she suffered a serious assault whilst in her own apartment and was badly injured. When she was discharged from the hospital she did not have the confidence to return to her apartment or live alone. It was arranged that she could have a bed sitting room on the top floor of the hotel with a separate office. From her salary most of the cost of living at the hotel is deducted. I am pleased to say that she is improving and her confidence is gradually returning.'

'This person is necessary? You are not just employing her because you feel sorry for her?'

'Not at all. If she lived elsewhere we would still ask her to work here. She is most efficient.'

Vasi did not add that it was due to Dimitra's friendship with Alecos that funds from "The Central" had been diverted. Having her work at the hotel was the most efficient way of monitoring her actions, making sure she had no access to the accounts and ensuring that such a thing did not happen in the future.

Vasi decided it would be diplomatic to change the subject. He would need to speak to Dimitra if the Russian did purchase the hotel.

'A certain number of vacancies amongst the staff occur each year,' observed Vasilis. 'When that happens would you continue to employ local people or be bringing in Russian workers?'

'That is a good question. Your manager and receptionists all speak a variety of languages. I do not think Russian is amongst them. If I could find a linguist that was also an accomplished Russian speaker it could be practical to add them to the list of employees if a vacancy arose. Russian people who have the money available to travel find all parts of Greece an attractive destination.'

Vasilis and Vasi looked at each other and nodded. The idea made sense.

'Likewise a good bar tender needs to know his drinks and how to prepare cocktails to a customer's satisfaction. He does not need to be able to hold a conversation. The same with the chef;

31

his culinary expertise is his most important asset. I would have no hesitation in employing local people for the more mundane jobs, but for those that need more than a modicum of knowledge I would advertise and the most successful applicant would be offered the position, regardless of his nationality.'

'Do you have any applicants in mind for the work you mention?'

Mr Kuzmichov shook his head. 'I am certainly not going to sack all the staff and replace them with Russians. I hope, provided I become the owner, that the staff will be happy working with me. I feel sure the only change they will notice will be the name of the owner on the headed notepaper.' He poured himself a glass of water. He was sure he had answered all their questions satisfactorily.

'There is one more thing. There must be a good deal of money on the premises each week and that would need to be taken to the bank. Who is responsible for that?'

'Very few people pay their bill in cash. Most transactions are done by credit card. Meals and drinks are added to their account by the room number they give. These payments go directly into the bank account. There is rarely more than two or three hundred Euros actually on the premises.'

'And you use the internet system of banking to pay your bills?'

'As soon as I have checked that the amount requested is correct I transfer the money to the local suppliers each week. I pay the utility and telephone bills along with the other staff wages, except for the chambermaids and cleaners, through the bank each month. The chambermaids and cleaners are paid in cash each week. I am sure you are familiar with the system.'

Evgeniy nodded. 'Now I would like to ask you a personal question. May I ask the salary that you draw each year?'

Vasilis smiled. 'That varies. I do not pay myself a set amount. At the end of the year I take into account the money that has come into the hotel and deduct any outstanding expenses. I then draw sufficient to pay my accountant and from the remaining balance pay myself fifty per cent. The remainder usually has to be paid to the tax man.'

'Yes, the dreaded tax man.' Mr Kuzmichov shook his head sadly.

'That does bring us to another small dilemma. You wish to use American dollars for the purchase and for me to have access to the funds they will need to be converted into Euros. There will be a charge for this and I am unwilling to pay the amount. I would prefer you to effect the conversion and then transfer the full amount to me in Euros.'

Evgeniy shrugged. 'If you wish, but I suggest before you make a final decision you check how much tax you will be expected to pay for the sale of the property. A charge against the dollar conversion could be to your advantage in reducing that amount.'

Vasilis and Vasi exchanged glances. 'I'll need to speak to my accountant,' said Vasilis.

'Are you still wishing to purchase my father's apartment?' asked Vasi.

'Certainly. I know I have not visited and seen it yet, but I do not have time to spend going around trying to find suitable accommodation and I cannot expect my wife to live in the hotel. I do not wish to live with my work either. It is far better to return to my own home at the end of the day. Obviously I would like to view it properly before I make a decision if that can be arranged.'

'You could return there with us when our meeting here has been concluded,' offered Vasilis. 'My wife and Vasi's partner are there and you would be welcome to stay and have a light lunch with us.'

'That is most kind and I will certainly take you up on your offer provided it is of no inconvenience. May I bring my wife?'

'Of course.'

'I have to warn you that she does not speak Greek or English, so you will have to excuse us if we carry on a conversation in our own language.'

33

Vasilis smiled. 'Both my wife and Vasi's partner speak only English and very little Greek.'

'That would be no problem to me. I speak many languages. It has become a necessity when dealing with business men from different countries. If it is no imposition I will collect my wife from our hotel and meet you at your apartment shortly.'

'You are not staying here?' asked Vasilis.

Evgeniy shook his head. 'I did not want to draw any attention to myself. I thought it better to stay elsewhere. The staff would be curious if they saw a guest meeting with the owner and speculation and rumours could abound. If our negotiations are unsuccessful they will be none the wiser. Provided you are satisfied with my credentials and my accountant is satisfied with the figures you have given me I see no reason why our respective lawyers should not draw up contracts immediately and our transaction completed by the end of March. Then will be the time for me to be introduced to your staff.'

Mr Kuzmichov rose. 'Thank you for your time and answering my questions. If more should occur to me I hope you will not mind me troubling you again?'

'Not at all. We will return to my apartment now and see you and your wife in a short while.'

'So what did you think of him?' Vasilis asked his son.

Vasi wrinkled his nose. 'I can't say I liked him, but it is a business arrangement and once he has bought the hotel we neither of us need to have anything more to do with him. I was expecting him to be better dressed.'

'Maybe he prefers to dress down or they may not have any decent suits in Russia.'

Vasi looked at his father scornfully. 'Putin is always smartly dressed. If Kuzmichov is as wealthy as he suggests I would have thought he could have afforded the same tailor.'

'I hope the staff will be happy working for him. He would be able to find replacements easily enough, but the older employees could have difficulty in finding work.'

'All the more reason for them to stay. You don't have to like your boss provided he treats you decently. I'll 'phone Saffie and say we are on our way and the Kuzmichovs will be joining us. I hope they haven't waited lunch for us. Do you realise we spent almost five hours with the man?'

Vasilis shrugged. 'It would probably have been a better idea to invite him to visit us about six after he and his wife had had some lunch.'

'That could have meant that they stayed all evening. We have an appointment at six thirty.'

'Do we? Who with?'

Vasi smiled at his father. 'I'm sure I can come up with a name. I had hoped we might be able to return to Elounda this afternoon but it would be more practical to wait until tomorrow and drive down then; less tiring for Cathy.'

Vasilis nodded in agreement. He did not relish the thought of driving down to Elounda that night.

'Saffie, we have just concluded our meeting with Mr Kuzmichov. He has gone to collect his wife and has accepted the invitation to come to the apartment so his wife can have a look and also have a light lunch.'

'Haven't you eaten yet? Cathy and I thought you must have eaten at the hotel. We had our meal ages ago. I'll get everything out of the fridge so that it is ready for when they arrive. I'm sure Cathy and I can sit and nibble at things just to be polite. What is his wife like? Have you met her?'

'Not yet, but however charming she may be we really do not want them to stay any longer than necessary. If they appear to be expecting to stay for the evening we have an appointment at six thirty.'

'Where?'

'Anywhere; a friend's birthday, a Christening, Wedding reception. Any excuse. Warn Cathy.'

Mr Kuzmichov handed his wife out of the car. She stood and looked around whilst waiting for her husband to take her arm. 'How do you want me to behave?' she asked.

'Badly; we do not want them to like us and think they are friends who can drop by at any time. I've told them you only speak Russian.'

'I wouldn't have thought it cold enough for her to need to wear a fur coat,' remarked Cathy.

'Probably done for show. Can't say the same for Evgeniy. He appears to have dressed down. I felt quite self conscious wearing a suit and tie. I'll let them in. By the way, Mrs K only speaks Russian,' and grinned at the look of dismay on Cathy's face.

Vasi helped Mrs Kuzmichov off with her coat, placing it carefully on a hanger before taking it into the spare bedroom and hanging it up in the wardrobe. He ushered the stocky, dark haired woman through to their living room, noting that she was as casually dressed as her husband in jeans and a blouse. It crossed his mind that before any agreement was concluded between them and his father the financial situation of the Kuzmichov's should be checked out again. Evgeniy did not look like a wealthy man, and his credentials could well have been falsified.

'This is my wife, Ludmila.' Evgeniy announced and she nodded briefly.

'Please, have a seat,' Vasi indicated the chairs. 'I will just check that everything is in readiness for our meal.'

He hurried through to the kitchen and beckoned Cathy and Saffron over to him and spoke very quietly.

'Just to warn you, Mrs K is nothing like I had expected.'

'What had you expected, Vasi?'

'A tall, athletic looking, attractive blonde.'

'And?'

'She's small and dark and could do with losing a few kilos.'

He raised his voice. 'Is there anything you would like me to take through for you?'

Saffron and Cathy exchanged glances. They had noticed the jeans and blouse that Ludmila was wearing and were pleased they had not made any effort to dress up.

'No, all is ready. The cheese pies have just come out of the oven and everything else can be served cold. I'll just bring in a jug of water.'

Ludmila Kuzmichov sat hunched in her chair helping herself to the various dishes that were on the table. Evgeniy was attentive to his wife, passing her plates and complimenting Cathy on her behalf for the food she had prepared. Cathy and Saffron hoped their lack of appetite would not be noticed and were pleased when they both saw that Vasi and Vasilis appeared ravenous and quite capable of clearing the plates along with their guests.

'I'll clear the table whilst you show Mr and Mrs Kuzmichov around, Cathy.'

Vasi looked at his watch. 'Goodness, is that the time already?'

Evgeniy looked at his watch. 'It is only five thirty.'

'We spent far longer talking at the hotel that I realised. No problem, I can always phone Yiorgo and Barbara and say we will be a little late.'

'You are going out?' Evgeniy frowned.

'Yes, but we do not have to be there for an hour or so. Plenty of time for you and your wife to look around the apartment. It is not that large.'

'I'll have some coffee ready for you before you leave.'

'We do not wish to be of any inconvenience to you.'

'Not at all. You can always come again and look around more thoroughly. If you decide to buy the apartment you would most likely want to come in and measure to ensure that your furniture fits.'

'As I am planning to purchase the apartment I will expect to buy the furniture that is here now,' said Evgeniy firmly, waving his hand around the room. 'I will not have time to go around choosing furniture with my wife. If my wife is happy with all she sees today then the deal can be agreed.'

'There are ornaments and pictures that are of a personal and sentimental value that I would not be willing to sell to anyone,' said Cathy firmly.

Mr Kuzmichov raised his eyebrows. 'There is no space for sentiment in business.'

'Not in your business, maybe, but I insist that we keep whatever we want in the way of decorative or sentimental items. Why would you want a photograph of my father or the collection of books that he wrote?'

'No doubt I will be able to find something to occupy the space they leave.' Mr Kuzmichov glared at Cathy and rose from the table. 'If you would be good enough to show us the other rooms, then we will need to delay you no longer.'

Cathy took her stick and led the way to the bedroom she and Vasilis shared. 'This is our bedroom with a bathroom en suite.'

Cathy stood there in amazement as Mrs Kuzmichov began to open the drawers and wardrobes, handling the contents, riffling through her underwear and sniffing at everything. It would never have occurred to her to do such a thing. The woman ran her finger along the window sill and then inspected it for dust. Finally appearing to be satisfied Mrs Kuzmichov said something unintelligible to her husband and he nodded.

'My wife thinks there will be sufficient space for her clothes and there doesn't appear to be any damp. Is the other bedroom any larger?'

Cathy shook her head. 'It is really only for guests and the bathroom is next door. Vasi and Saffron are using the room whilst they are staying with us.'

Mrs Kuzmichov gave the room a cursory glance and again opened the drawers and wardrobes, pleased to see that her coat had been hung carefully in an empty wardrobe and the other contained only a few items that belonged to Vasi and Saffron, along with bedding and towels stored on the shelves. She spoke again to her husband.

'Ludmila says that if there is insufficient space in the master bedroom for all her possessions she can store some of her clothes and shoes in here. We are very unlikely to have any visitors.'

'I am intending to take the bedding and towels with me as I am sure you would prefer to have new ones,' said Cathy firmly. 'You have seen the dining room so there is only the lounge and kitchen to see. We will go into the kitchen first and I will ask Saffie to take the coffee through to the lounge.'

Again Mrs Kuzmichov opened cupboards and pulled out drawers, looking at the make of the various appliances and shaking her head as she read the maker's logo on them.

'I will also want to take my electrical appliances. It would probably be more practical for you to purchase new ones. I have had these a considerable amount of time and I would be embarrassed if you bought them and then they stopped working after a few weeks.'

Mr Kuzmichov nodded. 'Yes, they do look old and cheap.'

Cathy opened her mouth to say they were the top of the range and then changed her mind. They might not be the latest models but they all worked perfectly.

'What else are proposing to take with you?'

'The cutlery, that was a wedding present from my father. I will also want my pots and pans, china and glassware.'

Mrs Kuzmichov frowned, drawing her dark eyebrows together and opened her mouth as if to make a comment and then changed her mind as her husband looked at her.

'It sounds as though we will have to re-equip the kitchen completely along with new bedding. I had expected to be able to move in with everything in place as it is now.'

'I don't plan to take the fridge, freezer, dish washer, washing machine, oven or hob. The other items are relatively inexpensive to replace.' Cathy set her mouth in a determined line. 'If you had not requested that we leave the furniture we would have emptied the apartment completely when we left.'

'If any of the items you leave cease to function within the first two months of my occupancy I would expect a refund. Why is this high stool cluttering up the kitchen, can it not go elsewhere?'

'I use it to sit on when I am working in the kitchen,' explained Cathy. 'I have difficulty in standing for any length of time.'

'Then that is something you could certainly take to your new home. We will have no need for that.'

'I will be only too pleased to do so,' replied Cathy frostily. 'From the kitchen you have access to the small patio at the back. In the summer we often sit out there for a meal or just a glass of wine during the evening.' Cathy switched on the light that floodlit the area. 'The chairs and table that we use out there we will leave, of course, along with the sun umbrella.'

'Quite pleasant,' remarked Mr Kuzmichov. 'Now, the coffee and then we will leave you.'

Cathy led the way through to the lounge where Saffron carried through a tray of coffee. Mrs Kuzmichov prodded the seat of the armchair before she sat down and then pummelled the arms with her hands.

Mr Kuzmichov spoke to his wife who nodded and replied. 'My wife says the chairs are reasonably comfortable. You are not planning to take those with you, I hope.'

Cathy shook her head. 'It would not be practical. They could be too large for the apartment we eventually move into.'

'I would like a complete itinerary of the items you are leaving behind. I would also like to know how quickly you can move out.'

'That is no problem,' Vasilis assured him. 'It is more practical for us to stay here at present, but once you become the owner we can move immediately and stay with my son until we find a suitable apartment. I am sure we could agree on a date that suits both of us.'

'How soon can I expect to receive the itinerary of the goods that are to be included in the price?'

'I am sure I could provide that for you within the next two to three weeks.'

Mr Kuzmichov frowned. 'Why so long?'

'I have other commitments and there is no immediate rush. Knowing how speedily lawyers work I cannot see the final transaction being completed for at least another month, possibly longer.'

'Time is of the essence for me. I will expect to be the owner of "The Central" and this apartment by the beginning of March. I will insist on a penalty clause should the time over run.'

Vasilis shrugged. It did not matter what Mr Kuzmichov threatened about penalty clauses that would be in the hands of the lawyers to sort out. 'I will make that known to my lawyers and I am sure they will do their best to oblige.'

Mr Kuzmichov spoke to his wife and she handed him her empty coffee cup which he placed on the tray. Ludmila took her husband's hand and rose easily from the armchair. Vasi collected her fur coat from the wardrobe and held it whilst she thrust her arms inside.

'It has been a pleasure to meet you,' smiled Saffie and Mrs Kuzmichov said a word that Saffie did not understand. Evgeniy smirked and Saffron had an idea that the word had not been complimentary.

'I will be in touch as soon as our lawyers have completed the contracts for the hotel and the apartment,' Mr Kuzmichov assured Vasilis. 'If I have any queries I will call you. I have your mobile number.'

Vasilis nodded. He hoped the man would not call at an unreasonable hour. 'I look forward to hearing that everything has been completed without any problems arising and we can make a date to sign our respective contracts.'

'What a horrible couple,' remarked Cathy as Vasilis returned to the lounge. 'They're not a bit like I expected.'

'I was surprised when he turned up looking like a tourist rather than a business man. Vasi and I felt very over dressed.'

'I do wish you were not selling the apartment to them. I have a feeling that nothing here will ever be good enough for them.'

'When I make up the itinerary I will give the approximate age of everything and the current condition. Vasi probably has the original receipts for the kitchen items from when he had them installed.'

Cathy shook her head. 'I don't think it would be a good idea to give him those. He would know exactly how old they all were and would probably claim they were outdated. Everything is working perfectly at the moment.'

'I will insist that if they find anything unsatisfactory they have to prove that the fault was there when they purchased and also that they only have two months in which to make a claim.'

'Have we got any large boxes around, Vasilis?' asked Cathy.

'No, why?'

'I think it would be a good idea to commence packing some of our personal possessions and removing them to Elounda tomorrow. I do not want that woman pawing through any more of my belongings. She actually took my underwear from the drawers and sniffed at it. I felt quite violated.' Cathy shuddered. 'I wouldn't dream of putting used underwear back into the drawers.'

'She sniffed at it? Why would she sniff at your clean underwear?' asked Saffie.

'Her husband implied that she was checking whether there was any damp in the drawers or wardrobes. She didn't even ask if she could open them and look inside. So rude.'

'Maybe it is customary to do that in Russia,' suggested Vasi.

Cathy shook her head. 'I found out that Greek people tend to be inquisitive, but I have never known them to open a cupboard and inspect anyone's clothes. They would be more interested in where we bought the cupboard and how much it cost.'

'And then they would tell us where we could have bought it more cheaply,' grinned Vasi. 'Why don't you pack up your summer clothes into a spare suitcase and we can certainly take those down tomorrow and store them for you.'

'I don't think she would be interested in keeping them. She's at least three sizes larger than me.'

'Three!,' scoffed Saffie. 'More like six.'

'It's my photographs and the letters I have from my father and Rebecca that I don't want her going through. Clothes can always be replaced.'

'Would it make you happier if I 'phoned "The Central" and asked if they have any large boxes? I could go and collect them.'

Cathy smiled at her husband gratefully. 'If they have I could start packing other things away tonight.'

'I'm willing to help if you just pass your summer clothes out to me. I promise not to sniff them, only fold them and place them in the case,' offered Saffron. 'The more we could take down tomorrow the happier you would be.'

'I'll come with you, Pappa. I think we need to have a few quiet words.'

Vasilis raised his eyebrows, but asked no more until he and Vasi were in the car. 'What's troubling you?'

'Are you sure this Kuzmichov man has the money he claims and is in a financial position to purchase the hotel and apartment?'

'I asked for a financial check as soon as he made the proposal. It came back assuring me that he had more than enough collateral.'

'He and his wife just did not come across as people who were wealthy. I think you should ask for a further check. Whatever they had in the bank originally could have been withdrawn.'

Vasilis sighed. 'I hope your fears are groundless. I'll ask for another check if it concerns you and insist that all the financial transactions are in place before I sign the contracts.'

'Right up to the very last minute. There is just something about that man that I do not trust.'

January 2015
Week One – Thursday

Cathy looked around the apartment. Vasilis had collected boxes from "The Central" and whilst she and Saffron packed her summer clothes into a suitcase Vasi and Vasilis had filled a box with photographs and books. They then began to wrap ornaments carefully in towels before placing them in the boxes which they stacked at the side of the room.

'It doesn't look like home any more,' said Cathy sadly.

Vasilis placed his arm around her. 'I'm sure we'll find somewhere equally as nice, maybe better, in Elounda. If there is nowhere suitable I'll look for a plot of land along the coast road and we can build our own apartment.'

'That would take months to complete, Vasilis.'

Vasilis shrugged. 'At least we know we have somewhere to live until in the immediate future. We'll just have to behave so that our landlord doesn't ask us to leave.'

Vasi looked at his father reproachfully. 'I still think of it as your house and you know you are welcome to stay as long as you want. Are we ready to load up? I don't want Evgeniy Kuzmichov paying us a surprise visit.'

Cathy looked at Vasi in horror. 'Do you think he might?'

'I can't think why he should, but I'd rather not take the chance by hanging around.'

'I think Mrs Kuzmichov understands English,' remarked

Cathy. 'When we were in the kitchen discussing the appliances she appeared to be listening intently and often on the point of saying something.'

'Why would she pretend not to speak the language?' asked Saffron curiously.

Cathy shrugged. 'Maybe she hoped to hear us say something detrimental about the apartment or hotel that she could pass back to her husband, or even a personal comment about one of them.'

Saffron giggled. 'If they come again you could make all sorts of derogatory remarks about people who underdress to try to make people think they have no money, without mentioning any names, of course.'

Cathy smiled back conspiratorially. 'I could copy some of my modelling photos and leave them here for them. What about a life size one of me in a bathing suit? I could hang it in the bedroom. I don't think she would want her husband to look at that each night and start comparing it with her. She's no beauty and could do with shedding a few pounds.'

'Wow,' said Vasi. 'The cats have got their claws out and sharpened. Forget her. Let's get down to Elounda before you think of any more nasty tricks you could play.'

Vasi and Vasilis carried the boxes up to the spare bedroom whilst Saffron made coffee for the men and tea for her and Cathy.

'Can we leave all our belongings stored in the spare room?' asked Cathy. 'There's no point in unpacking everything as we will only have to repack when we move again. I've packed a separate case with our winter clothes and anything we will need whilst we are here for a few days.'

'They won't be in our way,' smiled Saffron, 'And you know you can stay as long as you want.'

'I thought we ought to drive around and see if we can spot anywhere suitable to live. If I didn't have to live in a ground floor apartment and know I would eventually have to rely on a wheelchair to get around it would be far easier.'

'Why don't we invite ourselves over to Marianne and Giovanni? They might well know of somewhere.'

'I don't want to live as far out of Elounda as they do. It would make me dependent upon Vasilis driving me wherever I wanted to go. I need to be reasonably close to the shops like I am in Heraklion.'

'Have you considered getting an electric wheelchair?'

'It would be practical, but I still couldn't live up here; even with an electric chair the hill would be too long and difficult to negotiate safely.'

'I wasn't suggesting that, but it could mean you could live in one of the roads behind the town where the road begins to rise and you could not possibly cope with it in a hand powered chair.'

Cathy nodded. 'It's a good idea. It could make finding somewhere suitable to live easier.'

'How is Vasilis planning to spend his time once he no longer has to think about "The Central"?'

'I don't know. At the moment he is so engrossed with the sale and moving that he hasn't thought any further ahead. I just hope he won't end up bored.'

'Vasi could well appreciate his help with the local hotels or "The Imperia". I know once he has made "The Imperia" a going concern he wants to think seriously about us moving elsewhere and turning this house into a self catering establishment for summer lets.'

'I'm sure Vasilis would like to be involved in his plans. Whilst we look for an apartment we could look for anywhere that you two might consider suitable.'

'That would be a help,' smiled Saffron. 'We've only talked about it so far. Olive picking will start next week so we certainly won't have time to go out and around. I'm hoping Monika will come up and help me again as she did last year. It was a novelty to her, but I'm not sure she enjoyed the actual picking. Of course now she has started the lending library at the bookshop she may not have the time.'

'I could always stay and help you with making up the refreshments.'

'If you are here with me helping to fill baguettes how are you going to be out looking for an apartment?'

Cathy shrugged. 'We can always go out in the afternoon. Elounda isn't that large. Within two or three afternoons we will have driven around every likely location and probably found somewhere.'

Saffron did not share Cathy's optimism. 'I'll call up to the men and tell them that the coffee is ready.'

Vasi was talking on his mobile as he entered the lounge and Saffron guessed he was speaking to Yiorgo. He closed his 'phone and gave a relieved sigh.

'Yiorgo says everything has gone according to plan and no problems have arisen. I thought I'd go down and check when I've had my coffee.'

'May I come with you?' asked Vasilis. 'I'd be interested to see how you have converted and decorated.'

'I was just about to start preparing some lunch,' remonstrated Saffron. 'Can't you have that first? Once you get down there we'll probably not see either of you again for hours.'

'I promise we'll not stay that long. Give us two hours at the most.'

'If you're not back by then Cathy and I will have eaten and you'll have to make do with the left overs.'

Vasilis's mobile 'phone rang and he grimaced as he saw the number come up. 'It's Evgeniy.'

'Let it ring and go to voice mail,' advised Vasi. 'You're not obliged to answer him.'

'I'll see what he wants and then phone him back if necessary.'

Vasilis listened to the message and frowned. 'He says he's at the apartment and there is no one there. He doesn't actually say what he wants.'

'Give it five minutes and then answer him. Tell him you were driving and cannot always get a signal as you go through the mountains. Thank goodness we left early or we may have had to spend time being sociable to him.'

'I hope he hasn't withdrawn his offer for the hotel.'

Vasi shrugged. 'If he has then you withdraw from the agreement that he can purchase your apartment.'

Vasilis sighed. 'I'll have to speak to him. It will worry me until I know what he wants.' Vasilis pressed in the numbers to return the call. 'Hello Evgeniy, you just tried to call me?'

'Yes. Where are you?'

'I have driven down to my son's house. We have to go through the mountains so that is probably why your message went to voice mail. How can I help you?'

'When will you be back in Heraklion?'

'I'm not sure. We have no definite time limit on our stay here.'

'I wanted to go to "The Central" and have a look at the conference rooms that you mentioned. I know I should have asked when we had our meeting the previous day, but there was so much to discuss that it slipped my mind.'

'They will still be there when I return and we can arrange a visit then.'

'You cannot come back now?'

'No, definitely not. If it is important that you inspect the rooms now I can call the manager and ask him to show them to you. I'll tell him you are thinking of booking them and want to see the facilities offered.'

Mr Kuzmichov hesitated. 'I suppose that could be helpful. Arrange for me to be there in an hour.'

'I'll do my best. If there is any problem I'll call you again.'

Vasilis shook his head as he finished the call. 'He wanted me to return to Heraklion so I could show him the conference rooms at "The Central". I've agreed to ask the manager to show them to him.'

'I suppose we should have offered to take him up there. Make your call, then switch off your phone and we'll go to "The Imperia".'

'I don't like to leave it switched off in case Cathy needs me.'

'Pappa, Cathy is safely here with Saffron. If there is any problem Saffie could 'phone me and I would bring you straight back. You do not have to be at that man's beck and call; you are not one of his employees.'

'You don't have to worry, Vasilis. We are not planning to go out anywhere this afternoon and I won't let Cathy attempt to do the stairs until you are both here to help her,' Saffron reassured him. 'We are going to contact Marianne and see if it would be convenient for us to pay them a visit tomorrow afternoon. 'Phone the manager and then do as Vasi says and switch off your mobile. You can always check it for messages at regular intervals, but if there's one from Evgeniy Kuzmichov I suggest you ignore it until you return here.'

Reluctantly Vasilis switched off his mobile 'phone after speaking to the manager at "The Central" and slipped it into his pocket.

Vasi parked outside the entrance to "The Imperia" and unlocked the door. 'The one draw back is nowhere convenient for customers to park. It isn't that far from the main car park for them to walk up but if it's raining hard they are not going to be happy doing that.' He stood to one side. 'What do you think?'

Vasilis nodded. 'I like it. You've made good use of the space available and utilised the mementos from "Imperia Airways" as decoration. I'm pleased you haven't tried to make it all modern and up market. There's no need for any further embellishment.'

'That's what Saffie said. Ronnie helped with the design of the place mats I'm going to use. She suggested the finishing touch of a red stamp saying "damaged by sea water in air plane accident". They show the route that was taken by the sea planes and they have a short history on them in English and Greek along with the photos of the plane in flight and also landed in the bay. I'll get one out to show you. They arrived three weeks ago but Yiorgo may have stored them elsewhere whilst I've been away.'

'I see you have had the photo of Churchill framed. That looks better than when it was just stuck on the wall. Where is the one of Gandhi?'

'I'm trying to decide whether I should put that up as well.'

'I think you should. It's part of the history of "The Imperia".'

'Here they are.' Vasi opened a large box that was beneath the bar and pulled out a place mat to show his father. 'What do you think?'

'They're larger than I expected.'

'I'm hoping they will save spills on table cloths or stains on the wooden tables so the larger the better. If "The Imperia" is successful I plan to have a transfer on the china showing the sea plane. At the moment everything is white, a cheap bulk buy.'

'Provided customers don't take them away as souvenirs.'

'Eventually I'd like to have all the cutlery engraved with a sea plane on the handles. Some will be bound to go missing, but I'll claim for them on my tax return each year. I'll have to take things slowly as I'm going to need a considerable amount to get the side of the building underpinned and made safe. Once that is done I can think about the upper rooms.'

'What are your long term plans for those?'

'I'm not sure yet. I could make them into bedrooms but that would mean being open during the summer. Yiorgo is more than happy to be the manager here during the winter months but as soon as the season starts he will want to be back on the boat and doing the Spinalonga trips.'

'You could make them into an apartment and let that.'

'I could, but I would need to have a separate entrance made

at the side and would you want to live above a taverna? It could become quite noisy.'

'One of your employees could be happy living there. They would be working and not notice any noise.'

'Except on their evening off,' smiled Vasi. 'The upper floor being made safe is a long way off yet. Plenty of time to consider how to use it.'

Vasilis sat up on one of the bar stools. 'Can people take their drinks down to the tables?'

Vasi shook his head. 'Only if they are also ordering a meal. If I find that locals are congregating down there just to drink I will place "reserved" on the tables and remove the notices when customers who wish to eat arrive. Would you like a drink? I want to check the kitchen area and ensure all is in order there.'

Vasilis shook his head. 'No, I'll not interfere with your display of unopened bottles. When is the grand opening? I'd like to bring Cathy up and I'm sure Saffron would want to join us.'

'I've arranged to throw a private party on Sunday. I've already arranged for Marianne, Giovanni, Bryony and Marcus to come and they say they can manage to bring Uncle Yannis and Marisa along with Uncle Andreas and return them home when they are tired. John and Nicola have said they can only call in briefly and will then have to take the children home. Nicola is strict about bed times.'

'What about Monika and her mother?'

Vasi nodded. 'Of course. I've also extended the invitation to Theo.'

'Theo? Do I know him?'

'I'm not sure. He has the taverna in the square at Plaka. He went to Monika's rescue when her ex-husband arrived in her shop and threatened her. I've also asked Ronnie and Kyriakos.'

'Quite a gathering.'

'Mr Palamakis and his sons and grandsons are also invited, but I'm not sure if they will come. They seem to think that they should not mix socially with the people who they work for. They may well make an excuse and then arrive the following night when "The Imperia" will be open to everyone. I've employed two extra bar staff for the first two weeks as I am expecting quite a lot of the locals to visit out of curiosity. I have bookings for every table for the first week so it is going to be busy when we open on Monday.'

'I hope it lasts.'

'There are so few tavernas open at this time of year that I think we will be popular.'

Saffron called Marianne who was delighted to know that Cathy and Vasilis were in Elounda. 'When are you visiting us or would it be easier if we came to you?'

'No, we'd like to come to you then we can say hello to Uncle Yannis and Marisa. I expect Nicola and John will be around with the children and Cathy will certainly see a change in them since she was down here last.'

Marianne laughed. 'They're under threat of good behaviour at the moment or they won't be allowed to go to "The Imperia" on the opening night. John says they'll not stay long. The children will only become bored and want to play chase or something similar around the tables. Why don't you all come up for lunch tomorrow?'

'May we? I'm going to accept and hope that neither Vasi nor Vasilis suddenly has something unexpected to deal with.'

'Is that likely?'

'Well, Vasi is stressed that something might go wrong with his plans for "The Imperia". He and Vasilis are down there now. Vasilis is also in the midst of negotiations to sell "The Central". I'm sure he'll tell you all about that tomorrow.'

'He's selling? To a local?'

'No, a Russian. I've met him and I was not impressed. His wife is horrendous and I'll not spoil Cathy's story by telling you about her behaviour.'

'Now you have made me really curious. Is Cathy there? Can she tell me now? You know what it's like; we'll all start talking and I'll forget to ask her.'

Saffron smiled. 'I'll pass the 'phone to her.'

Cathy took the mobile and began to tell Marianne about the way Ludmila Kuzmichov had gone through her underwear and even lifted items out of the drawers and sniffed at them.

'What! That's unbelievable. I would have slammed the drawer shut on her fingers.'

'If Vasilis was not so anxious for the sale of "The Central" to go through I probably would have done. I was so taken aback that I just stood there getting more and more angry.'

'They definitely want your apartment? She wasn't just being nosy?'

'No, they say they want it signed over to them at the same time as "The Central" so they can move in immediately. Mr Kuzmichov was not very pleased when I said I would be taking my kitchen appliances and the other equipment with me. He expected us to leave it fully equipped and furnished for him. I didn't tell him that I also planned to take the bedding and towels. I haven't spoken to Vasilis about it yet, but I want to leave the day before the contracts are signed and give the keys to the lawyers along with the inventory he is demanding of all that we have left behind. It will serve that woman right if they have to spend a night on a bare mattress and don't have a towel to dry their hands on.'

Marianne laughed. 'Why don't you remove the beds, then they'd have to sleep on the floor.'

'If I knew the size of the apartment that we will eventually move into I would do so. There's no point in us bringing them down here and finding they are too big for the bedrooms. We're leaving the lounge and dining room furniture also.'

'Have you found an apartment?'

'Not yet. Monika saw one that she thought might be suitable as it had a ramp up to the doors and the entrance was quite large.

Vasi went to look and the owner is in hospital. Vasilis has said that if we cannot find one he'll buy a plot of land down by the village and build us a new house there.'

'I'm sure he would, but land anywhere along the coast and close to Elounda is at a premium and then you have to get permission to build.'

'I'm sure he would find out if there were any building restrictions before he purchased. If the worst comes to the worst we will have to stay up here and I'll need to have a stair lift installed.'

'You could probably come and stay with us for a while. We have a spare room and it is equipped with the aids that we had installed for Aunt Anna.' As soon as Marianne made the offer she realised that all the boxes containing Uncle Yannis's pottery that had been moved from his shop in Plaka when Monika turned it into a book shop were stored in there.

'That's kind of you, Marianne, and I'll tell Vasilis, but I hope we won't have to take advantage of your offer. I'll hand you back to Saffie and you can arrange between you the time it will be convenient for us to arrive.'

'May I tell Bryony about your Russian woman?'

'Of course, tell Nicola and Marisa also and then let me know tomorrow what they said about her.' Cathy shook her head at Saffron when she closed her mobile. 'It's very kind and thoughtful of Marianne to offer us a room in their house, but I would hate being amongst so many people all of the time. I'm used to it being just Vasilis and myself and an occasional visitor.'

Saffron smiled sympathetically. 'I know what you mean. I'm quite happy to be in the shop and chat almost non stop to customers, but I really appreciate coming home and spending our evening quietly.'

'We'll try not to intrude on you.'

'Oh, present company excepted. You and Vasilis are no trouble and I'm enjoying having some company. Since Vasi started to get

"The Imperia" ready for opening I've hardly seen him. I'll make a cup of tea for us now we've spoken to Marianne.'

Vasi and Vasilis returned to the house and entered the lounge. 'I might have guessed that you would be having a pot of tea,' smiled Vasi. 'Saffie has tried to convert me without success.'

'I don't mind it occasionally, but it certainly cannot take the place of coffee.'

'It's just a question of educating your taste buds,' smiled Cathy. 'You see, I am all in one piece. There was no need to worry about leaving me and switching off your mobile.'

Vasilis looked at his wife and groped in his pocket. 'I'd forgotten I'd switched it off,' he said guiltily. 'It says three missed calls. They're all from Kuzmichov. What's his problem now?'

'Wait until he calls again to find out. He could just be saying thank you for arranging for the manager to show him the conference rooms.'

Vasilis placed his mobile on the table in front of him, staring at it fixedly as if willing it to ring.

'We've spoken to Marianne,' announced Saffron. 'We've been invited to go for lunch tomorrow and I've accepted.'

'Did you ask if they knew of anywhere suitable for us to live?' asked Vasilis.

'I thought it better for you to speak to Giovanni tomorrow. She did say we could go and stay with them if we became desperate.'

Vasilis shook his head. 'That won't be necessary. We can always stay here.' As he spoke his 'phone rang again.

'Where have you been? I've been trying to speak to you.' Mr Kuzmichov sounded thoroughly annoyed.

'I do not always have my 'phone switched on when I am in a business meeting.'

'I would have thought our business took priority over anything else.'

Vasilis raised his eyebrows and made no comment and Mr

Kuzmichov continued. 'I've looked at the conference rooms. I see there are some other rooms up on that floor. What are they used for?'

'Dimitra uses two of them. One is her personal room and the other her office. The room next to her is used by the sewing ladies.'

'Sewing ladies? What do you mean?'

'We were spending a considerable amount on renewing items that only needed to be repaired. There are three ladies who stitch the hem of a curtain or bed cover if it has come undone, or a pillowcase where the seam has split a little. When we have a consignment of new bedding and towels delivered they machine embroider the name of the hotel on each one. It prevents pilfering.'

'And the others?'

'One is shelved out and used as a store room. The others are bedrooms that can be used by guests if those on the lower floors are already occupied'

'Suppose I wanted to convert one of the conference rooms into bedrooms? Are there any regulations against this?'

'Not that I know of. The conference rooms were there when I first bought the hotel and they bring in a considerable income, particularly during the winter months. Personally I would think twice before making one of them into three or four more bedrooms. I can ask someone tomorrow if they happen to know of any reason why you would not be allowed to do that, or, of course, you could ask a building inspector.'

'As the current owner I would have expected you to know the regulations.'

'I have never felt the need to make the alterations you are considering so I have never investigated the regulations for conversion.'

'I will call you tomorrow when you have spoken to this person whom you think will know the answer.'

'No,' replied Vasilis firmly. 'I don't know what time I will be seeing him. I will call you. Was that all you wanted to ask me, Mr Kuzmichov?'

'For the present, yes. If anything else occurs to me I will call you.'

Vasilis closed his mobile with a sigh. 'Now he wants to know if he can convert one of the conference rooms into bedrooms. I'll ask Uncle Yannis tomorrow if he knows of any legal restrictions. The sooner we have agreed the sale the better. I do not want to have continual calls from that man.'

'Then switch your 'phone off again. You can see if you have missed a call and if it isn't from him you can always call them back.'

'Has he ever said why he wants a hotel?' asked Cathy. 'I would have thought he had enough to do with his import and export business.'

'He told me he planned to gradually wind down his import and export business over the next few years so he could spend more time with his wife.'

'I don't know who I feel most sorry for, him or his wife. I wouldn't want to spend time with either of them. If you weren't desperate to sell I'd recommend taking the hotel off the market and tell Kuzmichov that you've changed your mind.'

Vasilis shook his head. 'Much as I would like to do that his was the only enquiry I had. Now I've made the decision to retire I'm looking forward to some free time. The fact that he also wants to buy the apartment actually simplifies matters. We won't have to hang around in Heraklion waiting for it to be sold. Once we have found somewhere down here to live I'll be able to accompany Cathy into the town whenever she wants and please myself how I spend my spare time. I thought I might try my hand at fishing.'

'Fishing?' A chorus of voices greeted Vasilis's statement.

'Why would you want to go fishing?' asked Cathy.

Vasilis shrugged. 'Why not? I'm thinking of sitting on a jetty in the sun and just waiting for some passing fish to take the bait. I'm not planning to be a fisherman out on a boat in all weathers.'

'I should hope not.' Cathy was relieved. 'I wouldn't want to be sitting at home on a stormy night wondering if your boat had sunk and you were drowned.'

Saffron shuddered. 'That is too awful to contemplate. Those fishermen's wives must go through agonies when their husbands are late home.'

'Manolis never seemed troubled by the weather. It was a rare occurrence for him to stay in the harbour,' remarked Vasi. 'By the way, before you finally leave Heraklion are you planning to visit your father's memorial?'

Vasilis nodded. 'I know Cathy wants to and I thought we'd make a full day of travelling up and back, maybe next week or the following one. We'll see what the weather is like. I don't relish driving on icy roads. If the weather did deteriorate unexpectedly I'd stop overnight somewhere.'

'You shouldn't have a problem. We're starting olive picking next week and the weather is usually good then.'

'I've offered to help Saffie with making up the baguettes for the workers,' frowned Cathy. 'I thought we would be staying down here so we could look around for a suitable apartment. Surely we could put off a visit to the memorial until after that. I don't want to let her down.'

'We don't have to go before we leave Heraklion. We can go later in the year and stay up in the area as long as we wish. I should be a free man by then.' Vasilis smiled complacently.

January 2015
Week One – Friday and Saturday

'There's no need for us to take two cars,' said Vasilis, 'provided you and Saffie don't mind sitting in the back. Mine has more leg room for Cathy.'

'No problem. We're not going far anyway. Is your 'phone switched off? You don't want Kuzmichov 'phoning you whilst you're driving.'

'I have had it off since I spoke to him last night,' smiled Vasilis. 'I haven't any missed calls so he is obviously being patient and waiting for me to contact him later. Personally I think it would be crazy to turn one of the conference rooms into more bedrooms. Most people prefer to stay on the lower floors. Maybe he isn't such an astute business man as he thinks. A two day conference brings in far more than four extra bedrooms would even if they were occupied most of the time.'

'Forget him, Vasilis. Let's just go to Marianne's and enjoy a relaxing day with the family.'

'I can't. I said I would ask Uncle Yannis if there were any restrictions on the conference rooms when he bought it.'

'Alright, you can talk to Uncle Yannis and we can discuss the delightful Ludmila's behaviour, but not the whole afternoon. We want to ask Giovanni if he happens to know of anywhere that would be suitable for us to live, remember.'

'If you drive slowly, Vasilis, we can keep a look out as we

drive along. Vasi and I didn't go any further than the car park where they hold the market. It's all tavernas or gift shops from there on towards Mavrikiano. They are all closed down at the moment so it's quite hard to tell if they are refurbishing or closing permanently.'

'If you see anywhere that you think could be a possibility I can always draw over and we can have a better look. Are you ready, ladies?'

Vasilis drove slowly through the deserted town, past the harbour area and municipal beach, and took the road that led to Plaka. At one time it had been a pleasant drive with hedges on both sides and hills in the distance. Now the whole area had been developed for the tourist trade. Shops and tavernas finally gave way to self catering establishments and private villas. It was impossible to tell from the facades of the shops and tavernas whether they would be opening again in the spring.

'We'll just have to come along and see if we can find anyone working who can help us. Giovanni might know if one of them has closed permanently.'

'I wouldn't want to live out any further than this,' frowned Cathy. 'Even from here it could be difficult for me to get into the centre of Elounda on my own.'

'Out of the question,' said Vasilis firmly. 'I think we should definitely look for somewhere in the town.'

Marianne ushered them into the lounge. 'Uncle Yannis and Grandma Marisa are waiting for you. Giovanni and Marcus are up at the apartments, but have promised to return in about an hour. John and Nicola have just returned from taking the children out for a walk to calm them down a bit before they join us and Bryony will bring some coffee through now you have arrived.'

'I want to have a word with Uncle Yannis so now could be a good opportunity.' Vasilis and Vasi shook hands with the two elderly relatives whilst Cathy and Saffron kissed their wrinkled cheeks.

'So what do you want to talk to me about?' asked Yannis. 'Do you want to buy some of my pots? I have plenty here that you can choose from as I had to move them from the shop when Monika decided to rent it from me.'

Vasilis shook his head. 'I really have nowhere to put any more. I have decided to sell "The Central" and I have a buyer who wants the sale completed by March if possible.'

'Would he be interested in buying some of my pots? John has some idea about putting them for sale on the internet. I'm not sure how that works, but John seems to know all about it. He's certainly given me a job. I've had to go through all my old invoices and make a list of the cost of them. Once I've completed that he says he'll check how much replicas are being sold for at the museum and we'll offer them for less than the current price.'

'I could mention the pots to him,' said Vasilis, thinking it unlikely that Mr Kuzmichov would be interested. 'He called me yesterday and asked if there were any restrictions on the conference rooms. He's contemplating turning one of them into bedrooms.'

'Whatever for? I changed the bedrooms that were there into conference rooms originally. Bedrooms up there were wasted. No one chose to be on that floor and it was rare that we were so full that they had to be used.'

'You converted them?'

Uncle Yannis nodded. 'Seemed a practical thing to do.'

'So did you have to comply with any building regulations?'

'I didn't ask. It was my hotel so I could do as I pleased.'

Vasilis smiled. He had worked on much the same principal when making changes to any of the hotels he owned. 'So as far as anyone knows they are still bedrooms?'

Uncle Yannis shrugged. 'I expect so. No one has ever mentioned them. When the dividing walls were removed I had steels put in to support the roof.'

'What about the plumbing for the toilets?'

'Just extended the pipe runs from the nearest bedroom and cut off the water supply to the others. Same with the electrics. I had the original wiring removed and made sure all the fire and safety regulations were carried out.'

'So it would be quite a big job to convert them back to bedrooms?'

'And expensive. It would be years before the cost was recovered. Has the man any hotels elsewhere?'

Vasilis shook his head. 'He's a Russian and his business is import and export. He must have been successful as he has no problem with paying my asking price. He also wants to buy the apartment in Heraklion so he and his wife have somewhere to live locally.'

'Have you agreed to sell to him?'

'Verbally the sale of the hotel and the apartment have been agreed. Our lawyers have been instructed to draw up the necessary legal papers. Kuzmichov is anxious to complete as soon as possible.'

'Where will you live if you don't have the apartment?'

'Cathy wants to return to live down here and we are looking for somewhere suitable. I'm hoping Giovanni might be able to help me there. In the meantime we can always stay at the house with Vasi and Saffron.'

'Giovanni only has the self catering apartments and they're not suitable for winter living.'

'Plaka is too far out for Cathy. Ideally we would like to live in Elounda.'

Vasi leaned forward. 'We could ask Mr Palamakis if he knows of anywhere that is closed and not having a refurbishment. We should have thought of that before. Shall I call him?'

'Not now.' Cathy shook her head. 'If he mentions anywhere Vasilis will want to go dashing off to have a look. This is supposed to be a relaxing and enjoyable afternoon.'

Bryony, having finished placing the coffee, water and a plate of biscuits on the table, took a seat beside Cathy. 'I want to know more about the Russian's wife.'

'You have to see her. I was expecting a tall attractive Russian woman. She's short, overweight and has quite a dark complexion.'

'She may not be Russian as we think of them. It is such a large country she could have come from one of the other countries that originally made up the area.'

'That's a possibility I hadn't thought of,' admitted Cathy. 'Not that it makes any difference where she comes from. I disliked her when I first saw her and her subsequent behaviour certainly did not endear her to me.' Cathy delighted in telling the story of Ludmila Kuzmichov's examination of her drawers and cupboards again whilst Marisa sat and "tutted" at intervals and Bryony tried to stifle her laughter.

'What a shame that you didn't have a mouse trap in one of the kitchen cupboards so she caught her fingers.'

'Thankfully I have never seen any sign of a mouse.'

'Pity you didn't have insects in containers in the fridge. That would probably have freaked her out.'

Saffron laughed. 'They'd just had some lunch with us. Cathy could have said that we were insectarians and the only meat we ate came from insects. They would probably have both made a rush for the bathroom.'

'It's all very well for you to laugh,' said Vasilis, 'but I don't want the sale of the hotel to fall through.'

'When are you meeting with him again?' asked Uncle Yannis.

'I've no idea. I have to 'phone him to tell him about the conference rooms and bedrooms, but that can wait until later. I told him I was seeing someone I could ask, but I made no mention of time.'

'Do you think he's trying to find an excuse to withdraw from the sale?'

Vasilis shook his head. 'No, I don't think he realises just how profitable the conferences are. He's seen the annual turnover figures for the hotel. I had to disclose those, but he hasn't received a breakdown of the amount received from guests, conferences and casual diners. He grilled us for hours yesterday about the way the hotel was run and why we needed certain staff. It won't surprise me if he gets rid of some of them and tries to manage with fewer chambermaids and cleaners.'

'He could bring in Russian staff.'

Vasilis shrugged. 'Who he employs will be nothing to do with me. We did discuss the advantage of having a receptionist who had Russian along with the other European languages.'

'We've noticed more Russian visitors down here,' said Marianne, 'so that could make sense. Some of them have bought very expensive properties and then they only stay for a few weeks each summer. Would anyone like more coffee? I'm expecting everyone else to return any minute and then we can have lunch.'

The afternoon passed pleasantly. Elisabetta and Joanna had spoken hesitantly to Cathy and Saffron in English, but Yiannis decided he was too shy to approach them and sat on Nicola's lap, despite their attempts to attract him. Having had lunch Uncle Yannis and Marisa retired to their rooms for a rest and Nicola took the children to their rooms to play whilst Yiannis had his afternoon nap. Vasilis took the opportunity to ask Giovanni if he knew of any suitable property that might be available to purchase.

'We don't want to rent and then find we have to move after a few months. We might just as well stay up at the house.'

Giovanni considered. 'I know of a house in Plaka that is on the market. I don't think it would be suitable for Cathy, though, as it opens onto the main road. There could be a back entrance, of course.'

'We don't want to be in Plaka,' said Vasilis firmly. 'The whole idea of being in Elounda is to give Cathy some independence so she can come and go as she pleases.'

'The only other property I know about for certain is a taverna that is just along from the municipal beach. Someone may have put in an offer, of course, but there are any number of tavernas along there and some of them are struggling to keep going.'

'I certainly do not want to run a taverna.'

'Just because it has a catering and liquor licence you wouldn't have to keep it as a taverna.'

'Tell me exactly where it is and we'll have a look on the way home.'

'Easier for me to drive back along with you and show you which one. They're all closed down at the moment.'

'I don't want to be a nuisance and drag you out.'

'It's no problem, but we ought to go now whilst it is still light. The ladies can stay here and chat and if you consider it to be a possibility you can always take Cathy along there tomorrow to have a look.'

'Well, if you're sure it's no trouble.'

Giovanni looked at Vasilis scathingly. 'If it was going to be a trouble to me I wouldn't have offered.'

Giovanni drove swiftly to the outskirts of Elounda and then slowed. 'It's one of these. There's a gift shop and then an access road through to the houses behind. On the other side there's a general store and then another small road. There it is.' Giovanni waited for a car to pass them and then parked. 'It was run by a family for years, but their children have married and moved away. As the parents became older they tried to keep it running by employing staff but eventually it became too much for them. They gradually cut down on the evenings they were open and customers began to go elsewhere. The other problem was insufficient parking. There's only enough space for three cars to pull off the road and visitors don't want to walk far at the end of an evening out.'

Vasilis looked at the premises. There were three steps leading up to a large patio area which had some wooden uprights supporting a sagging roof with bedraggled plants in pots beside them. At the back of the patio there were glass doors, but more than that it was impossible to see. He shook his head.

'Cathy couldn't manage those steps.'

'You could probably have a ramp made. Let's have a look and see what there is inside.'

Reluctantly Vasilis followed Giovanni up onto the patio. This was a waste of time. The premises were not suitable.

'Look at that,' Giovanni pointed to the side of the patio. 'There's a ramp leading to the road.'

'It wouldn't be wide enough for a wheelchair.'

'A couple of bricks knocked out from the wall and it could easily be widened.' Giovanni pressed his face up close to the glass patio doors. 'All the cooking equipment is still in there along with the tables and chairs.'

'I've told you I don't want to run a taverna.'

'No, but think of the space once it's been removed. You'd have a large lounge leading out onto the patio. There must be two or three rooms behind that could be made into a kitchen, bedroom and bathroom.'

'You'd be very exposed if you sat out on the patio.'

'The wall just needs to be built up a little higher, bit of trellis and some climbers and you wouldn't be seen by passers by. Take off the roof and have a large umbrella. Ideal. Lovely view across the bay.'

Vasilis turned to look, but it was already too dark to make out more than a few boats tied to the jetty and the lights of Elounda beginning to be turned on.

'It's a possibility,' he said to Giovanni, not wanting to hurt his friend's feelings. 'I'll bring Cathy along tomorrow and see what she thinks. Is the owner contactable should we want to look inside?'

'I expect there's a notice with his details somewhere. If not someone from the general store can probably help you.'

'Well?' asked Cathy when they returned.

'It has potential. We'll drive along there tomorrow and you can see for yourself. There's no point in stopping to look in the dark.'

Vasilis was just about to suggest that he and Cathy drove along to the taverna when he remembered that he had not telephoned Mr Kuzmichov as he had promised. 'I'll have to speak to him first.'

'Tell him you arrived home too late to 'phone him last night and then wanted some more clarification about the regulations this morning.'

Vasilis shook his head. 'I'll let him assume I was too late last night and was sleeping off a hang over this morning. I'll only trip myself up if I start to try to make excuses. I'll try not to be too long.'

Cathy smiled. She did not really mind how long Vasilis was on the phone to the Russian. She was warm and comfortable sitting on the sofa reading a magazine.

To her surprise Vasilis was speaking to Mr Kuzmichov for no more than fifteen minutes.

'That was quick!'

'He seemed satisfied when I said there were no known regulations in place regarding converting a conference room back into bedrooms.'

'Didn't he want to know who had changed the layout originally?'

'I was quite honest. I told him it was done by the previous owner when he first bought the hotel. I didn't bring it to his attention that the building regulations have been updated and are much stricter now than they were then. It would be in his own interest to leave things as they are. Once the inspectors start to nose around they'll probably find all sorts of things that don't comply with the new specifications and they will demand that he changes them to bring the premises up to date.'

'You never had a problem?'

'I made sure that my fire doors were not blocked and the signs were visible. The extinguishers were checked annually along with an electrical check. I never proposed doing any alterations that would need a visit from the building inspectors. Make sure you are you wrapped up warmly. It looks quite windy out there.'

Vasilis drove Cathy along to the taverna he had visited the previous evening with Giovanni. 'It used to be a taverna and there would be quite a bit of work needed to turn it into a home. I'll see if I can find the owner and ask him to open up for us. All the kitchen equipment would need to be removed, of course. A new kitchen area could be constructed and it would still leave a very large lounge and dining area. See what you think if we are able to go inside.'

'I'm not sure about those steps,' demurred Cathy. 'I could manage to walk up and down them at the moment, but once I am dependent on my wheelchair they would be impossible.'

'There is a ramp at the side. It would need to be widened to take your chair, but that would be no big job.'

Cathy stood on the patio and looked around. 'There's a lovely view, but it would be like living in a goldfish bowl. Everyone would look at you as they walked past.'

'Giovanni suggested making the retaining wall higher and putting up some trellis with plants growing up them.'

'The roof looks ready to collapse.'

'We wouldn't need a roof over the patio. We're not likely to want to sit out here when it's raining. That could be taken down and a large umbrella could be fixed out here to give shade.'

Cathy looked through the glass doors. 'All the table and chairs are stored in there. It's quite difficult to get an idea of the size of the room.'

'Do you want me to see if we can go inside?'

Cathy considered. 'I suppose we should. We can't really make an informed decision just by looking through the window.'

'I can't see a 'phone number anywhere. I'll go into the general store and see if they can help. I won't be a minute.' Vasilis ran down the steps and entered the shop, exiting a short while later with a woman who pointed down the access road at the side of the property.

Vasilis returned to where Cathy was leaning against the wall. 'She says there is quite a large garden at the back and Manolis is probably out there. I'll go and have a look.'

Vasilis used the ramp to walk down to the access road and along to where he could see man tending the garden at the rear of the building. 'Hi, are you Manolis?'

The man looked up. 'That's me.'

'I believe you want to sell your taverna. Would it be possible for my wife and I to go inside and have a look around?'

'Go round to the front and I'll come and open the door for you.'

Vasilis returned to where Cathy was waiting patiently.

'He's coming to open the door. We could see some chairs inside so you could sit down whilst I look around. If I think you'll be interested I'll come and fetch you.'

Cathy nodded gratefully. She found standing for any length of time incredibly tiring and painful.

Manolis opened the door and looked at them curiously as they walked inside. They did not look like prospective taverna owners. He placed a chair for Cathy and stood facing them.

'As you can see, the kitchen area is fully equipped for catering. During the winter months tables and chairs are arranged inside and the locals visit for meals. During the summer, of course, it is mainly tourist trade and they usually want to sit outside. We can cope with twenty tables, that's approximately eighty diners.'

'Do you get that many every evening?' asked Vasilis curiously.

'Not every night. Custom fluctuates. Over there are the customers' toilets. Well away from the cooking area. Do you want to see them?'

'Not at the moment.'

'Through the door at the back there is a large storeroom and an area where vegetables and meat can be prepared before bringing it through to be cooked. There is also our own toilet that backs on to the ones for the customers and a door that leads out into the garden. We grow a good deal of our own produce.'

'I'd like to see those rooms.'

Vasilis followed the owner through the door. The store room was spacious and had shelves down one side and the back wall. The preparation room was even larger and had a stainless steel table along with a smaller wooden one and a sink over by the wall with another work top.

'The meat is prepared on the steel, the vegetables on the wood and pastry on the marble slab over by the window,' explained Manolis and Vasilis nodded. This was the same hygiene system that was used in the kitchen of "The Central".

'So where do you live?' asked Vasilis.

'Upstairs. Not sure how tidy it will be as we weren't expecting visitors, but you're welcome to come up and have a look.' Manolis opened a door on the far side of the room and a flight of steep stairs were immediately exposed. He switched on a light and led the way to the top where he opened another door. 'Anna, are you respectable? We have a visitor.'

Manolis led the way into the room that was used as a lounge and Vasilis was surprised at how much smaller it was than he had expected. Almost half the area was taken up by a balcony that ran the width of the building. From the ground the balcony could not be seen, but would be ideal to sit out on in the summer to eat. There were two other rooms, one serving as a bedroom and the other the kitchen where Manolis's wife was employed with something in the sink.

'You'll have to excuse her, she's washing a squid ready for our meal this evening. I caught it yesterday and we want to eat it whilst it's fresh.' Manolis opened another door and exposed a small cloakroom. 'Useful to have one on this floor. Saves having to go up another flight.'

Vasilis followed Manolis up yet another flight of steep stairs and was shown three bedrooms and a bathroom. 'We only use these bedrooms when any of the family come to stay.'

'It's certainly very spacious,' admitted Vasilis.

'Ideal family home and a good business down stairs.'

'I'm sorry. I think I have rather wasted your time. My wife and I are actually looking for an apartment reasonably close to Elounda. I did not realise there were two floors above the taverna. There is no way my wife could manage the stairs.'

'You could probably have a lift fitted.'

'Very likely, but when I looked through the windows I thought I would be able to convert the taverna into separate rooms where we could live on the ground floor.'

'So you wouldn't plan to open the taverna?'

'I have retired. A taverna is hard work and I would not want to be involved. We are planning a quiet, sedentary life. I would certainly not want to be responsible for your large garden. My wife wants to be able to use a wheelchair if she wishes to be independent of me which is why I thought the taverna premises could be suitable. Had I realised how extensive the property was I would not have bothered you.'

Manolis shrugged. 'It was no trouble. If you hear of anyone wanting a taverna please ask them to contact me. Although ideally I would like to sell I would be willing to rent and my wife and I could live upstairs.'

'I'll mention it to some of my acquaintances. One of them could be interested.' Vasilis extended his hand. 'I should now return to my wife. She is probably quite ready to return home and have rest.'

'Where are you staying?'

'With my son at present, but it isn't ideal. Once again there are stairs that have to be dealt with.'

Once in the car Vasilis shook his head at Cathy as she looked at him eagerly. 'Manolis has very kindly shown me over the whole building. What was not evident from the road are the other two floors above. It would not be a practical proposition for us unfortunately.'

'That's a shame. I was becoming quite enthusiastic about your idea of the trellis work and umbrella on the patio,' smiled Cathy. 'I've been watching the sea. It's quite rough.'

'For anyone wanting to start up their own taverna this would be ideal. Manolis would be willing to let the ground floor and he and his wife would stay living above. There are three bedrooms and a bathroom on the top floor so plenty of space if their family wanted to visit. I'll let Giovanni know. He may know of someone who would like to rent a taverna.'

'Don't tell Vasi.'

'Why not?'

'Once he has "The Imperia" running in the winter months he could well want to turn his attention to a taverna catering for the summer visitors. He must not take on too much.'

'I could always help him.'

'Vasilis, if you are going to be working you might just as well continue to run "The Central". The whole idea of you selling it was so you could take life more easily and have some free time. You're seventy three, remember, not thirty three.'

Vasilis grinned sheepishly. 'I wasn't considering anything like a full time job; just a helping hand if Vasi needed it.'

'You know what you're like. Once you became involved you would have ideas for all sorts of improvements and eventually ending up running it.'

'I might be getting old, but my mind is still active.'

'Then let your mind become interested in things other than tavernas and hotels. I'm not saying that you should never help Vasi, but keep a distance between his businesses and yourself. At the moment I'm interested in finding somewhere open where we can have a snack lunch and then I'd like to drive across the

Causeway provided the sea is not coming over the road too much.'

Vasilis turned from the main road into the car park at the square. 'I think we should be able to get a gyros if you are happy with that. They look as if they are open.'

He returned a short while later bearing two large gyros and he and Cathy sat in the car eating them. 'A shame to have to sit inside,' remarked Cathy, 'but with this wind blowing we'd probably lose the filling.'

Having finished the gyros and disposed of the soiled napkins into the rubbish bin, Vasilis drove back to the main street and then onto the pedestrian precinct that ran past the tavernas. 'I must say it's a pleasure to be able to do this rather than have to use the main road.'

'Even in the summer I'd be able to ride along here if I had an electric wheelchair.'

'It would certainly be preferable rather than using the main road. I'd not be happy with you trying to avoid the coaches and lorries that come through or having to negotiate that horrible turn from the main road to get down to the coast.'

They could see that the waves were being blown onto the Causeway road. 'We'll see how far over the sea is coming. I don't want to get sea water into the engine and find we are stuck there.'

'It probably looks worse than it actually is, but you can judge the risk as we drive along.'

Vasilis drove cautiously. Although all the tavernas were closed down there could be a pedestrian or someone working outside their premises. They dropped down lower and Vasilis stopped.

'I'd forgotten this patch of rough road. I'd better turn back or you'll be jolted to pieces. I don't want you to end up in pain for the remainder of the day.'

'It's only a short stretch. I'll be fine. We can always drive back the other way,' Cathy assured him.

Vasilis drove on, reaching the tarmac section of the road and finally driving down to where the road ran and they could see that the waves were encroaching on the flat shore and spilling over onto the roadway.

'We should be able to get along here safely. If I think the Causeway is impractical we'll turn back and then use the main road.'

'Vasilis, stop a moment,' said Cathy after they had driven no more than a few yards.

'What's the problem?' Vasilis drew to a halt. 'Is it too rough for you?'

Cathy shook her head. 'Those houses there. One of those would be ideal for us.'

'They none of them have a ramp. I think they are accessed from the main road.'

'They all have a door that opens onto this road. A ramp would be quite simple to put in. Do you think any of them are empty?'

'Probably all of them at this time of year.'

'Could we find out who owns them and ask if we could look inside? The rooms might be hideously small, but they could be worth investigating.'

'I'll ask Vasi if he knows anything about them, but I don't think they are a practical option. Even with a ramp you would have to negotiate this rough stretch of road and when the weather is really bad the road down here can be impassable, also there is no patio where we could sit out. Are you ready to move on now?'

'I suppose you're right. It was just seeing the sea so close that gave me the idea. I have missed that whilst we've lived in Heraklion.'

There was no problem driving over the Causeway as the waves that covered the tarmac at intervals were not high or powerful. The usual parking area was just a large puddle and Vasilis was loath to drive through it out of consideration for his engine.

'There's no point in struggling through this to reach the Kanali as they're closed. We can drive a bit further along the road towards the white house and we can see if it is as rough on that side if you want.'

'I do wish I could get out and walk.'

'It's probably just as well that you can't. That wind is quite strong and you wouldn't want to be blown into the sea. It's bound to be freezing.'

'I wouldn't want to be blown in at any time. I'm sure I would end up battered and bruised. I do like to feel the wind on my face and blowing through my hair.'

Vasilis let down the passenger window and Cathy gasped and then pushed her head as far out as possible.

'That was really invigorating,' she said as she withdrew her head back into the car and Vasilis closed the window swiftly.

They continued to drive along the road until it finally ended in a muddy cart track. 'I'll have to reverse back to that gateway to turn and hope not to get stuck in the mud,' observed Vasilis. 'I don't really want to call out the recovery services. Just too humiliating.'

Cathy laughed. 'You could always call Vasi and ask him to come with a rope and pull you out.'

'That would be just as embarrassing. Hold on. This could be bumpy.'

To Vasilis's relief the car turned reasonably easily back onto the tarmac. 'Time to go, I think. By the look of those waves the wind is gathering strength. We'll return by the hill that leads us into the main road rather than the beach road.'

'Back home for a nice cup of tea,' and Cathy smiled at the look of disgust on Vasilis's face.

Vasilis drove back over the Causeway where the waves were now higher and spreading water and foam across the tarmac. Even when they reached the road that led past the self catering establishments and Vasi's hotel the sea was leaving large puddles and the shingle was being dragged away from the shore. Towards the end of the road where the steep hill led to the main road there were two empty plots of land that he had not noticed earlier due to the large rubbish bins that stood on the road in front of them. He would speak to Vasi and see if he knew who owned them.

January 2015
Weeks Three and Four

Kuzmichov telephoned his brother in law. 'All is going to plan regarding the hotel and apartment. Have you made progress?'

'I have a number of eager customers. I'm planning to set sail tomorrow as the forecast for the week is good. Panos will be with me. He knows the area well and we'll investigate the drop off point that he thinks will be suitable before proceeding on to Heraklion.'

'How far away from Heraklion is it?'

'A convenient distance. I'll give you the details when we meet and we can also drive down for you to see for yourself.'

Vasilis and Cathy drove back to Heraklion in the early afternoon after they had lunched with Saffron and Vasi. Cathy had enjoyed helping to make up the baguettes, pleased that Monika had closed the bookshop so she had been able to join them. Vasilis had driven the truck loaded with olives down to the weighing centre, feeling he was doing something useful although he had no desire to pick the olives or climb the trees as the men did to prune the branches.

'We were certainly lucky with the weather,' remarked Vasilis. 'Rain is forecast for tomorrow and you can see the clouds gathering over the hills.'

'Once we are back home I don't mind,' smiled Cathy. 'We can have a nice quiet evening in together, just the two of us.'

'Didn't you enjoy going to the opening of "The Imperia" and seeing everyone?'

'Very much, but I would not want to do that every day. I was very pleased to sit down in the kitchen and help make up the baguettes during the remainder of the week. That is more the life that I envisage for myself when we have moved down here; visiting friends and having them visit me, joining in when I can be helpful with the daily events.'

'What did you think of Theo?'

'I hardly saw him. You men kept together as usual. He seemed pleasant enough when Monika introduced him.'

Vasilis chuckled. 'I'm not sure which lady he has his eye on, Monika or her mother, Litsa.'

'What makes you think he is interested in either of them?'

'He kept looking around and checking who they were with.'

'What makes you think he was 'checking'? asked Cathy curiously. 'He was probably just looking to see if their glasses were full and they had something to eat.'

'Vasi and Yiorgo would have made sure they were well looked after. I thought it was a superb evening. Everyone appeared to enjoy themselves and admire the new interior décor. The food was delicious; he's obviously found a good chef.'

'Are there any books at "The Central" that would be suitable for Monika? I'm sure Kuzmichov will not know you have removed them provided he has not looked in the cupboard beneath the shelf.'

'I'll collect some tomorrow when I go in,' promised Vasilis.

'I heard Uncle Yannis trying to sell some of his pots to Vasi and when Vasi refused he tried to persuade Uncle Andreas to take some.'

'Where would he put them in his tiny house?'

'That's what he said. When we've found somewhere suitable to live maybe we could take one or two off his hands,' suggested Cathy.

'We have to find somewhere first. We were not very successful on this visit. At least we can stay with Vasi and Saffie indefinitely.'

'I'm sure something will turn up. I don't want to end up living with them permanently.'

'That won't happen,' promised Vasilis. 'I've told you, if we cannot find anywhere that suits us I'll buy some land close to the village and build a house near to the shore. I should have thought years ago when I built the current house that it was not going to be practical to live up on the hill for ever.' Vasilis did not mention to Cathy that he had approached the owner of the land on the road leading to the Causeway with a view to purchasing an area where he could construct a house and was awaiting a decision.

'Do you think Kuzmichov is going to contact us once we're home?' asked Cathy.

'I hope not. He has no reason. I 'phoned him back about the conference rooms and I didn't tell him when we planned to return. I cannot bring myself to call that man Evgeniy as if he was a friend.' Vasilis shook his head.

'Nor I and I certainly do not want to be a friend to the objectionable Ludmila.'

'Once he has purchased the hotel and the apartment there is no reason why we should ever have to see them again.'

'Can you bring some more boxes back from the hotel so I can continue to pack?'

'I don't want you wearing yourself out. I can always help.'

'I know you will, but once we're home you will want to visit "The Central' and check with the manager that all has run smoothly whilst we were away.'

'I did 'phone him every day,' admitted Vasilis. 'I'll contact my lawyer tomorrow. Once I know the sale is definitely going through I'll have to hold meetings with the staff and introduce them to Kuzmichov.'

'That is why I need the boxes,' smiled Cathy. 'It will give me something to do whilst you are busy with business meetings.'

Ivan Kolmogorov telephoned Evgeniy Kuzmichov. 'All is well. We should be in Heraklion harbour by mid-day. I'll have to go through the usual formalities but I don't envisage any problems. Come down about two and we can discuss our arrangements. Bring Ludmila with you. She needs to know what is expected of her and bring some sandwiches. We don't want to have to break off our discussion by having to go out for a meal.'

'I'll take you up to the hotel this evening and buy you dinner. It's open to non residents. I'll book a table for four at eight.'

Evgeniy rubbed his hands together. The idea that he and Ivan had thought up at the end of the summer was coming to fruition and should certainly increase their personal fortunes. Since the introduction of sniffer dogs concealing supplies of cocaine in the lorries that travelled across Europe had become almost impossible however well hidden they were and the searches for hidden armaments was more thorough than in previous years. So far he had been both cautious and fortunate. He knew his lorries could be stopped and searched at any time and for the previous six months he had ensured they held nothing incriminating. Now was the time to explore a different profitable venture.

Evgeniy, Ludmila, Ivan and Panos sat at the table in the lounge area of Ivan's boat with a plate of sandwiches before them and a bottle of wine.

'Where shall we start?' asked Evgeniy.

'I've made contact with about almost a hundred professional people who want to leave Syria and have the money to pay for an unorthodox exit. Once the fighting started over there they had the foresight to move their money into American dollars. I have met with them all individually as I did not want to draw attention to either them or myself by meeting in a group. More than three people together are viewed with suspicion. They have up to date Syrian passports, but are not permitted to leave the country legally and seek refugee status or asylum elsewhere. They are gradually withdrawing money ready to pay for their travel to a new life.'

'Where do they want to go?' asked Ludmila, speaking perfect Greek.

'Their main preference is England as they all speak the language fluently. A few have mentioned France or Germany. I think it would be best to concentrate just on the English speakers first. We can diversify later.'

Evgeniy nodded. That idea made sense. 'What about their families?'

'These are all unmarried men. We don't want women and young children around to complicate the situation or their elderly parents. No more than six at any one time will make the journey. When they have reached their destination it will be up to them to arrange for any family members to join them.'

'Why only six? Boats are going across from other places loaded with considerably more.'

'If we were stopped the authorities would have good reason to be suspicious if there were a large number of passengers on board. The greater the weight the slower we would travel. Besides, my boat only sleeps four and there will be eight of us so we can sleep in shifts. I am also not prepared to overload my boat and put lives at risk.'

'How do you plan to bring them out without attracting suspicion?'

'I will invite them to come aboard for lunch, wearing at least two shirts and two pairs of trousers and extra underwear and socks. They will need to have the money with them. I will explain the arrangements to them and also the costs. If they still want to participate in the venture they will leave their surplus clothing in the cabin along with the full amount of their travel expenditure. They will also be given instructions that must be strictly adhered to.'

'Suppose they refuse and then go to the authorities?'

Ivan smiled. 'That would mean they had to admit to trying to leave Syria illegally and could be arrested. I will not have taken their money so I cannot be accused of stealing from them. These men are desperate to leave Syria; they want to go to another country that will welcome their expertise.'

Evgeniy frowned. 'What are these instructions that they must agree to? Will there be a written agreement?'

'Nothing at all will be written down. Assuming they have agreed to travel with me, they will be instructed to purchase black deck shoes or trainers without flashes or logos, black wind cheater, again no maker's logos and a black roll neck jumper. I am assuming they all have a pair of black trousers.'

'It can be quite difficult to purchase trainers and a wind cheater without a logo,' frowned Ludmila.

'If they have to purchase something with a logo it needs to be possible to remove it or block it out. I will explain this to them. Once their purchases are complete they will return to the boat on a given evening and at a particular time. They will wear as much underwear as possible under black trousers and a white shirt over their black roll neck. They can carry the windcheater over their arm. They can bring whatever extra money they wish with them. If they are questioned they say they are attending a small private party on board. They will not have anything with them except their passports, papers and certificates that confirm their expertise in their chosen occupations, some money and their mobile 'phones.

'They will retire below and remove their surplus clothing and the black jumper but wear their white shirt. Their 'phones will have the batteries removed, each 'phone placed in a separate bag and locked in the safe. The boat will be lit up, people will be seen moving around on deck until the early hours of the morning. I will then pull up the gang plank and cut all the lights. The boat will then be in darkness and once I am happy that no one is going to come and challenge me Panos will quietly untie our moorings and

I will sail out of the harbour and down the coast. The men will not be allowed back up on deck at any time without my permission.'

'And if you are challenged?'

'I will say the men have had rather a lot to drink and are recovering before returning ashore.'

'Suppose you are stopped by the coastguards the following day?' asked Evgeniy.

Ivan shrugged. 'No panic. I am taking my friends for a sail. Once we have sailed down the coast as far as possible I will make for the open sea and begin the crossing to Crete. Whilst confined below they can spend their time unpicking manufacturers labels from all their clothes, both old and new. Once we are out of sight of the land the men will be allowed on deck to stretch their legs and get some air. At that time we will still be in Syrian waters for at least another twenty four hours. When I enter Greek waters I will replace the Syrian flag with the Greek one and the men will only be allowed on deck for a short while provided there are no other boats in the vicinity.'

'How long will it take you to sail over?'

'I estimate three days before we reach the drop off point provided we have a fair wind and also use the engine. That will mean we can make a journey every ten days, approximately three each month.

'What about food and water if you are delayed?' asked Ludmila.

'The boat will be stocked with sufficient victuals to last for at least ten days and basic toiletries will be supplied.'

'You seem to have thought of everything,' Evgeniy complimented his brother-in-law and poured another glass of wine for each of them whilst Ludmila helped herself to another sandwich.

'Now you begin to enter the picture,' smiled Ivan. 'You need to order a large black car, preferably a Mercedes, but it must have tinted windows so no one can see in and be capable of seating six passengers. You will probably have to order this from Athens and have it shipped over. You will arrange to have the driver's seat modified so it can be lifted to expose a reasonable sized storage space below. If they query the reason you tell them that you will be carrying large amounts of cash from your hotel to the bank and want to feel secure. You will garage the car at the hotel and use it on airport runs to personally collect or deliver travellers. That way the car will become a familiar vehicle and not cause comment.'

'What is the purpose of the space beneath the driver's seat?' asked Evgeniy.

'I will explain the reason in a short while. Ludmila will purchase suitcases that are of an acceptable size as hand luggage on board an aircraft. Get each one from as many separate shops as possible.'

'Any particular colour?' asked Ludmila.

'No, but they must be plain colours without any decoration on them to make them distinctive. Two different blues and greens along with a black and a red maybe. The choice is yours. You will also need black trousers and jumper for yourself unless you already have them in your wardrobe and also a black baseball cap.'

'That will be difficult to find without a slogan of some sort on it.'

'If it is embroidered you can unpick it, if it is a stencil you can turn the cap inside out.'

'Where are you planning to land your passengers?'

'Once we arrive off the coast of Crete I will drop anchor a short distance out from the shore. It's probably better if Panos explains the procedure to you. We checked on the area before we came on to Heraklion and it seems ideal.'

Evgeniy and Ludmila looked at Panos expectantly and he placed a map of Crete on the table.

'This is Heraklion where we are at the moment. We will not be coming here. Our destination is further down.' Panos traced the route across from the Syrian coast to Crete. 'When we reach the Eastern coast there is a large inlet. We will sail in as far as practical and anchor. On one arm of land there are hotels and villas and on the other there is only a taverna. Once the taverna has turned off their lights and we are sure the staff have left we will motor as close to that shore as possible and anchor. Three men will climb into the dinghy that we carry and I will row them through a small canal to a secluded bay.' Panos placed his finger on the appropriate spot on the map.

'The men will leave the dinghy and wait on the shore whilst I return for the other three. They will all be dressed entirely in black and have their other clothes in black carrier bags. If Ludmila leaves Heraklion at about one in the morning she will have sufficient time to drive the Mercedes down to collect them. Any change to our plans and Ivan will telephone her. She will then leave the car and walk to the cove to await my signal. When she sees two flashes from my torch she will confirm she is there by flashing her torch three times. That will be the only time she uses it. I will not land the men until I have had that confirmation. Ludmila will wait with the first three men until I arrive with the others. They will have had it impressed on them that they must wait with her in silence. When I land the second group of men I will throw over to Ludmila a bag that contains their mobile 'phones and the money. Ivan will already have deducted our share. I row back to the boat, haul up the dinghy and we will motor back out to sea. Job done.'

'How long will it take to bring the men to the shore?'

'I estimate an hour, but it could be a little longer depending upon the wind.' Panos then continued. 'Ludmila, will also be dressed in black and with her hair pinned up and hidden underneath the cap. Make sure you purchase one that is large enough for you to do so,' he said and Ludmila nodded. 'She will take the men to where the car is parked. The bag containing their 'phones and the money will be placed in the cavity that is beneath the driver's seat. The men will place all their possessions into a case and change their black roll neck for a white shirt. This must be completed as swiftly and silently as possible. Ludmila will then drive back across the Causeway, along the coast road and up the hill away from Elounda and join the road that leads to Heraklion.'

'How far from Heraklion is the place where Ludmila is collecting them?' interrupted Evgeniy.

'About an hour and a half. We can take a drive down there tomorrow and you can see the exact location and also the area where Ludmila will park whilst she waits and where the men will change and pack their cases. That should not add more than ten minutes to the journey. Ludmila will drive back to Heraklion and meet you, Evgeniy, at a designated spot. She will leave the car, taking the bag containing the money and the mobile 'phones with her, and you will drive the men to the hotel as if you have collected them from the airport. By then it will probably be six in the morning. You will take their cases from the boot and they will take them up to their rooms.'

'What about registration at the hotel?' asked Evgeniy.

'They are your private guests. They do not need to register as they will pay you for their stay in cash. You settle them in their rooms, order a light meal from the dining room and wait until it is delivered. You then leave them to shower, rest or whatever and arrange a time when you will return to advise them what will happen next.'

'So what will happen next?' asked Ludmila.

'Evgeniy will have arranged for Rashid to come at short notice and take a photograph of each man. This will be inserted into their new British passport that he will make up. This will enable the men to leave Crete or Greece and enter Britain without any questions asked. They will be met at the airport on their arrival and escorted to a cheap boarding house and after that they are on their own.'

'Who is meeting them?' asked Ludmila.

'Nassam. He has a London taxi capable of carrying six people. He will charge each man fifty pounds sterling for meeting them and taking them to the boarding house.'

'How are they going to pay for their lodgings?' asked Evgeniy.

'I have worked out the costs involved. I will be asking each man for twenty thousand dollars. Ten thousand will cover the cost of the sea voyage,'

Evgeniy held up his hand and stopped his brother-in-law. 'Why are you charging so much for the boat ride?'

'It is less than is being charged for a trip across the English Channel in an overloaded dinghy and being dumped ashore with no knowledge of the area and risking immediate arrest. I have agreed to pay Panos three thousand for each man we take across and I have to cover the cost of the fuel and their food. That leaves ten thousand to cover their ongoing expenses.

'Each man will pay two thousand dollars for his passport. You will make regular visits to the bank and change a minimum of three thousand dollars into Euros; vary the amount you withdraw each time. This will provide each man with five hundred Euros. This should be sufficient to cover the cost of their flights, their luggage and new shoes. A further three thousand dollars of the remaining money will be changed into sterling, again five hundred for each man. Make sure you use a number of different exchange bureaus and vary the amounts each time. The sterling will be given to them when they depart for the airport along with their mobile 'phones. That should leave seven thousand dollars to cover their expenses whilst they stay at your hotel.'

Evgeniy was writing down the figures on a piece of paper watched by Ludmila and she shook her head. 'Suppose for some reason they are unable to leave Crete within the time scale you envisage? That would mean the hotel was subsidising them indefinitely and we would be out of pocket.'

'At worst they should have a delay of no longer than one day depending upon flight availability. If I am delayed at sea due to bad weather I have to stand the cost of feeding them.' Ivan shrugged. 'We just have to hope that everything goes smoothly.'

'How are their flights going to be arranged?' asked Evgeniy. 'I certainly do not want to start booking their flights on my personal computer or the one at the hotel.'

'Ludmila will take the men to a travel agent, posing as a travel consultant, and purchase a flight for each of them. She will then take them to a shoe shop to buy a pair of conventional shoes. This will leave the men with a few Euros in their pocket. Evgeniy, you will drive the men to the airport in the Mercedes where the sterling and their mobile 'phones will be given to them, but they must not make any calls until they are safely in England. You help them to check in and bid them farewell, safe journey and the like. You watch from a distance until they have passed through security and then return to the hotel.' Ivan sat back and smiled complacently.

'What happens if they are stopped at security?'

'Evgeniy must leave the airport immediately. The men would look for him to help them so it is far better that he is not in the vicinity. They will not have his 'phone number or that of the hotel. It is unlikely that anyone would believe their story of sailing across to Crete, being taken to a luxury hotel and having false passports to allow them entry into Britain. They have no proof and you would confirm that their story was a tissue of lies.'

Evgeniy nodded, satisfied that he was unlikely to be implicated in any way. 'Who pays for this Mercedes that I have to buy?'

'Put it through the hotel expenditure. You'll be making near enough forty two thousand for each trip we complete.'

'Less the cost of petrol and the food they eat.'

'I'm sure you can absorb that in your expenses. Not a bad return for very little expenditure. If we can do three trips a month, weather permitting, from March until the end of October you're looking at approximately a million, probably a bit more, and it's money straight into your pocket. Any more questions regarding the project or shall I open another bottle and we can drink a toast to our success? I'm looking forward to visiting your hotel this evening and having a meal and tomorrow we will hire a car and drive down to the Bay of Mirabello.'

Cathy manoeuvred her three wheel walking support carefully through the front door of the apartment; placed her stick into the holder, and checked that she had her mobile 'phone, purse and keys in her bag before closing the door. Vasilis had gone into the hotel and she was quite capable of going down the road and around the corner to her local shops alone.

As she rounded the corner she nearly bumped into a group of people who were standing there talking.. 'I'm so sorry,' she apologised as she stopped abruptly. 'Oh, Mr Kuzmichov, what brings you here?'

'I was just showing my friends where our new apartment is located. Where are you off to?'

'I'm going shopping. I need to stock up on a few items as we have been away. As the area is flat I can go out independently. I am able to do my shopping without having to impose on Vasilis.'

Kuzmichov nodded.. 'An ideal location. Well, I'll not detain you any longer unless I can be of assistance to you in any way.'

'Thank you, but I can manage. I am known at the shops and they are always willing to pack my bags and place them in the carrier for me.'

Cathy continued down to the end of the road. From where the group had been standing they would not have been able to see the apartment and she had certainly not seen them until she turned the corner. She was sure she had heard a woman's voice and it could only have been Ludmila speaking in Greek. The conversation had stopped abruptly and Ludmila had given her a thin smile.

Ivan turned to Evgeniy. 'I think it would be better to change drivers down by the shops rather than here on the corner; you cannot see if there is anyone coming.'

'Provided they haven't started to open up.'

'If that is the case then Ludmila must drive a little further down where she will be less likely to be noticed. If you consider it to be a problem a new venue can be arranged. Now, shall we go and hire a car and Ludmila can drive us to the drop off point.'

'Me? I don't know the way.'

'It is quite a straight forward journey until you reach Elounda. Panos will direct you then. You need to become familiar with the route.'

Ludmila drove steadily out of Heraklion and at Panos's instruction took the road through the mountains that was signposted as leading to Aghios Nikolaos.

'You just keep going straight down this road until you reach a roundabout and traffic lights There is a sign that shows the road to Aghios Nikolaos is to the right. You take the fork to the left where the sign says Elounda.'

Ludmila took the road to the left. So far the drive had been as straight forward as Panos had said.

'Just continue along this road and I'll tell you when to draw in,' said Panos. 'From there you will be able to see the drop off area.'

It seemed a considerable time before Panos finally directed Ludmila to pull in to the side of the road where there was an area for tourists to stop and take photographs of the picturesque bay.

'If you arrive earlier than expected you can always sit here for a while. If anyone should stop and ask if you need any help you just tell them you are taking a short break from driving and there is no problem. Now, everyone out and I will show you the area from up here. It is a spectacular view.'

Dutifully Evgeniy, Ivan and Ludmila followed Panos over to the safety barrier.

'The buildings down there are Elounda.' He pointed to the left. 'Look across the water and you will see that expanse of land opposite which is actually an island. It is joined to the mainland by a Causeway. At the end of the Causeway is a small canal that can be used to access the bay by the small boats to save them having to sail around. That is where I will take the men through in the dinghy and land them.'

'How do I get there?' asked Ludmila.

'You drive over the Causeway.'

'Are there lights on the Causeway?' asked Ludmila. The thought of driving across the narrow road in the dark was daunting.

'You will see that the Causeway is actually wider than it appears from up here and it is lit. You will be able to drive over there and back without using the lights on the car. We will drive across and I will show you where the men will land and also the area where you can park the car.'

'Why don't you sail into the harbour?' asked Evgeniy noticing the collection of boats of various sizes that were moored there.

Ivan shook his head. 'There are people around in that area at all hours of the day and night. The men could be seen leaving the boat and a Mercedes waiting to pick them up would be a talking point amongst the locals. We need to be as invisible as possible.'

'Seen enough?' asked Panos. 'If so we will drive on towards the village and you must be prepared to make a very sharp right hand turn, Ludmila. I will tell you when it is coming up. In the season this road is full of traffic and it can often be easier to drive into the village, turn and drive back up.'

Ludmila nodded, her hands gripping the steering wheel. It was going to be very different making the journey at night.

'Indicate well ahead and slow down. Now turn.'

'Down there?'

'That's right. Just take it slowly in case there is someone coming up.'

'Is this road often used?' she asked.

'Continually. It leads to some self catering apartments and hotels then on to the Causeway. There are two small churches that are accessed from there where the locals go for services on special occasions and tourists go walking. They also walk or drive across to go to the taverna and look at the remains of the Roman Basilica.'

Once having negotiated the turn and short steep hill Ludmila found she was driving along a well kept road with the sea on one side and buildings that looked derelict on the other. The buildings ended and there was sea on both sides of the road.

'You are now on the Causeway,' announced Panos. 'Drive across the bridge and park near the windmill. We will then get out and walk for a while.'

'There is someone else already here,' remarked Evgeniy.

'They have probably driven over to take a walk the same as us. If we meet them just smile and say hello.'

Panos led the way along the road to where there was a small sheltered beach and Ivan, Evgeniy and Ludmila followed him dutifully to where there was a small bay with rocks on one side and a stone jetty on the other. 'Here it would be very difficult for anyone on the shore to see you. The Causeway lights do not penetrate this far and everyone will be wearing black, remember.'

'How will the men get ashore?'

'I will paddle in as far as possible and they should be able to jump onto dry land. If Ludmila has not returned my signal I will stay a short way out and keep trying until she answers me. If I do not receive the signal at all I will return the men to the boat and you will be 'phoned, Evgeniy to explain her absence.'

'Suppose the car has broken down?'

Ivan gave Evgeniy a steely glare. 'A brand new Mercedes should certainly not break down. If such an eventuality occurred Ludmila must phone you immediately and you must phone me. There is no point in risking the journey for nothing.'

'Where do I park?' asked Ludmila.

'This road leads to the hotel you may have noticed from the shore. It caters for bed and breakfast so there could be staff and tourists around even at night. Under no circumstances do you use their car park. A Mercedes would be far too noticeable. You will park behind the windmill, close to where we have parked now. At times the other windmill is occupied but no one is likely to be up and around at the time you will be here. Switch off your lights when you drive in and cut your engine as soon as possible. There are no street lights there and you will not be seen from the shore.' Panos led them back towards their car, talking as he went. 'The taverna is very popular with the tourists. We will have to wait until the lights have all gone out and the staff have left for the night before I can start to bring the men ashore. You can see the canal that I will use; it goes beneath the bridge and then joins the bay. Sometimes, depending upon the time of the month, the water can be too low even for a dinghy to pass through. If I find that is the case I would have to drop the men at the end and they would have to scramble up the rocks.'

'Why don't they do that anyway?'

'It is not ideal. They could slip and injure themselves and the area is rocky. If the dinghy was holed it would ruin our plans and I might not be able to return to the boat. It is far better for Ludmila to meet them on the beach and bring them round here to the car.' Panos waved his hand in the direction of the windmill.

'Can't she park closer to the beach area?'

'If she is parked there it is possible for her to be seen from the shore due to the lights on the Causeway. The windmill is a far better spot. They will be told to transfer their clothes from the carrier bags into the cases as swiftly and quietly as possible before getting into the car. Now, Ludmila will tell me exactly what she has to do when collecting the men.'

Ludmila repeated her instructions to Panos's satisfaction.

'Suppose I am stopped by the police?' asked Ludmila.

Panos chuckled. 'There are no police in Elounda as they have no crime. During the day they drive through and then return to Aghios Nikolaos. Provided you do not exceed the speed limit when driving back to Heraklion on the main road the police should have no reason to take any notice of you. There is always a considerable amount of traffic going to Heraklion airport. You will be just one of many using the road in the early hours.

'We will now drive back across the Causeway and up the hill to the main road. We will then go down to the village, drive around as if we are visitors who have lost their way and return up the hill following the signs for Aghios Nikolaos.'

'Could we stop for something to eat in the village?' asked Evgeniy.

'There will be few places open and a tourist would be remembered out of season. You do not want to attract any attention to yourself. We will drive on towards Aghios and have something to eat there. We will have a leisurely meal followed by a stroll around the town until it is dark. Ludmila will then drive us back to Elounda and across the Causeway so she can see the route in darkness. Over the next few weeks I expect you to hire a number of different cars from rental places and drive down during the day to familiarise yourself with the route and then make some journeys at night. Evgeniy can always accompany you at first.'

Vasilis returned from "The Central" with four large boxes of books that he had taken from the cupboard. 'There are still some more in there and I'm sure I could take some from the shelf without anyone noticing.'

'Monika will be thrilled. We can take them down to her the next time we visit. Did you manage to bring any empty boxes for me to pack our belongings?'

'I brought two'

'We'll need more than two!'

'I know, but I don't want you overtiring yourself. There's plenty of time to pack.'

'There's only a month and the apartment will have to be thoroughly cleaned through when we leave. I know it isn't dirty, but I would not want the Kuzmichovs to find a speck of dust anywhere. Do you think there's a reliable cleaner at "The Central" who would be willing to come in?'

'I'm certain I can find someone. We can arrange for her to visit and clean the spare bedroom thoroughly when we have moved everything we want from there. For a final clean through we could arrange that to coincide with our visit to Rethymnon and we could always go and stay at "The Central" for a couple of nights when we return.'

Cathy smiled. 'I've had a wicked idea. As we are taking the bedding and towels with us along with the china and cutlery would it be possible to 'borrow' some from 'The Central".'

Vasilis frowned. 'Why would we want to do that? We won't be here.'

'I know, but the bed could be made up and they would have towels and some plates and cups to use.'

'They will have "The Central" logo on them.'

'You could leave them a note to say the items are on loan from "The Central". After all, they will be Evgeniy's possessions by then so it will be up to him if he keeps them.'

Vasilis looked at his wife in amusement. 'You have a very devious mind on occasions. Kuzmichov was obviously displeased that we would not be leaving everything here for him. He could look on it as a gesture of good will from us.'

'I saw Kuzmichov and his wife today. They were standing round the corner talking to two men and I nearly ran into them. Kuzmichov said he was showing his friends where the apartment was, but from where they were it was impossible to see it.'

'They may have walked past earlier and you didn't notice them.'

Cathy frowned. 'I'm sure I would have seen them. I was sitting in the window.'

'Reading?'

'No,' Cathy shook her head. 'I was painting my nails. The light was just right. I was looking out of the window as I waited for them to dry. It just seemed a bit odd, that's all. If they wanted to show their friends their new apartment I would have expected them to stand opposite, not round the corner.'

February 2015
Week One

Vasilis closed his mobile 'phone with a pleased smile. The owner of the land down by the seafront road leading to the Causeway was willing to sell and the man already had permission to build on the site. The price he was asking was ridiculously high, but the cost of prime building land was rising continually. It could be a good investment, although it did not solve the immediate problem of where he and Cathy could live until he had built some suitable accommodation on the site. He would keep the knowledge to himself until he had signed the contract during the next week. He would then need to have plans drawn up and approved.

'How is the packing coming along?' asked Vasilis of Cathy.

'The spare bedroom only has the items stored in there that we are taking down to Elounda. I have also packed all your summer clothes along with the few of mine that were still here.'

'In that case I will telephone Vasi and say we will be going down this week. We can take the boxes of books for Monika at at the same time.'

'Can I tell her?'

'Of course. Ask if her friend Eirini at "The Central" would be willing to come and do some cleaning here. According to Monika the lady was in need of some extra money which was why Monika asked for her to be appointed as a chamber maid rather than herself. If she is agreeable she could come in whilst we are away in Elounda.'

Eirini accepted the offer from Vasilis gratefully, but was concerned about the time she would have to ask to have off from the hotel.

'I will give you a key and you can go to the apartment as it suits you. We only want the spare bedroom and adjoining bathroom cleaned at present. It's more than just a dust and hoover job. The windows will need to be cleaned inside and out along with the blinds and the paintwork washed. If you find any marks on the carpet they will need to be removed. If you haven't managed to finish by the time we return you can always come in whilst we are there.'

'How long do you plan to be away?' asked Eirini.

'At least four nights, possibly five. If you give me your telephone number I can call you so you know when we will be back.'

'If I went there when I've finished at "The Central" four evenings should be quite enough time for me to clean everything. May I also have your telephone number so I can advise you when I have finished?'

Vasilis handed Eirini his business card along with a key to the apartment. 'Use my mobile number. If it is switched off leave a message and I will get back to you as soon as I can. There should be everything you need in the way of cleaning materials in the apartment, but buy anything you find you need and give me the receipts.'

Eirini placed the key and card safely into her purse. If Mr Iliopolakis was pleased with her work he might want to employ her permanently as a cleaner for him and his wife.

Ludmila was beginning to feel more confident. On three occasions she and Evgeniy had hired a car from separate garages and driven down to Elounda. The first time they had driven to Aghios

Nikolaos Ludmila had purchased two suitcases that could be taken on board an aircraft as hand luggage and Evgeniy converted a thousand dollars into sterling.

'If I knew exactly what that woman was taking from the kitchen we could probably buy some replacement items whilst we are down here,' she grumbled.

'There's bound to be a better selection in Heraklion. Look on the internet and find some bargains. You'll have plenty of time. Unlike me, you'll only be working two or three nights a month and a short while during the day. Not only will I have to make a show of running the hotel I will need to spend some time with the men whilst they are staying. I don't want them to become bored and go wandering off into the town on their own.'

'You can't be with them all day and all night,' remonstrated Ludmila.

'I will impress upon them that they must not go down into the hotel unless I am with them and if they attempt to leave by one of the fire exits an alarm will go off. If these men are as desperate as Ivan says to get to England they won't want to jeopardise their chances by doing something foolish and drawing attention to themselves.'

'It wouldn't hurt to look around when we've had some lunch. I want to drive on to Elounda when it's dark to ensure I can find that turn off and drive across the Causeway safely.'

'You found it easily enough when Panos was with us and you had no problem when we've driven down since. I can always keep a look out for the turning.'

Ludmila shook her head. 'You won't be with me, remember. I have to know exactly how to do this when I am alone. After this run I plan to come down by myself when it is dark.'

'A Mercedes is considerably larger than a saloon car. Will you be able to cope with it?'

Ludmila gave her husband a scathing look. 'I managed perfectly well to drive a lorry load of equipment across Turkey for you, besides, you still have to buy the car.'

'It's a shame we can't arrange to have goods here that are needed in Syria. Ivan could take them across each time he returns.'

'If I had been stopped when I was in Turkey I could have denied all knowledge of the contents of the lorry, told the authorities that I didn't load it and had only been employed to drive. Whatever enquiries they made they would have continually come to a dead end. You know exactly how to cover your tracks. Ivan has to return to a port and his boat could be searched. He couldn't very well deny any knowledge of armaments that were found on board.'

'So what excuse are you going to make if you are stopped and found to have six Syrian men in the back of the car?'

'I am just the driver taking them to the airport. I received a phone call and was told where I should meet them. I do not know where they were staying or any other details about them, besides Panos said there are no police patrols in Elounda and the main road will be full of traffic with people going to the airport. Why should they decide to stop me?'

Evgeniy shrugged. There was no reason why his wife should be stopped, but in the eventuality of that happening he would claim that she was often asked to drive people to the airport using the Mercedes as a status symbol. He had not bothered to keep a record of the names or telephone numbers of those who had instigated the request and there had never been any problem in the past. If pressed for information he would give a list of most of the hotels in the area along with their telephone numbers and he was convinced the police would give up trying to implicate him and Ludmila.

Vasilis loaded the boxes and cases into his car and called Eirini. 'We are leaving this afternoon so you are welcome to arrive whatever time you wish to clean the spare bedroom and bathroom. Please make sure you clean inside the wardrobes and drawers.'

'Of course. I will telephone you when I have finished, Mr

Iliopolakis. If there is anything not done to your satisfaction when you return I will obviously come and put it right free of charge.'

'I'm sure everything will be fine. You are not to work until you are exhausted each evening.'

Eirini smiled to herself. She would ensure that the bedroom and bathroom were spotless when Mr Iliopolakis and his wife returned, but she was not expecting to find the area dirty. She would clean the inside of the bedroom window that night and wash the paintwork. The following evening she would wash the blind and have time to remove everything that was in the wardrobe and drawers before she cleaned them. By the time she had replaced everything and hoovered the room it would not leave her time to clean the bathroom area and tiles. The bathroom could wait until the following day and once she had finished the cleaning she would polish the chrome fittings. That would leave her one more visit to put the final touches to everything and clean the outside of the window, provided it was not raining.

When Eirini entered the apartment she was struck by how few personal items appeared to be around. She had expected to see pictures and ornaments everywhere, but it looked almost unwelcoming. Entering the kitchen she noted there were up to date appliances, but few other items. She had not expected Mr Iliopolakis and his wife to live such a Spartan existence. In a long cupboard in the kitchen she found a bucket and the cleaning materials she needed along with a hoover and small step ladder.

Investigating further down the hallway she found a bathroom was behind the last door she opened and a bedroom next door. There were no toiletries in the bathroom that needed to be removed and the bed had been stripped bare except for a mattress and four pillows. Curiously she opened the wardrobe doors followed by the drawers in the chest. Everything was empty.

Eirini shrugged. It was no business of hers. Maybe they were planning to have the apartment redecorated and that was why everywhere looked so bare. It would certainly make her cleaning easier. She carried the step ladder down to the bedroom and placed it in front of the window, pulling up the blind. She should manage to clean that along with the window, the wardrobe and the drawers that day.

Mr Iliopolakis had not mentioned the amount she would be paid and she assumed it would be the same rate as she received for her chamber maid services at the hotel. She must keep account of her hours to present to him upon his return.

Within three hours she had cleaned everywhere in the bedroom and moved into the bathroom. She would clean that window and the blind that evening before returning home. The bathroom she should be able to complete the following day and then she would only have to wash the tiled floor and hoover the bedroom, along with cleaning the outside of the windows. The work was not going to be as lucrative as she had envisaged.

Monika was delighted when Vasilis and Cathy arrived with four large boxes of books.

'Would you like me to ask Theo to help you in with them? I believe he is over at the taverna.'

'Thank you, but I can manage. You just show me where you would like me to put them.'

Monika looked at the large central desk. It was already covered in the books she had salvaged from the self catering apartments and local hotels. 'I think the only space is on the floor. I am trying to get the shelves reorganised whilst I am only open for a short while as a library service hence the mess there is everywhere.'

'I had hoped I would be able to bring you a few more, but you seem to have plenty.'

'I'll be grateful for any. Because the people can borrow the books for a small fee and have money returned to them when they bring them back they are often ruined and I have to throw them out.'

'Maybe you should charge more and give them less money back.'

Monika pulled a face. 'I need the little it brings in to cover my winter rent. It's better to throw a few books away than refuse to lend them. I shouldn't complain; I have only paid a few Euros for a quantity of used copies. I certainly would not lend out any new books. They are for sale only.'

'You could do with someone to help you with the sorting.'

'I come in on the days when I say I am closed and often stay on late. The sorting is not the problem; it is making a comprehensive list on the computer that takes the time. Theo is very kind. He usually brings me over a sandwich lunch and often stays on to help for an hour or so.'

'Couldn't your mother help you?'

'She only reads Greek,' smiled Monika. 'Even if I ask her to put books on the shelf in alphabetical order of the authors she becomes confused with the Greek and English alphabet and I have to sort them out a second time. I have assured her that she is more help to me if she cooks me a meal each evening. I'm sure I will be organised by the time the season starts.'

Vasilis smiled. He knew the problems that Cathy would have if she was asked to put Greek books in alphabetical order.

Vasilis arrived promptly at the lawyer's office in Aghios Nikolaos and was asked to wait until Mr Lucanakis arrived. After ten minutes he was considering telephoning the man to check that he was planning to arrive shortly and the deal was still going ahead. The door burst open and a florid faced man rushed through.

'I'm late. Is Mr Iliopolakis here?'

'I am Mr Iliopolakis.' Vasilis rose and extended his hand. 'Are you Mr Lucanakis?'

The man nodded and sank heavily into the chair next to Vasilis. 'I'm sorry. My car broke down and I had to wait for a taxi to arrive and bring me here. Give me a few minutes to recover my breath and then we can tell the lawyer we have both arrived.'

'Take your time.' Now the owner of the land had arrived Vasilis was no longer worried that the man had decided against selling.

Both men sat in the lawyer's office and tried to listen intelligently to the information he read out to them from his papers. 'Are you both in agreement with the arrangement?' he asked finally.

'I would like to have a quick look at the contracts before I place my signature to them.' Vasilis stretched out his hand. 'I am conversant with property transactions and there can sometimes be something detrimental to the purchaser in the small print.'

Vasilis scanned the first pages quickly and then concentrated on the wording of the purchase of the land. He frowned. 'There is no mention here of permission to build on the land. I was under the impression that has been granted.'

'That is in a separate document,' announced the lawyer smugly.

'Then before I sign I would like to have sight of that also. The land, without permission to build, would only be a useful financial investment, but I want to be able to build a house for my wife there. She is disabled and it is extremely difficult to find suitable accommodation. Halls and doorways are often too narrow for a wheelchair or the property is up a flight of steps.'

The lawyer handed over four sheets of paper with a Prefecture seal on the last page along with two signatures. Vasilis nodded. 'That seems all in order. I do have one other question. At present there are two large rubbish bins outside. I need to know they will be moved elsewhere. There is no way I wish to look out on them from my windows.'

'I agreed they could stand there,' said Mr Lucanakis. 'The hotels and tavernas use them.'

'Then the agreement must be revoked before I purchase the land. I imagine the aroma arising from them, particularly during the summer months, would be most obnoxious. Who did you make this agreement with?'

Mr Lucanakis shifted uncomfortably in his chair. 'Well, the

local people. They had no desire to have rubbish bins outside their hotels or self catering apartments. It was just an empty plot of land and the rubbish collectors had no issues.'

'So you only have a verbal agreement?'

Mr Lucanakis nodded.

'Then I expect the rubbish bins to be removed permanently to a new location well away from your land by this time next week. Provided that is complied with I will be happy to go ahead with the purchase.'

'I'm not sure if I will be able to contact the local traders. Many establishments are closed down and the owners away.'

'Then contact the rubbish collectors and tell them the bins have to be removed elsewhere now you are selling. You only allowed them to be there as a courtesy and convenience. Once that has been done we can proceed with our business.'

'They might object.'

'You have to over-ride their objections. You wish to sell and I wish to buy. The bins have to go as I will need access to the site for machinery and building materials. That is not unreasonable.'

'I'll see what I can do,' sighed Mr Lucanakis.

Vasilis turned to the lawyer. 'I apologise for wasting your time this morning. Please make a further appointment for Mr Lucanakis and myself for this time next week. If you are unable to get the bins removed permanently, Mr Lucanakis, please contact me. There is little point in having an appointment if I am unable to go ahead with the purchase.'

Annoyed at having a wasted morning Vasilis walked back to his car. He was sure Mr Lucanakis had been paid by the taverna owners for the convenience of having the bins in front of his land.

Although Vasi had heard nothing from the man whose neighbour was in hospital Vasilis decided to call and see if he was around. He wanted to go ahead with the purchase of the land as he was convinced it was a good investment, but he also wanted somewhere he and Cathy could live until he had managed to build a suitable property.

The apartment still showed no sign of occupation, but he knocked loudly on the door and stood looking around hoping the neighbour would appear. Everywhere appeared to be deserted and he knocked again and called 'Hello. Is anyone in?'

Vasilis stood back and waited. A woman lifted the corner of her curtain and looked at him curiously. Deciding he had nothing to lose Vasilis crossed the road and knocked on her window. The curtain was raised again and she looked at him suspiciously.

'Please would you open the window so I can speak with you.'

The curtain dropped back into place and although Vasilis stood there hopefully the window was not opened. Just as he was about to give up and leave the front door opened and a man glared at him.

'Why are you being a nuisance to my mother?' he asked.

'I do apologise. I am trying to contact a man who lives near the empty apartment across the road. I hoped your mother might be able to help me.'

'Have you knocked on his door?'

'I'm not exactly sure which is his house. My son spoke to him a few weeks ago.'

'Then I propose that you go and try the houses over there. No point in disturbing my mother.' The door was closed abruptly in Vasilis's face.

Feeling embarrassed Vasilis returned to his car. He had certainly not wished to distress the lady. He drummed his fingers on the steering wheel. There were no shops or tavernas open in the vicinity where he could make enquiries. He would have to return later in the day and start knocking on doors.

Time was beginning to run out for him. He needed to complete the purchase of the land the following week and return to Heraklion to make the itinerary for Kuzmichov of the items he and Cathy were leaving behind. He then needed to hold meetings with the staff at "The Central" and inform them that he was selling up and arrange for Kuzmichov to come in and be introduced as the new owner. He was relying on being able to stay at the hotel once he and Cathy returned from visiting the memorial her father had had erected for his first wife and child up past Rethymnon. In that final week whilst they were away he wanted Eirini to complete the cleaning of their apartment. He hoped his faith in the chambermaid was not misplaced and she would have left the spare bedroom and bathroom spotless.

He opened his mobile 'phone to call Cathy and then thought better of it and pressed in Vasi's numbers instead.

'What's wrong, Pappa?' Vasi sounded anxious.

'Nothing. I'm down in Elounda by the apartment that is empty. Can you remember where the man lived that you spoke to?'

'I'm not sure. I didn't take a lot of notice. Either two or three houses further up I think. Why?'

'The apartment is still empty and I thought I would ask if the owner had made any decision regarding selling. If so I'd like to have a look inside before bringing Cathy down to see it. If the interior doorways are too narrow for her wheelchair to pass through it will be out of the question.'

'So knock on a few doors.'

'No one appears to be around.' Vasilis sighed. 'I'll come back down in an hour or so. Even if I am able to contact the neighbour he may not have keys to the property. Are you at the house? If so, tell Cathy I'm on my way.'

Eirini looked around. She had done the work required of her and did not like to start cleaning the lounge without the permission of Mr Iliopolakis. He could have personal items in there that he would not want touched. She took his card from her purse, looked around the lounge and with a little giggle she sat down on the sofa and removed her shoes, tucking her legs up beneath her. She would pretend for a few minutes that she lived surrounded by this luxury.

'Mr Iliopolakis, this is Eirini,' she said hesitantly as Vasilis answered.

'Is there a problem?'

'No, none at all. I just wanted to tell you that I have finished the cleaning you asked me to do. Is there anything else you would like me to clean for you.'

'Just a minute.'

Eirini could hear Vasilis speaking to someone, but was unable to distinguish the words.

'If you are willing to do some more my wife says there are three empty drawers and one of the wardrobes in the main bedroom that could be cleaned. The others will need to be done when we have removed our possessions. She also said the windows in our bedroom and the lounge could be cleaned inside.'

'Certainly. Would you like me to start to wash the paintwork along the hallway and in those rooms?'

'Well, yes, I suppose you could. It will be less to do later.'

'There is only one problem, Mr Iliopolakis. Everywhere is so clean that you cannot see where I have done any work.'

Vasilis laughed. 'I'm pleased to hear it. I could probably have walked out without having any cleaning done, but the purchaser is a rather particular person and I would not want him to be dissatisfied when he moves in.'

'You are selling this lovely apartment, Mr Iliopolakis?'

'Yes, Eirini. My wife wishes to return to Elounda where we lived originally. We will be back on Monday afternoon and I will speak to you again then. I will pay you all I owe you to date and we will arrange for you to come in again when we have finally finished packing everything up.'

'Yes, thank you, Mr Iliopolakis.' Eirini closed her mobile 'phone and looked around the lounge. If the apartment was being sold that could explain why there were no pictures or ornaments around.

Marianne made her weekly telephone call to her mother. 'Hi, Mamma, how are you this week?'

'I'm alright.'

'Are you sure? You sound a bit down.'

Marianne heard her mother give a deep sigh. 'It's Helena.'

'What has she done now?'

'She told me she has been seeing a therapist and he has told her she needs a focus in her life that makes her feel useful and valued. I agree with that. Since the boys left home she only has her local committees and she appears to fall out regularly with the other participants and then she resigns in a huff. The problem is that she has decided to make me her focus.'

'You?'

Elena sighed again. 'She has decided that I need looking after. She descends upon me at all hours. She insisted on doing my shopping the other week and bought all sorts of items that I dislike. She bought me some pears and insisted they would be better for me than grapes. I don't like pears so I gave them to a neighbour. I hate Tofu and Quorn but she said they would be better for my health than meat or fish.'

'So tell her to take them and use them herself if she considers they are part of a healthy diet.'

'She refused and insisted they were for my own good and I must eat them. I threw them away. Such a waste of money. The other morning she arrived whilst I was still having my early morning coffee and watching the news. I was not showered or dressed and she said I was no longer capable of looking after myself properly. I am perfectly capable. I just have a routine. There is no need for me to be up early nowadays so I take my time. I certainly don't spend all day in my dressing gown sitting watching the television.'

'Have you told her that she is not welcome to come before a certain time?' suggested Marianne.

'I tried, but she said she needed to visit me early some days to ensure I was alright before she went about her own business.'

'Has she got a key?'

'No.'

'Then don't answer the door.'

'She says if I don't answer she will assume that I have collapsed and would call nine one one and ask the police to come and gain access.'

'That is ridiculous. Maybe it would be better if you gave her a key.'

'I don't want to. It would take away my privacy. She would be able to just walk in whenever she pleased.'

'Have you spoken to Greg?' asked Marianne.

'Yes, he asked me to humour her for a while and that she was certain to find something else to occupy her soon and leave me alone.'

'That's all very well, but in the meantime she is making your life a misery.'

'She suggested last week that it would be practical if she and Greg moved in with me. That way she could look after me.'

'I hope you said no.'

'Of course I did, but she then said my house was too large for me to look after properly now and it would be to my advantage to have some live in help.'

'Are you finding it difficult to look after the house?' asked Marianne.

'No. I make sure the kitchen and bathroom are always clean every day. I dust and hoover my lounge and bedroom at least once a week and the other rooms that I no longer use I clean occasionally. I admit that I am probably not as meticulous as I used to be, but there is only me here.'

'Do you cook yourself a proper meal each day?'

'Yes, unless I am meeting friends for lunch; then I just have a snack in the evening.'

Marianne considered her mother's words. There was only one way to find out if Helena's actions were justified. 'I think you need a change of scene. The men are busy at the self catering apartments ensuring all is in order for the coming season. Bryony and I share the cleaning and cooking between us with help from Nicola when she isn't busy with the children. I'd like you to come and stay with us for a few weeks. That will get you away from Helena. By the time you return she will probably have found a new interest.'

'Can I? I didn't want to ask. You're always so good about having me for a holiday during the summer months.'

'Mamma, you know you are welcome to come and stay at any time and for as long as you wish. Uncle Andreas is living out here and I know he will be pleased to see you. You'll need to bring some warm clothes with you as it is still quite cold most days. If I look into flights for you how soon can you travel?'

'I would only need two or three days to ensure that the fridge is empty and everywhere is clean.'

'Never mind the cleaning. You start packing and I'll e-mail you later and tell you when you are leaving.'

'Shall I tell Helena?'

'No. You don't want her deciding that you cannot travel alone and insisting that she accompanies you. I'll call her when I know you are safely on the 'plane.'

'She'll be furious.'

Marianne shrugged. 'That will be her problem. E-mail me your passport details and leave everything with me. I'll 'phone you later to tell you the arrangements.'

Marianne ended her 'phone call to her mother and called Giovanni.

'What's up?' he asked. It was unusual for Marianne to call him whilst he was working up at the apartments.

'I've just invited my mother to come to stay.'

'What now? At this time of year?'

'She's having a hard time with Helena. I'll explain everything to you later. I'm going to book her a flight so she can leave within the next few days.'

'What about a stop over in London? Do you want me to come home now?'

'I'll sort it; don't worry. I'll just need Uncle Yannis to move some of his boxes of pots from the room where he has stored them.'

'I thought John was supposed to be photographing them and putting them on e-bay to sell.'

'They both seem to be dragging their heels over that. Uncle Yannis insists that he needs to know how much he paid for them originally and how much the museum shops are charging.'

'I'll ring John and ask him to come home now. He'll have to insist Uncle Yannis makes a start on the project now before the season begins as he won't have time to deal with it then.'

'I think that is why Uncle Yannis is being so slow.'

'Tell him the pots either have to go soon or I will take them to the tip.'

'You wouldn't.' Marianne was horrified at the idea.

'Of course not, but explain that your mother is coming over and you need the space. You talk to him whilst I explain the position to John.'

'I was going to start to look up flights.'

'You can do that later. Arrange to meet her at the airport and have an overnight stop in London.'

'Me?'

'Why not? She's your mother. You could even stay over there for a week, have an impromptu holiday.'

'I wouldn't want to be there without you for that long. Over night would be sufficient for her to rest after the first flight.'

'Whatever suits you best, but you can spend longer in London if you want.'

Marianne closed her mobile 'phone, grateful that she had such an understanding husband.

'Dad says Grandma is coming to stay? Why on earth does she want to come at this time of year?' asked John.

'She wants to get away from your Aunt Helena for a while.'

'That does not surprise me. I understand that I have to bully Uncle Yannis to get on with selling his pots?'

'That's right. They'll have to be moved so the room where they are now can be made ready for your grandmother. It's a good opportunity to insist that some are put on e-bay. Once a few have sold Uncle Yannis will be happier about putting them all on.'

'They're not likely to sell over night. There are far too many.'

'Some of the boxes will have to be moved into his room and others will just have to go wherever we can find a space.'

'Why don't we ask Vasi and Saff to store some for him?'

'That's not possible at the moment. Vasilis and Cathy are storing their belongings with them. Just see what you can do about putting them on e-bay.'

'If they sell they will have to be securely packed and taken to the post office or a collection arranged,' warned John.

'We'll cope with that when the necessity arises.'

Grudgingly Uncle Yannis produced the list that he had made so far of the amount he had paid for each pot originally and the price the museum shops were asking.

'We ought to ask the same,' he said truculently.

John shook his head. 'People buy on e-bay expecting a bargain. Your prices have to be lower than those currently being asked. Let's make a start. You show me which ones you've valued and then I'll take a photograph. When I've done that we'll sit down together and work out a reasonable asking price and decide whether the packaging and delivery is to be extra or included.'

'It isn't cheap to send them anywhere.'

'I know, but if people see free post and packaging they are even more inclined to think they are getting a bargain and in many cases we can incorporate that into the asking price.'

Uncle Yannis followed John into the spare room and John looked around in despair. 'They need to be sorted out into which kind of pot they are and then we come up with a simple labelling system.'

'They are labelled.'

'You know exactly what the label means in relation to the contents, but I don't. If we make a start on the large pithoi and label the boxes A1. When I've photographed them we can move them to one side and I'll start on another collection that we can label A2 or B1.'

'Some of them have different designs on them.'

John sighed. 'Right. We'll label the pithoi collection as A1 and when I've taken a photograph we'll attach a copy to the outside of the box so we know what the inside contents look like. How does that sound.'

'I suppose so.'

'Don't be too enthusiastic, Uncle. I've agreed to do this to help you and also to help Mum to clear the room ready for when Grandma comes to stay.'

Uncle Yannis shook his head. 'I just don't understand how the system works, this putting photographs on a computer and expecting people to want to buy the items is beyond me.'

'You don't have to worry. I'll deal with all of it, but I need your help at the moment to sort them out. We can agree on the price later before we advertise them and also put a reserve price on them.'

'What does that mean?'

'You ask a hundred Euros for a pot and say that you will not accept less than ninety five. If anyone tries to buy for less they are refused.'

'Many of them are worth more than a hundred.'

'I was only using that as an example. Come on, let's make a start. Once you've seen exactly what I'm doing you'll understand.'

Marianne sat at her computer and began to look up flights from New Orleans to Washington or New York where she would be able to get a connecting flight to England. She wondered if her mother would have sufficient time to collect her luggage and find her way to another departure gate before it closed. Finally she called the airline and asked for their advice.

The woman she spoke to was helpful. 'If it was my elderly mother making the journey I would book assistance for her. This would mean that she was escorted to the gate she needed and her luggage would be collected for her and placed on board.'

'Suppose for some reason her inward flight was delayed. What would happen then?'

'The arrangements regarding helping her would stay in force until they were signed off as completed. Obviously if her inward flight arrived too late for her connection she would be given priority on the next flight. If necessary she would be accommodated in a hotel for the night. No one would expect her to sleep at the airport. Will your mother also require assistance when she arrives in London?'

'Is that possible? She would probably find it considerably easier if she did not have to struggle with luggage or have a long walk through the terminal to where I will be waiting.'

'I'll book it for you and send you confirmation by e-mail.'

'No,' panicked Marianne. 'I haven't booked my flight from Crete to London yet and I'll have to go via Athens.'

'Then I'll put your requirements on hold. You connect with this department when you have the details of your departure and we will update everything.'

Marianne gave a sigh of relief. All she needed now was a flight to Athens and an onward flight to London. It would be better for her to arrange to arrive a day before her mother just in case she was beset with any delays.

John placed the photographs he had taken onto his computer and printed off copies. 'It would be much quicker without Uncle Yannis,' he complained to Nicola. 'Each box we open he insists on examining the pot minutely before I photo it. He then tells me where the original was found and how much he paid for the replica. All I need at the moment is to make sure it is undamaged and photo it back and front. He can give me all the other details when we advertise it on e-bay.'

'Do you think they will sell?'

'I hope so. Mum needs the room emptied and they are going to be stored all around the house.'

'I think they should all go into his room. Once he realised how inconvenient they were he would be only too keen to sell them.'

'He wants to sell them, but he doesn't understand the system. He is used to people being able to look at them in a shop and deciding which one they want.'

'Can I help at all?'

'I'll tell him he needs a break and you have some coffee and cake waiting for him and Grandma Marisa in the kitchen. If he can be kept in there for a while I'll be able to finish the large pithoi in no time. I'm going back now to stick these photos on the outside of the box. That way we'll know exactly what is inside without having to continually open them when someone shows an interest.'

'Shouldn't you advertise the dimensions?' suggested Nicola. 'Someone might think the pot is considerably smaller than it actually is and having bought it find it far too large and want to return it.'

John nodded. 'I believe all the pithoi are near enough the same size. How about if I take a photo of Uncle Yannis standing next to one? That would show how big it is.'

'That's a good idea, you could use that as an advertisement. "Yannis Andronicatis is selling his amazing collection of museum replicas at bargain prices", but I still think you ought to give the approximate measurements. Uncle Yannis could be very tall or very short.'

John sighed. 'That will mean unpacking those I've already photographed. Why do you always come up with good ideas that mean more work for me?'

February 2015
Week Two – Monday, Tuesday & Wednesday

Each day Vasilis asked his son if the rubbish bins had been removed and Vasi shook his head. 'They are still in the same place. What's your interest?'

'I haven't mentioned this to Cathy yet, but I want to buy one of the plots of land down there and build a house. I had hoped to sign the purchase papers last week but I am insisting the bins are removed. I'm not prepared to have them outside looking unsightly and smelling to high heaven in the summer. Apparently the land owner has a private agreement with the taverna owners and rubbish collectors.'

'Has he?' Vasi raised his eyebrows. 'You should have told me that earlier. I'll soon sort it out. I will speak to the rubbish collectors and if they refuse to be reasonable I will tell them I am going to the local Prefecture Council and say they have accepted a bribe to have the bins placed there rather than in their original location. They know it is illegal to move them from a designated area without permission. I thought you were interested in the apartment in Elounda.'

'I am, but I've still not been able to contact the owner or the neighbour you spoke with. We must go back to Heraklion tomorrow afternoon as I have to help Cathy pack up the kitchen equipment and make an inventory. I also need to make arrangements to go into "The Central" and talk to the staff.'

'You have three more weeks before you sign the hotel over.'

'I know, but I've promised to take Cathy up to Rethymnon. Whilst we're gone the apartment will be thoroughly cleaned and we will then stay at "The Central" until all the legalities have been completed.'

Marianne telephoned her mother. 'Everything is arranged. You order a taxi to take you to the airport on Wednesday morning. You need to arrive at eight at the latest to check in. Your ticket will be waiting for you at the information desk and I have also arranged that you will have assistance.'

'What does that mean?'

'Your luggage will be taken from you to the check in desk. Your paperwork will be checked to ensure it is in order and then you will be driven to the departure gate.'

'Driven?'

'It could save you a long walk and ensure that you arrive in time to board easily. When you arrive in Washington you will be met again by a courier who will collect your luggage and take you to the departure gate. Once again your luggage will be checked in for you and all you have to do is show your ticket and go on board.'

'Suppose my flight to Washington is delayed?'

'If that should happen you will be given priority on the next flight out and if that is not until the next day there will be accommodation arranged for you at the airport hotel. Telephone me from the departure lounge and let me know that you are there and everything is going to plan. When you arrive at Heathrow you will be given assistance again and I will be waiting in the arrivals area to meet you.'

'You will?'

'Yes. The flight to Athens is not until the following day so I have booked us into a hotel for an overnight stay. You will need to rest as you know you will be tired and also have jet lag.'

'I hope I will be able to sleep on the flight.'

'That will be good if you can. I will have arrived the previous day and once you are on the flight to Washington I will telephone Helena. It will be far too late then for her to interfere with your plans.'

'It all sounds so easy. If I have to be at the airport by eight I'll order a taxi for six thirty.'

'You don't need to be there that early.'

'I know, but if Helena decides to pay me an early morning call she will not find anyone at home. If she is foolish enough to call nine one one and they do come and break in she will look rather stupid when she finds I am not there. I'll leave a note for her, just in case.'

Before driving in to Aghios Nikolaos Vasilis drove down to where the apartment was situated. He would make one more attempt to contact the neighbour before he drove into the town to meet at the lawyer's office. He parked a short distance away and knocked at the house next door to the empty property. Not receiving any answer he knocked on the second house and a woman with a baby in her arms answered him.

Although she admitted to knowing the owner of the empty property she had no idea how to contact him and suggested that he tried the man who lived next to her.

'We haven't lived here long but I know Panayiotis and Giuseppe were friends. Panayiotis might be able to help you as he said he was visiting Giuseppe in the hospital last week. He may have left for work, of course.'

Thanking her Vasilis hurried back next door. And knocked again. Even if he managed to locate the correct neighbour he would not have time to view the apartment before keeping his appointment in the town, but he might be able to return afterwards.

To his relief a man came to the door and Vasilis explained that he was interested in viewing the apartment.

The man scratched his head and stifled a yawn. 'I'm not sure.

There was someone else here the other week who wanted to view it. I've been looking for the card he gave me so I could contact him.'

'I believe that was my son. I can give you a contact number for him and I am sure he will confirm that I am his father and the person who is interested in looking inside to see if it would be suitable for my disabled wife.'

'I can let you in to have a look. Giuseppe gave me the keys when he went into hospital. He was hoping to let the apartment out during the season but if you are interested in buying I'm sure he would be happy to sell. It would relieve him of the responsibility. He's decided he wants to return to Italy where his sister has offered to look after him. He managed when he had only had one leg amputated but now the other has gone it is impossible for him to live alone. I told him that he needed to redecorate before he could expect to rent it out, but he said he was unable to consider doing that until later. I helped him clear the front room and put the furniture into the bedroom in readiness.'

'Would I be able to return a little later? I have an appointment in Aghios Nikolaos in half an hour.'

'What time? I can't hang around all day.'

'I should certainly be back by twelve.'

The man nodded. 'Provided you are not late. I have to be at work by two.'

'I'll make sure I am here. I may even manage to be a little earlier.'

Before taking the road that led to Aghios Nikolaos Vasilis dropped down to the seafront road. To his relief he saw the rubbish bins had been removed. Once the agreement for the sale of the land had been completed he would return to Elounda and visit the apartment. If he thought it was suitable he would telephone Cathy and ask either Saffron or Vasi to drive her down to view it for herself. He would then take her down to show her the plot of land where he planned to build their house and was looking forward to her reaction to his news.

Vasilis arrived at the lawyer's office no more than five minutes late and was relieved to see Mr Lucanakis already there.

'I've arranged to have the bins moved,' Mr Lucanakis greeted him with the news before saying good morning.

'I'm pleased to hear it. There should be no problem now in signing the purchase agreements.'

'How are you going to pay me? I don't want to wait weeks whilst you arrange a bank loan and get the money transferred.'

'The funds are already available,' Vasilis assured him. 'We can visit the bank and an immediate transfer to your account arranged. I am pressed for time today so I would like to have all our transactions completed within the hour.'

Mr Lucanakis nodded. He would be only too pleased to have the money in his account that morning.

Vasilis drove back to Elounda, arriving shortly before twelve and made his way to the apartment and knocked on the neighbour's door. The man opened it with a bunch of keys in his hand.

'I called Giuseppe and he has told me the asking price.'

Vasilis nodded. He had more than sufficient funds available even if Kuzmichov withdrew from his purchase of the hotel.

'Would you have a rule, by any chance? I need to ensure the internal doorways are wide enough to accommodate a wheelchair if necessary.'

'Bound to be. Giuseppe used a chair.'

Panayiotis closed his door and opened the door of his neighbour's apartment.

Vasilis looked around. The living room was spacious, but there were marks on the walls where the furniture had stood and more by the doorway where the owner had obviously misjudged the width of his wheelchair on occasions. At the far end was a door that led out to a patio area, although it had weeds growing through the paving slabs.

The kitchen doorway was certainly wide enough for a

wheelchair, although once in it would be necessary to go out backwards; there was insufficient space to turn. Vasilis nodded. He was not interested in the condition of the appliances. He would prefer to renew the washing machine, dish washer and refrigerator. The cooking hob looked reasonably clean, but again, that and the oven could be replaced along with the sink.

The bathroom presented more of a problem. There was a shower attached to the bath taps and a handle hanging down from the ceiling above a plastic chair. That was obviously the way the man had overcome the problems of getting in and out of the bath for a shower.

'Here is the bedroom,' said the neighbour opening the door. 'As I said, the furniture from the living room is stored in here at the moment, but it is quite a large room.'

Vasilis nodded. 'I really need a rule to ensure there is sufficient space for a double bed and a wheelchair if necessary.' At present Cathy was quite capable of walking around inside their apartment with the aid of her sticks, but the day could come when she was entirely dependent upon a chair.

'So what do you think?'

'It's a definite possibility. I'm going to 'phone my wife and ask my son to bring her down to have a look. The decision will be hers.'

The man looked at his watch. 'I can't stay much longer.'

'She will only be a few minutes and I'll ask her to bring a rule with her. Assuming she finds it acceptable how do I get in touch with the owner?'

'I can give you his mobile number.'

Vasilis nodded as he pressed in the numbers to contact Cathy. He spoke to her briefly, stressing that she must arrange to come down immediately. He took another business card from his wallet.

'Please, his name and 'phone number and also one where I can contact you. If you need to leave before my wife arrives are you able to leave the keys with me? I'll lock up when we leave and arrange for my son to deliver the keys back to you at a time to suit you.'

Panayiotis looked at Vasilis doubtfully. 'I feel responsible for the property.'

'You have my card, you can trust me. At least give me the telephone numbers.'

Panayiotis shrugged. There was no harm in giving the man the telephone numbers he requested but he was not prepared to leave the keys in the man's possession. He was due in at work at two that afternoon and he could not be late.

Whilst they waited for Cathy to arrive Vasilis looked around the apartment again. The little yard at the back, once cleaned and with some plants around, could be an attractive area to sit out in during the summer whereas the front windows only looked down the street. The cupboard at the end of the hallway should just about be large enough to make into a cloakroom for guests. He would need to spend a considerable amount of money bringing the apartment up to an acceptable standard, but once refurbished when they left it could easily be let out to summer visitors or local residents.

He drew a breath of relief when Vasi drew up outside and helped Cathy from the car. She looked at the exterior and smiled as she handed Vasilis the rule she had brought with her.

'I'm certain the front entrance will be wide enough.'

'Come inside and see what you think of the rooms. It needs to be decorated and a few alterations made, but provided you can see past the defects and you think this will be suitable for you I have the owner's telephone number.'

Cathy nodded in approval at the size of the main living room. 'I would be able to keep my walker over there by the door. There's plenty of space. Will I be able to get into the kitchen and bathroom?'

'The owner used a wheelchair so that should be no problem. I asked you to bring the rule as I want to take a few other measurements.'

Cathy wrinkled her nose as she entered the bathroom. 'I couldn't possibly cope with that arrangement of a chair in the bath. Suppose it slipped?'

'We would have that taken out and a shower installed the same as you have at home now.' Vasilis measured the width and length of the room. 'There should be no problem getting one to fit.'

'How do I get in here?' asked Cathy as Vasilis opened the bedroom door.

'The owner has his furniture stored in here at the moment. I just need to measure the area to ensure that there would be enough space on either side of the bed. I don't want to have to continually climb over you. The only real problem is the kitchen. If you do eventually need to use a chair you can go in easily, but there would be insufficient space to turn it around.'

'I'm sure I could soon learn to negotiate it backwards,' Cathy assured him. 'I might bump the doorway a few times at first so you would need to have a pot of paint handy to erase the marks I leave. If we do live here I would like some different tiles. That acid yellow puts my teeth on edge.'

Vasilis smiled in relief. 'So you think this is a practical proposition?'

'I certainly do, provided the appropriate alterations can be made. Is the owner willing to sell?'

Vasilis turned back to Panayiotis. 'As far as I am concerned I am willing to buy the apartment as it stands. The furniture needs to be removed, of course, but I'll be responsible for redecoration. How quickly can I contact the owner?'

'I've given you his 'phone number. You could call him in about an hour.'

Vasilis frowned in annoyance at the delay. 'I had hoped to drive back to Heraklion this afternoon.'

'A telephone call does not take all afternoon. You should have plenty of time.' Panayiotis did not disclose that he planned to telephone Giuseppe immediately and let him know that he had a prospective buyer for the apartment. He would also advise Giuseppe to add a few hundred Euros to the asking price he had mentioned earlier.

Vasilis shook hands with Panayiotis. 'Thank you. I appreciate your time. I will call you this evening.'

'I'll not be home until ten thirty at the earliest. You'd do better to call me tomorrow morning.'

'That is no problem.' Feeling highly satisfied Vasilis helped Cathy into his car.

'Do you really think it will be suitable?' asked Vasilis anxiously.

'I think it could be a lovely apartment once work has been done on it. I received the impression that it had been updated about ten or more years ago and never touched since. Where are you going now, Vasilis? You should have turned left, not right.'

'There's something else I want to show you before we leave Elounda.' Refusing to say any more Vasilis drove up the hill and then took the steep left hand turn that led down to the coast road. He drew up outside the empty plots of land and smiled at Cathy.

'What do you think?'

'What do you mean?'

'Would you like to live here?'

'In a tent?'

'I bought one of the plots of land this morning. It has building permission so all we have to do is employ an architect and tell him our requirements.'

'You bought it? I thought we were going to live in the apartment.'

Vasilis nodded. 'It will take a year or maybe longer to get a house built on the site and we need somewhere to live in the meantime.'

Cathy gave a contented sigh. 'I was becoming concerned that we would be living with Vasi and Saffron for ever more. I know they make us feel very welcome, but it's not the same as when we are in our own home. I feel like a visitor. Saffron won't let me lift a finger and I'm becoming thoroughly lazy.'

Vasilis chuckled. 'Don't worry. I have work planned out for you once we are back in Heraklion. We need to pack up the kitchen equipment and make a start on the inventory. I'll have to go into the hotel and talk to the managers then make time to speak to the other members of staff. Once I have done that and the inventory is completed we can go down to Rethymnon and arrange for the rest of the apartment to be cleaned ready for Kuzmichov. When we return we'll stay in "The Central" until the final papers have been signed.'

'Can we do that?'

'Of course. Until we have both signed the sale and purchase agreements the hotel still belongs to me.'

John began to unload the pots from their boxes.

'What are you doing?' asked Yannis.

'Nick said we ought to put the dimensions of the pots on the site so people know exactly how big they are.'

Yannis nodded. 'Of course, but there's no need to unpack them. The details are on the label on the bottom of the box.'

John sighed in exasperation. 'Why didn't you tell me before?'

Yannis shrugged. 'You insisted that you knew exactly what you were doing.'

'Right. Well before I put these back in their boxes I want a photograph of you standing between two of them.'

'Whatever for?'

'Another of Nick's ideas. We make up an advertising site saying these are your amazing collection of pots that you are now selling off at bargain prices.'

'I wish you'd stop calling them pots,' complained Yannis. 'Apart from the pithoi there are amphorae, kylixes. The small ones are ickythoi that would have held oils or perfumes, and many of the others are classified by the style of their decoration, Attic ware or geometric design.'

John gave his Uncle Yannis an exasperated look. 'I know as much about pottery as you do about photography. I'm happy to list them under their correct title, but when I talk about them they are pots. I'll make a start on the web site tonight and say there are more pots of various styles and dimensions that will be added to the site daily. It may mean that people wait until they have seen the whole collection before they start to buy, but knowing that there are more being added will also make people curious to keep going back into the site. Every day we will put a 'sold' sign on some of the pots and that should encourage the hesitant purchasers to make their bid.'

'But they may not have sold,' demurred Yannis.

'The purchasers won't know that any more than they know how many you have of each design. If anyone queries the sales you can honestly say you have more than one of the replicas.'

'I suppose so.'

'Right, stand over there and I'll place a pot on each side of you.'

'Should I go and put a suit on?'

John shook his head in amusement. 'There's no need for you to dress up. Nicola and I will design the web site tonight and then we can add some more photos of the pots, I'll show it to you tomorrow and see if you approve. Today we have to start moving furniture around to make space for these pots to be stored elsewhere. We'll move the pots that have been photographed into your room and then start on the next batch.'

'Into my room?'

'We have to clear the spare room today so Bryony can get it ready for Grandma Elena to come to stay. She can't do that whilst it's full of boxes of pots.'

'There's not enough space in my room,' said Yannis firmly.

'We'll make some space. We'll spread them out around the house, but we need to ensure that we keep each size and design together in one place if possible. We don't want to have to spend hours searching for one when it has been ordered. I don't expect you to move them. Marcus, Dad and I will do the heavy work.'

Yannis sighed. 'When do you want to start?'

'Right away. I'm going to weigh a pot and then I'll ask Dad and Marcus to help with moving them. Once that has been done we can continue taking the photos.'

Vasilis telephoned Giuseppe Bordelli, delighted to find that he was more than willing to sell the apartment he owned in Elounda to him and relieved that the man was in hospital in Aghios Nikolaos.

'How soon can you arrange for a lawyer to come to visit me in the hospital and draw up the agreement?'

'I can telephone mine in a few minutes and call you back to let you know. I am not able to return to Elounda until the end of the month as I have commitments here. In the meantime you could contact your lawyer so everything is ready for our signatures at the beginning of March.'

'How will the payment be made?'

'A direct cash transfer from my bank to yours.'

'Cash? You don't have to arrange a loan?'

Vasilis smiled to himself. There were few people in the same position as himself able to use his capital to pay for expensive transactions rather than have to pay the interest that would accumulate on a bank loan.

'I have placed sufficient funds to one side. Cash is no problem. I just need to know about the furniture you have stored in the apartment. I understand that you plan to go to Italy. Do you want it shipped over to you?'

Giuseppe chuckled. 'I'll have no need of that. I'm going to live with my sister. I'll speak to my friend Panayiotis. He can have anything he wants and dispose of the rest. He may know some people who are in need of furniture.'

'I'll leave that in your hands and let you know when to expect a visit from my lawyer.'

Cathy spent the morning in the kitchen of their apartment packing her appliances into boxes ready for Vasilis to place in their car when they finally left. It was a nuisance to have to take them up to Rethymnon with them, but as far as she knew Vasilis was not planning another trip down to Elounda during the week. She was excited at the prospect of redecorating the apartment and even more excited about the prospect of him building a new house down by the shore.

She looked around. What else should she take with her? The electric toaster was old and she debated on leaving it finally deciding she would take it. Ludmila would probably want a new one. The ironing board could stay, but she would take her steam iron.

She studied the cutlery that she used in the kitchen. That could easily be replaced along with the china and glassware. They had already packed the dinner service and cut glass items, along with the canteen of silver cutlery that her father had given them as a wedding present.

Taking a pad of paper and a pen she began to make a comprehensive list of the pots, pans and baking trays that would remain. If her new oven was of different dimensions they could be useless. She would ask the girl Vasilis had employed to clean the spare bedroom and bathroom to ensure that everything was dust free before she replaced them in the cupboards after cleaning. The girl had done a good job and she hoped everything would be spotless when the Kuzmichovs moved in, although she was sure Vasilis would insist on checking.

John sat with his Uncle Yannis at the computer. 'Here is the web site that Nick and I have designed. Have a good look at it and tell me what you think.'

Yannis studied the wording and the photographs. 'What does this say?' he asked.

'Exactly the same as the Greek, except that I have translated it into English and I checked the Italian translation with my father. I'll ask him to look it over again to ensure I haven't made any typing errors. He has also suggested that I put the same information on in French.'

'What for?'

'When we put the web site on live it will be available all over the world. We can't put every language on, but the computer is clever enough that if you only speak Mandarin you can ask it to translate for you.'

'There are no prices. How are people going to know how much they have to pay?'

'We have to work on that. I'm going to weigh one of the boxes on the bathroom scales and then check on the post office site the cost of sending it to anywhere in the world. We need to make it clear to purchasers that they have to pay extra for the transport so we have to get it as accurate as possible.'

'Suppose it gets broken?'

'We take out insurance to cover such an eventuality. If it arrives with as much as a chip we make a claim.'

'That's all very well, but how do we know it was due to mishandling? It could have been done by the person who bought it.'

'They will have to take a photograph of the damage and send it to us within twenty four hours of receiving the pot. You had to do this when you received goods from the manufacturers or sent them to customers. I think I've covered every potential problem.'

Yannis nodded. He had never had any complaints from customers and only once had he needed to ask for compensation for a pot that the delivery man had dropped.

'Provided you're happy with this I'll add some more photos this evening and then we can start to concentrate on pricing. By this time next week we should be up and running.'

Elena telephoned Marianne. 'I'm in the departure lounge at New Orleans. A nice man has made himself known to me and has said he will come to collect me when it is time to go on board. I'm not 'phoning you too early am I?'

'Not at all,' said Marianne, stifling a yawn. 'I'm getting ready to leave. Giovanni is going to drive me to Heraklion and I'll be at Heathrow to meet you when you flight arrives.'

'When are you going to 'phone Helena?'

'I have your flight number and I'll check that you have taken off then call her. Make sure you have your mobile switched off so she won't be able to call you. Unless there is any problem there is no need for you to switch it back on until we meet at Heathrow.'

Marianne telephoned Helena as soon as she had checked that her mother's initial flight had taken off.

'I'm not calling you too early am I Helena? I hope I haven't woken you.'

'Of course not. I'm always up early. I like to make sure that Greg has had a good breakfast before he leaves the house. Then I have to visit mother.'

'That was what I wanted to talk to you about. Mother ….'

'I know,' interrupted Helena. 'I am very concerned about her. I've been shopping for her and buying her healthy food, but I'm not sure if she is eating it as I told her. She has seemed very jittery and nervous the past few days. I really think her mental faculties are failing. I've told her she needs someone to look after her. I've told her it would be practical for Greg and me to go and live with her. She doesn't like the idea, but I'll try talking to her about it again today. I'm sure she'll eventually see that it is the only practical solution.'

'Helena, listen, there is no point in you going round to *our* mother today. She isn't there.'

'What do you mean? She isn't there. Of course she is there.

Where else would she be? If she had been taken ill during the night I would have been notified. After all, I am her contact number as her nearest relative as you are so far away.'

'There's nothing wrong with her. She's on board a plane bound for Washington.'

'Washington?' Marianne heard Helena gasp. 'Whatever for? It just proves I am right about her faculties failing. I'll catch the next flight out and bring her safely back.'

'By the time you arrive she will be on her connecting flight to England. She's coming to Crete to stay with us for a while.'

'What! That's impossible. She isn't capable of making her way across London alone.'

'I am leaving this morning and by the time Mamma arrives I will be at Heathrow waiting to meet her.'

'I don't believe this. How could you behave so irresponsibly? You should have asked my permission.'

'Helena, she is my mother as well as yours. I do not have to ask your permission. I arranged for Mamma to be met at New Orleans by a courier so she would not have to deal with her luggage or have any boarding problems. The same will happen when she arrives in Washington. She will be taken to the correct boarding gate and escorted onto the plane.'

'You can't rely on that. Anything could happen to her. There could be delays and then she'll panic and not know what to do. Even if she arrives safely she'll be totally exhausted.'

'I've booked us into a hotel and she will have all day to rest before we fly out the following day. I'm sure she will cope admirably.'

'No, it isn't possible. No wonder she has been so nervous these last few days. Cancel the arrangements immediately and have the airport at Washington put her on a return flight to New Orleans.'

'No way.'

'Then give me her flight details and I'll do it.'

'Helena, Mamma wants to come to Crete. I will telephone you

from Heathrow to tell you that she has arrived safely. I have to go now. Giovanni is waiting to take me to the airport. I'll speak to you again after I have met Mamma.'

Marianne terminated her call and smiled at Giovanni. 'I just hope Helena is wrong about Mamma becoming incapable otherwise I could regret this decision.'

'If we find the situation is too difficult to deal with you will have to phone Helena and admit that she was right.'

Marianne pulled a face. 'That could mean that I had to escort Mamma back to New Orleans and face Helena when I arrived so let's hope it doesn't happen.'

February 2015
Week Three – Thursday and Friday

Vasilis left Cathy looking at the computer sites advertising kitchen tiles and shower units whilst he drove to "The Central" and after greeting the staff who were on duty went upstairs to see Dimitra. She looked at him nervously as he entered her room.

'Good morning Mr Iliopolakis. Is anything wrong?'

'Certainly not with your work, Dimitra. I just wanted to speak to you before I had a meeting with the managers.'

Dimitra frowned. 'Is there a problem?'

'I hope not. May I sit down?'

'Of course.'

'I wanted you to be the first person to know that I am selling the hotel. I didn't want you to hear it from any of the other staff as word went round.'

'Selling?'

Vasilis nodded. 'My wife wants to return to Elounda where she has a number of friends. It is not practical for me to commute from there so I decided the time had come to retire.'

'So you plan to sell the hotel?' Dimitra looked stricken.

'It is already sold. The new owner is due to take possession in two weeks. I have explained to him the work that you are responsible for and earning a very low wage as you live in the hotel.'

'Does he want me to leave? Where can I go? I don't want to

live alone anywhere. I wouldn't feel safe.' Dimitra's lower lip trembled.

'Mr Kuzmichov has not mentioned making any staff changes and I feel sure he would want to become conversant with the running of the hotel before he considered he could improve the efficiency and income. I don't think you have any need to be concerned. Should you no longer be happy living here or working for him please contact me and I will do my best to make some other arrangements that suit you.'

Dimitra's eyes swam with tears, making Vasilis feel uncomfortable. 'Do you have to sell the hotel? There never seems to be a problem when you go away for a while.'

'That is because I telephone the manager each day and he deals with everything on my behalf. Having decided to retire I do not want the responsibility any longer.'

'Couldn't Mr Vasi take over? He was the manager when I first came here.'

Vasilis shook his head. 'He has more than enough to keep him busy down in Elounda. I made him a manager at this hotel for him to gain experience. He was very happy to do that then and the arrangement worked admirably for a number of years. When my wife and I bought his apartment in Heraklion it meant he had to drive up here and I had to drive down to Elounda. It was not practical so it was decided that this hotel would return to my control.'

'If he returned to Heraklion he wouldn't have the journey and he could be the manager again.'

'That is not possible. He has the hotel in Elounda and another in Aghios Nikolaos, along with other business interests in the area. Also his partner has a business in Plaka and she would need to live in Elounda. She could not be expected to drive back to Heraklion in the season as she is often still open at nine or even ten at night.'

Dimitra looked at him desolately. 'So you really are selling?'

'The final papers will be signed in two weeks. I will advise the other members of staff of the situation and I will also arrange for Mr Kuzmichov to come and be introduced to everyone. It is doubtful that he will remember everyone's name, but at least all of you will know what he looks like when he walks through the doors. Remember, Dimitra, if you experience any problems you can call me.'

The tears were now running down Dimitra's face and she sniffed dolefully. 'You've been very good to me, Mr Iliopolakis. You could have had me sent to prison, although I truly did not know what Alecos was doing with your accounts.'

Vasilis shifted uncomfortably. 'That is all in the past. No one knows about the problem. Now, dry your eyes, make yourself a cup of coffee and return to your work. I'm sure you will not notice that Mr Kuzmichov is around.'

'I have been getting more confident recently. Some days I go to the bakery on the corner and buy a sandwich for my lunch and three times a week I make myself go down to the dining room for an evening meal rather than having it sent up. I'm not sure I will feel comfortable doing that if the new owner is down there.'

'I think it is unlikely that he will be spending his evenings at the hotel. He said he wanted the apartment so he could have more time with his wife. See how it goes, Dimitra, and remember you can call me if you have a problem.'

Vasilis went to Mrs Planatakis's office and broke the news that there was to be a new owner of the hotel.

'Would it be possible for you to organise the chambermaids and cleaning staff to all be assembled at ten tomorrow morning? I am sure that by then word will have got around, but I feel it is only polite that I should tell them personally. I will be bringing Mr Kuzmichov in to meet everyone next week.'

'That should be no problem. I will place a notice on their rota board and also ask the receptionists to tell them when they arrive for work.'

'You won't forget the sewing ladies?'

'Of course not. I can place a notice on the door of their room. Provided they all arrive before ten they should see it. I'm sorry you will no longer be around, Mr Iliopolakis. I hope you will call in from time to time just to say hello.'

'I am not going to be living in Heraklion, but if I do have occasion to come up to the town I will certainly visit. My wife and I will be staying here for a few days at the end of the month. Not only have I sold the hotel I have sold my apartment also to the new owner. We are gradually removing our belongings and plan to visit Rethymnon next week. During that time the apartment will have been thoroughly cleaned so we would not want to go back there to stay.'

'Of course not. I hope you will find your stay here satisfactory.'

'If I don't I have no one to lodge a complaint with!' smiled Vasilis. 'There is one other thing; I want to borrow some bedding and towels from the hotel to leave in the apartment for Mr Kuzmichov and his wife. I imagine they will very soon buy some of their own and return them.'

'Whatever you say, Mr Iliopolakis. Until you have actually sold the hotel the bedding belongs to you.'

'Yes, I suppose it does,' mused Vasilis. 'I've just never thought of it like that. Before I go downstairs and speak to the managers can you tell me which floor the chambermaid Eirini is working on, please?'

'Is there a problem? Has a guest complained about her work?'

'There is no problem. I just wish to have a quick word with her and then I will speak to the managers and receptionists. Now, where will I find Eirini?'

'Second floor.'

Mrs Planatakis looked after Vasilis as he hurried off. Why would the man want to speak to a chambermaid before having a meeting with the managers? Was he planning to make a number of the staff redundant?

Vasilis found Eirini making up the bed in the guest's room with clean sheets.

'I'm sorry to interrupt you, Eirini, but I need to pay you for the work you did in the apartment and arrange for you to come again.'

'It was a pleasure, Mr Iliopolakis. Everywhere was already so clean and tidy, except the outside of the windows, of course. I spent no more three hours there the first two days and two hours the final day.'

'So I owe you for eight hour's work?'

Eirini nodded and Vasilis handed her a hundred Euro note. 'I haven't any change up here with me, Mr Iliopolakis. We're not allowed to bring money up to the rooms with us.'

'Stupid of me. I forgot my own rule. Could you just tuck that somewhere discreetly out of sight? I don't want any change.'

Eirini looked at the note. 'It is too much, Mr Iliopolakis.'

'It is the amount I want to give you. I would also like you to go to the apartment again next week. We will have removed all our belongings that we plan to take with us and will not be returning there to live. There will be some furniture around. I'm not sure how long it will take you to clean our bedroom and bathroom, along with the lounge and the kitchen. All the cleaning materials will be in the cupboard as they were before and if any of them would be of any use to you please help yourself when you have finished.'

'I couldn't do that, Mr Iliopolakis. The new owner might realise they are missing and I would be accused of stealing them.'

'Mr Kuzmichov will not know as we will not be leaving him a list of half empty containers of cleaning fluids and cloths. Once again it is a question of ensuring that the cupboards, drawers and paintwork are all clean ready for the new owner to move in.'

'That will be no problem, Mr Iliopolakis.'

'There is just one other thing. I plan to borrow some bedding and towels from the hotel and leave them in the apartment. Would you be good enough to make up the bed in the master bedroom on your last visit?'

Eirini looked at Vasilis doubtfully. 'I wouldn't want anyone to think I had stolen them.'

'Of course not. I have spoken to Mrs Planatakis and I will take them with me today. I will leave a note for the new owner to say the items have been borrowed from the hotel.'

'Suppose he doesn't return them?'

Vasilis shrugged. 'That is his problem. I am gradually calling meetings for all the staff to inform them that I am selling the hotel. The man who has bought my apartment is also going to be the new owner of the hotel.'

'Oh, Mr Iliopolakis. I'm sorry to hear that. I thought it was just your apartment you were selling.'

'I'm retiring and my wife and I are going down to Elounda to live. We are leaving tomorrow afternoon to drive to Rethymnon so I would like you to keep the keys. We will not return to the apartment so I would be very grateful if you were able to go in and finish all the cleaning before the end of the month.'

'Of course, Mr Iliopolakis.'

'My wife and I are planning to be guests here for a few days. I will make sure I see you and pay you before we leave. You can return the keys to me then. Now, tuck that away safely somewhere.'

Vasilis pressed the note into her hand and Eirini turned her back on him as she folded the note and placed it inside her bra. She had not expected to be paid more than the rate she received for her work as a chambermaid.

Marianne stood in the arrival lounge at Heathrow and scanned the board that showed which flights had landed. She had four missed calls from Helena and when she knew her mother was safely with her she would call her sister with the information.

The passengers from her mother's flight number began to stream through, pulling their luggage with them and then there was a lull. Marianne's heart lurched. Surely her mother had boarded the flight and not changed her mind at the last minute?

A buggy arrived bearing four people and stopped whilst the courier alighted and collected luggage trolleys.

'Marianne, Marianne, I'm here.'

Marianne sighed with relief and went forward to greet her mother.

The courier returned and grinned at her. 'Does this lady belong to you?'

'Yes, she's my mother.'

'Then I'll hand her over into your care.' He placed Elena's case on the trolley and helped her to climb down from the buggy. 'Enjoy your stay in London.'

Marianne hugged her mother. 'I'm so pleased to see you. How was your journey?'

'So easy. I was looked after wonderfully. I didn't have to worry about anything at all.'

Marianne began to push the luggage trolley towards the exit. 'We'll take a taxi to the hotel and once we're in our room you can 'phone Helena and tell her to stop worrying. She was furious when I called her this morning. She said I should have asked her permission for you to travel.'

'Utter rubbish. When I've spoken to her I'd quite like some breakfast, or is it nearly lunch time? I'm not really sure what the time is.'

'You can have whatever you prefer. A breakfast or a lunch. Then I expect you would like to have a rest. I can sit and read whilst you sleep.'

'I don't feel the least bit tired. I think I slept through most of the flight.'

'It may catch up with you later.'

'I'd rather stay awake and just have an early night. What time is our flight tomorrow?'

'Eleven, but we have to be at Gatwick by nine so you won't be able to have a lie in. We'll be in Athens in the afternoon and then have to wait for our connecting flight to Crete. I'm going to book our luggage straight through so all we will have to do is find the correct boarding gate.'

'Am I going to have a ride on a buggy again?'

Marianne laughed. 'I can try to book one for you, but it might be a little late now. I should have thought about that before.'

'I'm quite capable of walking, it was just so nice to be looked after. I felt very important.'

Elena and Marianne waited for the food they had ordered to be delivered to their hotel room.

'I suppose I should 'phone Helena and tell her I have arrived safely,' sighed Elena.

'If she starts to give you a hard time pass the 'phone to me.'

'Hello, Helena. It's your mother 'phoning to say all is well.'

'Mother! Thank goodness. I've been worried to death over you. Where are you? Shall I come and fetch you? Marianne told me some story about you flying to London.'

'Marianne told you there was nothing to worry about. I am sitting in a very pleasant hotel room with her. We are waiting for a meal to be sent up to us.'

'What on earth made you decide to go to Crete? It will be cold and wet over there at the moment. It would be far better for you to visit in the summer. I'm sure I could arrange a flight back to New Orleans for you.'

'You will do no such thing. I certainly could not face such a long flight again yet.'

'I told Marianne that it would be too much for you. When you've had the meal you've ordered you must go to bed and rest for the remainder of the day.'

Elena set her mouth in a determined line. 'I have no intention of going to bed. I slept on the plane. When we've eaten we're visiting the British Museum.'

Marianne looked at her mother in surprise. She had not expected her mother to want to go out into the city.

'You're what! Whose crazy idea is that? Marianne's I suppose.'

Elena winked at Marianne. 'Actually it is my idea. Why

should I want to waste an afternoon in bed when I can go and do something interesting?'

'Let me speak to Marianne,' replied Helena tersely.

'Hi, Helena. I told you mother would have no problem. She's fine. We've just ordered a big breakfast; egg, bacon, sausage, mushrooms, fried bread, beans; then we're going out.'

'You have no thought for her cholesterol. You should have ordered fruit and muesli.'

'I ordered what mother chose from the menu. She'll probably have fruit and cereal tomorrow morning as we have to leave early to be at the airport. One fried breakfast won't do her any harm.'

Marianne heard Helena sigh in frustration. 'You must insist that she rests this afternoon. You say you have to be up early for a flight tomorrow. She is going to be exhausted.'

'Nonsense. We're going to the British Museum. We'll not be late home so we can both have an early night.' Marianne knocked on the wooden dressing table. 'Oh, must go, room service has just arrived. I'll call you again when we are in Crete. Bye.'

Marianne handed the mobile back to her mother. 'You are getting me into trouble,' she smiled. 'Do you have high cholesterol?'

Elena shook her head. 'Not that I have ever been told. Do you mind if we go to the museum this afternoon? It doesn't have to be the British. It just seems such a waste to be in London and do nothing.'

'We can go wherever you want and if you suddenly get hit with jet lag we can always come back here straight away. Oh, that really is room service knocking this time.'

Vasilis spent the remainder of the day at "The Central". Having spoken to the managers, receptionists, catering and bar staff of his impending retirement and the sale of the hotel he spoke to the man who kept the car park swept and was responsible for collecting all the rubbish and taking it to the bins throughout the day.

'I expect you have heard by now that I am retiring and the hotel will have a new owner. I am sure I can rely upon you to work as conscientiously for him as you have done for me.'

The man nodded. Provided the new owner did not expect him to work longer hours or undertake any more menial tasks for no extra pay he did not mind who owned the hotel.

John had finally added the dimensions, weight and the estimated delivery costs of the large pithoi to the web site. It needed to be tidied up before he showed it to Uncle Yannis again, but it was doubtful that he would have time to give it any attention that day. He, Marcus and his father were still moving furniture around to make a space to stack boxes of pots without them looking too intrusive. They needed to get the spare bedroom clear as soon as possible so Bryony could go in and clean away the dust and make up the bed ready for Marianne's mother to arrive.

'I've made some space in Uncle Yannis's room,' said John. 'We need to move the rest of the big pots in before he starts to replace the furniture. I don't think we can put any more behind his sofa, but some can go into his bedroom. They can go the far side of Aunt Ourania's bed and will be hardly noticeable. After that I thought we should stack as many as possible of the smaller ones in the lounge and they can be the ones that I photograph next. There are an awful lot of those and Nick is organising our room. I thought it would be a good idea to take the smallest and lightest ones up to Marcus and Bryony. We don't want to carry the heavy ones up the stairs.'

Giovanni sighed. 'Until they all came here I had no idea he had so many up at the shop Whilst you're stacking them in the lounge I ought to go and make some space in our rooms. I have to drive to Heraklion later to pick up your mother and grandmother.'

'What time are they due to arrive?' asked John.

'Their flight lands at six so I doubt if we'll be back here before eight. They'll both be tired and your mother won't want to have to think about boxes of pots.'

'Here comes trouble,' murmured John as Uncle Yannis entered the spare bedroom.

'John, I need to have another look at the computer photos that you showed me yesterday. If you rigged up a light it might show off the decoration to better advantage.'

'We'll have a look at that tomorrow,' promised John. 'We have to finish clearing this room first.'

'They're not in the way in here. I don't like having them behind my sofa. It means I am sitting too close to my television.'

'We have to clear this room as soon as possible, Uncle. Grandma Elena is arriving this evening and she will need a bed to sleep in. If you feel you are sitting too close to the television I'll move the set back a bit so you're more comfortable.'

Giovanni was about to make a comment when John shook his head at him. The position of the television could not be changed but John was quite prepared to pretend to move it.

'Are you sure you've taken everything you want?' asked Vasilis. 'I don't want to ask Kuzmichov for anything we've left behind. I have a feeling he would either deny that it was here or say he had thrown it away.'

'I think so. You go and check that I've not forgotten anything. Have you written out the itinerary for him?'

Vasilis nodded. 'It was relatively simple, the bedroom and lounge furniture, kitchen appliances and the few odds and ends that we are leaving, including "some cleaning materials". I'm certainly not listing them individually as we have no idea what Eirini will be using. I told Eirini that she could help herself to anything that was left over. It won't hurt him to buy some new ones. I've also written a separate note saying the bedding and towels belong to "The Central".'

'What time do you want to leave tomorrow?'

'I've arranged to meet the rest of the staff tomorrow at ten. I doubt if I'll be very long with them so we should be able to

143

leave here at twelve and stop somewhere for something to eat on the way. Have you packed us a separate case with clothes and toiletries for whilst we're away and when we return to stay at "The Central"?'

'I'll put the last bits and pieces in tomorrow morning. When do you plan to introduce Kuzmichov to the staff?'

'I thought we could return on Tuesday and I'll call Kuzmichov and ask him to come in to "The Central" and meet the staff on Wednesday. I'll probably have to spend most of the day there with him.' Vasilis pulled a wry face.

'I'm busy that day,' announced Cathy firmly and Vasilis raised his eyebrows. 'I am not prepared to spend the day entertaining the delightful Ludmila. I would rather sit in the hotel room and read.'

Vasilis smiled. 'You could make an appointment for ten at the beauticians and they could do whatever it is they do to keep you looking beautiful. That could be followed by a manicure and pedicure. If I meet Kuzmichov at ten thirty I could take you to the beauty salon first and it could be a good idea if we arranged a time for me to collect you. That way I could get rid of him at a reasonable time and you would certainly not be able to spend the day with Ludmila.'

'I'll call a taxi to bring me back to the hotel. I would be bound to call you at an inconvenient moment. There's a sandwich bar two doors down and I can always get something for a snack lunch. The chef at "The Central" would not be amused if I sent half my meal back because I had eaten a large lunch.'

'We should be able to have Thursday to ourselves so if you wanted to go to look at tiles or showers we could certainly fit that in. I'll arrange to meet the lawyers and Kuzmichov on Friday, sign the final papers, check his money is safely in my bank and then hand him the keys of the apartment and the hotel. We can drive down to Elounda on Saturday and I'll see if I can arrange a meeting early in the next week to meet Mr Bordelli and have his apartment signed over to me.'

'I'm so pleased you are going to have something to occupy you. I was worried that you would soon become bored without the hotel to think about. I don't really think sitting on a jetty fishing would keep you occupied for very long and it really isn't warm enough to do that just yet.'

'I shall have more than enough to occupy me. I'm hoping Mr Palamakis will be willing to oversee the work on the apartment and I will also need to find a good architect to draw up the plans for the new house. Shall I go and get a Chinese takeaway for tonight? That way there will only be the breakfast cups and plates to wash tomorrow before we leave for Rethymnon.'

Marianne was relieved when they landed in Heraklion and she saw their luggage was sitting there waiting for them. She had a horror that it might have been put on the incorrect flight and would have to be traced and sent on to them. Depending upon the destination where it had ended up that procedure could take a number of days.

Giovanni was waiting for them and greeted Marianne's mother effusively. 'This is a most unexpected pleasure.'

'I'm sure you don't mean that, Giovanni, but you have to blame Marianne. It was her idea that I put some distance between myself and Helena for a while. I'll try not to be a nuisance.'

'You have never been a nuisance,' Giovanni assured her. 'I mean it when I say it is a pleasure to have you to come and stay. It also made Uncle Yannis realise he could not put off trying to sell his pots any longer. They were all stored in the spare bedroom and although John wanted to start advertising them to sell on e-bay Uncle Yannis was resisting. I finally told him that as you were arriving we needed the room cleared and if they were still there by this evening I would start taking them to the tip.'

'You wouldn't!' exclaimed Elena in horror.

Giovanni grinned. 'Of course not, but it made him get on with the job. He's been thinking about it for months and finding excuses.'

'We saw pots just like his at the British Museum yesterday. Do you think they are originals or replicas like his?'

'I believe they are the original ones that were found on the site and claimed by the British Archaeologists. I doubt if you would be able to tell the difference unless you were a specialist. Here we are.' Giovanni opened the boot of the car and placed the luggage inside. 'We'll soon be home now and you'll be able to go to bed.'

'I'm not a bit tired,' Elena assured him.

Marianne looked at Giovanni. 'Mamma may not be tired but I'm exhausted. I can't wait to get home.'

'Are you going to 'phone Helena and tell her your mother is safely here?'

Marianne groaned. 'I suppose I could do that whilst we're in the car driving down. If she starts to be a nuisance I'll tell her we're losing the signal due to the mountains and then turn my 'phone off. Mind you, she was so cross with me when I told her Mamma was coming here that she'll probably never speak to me again. I called her again yesterday morning to say Mamma had arrived safely and I cut her off then by pretending room service had just arrived with our late breakfast.'

Marianne waited until Giovanni had negotiated the traffic leaving the airport and then took out her mobile 'phone. 'Do you want to speak to Helena, Mamma?'

A gentle snore answered her and Marianne giggled and turned to Giovanni. 'So much for her not being a bit tired. It's finally caught up with her. I was ready for bed long before her last night. I just hope that a sleep now will not give her a new lease of life when we arrive home.'

February 2015
Week Four – Wednesday, Thursday, Friday

Mr Kuzmichov had not been pleased when Vasilis 'phoned him and said the only day he had available to introduce the new owner to the staff was on the Wednesday and that he had also arranged to meet with the lawyers to sign the final papers on the Friday.

'I would have expected you to spend at least a week with me so the staff could be introduced gradually. I cannot possibly be expected to get to know them all in one day.'

'Of course not. In the case of the chambermaids and cleaners it is just a courtesy meeting. The people that you need to know immediately are the managers, Mrs Planatakis and Dimitra. I arranged for the final signing to take place on Friday as I have business to attend to elsewhere. I hope that will be convenient for you.'

'I suppose it will have to be. This is very short notice. I will have to cancel some of my other arrangements.' Evgeniy had no other arrangements at all but did not see why he should fall in with Vasilis's plans without protesting. 'When will you give me the keys to the apartment?'

'On the Friday once the papers have been signed.'

'I would have liked them earlier. No doubt I will have to arrange for the apartment to be cleaned before we can move in.'

'That certainly should not be necessary. I have arranged for a cleaner to come in and I am sure it will be spotless when you arrive.'

'I certainly hope so. I do not expect my wife to have to spend her time cleaning. Have you completed the inventory?'

'Yes, everything we are leaving behind is listed, including the carpets. I look forward to meeting with you on Wednesday, Mr Kuzmichov and I trust there will be no reason why the sale agreements cannot be signed on Friday.'

'The money is waiting for you if that is what you are worried about.' Mr Kuzmichov closed his mobile without saying goodbye.

Vasilis had met the chambermaids and cleaning staff and as he had expected they already knew that he was leaving at the end of the month and they all expressed their regret that he would no longer be the owner. He told them he had arranged for Mr Kuzmichov to visit the hotel on Wednesday and meet all the staff briefly.

'It will obviously take him some time to become familiar with the running of the hotel and I am relying on everyone to be as helpful as possible to him.'

Before leaving he had booked a room for himself and Cathy, arranging to arrive on Tuesday afternoon and stay until Friday. He loaded their cases into the car along with Cathy's walker and light weight wheelchair and looked around to ensure they had left nothing behind.

'Ready?' he asked.

Cathy nodded. 'I expected to be sad to leave this apartment but once we started to pack everything away it no longer seemed like home. I'm looking forward to being in Elounda again now.'

'One more week, provided all goes to plan.'

They had driven to Rethymnon looking for a taverna on the way where they could stop for a meal but nowhere appeared to be open.

'We should have realised and brought some sandwiches with us,' said Vasilis. 'Are you very hungry?'

'I can wait until we reach the town. There's bound to be places open there.'

The hotel Vasilis booked them into apologised that they only served a breakfast out of season but could recommend a taverna a short distance away which opened at twelve and remained open during the evening. The meal they had was surprisingly good and Vasilis made a mental note to check that they would also be open on the Sunday. He did not relish the prospect of having to push Cathy around on the cobbled streets in search of somewhere to eat and she would have been unable to use her walker for very long without becoming tired.

'What would you prefer to do?' he asked. 'We could drive to the memorial tomorrow or spend the day looking at the selection of tiles and bathroom suites they have available here. Alternatively we go to the memorial on Sunday and then spend Monday looking around again.'

Cathy decided that Sunday would be the most practical day to visit the memorial her father had erected in memory of his first wife and son. 'Nowhere will be open on Sunday so it would be better to go that day. I've seen some tiles on the internet that I quite liked but I'd rather go to a shop and see their full range. I thought I might ask Ronnie for some advice. She did a wonderful job in designing Monika's book shop.'

By Tuesday Vasilis was convinced they had visited every shop in the town that sold ceramic tiles and was relieved that they were leaving that day. Cathy had been unable to decide whether she wanted pale green, pale blue or grey, a rippled effect or plain in the kitchen of the apartment.

'The bathroom will need to be re-tiled once the fitments have been removed so I could have pale green in there if I decide on grey or blue for the kitchen.'

'What about white? It would make the room lighter.'

Cathy shook her head. 'White tiles remind me of hospital bathrooms. I wouldn't want them in either place.'

'Well, you certainly do not need to make a decision yet. I still need to buy the apartment,' Vasilis reminded her.

'Do you think that will be a problem?'

'Bordelli seemed keen for the sale to go through as soon as possible. I'll call him once we are back in Elounda. The only difficulty will be arranging for the lawyers to visit him in hospital to obtain our final signatures. I'll check out of this hotel and then we'll have a lunch at the taverna before we drive back to Heraklion.'

Arriving at "The Central" Vasilis was delighted to find that they had been given a bedroom on the first floor. He took advantage of the parking space at the rear that was reserved for him and took their cases up to their room.

'I really need to visit a launderette,' announced Cathy as she unpacked. 'We're running out of clean underwear.'

'Place them in a bag and I'll speak to Eirini tomorrow. I'm sure she would take them somewhere close by for us.'

'Won't she think we're taking advantage of her?'

'She can always refuse but I think she is grateful for any extra money. When I said I did not need any change from the previous payment she did not argue with me.'

'Are you proposing to tell Kuzmichov that she cleaned the apartment?'

Vasilis shook his head. 'I wouldn't want him to know who to complain to if he is dissatisfied. I'll call in briefly on Friday before I visit the lawyers and check there are no problems, but I'm sure everything will be satisfactory. You ought to make your beautician's appointments ready for tomorrow. If I finish earlier than expected with Kuzmichov I'll call you and arrange to collect you.'

Vasilis was in the foyer of "The Central" in good time to meet Evgeniy Kuzmichov and was amused to see that when the man arrived he was still dressed casually in an open neck shirt and slacks.

'I thought it would be more friendly if we sat in the lounge and invited the staff to join us for a drink.'

'All of them?' queried Kuzmichov.

'No, only the managers, followed by the receptionists and then Mrs Planatakis and Dimitra. I'm not suggesting that we entertain the chambermaids and cleaners.'

'I will need a list of their names and occupations. I cannot be expected to remember all of them.'

'Of course not. I have asked Dimitra to run off the names of everyone on the payroll and the designation of their current job. She will bring that with her.'

'In that case I would like to meet her first. I can then make any notes that I feel necessary on the list.'

Vasilis shrugged. It would have been more courteous to meet the managers and receptionists before Dimitra. 'I'll call her. Whilst we wait for her would you like me to order a drink from the bar?'

Evgeniy hesitated. It could be a long morning so he should pace himself carefully. 'A coffee would be most acceptable at this time of the day.'

Dimitra arrived bearing a folder of papers with her. She shook Mr Kuzmichov's hand nervously and sat in the chair closest to Vasilis. Mr Kuzmichov immediately moved so he was sitting on the other side of her and Dimitra shrank back.

'Would you like a coffee or a drink of any kind, Dimitra?' asked Vasilis trying to put her at her ease.

She shook her head. 'Just a glass of water.'

'I'll ask for a jug and glasses. Others may prefer water whilst we talk. I've told Mr Kuzmichov that you have a list of all the employees. If you could hand them to him, starting with the list of managers.'

Her hands shaking Dimitra removed a page from the folder and handed it over. Kuzmichov ran his eye down the names and nodded. He looked at the other pages as Dimitra handed them to him and finally looked at Vasilis quizzically.

'Do you know all these members of staff by name?'

Vasilis smiled. 'I have to admit that I know very few of the chambermaids and cleaners by name. I have very little to do with them. Mrs Planatakis is in charge of their employment. I met with them last week and told them that I was leaving. I did not think you would want to be introduced to each one individually so I have asked them to wait in the foyer when they have finished their duties for the day and you can just say a general hello.'

'You, Dimitra,' Evgeniy pointed his finger at her, 'are in charge of checking the accounts for accuracy. Do you have copies of the accounts covering the previous two months?'

'Yes, sir.'

'Then maybe you would be good enough to run off copies for me now. I think they will be more use to me than a list of names.'

Dimitra looked at Vasilis who nodded. 'I had planned to give you the accounts for this month on Friday, but if you require them earlier that is no problem.'

'Friday will be a little late if I find the hotel is running at a loss and I wish to withdraw.'

Vasilis felt his heart miss a beat. Surely the man was not going to cancel the purchase at the last moment? 'I think you will find that the hotel is making a healthy profit and you need have no concerns over the annual turnover.'

'I was told that by the lawyer, but I like to check these things out for myself.'

'Of course. If you could put that in hand, Dimitra, and bring the balance sheets down when you have completed them. In the meantime Mr Kuzmichov can be introduced to the managers. As you go back upstairs please ask them to come over to us and invite them to order a drink from the bar.'

'Yes, Mr Iliopolakis. It will take me about half an hour to print them off.'

Vasilis moved his chair so Dimitra could leave the table without having to push past Mr Kuzmichov. Evgeniy tapped the papers he held in his hand.

'Are these lists correct? There are a number of people listed who have the same name.'

Vasilis smiled. 'No one has been duplicated. It is just coincidence that they have the same surname. You will see there are three employees with the name Iliopolakis, none of them are related to me or to each other.'

'I would not want to find subsequently that one person was being paid three salaries and only doing one job.' Kuzmichov glared at Vasilis.

'I can assure you that is not the case. Two of the managers happen to have the same surname and you will see they are two separate men.'

The managers arrived and took seats around the table. Two of them had a glass of wine and the others had requested a soft drink.

Mr Kuzmichov looked at the two who had the glasses of wine and frowned. 'Do you normally drink when you are working?'

'I am not actually on duty,' answered one of them. 'I worked last night and agreed to stay on to meet you, sir.'

Kuzmichov looked at the other man. 'Were you also on duty last night?'

'No, sir, but I am officially off duty within the next fifteen minutes. I would like to drink to Mr Iliopolakis's impending retirement and also to welcome you as the new owner of the hotel.' The man raised his glass. 'My good wishes to both of you.'

Kuzmichov nodded. 'You are?'

'Manos Giorgiadakis, sir.'

Kuzmichov ran his finger down the list of names and made a mark when he reached Giorgiadakis. The man was slick with his answers. He would need to be watched.

Having introduced each manager by name Vasilis sat back and left the talking to Evgeniy Kuzmichov. Each man answered his questions politely, all finally assuring him that they would work as conscientiously for him as they had for Vasilis.

Dimitra returned with the financial spread sheets and at a nod from Vasilis handed them to Evgeniy. 'Do you wish me to stay in case you have any queries?' she asked.

'That could save time rather than continually having to send for you to come down and join us.'

Dimitra once again sat down next to Vasilis. She hoped the Russian would not ask her to explain any of the figures. She knew they were correct but she also knew she could easily become flustered if he began to ask for explanations.

'Who is this?' asked Evgeniy pointing to a name that had "misc" written after it.

'That is Mr Lanassakis.'

'And what exactly does "miscellaneous" mean?'

'I could probably explain better than Dimitra,' offered Vasilis only to be met with a steely glare.

'I would prefer Miss Dimitra to explain. She should know what the term implies and you will not be here next week.'

Dimitra looked at Vasilis. 'That's fine, Dimitra. Mr Kuzmichov is quite correct that you should know the duties that he carries out.'

'Well,' Dimitra hesitated, 'He ensures that the car park is free from litter and no one has parked in one of the reserved spaces if it is not their entitlement. The chambermaids, cleaners and kitchen staff place their rubbish in designated areas and he has to collect it on a regular basis and take it to the bins. This can entail a number of trips with the kitchen refuse. Each morning he washes the front windows of the foyer and checks that all the lights are working. If a light bulb needed to be replaced he would bring his long steps and deal with it. Should a door or window appear to be stuck he is usually asked to attend to it. If he is unsuccessful we then have to call in a specialist which is costly.'

'And that is the extent of his duties?'

'He also sweeps the front of the hotel at frequent intervals during the day and ensures that the door mats are clean.'

'Not exactly taxing work.'

Vasilis cleared his throat. 'Mr Lanassakis is of low ability. He is conscientious and efficient in carrying out those duties assigned to him, but would be unable to complete any work that necessitated dealing with the public in a reading or writing capacity. That accounts for his job description as being "miscellaneous".'

'So why is he employed?'

'Someone has to carry out those menial jobs and it is a way of helping the less fortunate to make a living.'

'I would have thought the kitchen could have taken their own waste to the bins and either the chambermaids or the cleaners could have taken the hotel waste. One of the cleaners could also have responsibility for the car park and keeping the front area clean.'

Vasilis frowned. Was Kuzmichov planning to get rid of Lanassakis? 'He is paid less per hour than the cleaners. He is paid a set wage for the hours he is contracted to work without the option of any over time. I don't think any of the cleaners would be willing to undertake picking up litter from the car park or cleaning an area where an animal had fouled. It would be impractical for the kitchen staff to take their waste to the bins as it would mean removing their kitchen uniform and having a thorough wash upon their return to ensure they had not brought any germs back from the vicinity of the bins.'

Kuzmichov shrugged. He was not really interested in the work the man did but he did not want to find him hanging around in the car park when he arrived with refugees.

'I'll take these papers away with me and study them tonight. If I have any queries I will contact you, Mr Iliopolakis. You may return to your duties Miss Dimitra.'

'Thank you, sir,' muttered Dimitra, only too pleased to have been dismissed.

Kuzmichov questioned the receptionists about the languages they spoke and their knowledge of the local area and amenities.

Maria nudged Tatiana who blushed and began to speak. 'We

all have college or university qualifications for our languages. It is quite rare for us to have a visitor with whom we cannot communicate. There is always an array of brochures advertising local areas that can be visited either independently or in an organised group. People who want more information usually bring a brochure to the desk and we are able to answer their queries, sometimes 'phoning the excursion organisers for further details. If a customer does not appear to know where they wish to visit we will take them to the brochures and make suggestions depending upon the length of their stay in the city.'

'Do you receive a commission from these excursion companies if you send customers to them?'

Tatiana looked at Vasilis. 'Not that I know of.'

Vasilis nodded in confirmation. 'We do not receive any commission from them and they do not receive any commission from us if they recommend this hotel. It would be very time consuming to keep the records and would result in little reward for either of us.'

'What about the taxis that you order for guests? Do you have an arrangement with one particular company and receive commission from them?'

'We use one company in preference to the others as they are so reliable, but we do not work on a commission basis.'

Vasilis could see the chambermaids and cleaners gathering in the foyer under the watchful eye of Mrs Planatakis. 'Do you have any more questions for the receptionists, Mr Kuzmichov? '

Evgeniy shook his head. 'If they would each of them tell me their full names, then they may return to their work.' He made notes against each name and Vasilis wished he could understand Russian to know what they said.

Mr Kuzmichov was introduced to Mrs Planatakis and confirmed that she was in charge of allocating the work on each floor to the respective workers.

'If they find a room has been left in an unsatisfactory condition by a guest what is the procedure?'

'The girl would advise me, I would check it out and report back to the manager on duty if there was actual damage. He would be responsible for adding an amount to the customer's bill to pay for the repair. Leaving it dirty is just annoying and time consuming but we cannot charge a customer for the extra time that would be needed to return it to our usual high standards of cleanliness.'

'How often have you had actual damage to any of the rooms?'

'It is very rare. Our guests are of a good calibre and if they have damaged anything accidentally they usually tell the maid. I would check the damage and decide if the customer should be charged.'

Mr Kuzmichov dealt with the chambermaids and cleaners quickly. He did not ask their names, but simply shook each one by the hand and said he looked forward to getting to know them over the coming weeks. Vasilis drew a breath. He would offer Evgeniy lunch at the hotel and introduce him to the kitchen staff afterwards and finally to Mr Lanassakis. After that there should be no reason for the man to stay any longer.

Vasilis shook hands with Evgeniy Kuzmichov and promised to meet him as arranged at the lawyer's office on Friday when the sale would finally be completed. He returned upstairs to the hotel room where Cathy was waiting for him.

'You look very glamorous,' he complimented her.

'Thank you. I enjoyed being pampered. Eirini has returned our washing. I asked her how much I owed her and she refused to take any money from me. I've told her she must add the amount to her bill for the cleaning and you would settle up with her before we left. How did the staff take to Mr Kuzmichov?'

'I think they found him somewhat intimidating. He asked some irrelevant questions that I had already answered for him. I'm not sure if he was testing their knowledge or hoping to find I had lied to him. He asked for the balance sheets for the previous two months and said if the hotel was running at a loss he would withdraw his offer on Friday.'

'Withdraw?'

'I think he was just saying that to unnerve Dimitra. He's seen the annual accounts and could find no fault with those. The hotel is making a healthy profit and he knows it.'

'Why would he want to upset Dimitra?'

'It was just an impression I had. She was horribly nervous, particularly as he sat so close to her and insisted that she told him the duties Mr Lanassakis carries out that classifies him as "miscellaneous" rather than listening to me.'

'You ought to go up and reassure her.'

'I will, I just wanted to check that you were safely home first.'

Vasilis found Dimitra sitting miserably in her office. 'I'm sorry, Mr Iliopolakis. I don't think I gave Mr Kuzmichov a very good impression.'

'I thought you were very efficient. You gave him all the information he asked for without a problem.'

'Do you think he will sack Mr Lanassakis?'

Vasilis shook his head. 'It would be very foolish of him to do so. He could find he was dealing with cleaning the windows and the car park himself. I'm sure none of the current staff would be willing to carry out Lanassakis's unpleasant jobs. He would soon have to employ someone else at greater expense. I don't think he will make any changes for quite a while. He has never run a hotel before so it will be a learning experience for him. Provided everyone continues to work conscientiously for him he should have no cause for complaint or feel the need to make any changes.'

'I didn't like him.'

'You don't have to like your employer, Dimitra. Just treat him with respect and you will have nothing to worry about.'

Vasilis sat in his lawyer's office. He had deliberately arrived early and was reassured to know that his lawyer had already checked with the bank and the money from Mr Kuzmichov was being held ready to transfer as soon as they were contacted and assured that the contracts had been completed.

Kuzmichov read the agreements through slowly and carefully before finally taking out his pen and signing. He passed the papers to Vasilis who also signed and then returned them to the lawyer for him to add his signature and an official seal.

The lawyer telephoned the bank and confirmed that the sale had been completed and the transfer of funds should take place immediately.

Vasilis waited until his lawyer nodded and closed the telephone. He took the keys for the hotel from his briefcase along with those for the apartment. 'Here you are, Mr Kuzmichov. I hope you will be very successful with the hotel and also find the apartment to your liking.'

Kuzmichov looked at the keys for the hotel which were all neatly labelled. 'I would have expected more keys,' he remarked.

'You have a master key that unlocks every bedroom door. I have given you the duplicates that I have always held to the external doors and the offices. Those for the kitchen, bar and conference rooms are marked. Whenever each area is not in use they are securely locked, but you can obviously gain access if necessary. I have written down the code for the safe and the managers also have a key and the code so they can deposit any sums of cash or valuables inside.'

'That will have to be changed.' Evgeniy spoke firmly. 'Staff cannot have access to the safe in my office. I will provide another where they can deposit anything as necessary and give the contents to me each morning when I arrive.'

'Whatever you wish. I can assure you that the staff who do have access are entirely trustworthy.'

'I should hope so.'

'There is just one other thing before we part company. My wife and I have been staying in "The Central" since Tuesday. We leave tomorrow morning. I will then pay for the meal we have this evening, our breakfast and our stay tonight.'

Vasilis expected Kuzmichov to say there was no need to pay, instead he nodded. 'Make sure you obtain a receipt.' Kuzmichov deposited the keys to the hotel in his briefcase along with his copy of the agreement of sale and rose. 'I hope you enjoy your retirement.'

Without thanking the lawyer or shaking hands with Vasilis he left the room and Vasilis sat back with a sigh of relief.

'Not the most pleasant customer I have had to deal with,' remarked the lawyer as he smiled at Vasilis.

'I agree, but I have been making the excuse that he is partly Russian. Do you have your bill prepared for me? I would like to pay you now before we leave Heraklion tomorrow.'

'It is all ready for you.' He knew Mr Iliopolakis always paid his debts immediately.

'Successful?' asked Cathy as Vasilis entered their room.

'Yes. It actually went through without any problems from Kuzmichov.'

'I'm so pleased. I asked room service to send something rather special up for us as soon as you left.'

Vasilis raised his eyebrows and Cathy produced a bottle of champagne.

'What would you have done if I had returned and told you he had withdrawn at the last minute?'

'Sent it back down and not told you. Open it, Vasilis. I've been looking forward to a glass all morning.'

Vasilis smiled. 'So who is paying for this?'

'What do you mean?'

'I told Kuzmichov that we had been staying here and would pay for our meal this evening, breakfast tomorrow and for one night. I expected him to say that it would be complimentary. He told me to make sure I obtained a receipt.'

Cathy shook her head in disbelief. 'He and his wife came to the apartment for lunch and you gave him lunch at the hotel. I ordered the champagne to be brought up as soon as your car arrived back so technically you paid for it as he had not signed the sale agreement by that time.'

'I just hope Kuzmichov never finds out,' said Vasilis as he poured them both a glass. 'Here's to our new life in Elounda.'

Evgeniy Kuzmichov called Ivan. 'All is completed.'

'Fine. When do you receive the car?'

'I've been told it will be delivered on Thursday. Everything else is in hand.'

'Good. Weather permitting I will set sail that day and call you when I arrive a short distance from the coast.'

March 2015
Week One

Ludmila looked around the apartment. 'They could have left a bit more for us,' she complained. 'The kitchen only has the basic equipment and the china and cutlery is cheap. The only bedding and towels they left come from the hotel. We would have done better to have rented somewhere furnished.'

'We've spent most of our years in rented apartments or hotels. I thought you would appreciate having a home of your own and furnishing it as you pleased. I'm planning to stay here for a number of years. I am now a respectable hotelier.'

'You're definitely planning to give up your other trade?'

Evgeniy nodded. 'We have been fortunate for a number of years and with the stricter checks and controls our luck would have run out sooner or later. Having the hotel gives me the excuse to place large sums of money into my account without awkward questions being asked. There are going to be plenty of refugees wanting to come to Europe whilst the area is in such turmoil. I'm hoping Ivan will decide to buy a larger boat then he can bring more over each time.'

Ludmila frowned. 'Could we cope with more? What about the transport up to the hotel?'

'You'd have to make the journey on two nights. No need for you to worry about that at present. Enjoy having some time to yourself so you can look on the internet and order whatever you want for the apartment.'

Vasilis 'phoned Giuseppe Bordelli and asked if he had consulted with his lawyer and made any arrangements for the man to visit him in the hospital.

'I was hoping to hear from you. I've drawn up a sale agreement and sent it to my lawyer. You can either collect it from him or he can send a copy over to you by e-mail. Have you pen and paper and I'll give you his details.'

Within half an hour Vasili was reading the agreement for the purchase of the apartment in Elounda. It was to be his responsibility to dispose of the furniture that Bordelli had stored there and the current owner was not to be held responsible for any damage or defects that were subsequently discovered.

Vasilis smiled to himself. Disposing of the furniture would be no problem. He would speak to the neighbour, Panayiotis, or simply arrange for a rubbish collection. He would ask Mr Palamakis to check the property over for any structural problems and as he planned to revamp the kitchen and bathroom area he was not concerned about the current condition.

Satisfied with the document he telephoned his lawyer in Aghios Nikolaos, advising him that he definitely wanted to purchase the property, provided no structural defects were found, and was forwarding the agreement on to him. He also warned him that it would be necessary for the lawyer to meet at the hospital to enable Giuseppe Bordelli and himself to sign a final agreement.

He hoped he could now contact the neighbour who had the keys and arrange for Mr Palamakis to meet them both there. Provided the builder did not find anything worrying in the structure he would be able to proceed rapidly with the purchase. If all went well it was possible that he and Cathy would be able to move into their new home in June or July.

John sat before his computer with Uncle Yannis at his side.

'So are you happy with the web site, Uncle? I've grouped the different types of pots you are selling together as you asked me to do.'

'I suppose so.'

'Well if you want anything changed now is the time to tell me. I am about to make it live.'

'Live?'

'Yes, put it on the computer and send it into the airways for everyone to see.'

'You are going to send it to everyone?'

John smiled. 'No, that would be a mammoth task. It will be placed on the computer and then I will also place an advert on to say that you are selling your collection of museum replicas. I'll add a few small photos and tell people to look at the web site.'

'Will they?'

John shrugged. 'I don't know. I can't make them. We'll check it later and see if there has been any response. I'll send it on to Vasi and ask him for his comments.'

'There is one thing.'

John groaned. He had just confirmed that the web site should be accepted and broadcast. 'What's that, Uncle?'

'We haven't photographed and listed the pots that Monika and Saffron have.'

John gave an audible sigh of relief. 'They're not important at the moment. They are the smaller ones and on show at the shops. Provided you get some sales they can be added later, besides, there really isn't any more space in the house to store them.'

'Yes, Elena chose rather an inconvenient time to visit.'

'Not at all. It made us get on with the project. I'd talked about it to you since the end of last season and you kept putting it off.'

'I'll be sad to see them go,' sighed Yannis.

John looked at his uncle in surprise. 'You can't see them now. They are packed away in their boxes.'

'But if I wanted I could get one out to look at.'

John shook his head in despair. 'I must go and get Skele. I can't expect Dimitris to bring him up here to me every day.'

'Do you want me to sit and look at the computer whilst you're gone?'

'There's absolutely no need. We'll close it down and have a quick look this evening to see if anyone has shown any interest.'

Although it was a lovely sunny day Elena put on her coat; it was probably not as warm out as it appeared.

'I'm going to walk into Elounda and meet Andreas,' she told Marianne. 'I'm not sure what time I will be back, but certainly before it becomes dark.'

Marianne frowned. 'That is quite a long walk for you. Would you like me to drive you in?'

Elena shook her head. 'I don't have to rush. I've told Andreas I will call him when I reach Elounda and there is sure to be somewhere open for me to have a coffee whilst I wait for him to come down to meet me.'

'Well if you want one of us to collect you by car when you are ready to come back just call me. It will be no trouble.'

'I'm going down to collect Skele, Mum. Is there anything you want from the village?' asked John.

Marianne opened the refrigerator door and checked on the amount of milk that was in there. 'No, thanks. We've no need of anything as far as I can see.'

'Where are you off to, Grandma?'

'I'm going to walk down to Elounda and meet your uncle.'

'Would you like a lift?'

'John!' exclaimed Marianne in horror. 'Your grandmother cannot ride pillion on your bike.'

'Why ever not? I'd go slowly and Grandma would be quite safe.'

Elena chuckled. 'If I was a few years younger I'd take you up on your offer. No, I'll enjoy the walk, thank you, John.'

Vasilis drove down to the seafront road and looked at the plot of land that he now owned. He walked over the rough ground, looked out to sea and frowned. From where he stood he had a view of the road and a small expanse of sea with the arm of land opposite. Now the rubbish bins had been removed cars were taking the opportunity to park in the space they had left. This was not what he had envisaged. In his mind he had planned a large patio at the front of the house which would give them a spectacular view across the bay. From the back patio of the house he had originally built up on the hill there was a far better view of the sea than the one he would have here. Feeling despondent he drove down to Vasi's hotel. He would look at the view that he had from the ground floor.

Being somewhat further around the bay the view was certainly better, but it did not come up to Vasilis's expectations. Had he made a big mistake? As he stood there a car drove past and onto the Causeway. Idly he wondered if the occupant was taking a dog for a walk. The Kanali was still closed so the taverna was not likely to be the object of their journey. He watched the car turn down the road away from the Kanali towards the bed and breakfast hotel and then lost interest.

Vasilis was still looking at the view Vasi had from his hotel when he saw the car returning. Evidently they had been misled by whoever had told them the bed and breakfast hotel would be open. As the car drove past Vasilis felt sure the driver was Ludmila Kuzmichov, but he could think of no reason why she would be driving around in the area and dismissed the idea. It was someone who resembled her.

To his relief he had not received any 'phone calls from Evgeniy querying anything or complaining about something at "The Central" and he hoped it would stay that way. The hotel was no longer his responsibility. He must now focus all his attention on the apartment and building a new house. His first job must be to contact Palamakis and arrange his visit to confirm that the apartment was not ready to collapse.

Vasilis drove back into Elounda, parked a short distance away from the apartment and then knocked on Panayiotis's door.

'I hope I'm not being a nuisance to you, But I have agreed with Mr Bordelli that I will buy the apartment. There is one proviso, I wish my builder to check there are no structural defects before I finally sign the agreement. When would it be convenient for you to give us access to the property?'

'I can be available any morning this week provided it is before one.'

'Bear with me whilst I call Mr Palamakis and see when he would be able to come.'

Mr Palamakis sounded reluctant when Vasilis spoke to him over the 'phone. 'I don't do very much work now. I leave it to my grandsons and just give them advice and check on them later.'

'I am not asking you to do any physical work. I would just like you to visit the apartment I am buying in Elounda and check that there are no problems that are going to cost me a fortune to put right. If there are I will try to get the asking price reduced. Would you be able to come along one morning this week? The owner is in a hurry to complete as he plans to go to Italy to live with his sister.'

'I can be there at eleven tomorrow,' replied Mr Palamakis. 'What is the address?'

Vasilis looked at Panayiotis. 'What is the address?'

Panayiotis chuckled and held out his hand for Vasilis's mobile. He asked Mr Palamakis to drive down the main street and park in the car park. 'We'll wait on the corner and look out for you. Mr Iliopolakis knows you so there should be no problem.'

He handed the 'phone back to Vasilis. 'Do you want to go inside now?'

Vasilis shook his head. 'There's little point in trying to do anything until Mr Palamakis has been and I have signed the agreement with Mr Bordelli.'

The walk down to Elounda was further and more tiring than Elena had anticipated. She sat on a seat a short distance from the church and called Andreas.

'I'm in Elounda, sitting by the church. I can't possibly walk up the hill to you until I've had a rest.'

'I'll come down and meet you. Stay where you are and when I arrive we'll find somewhere for some lunch. You may feel able to walk up the hill after that.'

Elena agreed, but from where she was sitting every taverna appeared to be closed. Maybe she should have accepted John's offer of a ride on his bike; she would certainly call Marianne and ask if someone could collect her when she was ready to return.

Andreas arrived and looked at his older sister in concern. 'You don't look terribly well.' he remarked.

Elena gave him a wan smile. 'I'm just tired. I only arrived yesterday evening and I think jet lag is catching up with me.'

'You should have stayed at home until you were completely rested. We'll go across the road for a quick lunch and then I'll pop you into a taxi to take you home. You can come up and see my little abode another day.'

Elena did not argue. She knew she would not be capable of walking back to the house and was loath to ask Marianne to come to collect her.

Yannis could not sit still. He walked from room to room and back to look at the closed down computer. Should he start it up again? He could be missing orders. He wished John would return to advise him. He realised that if he did see any orders appearing he would not know how to deal with them. He shook his head dolefully. His beloved pots could all be gone by tomorrow and he would never see them again.

Monika was busy sorting books when her mother arrived at the shop. 'Are you busy?' she asked.

'I'm putting the books Mr Iliopolakis brought down for me into order. Some are in such good condition that I am going to place them amongst my new book stock. You could help me if you have nothing better to do.'

'How can I help? You know I can't read anything except Greek.'

'All you need to do is look through every page to ensure there are no dirty marks or creased corners. You don't have to be able to read them.'

'Is that all?'

'Not exactly difficult. I just need to know that they are in perfect condition. It would be very embarrassing if I put them amongst the new books and then found someone had spilt something on a page or turned down the corner to keep their place.'

Litsa looked at the pile of books on the table. 'All those?'

Monika nodded. 'I don't expect you to be able to check more than a few, but whatever you are able to do would be a help.'

'I actually came down to tell you that I called on the baker where I worked last season and asked if I could have some work there again this year.'

'Did they agree?'

'They said I could have some hours until the schools broke up for the holidays. Their niece wants a holiday job.'

Monika pursed her lips. 'What did you tell them?'

'I accepted. It's better than nothing. I can continue to look around and see if there's anything available that would give me more hours. It's possible their niece will find a position in a boutique. I would have thought a young girl would prefer to work there rather than in a baker's shop.'

'You are not to accept cleaning or being a chamber maid, Mamma. I know how hard they have to work.'

'I could try the super market and see if they need any staff.'

'That would probably be shelf filling and means lifting heavy boxes from their stockroom out to the shelves. They would want you to work early mornings or late evenings. Why don't you ask Theo if he needs any extra staff?'

Litsa flushed slightly. 'He's a friend.'

'So? What difference does that make?'

'It could be awkward working for him.'

Monika raised her eyebrows and made no comment. She would take it upon herself to ask Theo if he was willing to employ her mother.

Panayiotis and Vasilis waited on the corner until they saw Mr Palamakis park his truck. He stood looking around uncertainly and Vasilis waved to him, finally attracting his attention and the builder crossed the road.

'What are you planning to do with this apartment?' he asked. 'Refurbish and let it out?'

'No, my wife and I want to live here.'

Mr Palamakis raised his eyebrows. 'I thought you were living up in Heraklion.'

'We were, but I've sold that apartment along with the hotel. I am now a retired man of leisure.'

'Lucky you! What's wrong with the house you have?'

'Nothing, but it is in an impossible position. Cathy wants to be able to visit her friends in the area independently from me. She certainly could not negotiate the hill down into the town.'

'So what are you going to do with your house? Are you going to sell it or are your son and his partner planning to stay up there?'

'They'll stay there at present, but they also have plans for the future. Come and have a look at this property and then I'll discuss something else with you.'

Panayiotis opened the door. 'Do you want me to wait?' he asked.

'Might as well. We won't be very long.'

Mr Palamakis walked from room to room, studying the walls and ceilings and finally returning to the kitchen. He turned on the taps to the sink and frowned. The water ran away slowly down the waste. Once the sink was clear he walked into the bathroom and flushed the toilet, watching the waste water disperse before he turned on the taps to the basin and the bath. Once again the water ran away slowly.

'There's certainly a problem there. Can we go outside and look at the patio? It could be that the drains are blocked near the surface with debris.'

Panayiotis unlocked the patio door and waited whilst Mr Palamakis inspected the drains, bending down and removing the leaves and general rubbish that had accumulated on top of them.

'Go inside and turn on the taps and flush the toilet,' he instructed Vasilis.

'All at once?'

'No, do them in rotation the same as I did.'

Vasilis obeyed and Mr Palamakis watched as the water entered the drains unhindered and then backed up, the residue only draining away slowly. He walked down the patio examining the slabs carefully.

'I think you have a cracked drainage pipe,' he informed Vasilis. 'You see those slabs that are damp? They will need to be lifted and the pipes examined. A piece could have broken off and be lodged inside which is causing the water to rise up to the slabs and hinder the discharge.'

Vasilis frowned. 'Can you unblock it?'

'Impossible to say until the slabs have been lifted and an inspection made.' Mr Palamakis turned to Panayiotis. 'I'll ask Giorgos to come and lift the slabs tomorrow morning if you are willing to give him access. It could be just one section that is the problem or it could be the whole run making dispersal into the main drain in the street a problem. He can take some photos on his mobile, send them to you and you can show them to the owner.'

'Provided he comes about ten and leaves at one I can be available,' agreed Panayiotis. 'He'll need to replace the slabs, not just leave them lying around.'

Vasilis sighed. 'I'm planning to renew the kitchen and bathroom, but I hadn't anticipated having to run new pipe work.'

Mr Palamakis shrugged. 'You may not have to renew all of it, but it should certainly be examined and the problem rectified before you install anything new.'

'What about the interior of the apartment? Did you see any problems there?'

'Nothing apparent. It just needs decorating.'

'So I can go ahead with the purchase?'

'I suggest you hold off on your decision until Giorgos has sent you the photos. You need to be aware that whatever the problem is with the drains it could be costly to resolve.'

'Would I be justified in asking the owner to reduce his asking price?'

'I would think so.'

'Would you be able to do the work?'

'I can't say without looking. If the whole run to the street drain needs to be renewed you'd do better to employ the drain maintenance company. If you find any fault after they say they have completed the work you can insist they return and put their work right.'

Vasilis nodded. 'I'll take your advice as always. We don't need to hold Panayiotis up any longer, but I would like you to come somewhere else with me.'

'Another apartment?'

Vasilis shook his head. 'No, I'm planning to build a new house and I want you to tell me if my ideas are feasible. It's down on the coast road towards the Causeway. We can go in my car and I'll bring you back to the car park afterwards.'

'Nice location,' remarked Mr Palamakis as Vasilis parked by the land he had bought.

'I've permission to build, but I'll need to have plans drawn up.'

'I can't do that. I'm not a draughtsman. I'm capable of drawing up interior alterations to a current building that satisfy the inspectors, but you will need an architect.'

'I'd like you to tell me if my ideas are practical. I know you helped Veronica Vandersham with the reconstruction of her house in Kastelli.'

Mr Palamakis shrugged. 'That was relatively easy. The structure was already there. Such a shame that it was burnt out just as it was nearing completion. What advice do you need here?'

'If you stand there and look out to sea your view consists of the road and a short expanse of water that makes the Long Arm look much closer than it is in reality. I don't like it. I want a view out over the bay. The only way I can do that is elevate the house.'

'Put it up on stilts, do you mean?'

Vasilis shook his head. 'I don't really want to do that. It would look incredibly ugly. I thought if the front area was banked up we could have a large patio that would give us the view I want. It would mean the house was about fifteen to twenty feet higher up than the road.'

'How high are you allowed to build?'

'Three floors maximum.'

'That would restrict you to two floors.'

'I'm not planning to build another floor on top. This is for Cathy. She needs to be on one level, so it would be a kitchen, dining room area and lounge leading out onto the patio. We would have a bedroom and bathroom en suite and a separate toilet for guests. We don't need any more than that.'

Mr Palamakis nodded, envisaging the building in his mind. 'To do that the ground would need to be banked up and a retaining wall built. You'll need a contractor who has heavy machinery to do that.'

'But it's feasible?'

'Costly and it would mean a long flight of steps up to the front door and patio area.'

'There's plenty of width. There could be a flight of steps, then a small landing and they could turn so they finally lead to a front door that opens immediately into the living area. At ground level I could park my car and have a conventional flight of stairs up to the rear of the building. Next to those stairs I would want to install a lift for Cathy.'

From his pocket Mr Palamakis drew a pad and pencil and began to sketch Vasilis's ideas. 'Like this you mean?' He showed the page to Vasilis.

'That's it exactly. There could come a time when Cathy is virtually confined to the house unless I take her out in the car. If there was a wonderful view of the sea from the patio she would have something to look at.'

Mr Palamakis tore the page from his notebook and handed it to Vasilis. 'Decide upon your architect and take this to him. Tell him this is how you want the finished house to look. He'll need to take precise measurements and don't forget that where you install the lift you'll have to dig down to allow for the mechanism.'

'Once the plans have been passed would you and your grandsons be willing to do the work?'

Mr Palamakis shook his head. 'It would be too large an undertaking for us. I'd be happy to complete some of the interior work, but we couldn't be responsible for the build. Footings will need to be dug and drains run down to the road. The building inspectors will need to be involved and pass each stage of construction. There's also the matter of the electricity to be considered. The electricians need to work with the builders to ensure that all the ugly wiring is hidden, but that you have access to junction boxes. I would also suggest that you had an emergency generator that would kick in automatically if you had a power outage.'

'I'm sure we could manage for a few hours without electricity.'

'I don't think your wife would be very happy sitting in the lift in darkness for an indeterminate of time. If such a thing did happen the generator would at least get the lift up to the house so she could get out.'

'Now you know why I needed your advice. How much to I owe you for your time today?'

'Are you going to ask my grandsons to work on the apartment if you buy it?'

'Of course.'

'Then I'll add the time I've spent with you today onto the bill then. I'll arrange for Giorgos to lift those paving slabs in the patio and we can see the extent of the damage there. If you decide against the purchase you'll just owe for his time tomorrow. What is happening with the furniture that is stored there at present?'

'It becomes my responsibility to dispose of. Panayiotis said he might know of people who would be glad of some of it.'

Mr Palamakis nodded. He would speak to Panayiotis; he had seen a rather nice looking table that could take the place of his old one.

Evgeniy inspected the Mercedes when it was delivered to him at the hotel. Despite having been brought over from Athens by the ferry there was not a mark on it. He opened the door and lifted the driver's seat to examine the cavity below. It should certainly be adequate for the money and mobile 'phones it was destined to contain.

He saw Mr Lanassakis was watching him and he called him over.

'This is the new car I have bought to transport our visitors to and from the airport. Please ensure that you do not scratch it or damage it in any way.'

'I'll not go near it.'

'On the contrary; you are going to have increased responsibilities.

I expect you to clean the windows and wing mirrors every day and if there is any mud on the wheels to wash it off. Make sure the glass over the lights is clean also. Inspect the interior, remove any rubbish that has been left inside and brush out the carpets. Once a week you will wash and polish the vehicle.'

Lanassakis nodded. 'Suppose I am doing the cleaning when you want to use it?'

'I will let you know if I will be needing the car during the day and the time that it must be ready for me. I am most likely to need it early in the morning to meet visitors so I do not see a problem. I am trusting you with a very responsible job.'

'Yes, sir,' replied Lanassakis. It might be considered to be a responsible job but he was unlikely to receive any extra money for ensuring that the car was kept immaculate.

Evgeniy called Ludmila. 'The car has arrived. I'll drive it around to the apartment and then you can see how it handles.'

Ludmila admired the car and slipped behind the wheel. 'Where shall we go?' she asked Evgeniy.

'Drive down to Elounda. You can see how easy it is to negotiate that corner. If there's a problem returning to the main road you can drive into the village and come back up the hill.'

'I'd like to go across the Causeway also.'

'No problem. You can drop me on the road whilst you go and park behind the windmill. I'll see how much of the car is visible from the road and also from the Causeway.'

Vasilis telephoned Mr Bordelli and explained that there was a problem with the drains at the apartment.

'I never had a problem.'

'I asked my builder to come and check it out. He reckons there is an obstruction in the drains, possibly due to where one has cracked. Some of the patio slabs will need to be removed to find the fault.'

'How long is this going to take?'

'His son is going to lift the slabs tomorrow and take some photos. I'll bring them in for you to see. I don't know how much it will cost to renew the drainage pipes if that is necessary. Are you willing to drop your price a little to cover the work?'

Bordelli gave a deep sigh. He knew there was a leak from his drains that was rising up into the patio and had hoped that the problem would not be discovered.

'I'll have a word with my lawyer and see what he advises.'

'Please do and let me know as soon as possible. I'd like to be in a position to complete the transaction with you by the end of next week at the latest.'

Ivan's arrangements had gone smoothly. The six men had arrived on board at different times during the week and deposited their money with him in the safe and the additional clothing they had been wearing they left in the cabin. He had assured them that he would not leave the port without them on board unless they were challenged by the port authorities at the last minute. If that happened they would have to arrange a different night to sail or even move further down the coast to a new boarding point. If any one of them decided the venture was too risky he would refund their money.

The men had obeyed his instructions regarding their purchases and the clothes they were to wear when coming aboard. He was relieved that the men had not been challenged as they arrived and he sent them below to remove their surplus clothing and return on deck wearing a white shirt. They stood around nervously, eating the food Ivan had provided, waiting for the signal to return below when Panos would draw up the gang plank and slip the mooring ropes. Standing below deck in darkness it seemed a long time to the men before Ivan started up the motor and the boat left the port unhindered.

Once out in open water Ivan handed over the controls to Panos and went below to where the men waited. He switched on the cabin lights and sat down opposite them.

'So far, so good,' he smiled. 'Remember, if we are challenged tomorrow I am just taking you out for a sail. The authorities should have no reason to stop us as we will only be a short distance from the coast. The reason you are all below deck is because you are feeling sea sick. Tonight you can decide which three of you sleeps in the bunks first. Panos will be joining you and I will take his bunk tomorrow whilst the other three sleep.'

'What happens if we run into a storm?' asked Salim anxiously.

'The weather forecast is good. A brisk wind to help us on our way but no storms in the offing. There are life preservers on deck and life jackets stored beneath the bunks. In the unlikely event that they should be needed I will sound the ship's horn three times and either Panos or I will come down and check that you have fitted your life jacket efficiently. I would expect you to stay below unless I gave the command to come up on deck. You will be much safer down here.'

'Suppose the boat begins to sink? I can't swim.' Salim was feeling extremely nervous.

'That is highly unlikely to happen, but if such an awful event did occur I would use the radio to alert the coastguards of our position and also send up flares. We carry a dinghy which would be used as a temporary measure until we were rescued. Your life jacket would keep you afloat until you were safely in the dinghy. Now, I suggest you help yourselves to anything else you would like in the way of food or drink and then retire for the night. The three of you who do not have bunks tonight will have to make do with sleeping in the chairs. We will still be off the coast of Syria tomorrow so do not come up on deck. I will be down here with you during the day catching up on some sleep. Any more questions?'

The men shook their heads. They were warm, dry and relatively safe, unlike many they had heard of who had tried to escape in an overcrowded fishing boat resulting in them having to be rescued and taken to a detention centre.

Vasilis looked at the photographs of the drains that Giorgos had sent through to him. A section had collapsed into the pipe causing an obstruction and forcing the waste water up into the patio area. Giorgos had lifted more of the slabs and the other pipes appeared to be intact. Relieved that the damage was no worse Vasilis requested that Giorgos renewed the faulty section and then tested the water flow to ensure there were no further problems.

Vasilis called Bordelli and advised him of the damage that Giorgos had found. 'Provided that is the only repair that is needed I'm willing to pay for it and not request a reduction in the purchase price.'

'I'll call my lawyer and tell him that you are prepared to go ahead with the purchase. Would Wednesday morning be convenient for you and your lawyer to come to the hospital for the signing?'

'I can manage that. I'll have to speak to my lawyer and confirm back to you.'

March 2015
Week Two

Yannis was disappointed; no one had replied to his web site advertising the selection of pottery he had for sale.

'You need to give it time, Uncle. It's only been up and running for a few days. People don't make snap decisions when something is expensive.'

'So you think I should reduce the price?'

'Certainly not. Wait for at least a month, maybe more, and then we'll think about price reductions or special offers if you've still not had any sales or interest shown.'

The refugees from Syria appreciated being able to sit up on the deck once they were out of sight of the land. It had taken them a while to get used to the movement of the boat and they all wore their life jackets. Ivan smiled in amusement. How would they have fared if the crossing had been rough? As the coast of Crete came into view he ordered them back below decks and joined them.

'Once it becomes dark we will sail in closer to the shore. There is a taverna on the promontory, but they are unlikely to be open for the season yet. In the early hours of the morning I will move in as close to the canal as possible and you will be going ashore. You will wear your black roll neck jumpers and carry the remainder of your belongings in a black carrier bag. Panos will carry down your bags into the dinghy and I will hold a light whilst three of you climb into the dinghy and join him. Panos will row you the short distance through a canal to a small deserted beach. You can decide who travels first. You will certainly not need your life jackets and they are to be left on board.'

'I can't swim,' Salim reminded Ivan.

'The sea is calm and you will be quite safe provided you sit still in the dinghy. Close to the shore the sea there is very shallow and the journey should take no more than fifteen minutes,' replied Ivan. 'Once through the canal Panos will row in as close to the beach as possible and you will collect your bags and jump ashore. There will be a woman waiting there for you. Panos will then return and ferry the remaining three men to join you. Once you are in the dinghy and on the beach you say nothing at all. Sounds carry at night across the water.'

There will be a car waiting to take you on the next leg of your journey. You will place a white shirt over your black roll neck and transfer your carrier bags into the cases she will provide as swiftly as possible. Once that has been completed she will drive you to Heraklion. In the unlikely event that the car is stopped you are travelling to the airport to catch your homeward flight; there are bound to be other cars and taxis making the same journey with visitors. Once in Heraklion you will be met again and escorted to a hotel. On leaving the car you are to remain silent until you are in your rooms. Do nothing that will draw attention to yourselves.'

'What about our money and mobile 'phones?' asked Ibrahim.

'All will be placed in a bag that Panos carries with him and passed over to the woman. She will be responsible for paying your further expenses. Once you are in the hotel you will be given instructions regarding your passports and flights. Another week should see you safely in England, with some money in your pockets and your mobile 'phones returned to you. Whilst you await your journey I suggest you all get as much sleep as possible during today.'

'I hope he will return our money and mobile 'phones. We

could end up stranded in this country otherwise,' remarked Salim pessimistically after Ivan left them.

Ibrahim shrugged. 'We have no choice but to trust him. So far everything has gone as he promised.'

Ivan waited until three in the morning before he motored swiftly towards the arm of land. Panos lowered the dinghy over the side of the boat and Ivan went below to tell the first three men to come up on deck.

Panos climbed into the dinghy first, carrying the bags containing the men's clothing whilst Ivan held the rope ladder steady and lit their way with a powerful torch. They climbed gingerly down into the inflatable dinghy and sat clutching the ropes at the sides whilst Panos rowed quietly away from the boat and across the short stretch of water and through the canal. Once into the bay he continued to row a short distance, then shipped his oars and flashed his torch twice. He was answered with three flashes and he immediately began to row in as far as possible to the sandy beach. When he felt the dinghy touch the ground he signalled to the men.

'Jump out onto the beach, one at a time,' he whispered.

Unable to see how far they needed to jump and off balance with the bag they carried, each man landed in the shallow water, soaking his shoes and socks and the bottoms of his trouser legs. Cursing inwardly they walked to where Ludmila was waiting and stood beside her. Ludmila placed a finger on her lips, reminding the men that they must not speak. They seemed to be waiting a long time before Panos returned with their three companions and threw a package across to Ludmila.

She beckoned to the men and led the way to the car, opened the boot, removed the cases and passed one to each man. 'Put on your white shirt and place everything else inside the case,' she ordered quietly.

Once the cases were replaced in the boot she opened the doors of the car for the men to climb inside and take their seats. She indicated that they must fasten their seat belts before she closed the doors quietly and checked that the door to the boot was firmly closed. Lifting the driving seat she placed the package she had received from Panos into the cavity and slid in behind the wheel.

'You may talk if you wish,' she advised them in Arabic as she drew away from the shelter of the windmill.

'Can we change our wet socks and trousers?' asked Ibrahim.

'We cannot spend the time for you to do that. You will have to be uncomfortable until we reach Heraklion.'

The men looked out of the car windows as they were driven across the Causeway and along the coast road to the steep hill that led to the main road. To Ludmila's relief she was able to draw out easily and drive along the winding road towards Aghios Nikolaos. The moon shone a certain amount of light onto the sea, but the men could see little else as much of the road was in darkness, lit occasionally by street lights. Upon reaching the junction the lights became more frequent and the area was well lit. Ludmila joined the traffic on the main road leading to Heraklion and drove steadily towards the town.

Ludmila had travelled the route on a number of occasions by now and knew that most of the traffic she would encounter would be going to the airport; few lorries travelled at night to make deliveries or transport materials. Within a short while the talking from the men had ceased and Ludmila had an idea that they were all sleeping. She wriggled her shoulders to release the tension she could feel building up; this was the easiest part of the journey, another hour and she would be able to go to bed.

She waited until she was in the outskirts of the town before calling Evgeniy to say that her arrival was imminent and as she drove slowly along the road that ran below their apartment she was relieved to see Evgeniy waiting on the corner.

Ludmila drew to a halt, opened her door and retrieved the package from beneath her seat before Evgeniy took her place behind the wheel. He raised his eyebrows at her and she nodded. The men began to stir now the car was no longer moving and Evgeniy spoke to them in Arabic.

'Five more minutes and we will be at the hotel. You will collect your cases from the trunk and follow me to where the elevators are situated. You do not talk at all. Three of you will enter each one and I will join you. You will press the button for the fourth floor. Do not get out until you have reached there and wait until I arrive with your companions. I will then take you to your rooms.'

To Evgeniy's annoyance he saw that Lanassakis was already in the car park sweeping the area assiduously as he drew up.

'I expected you to be cleaning the front windows. They take priority over the car park.'

'I arrived early. I have already swept the front and cleaned the windows,' answered Lanassakis.

Evgeniy frowned. 'The car will need your attention now. I have just used it for an airport run.'

'Yes, sir. Will you be needing it again in a short while?'

'No, but I would like it cleaned immediately.' Evgeniy had seen that the wheels were dusty and the windscreen had dead insect marks on it. That would be unlikely to happen on the short drive to the airport through the town.

The men followed Evgeniy into the hotel by the rear entrance and to the elevators. 'Fourth floor,' he reminded the men in English as the first three entered. 'You wait for me to arrive there with your companions.'

He led the six men way down the hallway and into the conference room, closing the door firmly behind him.

'Welcome, gentlemen,' he said, reverting to Arabic. 'I trust you had a pleasant journey. There are three bedrooms set aside for you on this floor. Two men to a room; you choose your companion. You will find toiletries waiting for you and you can change your wet trousers and socks. I imagine you would all like something to eat and drink so once you have changed please return to this room where I will be waiting for you. You can look at the menu and once you have decided what you would like to eat I will make a call to the kitchen and place your order. It will be brought up to you. Whilst you wait you can make coffee, tea or help yourself to a soft drink from the fridge. Bring your cases and follow me.'

Dimitra was puzzled. She had heard the elevator arriving and a short while later it returned again to the fourth floor. As far as she was aware there was not a conference booked to take place that week and it was far too early for the sewing ladies to arrive. Maybe a guest had pressed the incorrect button when returning to their room. She opened her door and looked out. On the carpet in front of the elevator doors there were wet patches and what looked like footmarks going down the hallway. Had one of the maids been sent up to do some cleaning and accidentally spilt some water? That in itself was a puzzle; they would have no need to bring any water up with them as there was water available in the conference room and also the unused bedrooms. She closed her door and hoped that if Mr Kuzmichov decided to visit that floor later in the day the wet patches would have dried out.

The men listened attentively to Evgeniy as they ate their food. He explained that they should not leave the fourth floor, but could congregate in the conference room or their bedrooms as they pleased.

'Please do not be noisy. You do not want to attract the attention of the staff. I will visit you throughout the day and you can order more food. Tomorrow a photographer will be coming to take photos ready for your temporary passport. It will show that you entered the country from Britain about a week ago. This is the passport you will use when booking your flight to England, to go through passport control in Heraklion and also at Gatwick.

'Once your new passports are ready you will be taken to book your flights and also to buy some leather shoes. You can also purchase other articles of clothing if you wish. I will have changed five hundred dollars for each of you into Euros so there will be no exchange problems. You will be given the amount remaining so that you have money in your pocket for your onward journey. A further five hundred dollars for each of you will be changed into sterling. This will be to help you make your way in your new country. It would be unreasonable to expect you to arrive with nothing. Your mobile 'phones will be returned to you once you reach the airport.'

'What happens when we reach Gatwick?' asked Ibrahim.

'You will be met by a friend and taken to a boarding house.'

'How will we know him?' asked Salim.

'He will be holding a placard with his name on it. You will look for Nassam. You will each of you pay him fifty pounds sterling for the taxi ride and then a week's rent in advance will be needed when you check in at the accommodation. After that, gentlemen, you are on your own to make a new life for yourselves.' Evgeniy smiled at them. 'I will be escorting you to the airport and once you have gone through security I can only wish you well. I will leave you now to finish your meal and return to your rooms where you can shower and also get some sleep. I will come back,' Evgeniy glanced at his watch, 'at two. You will be able to order some more food then and we will discuss the arrangements for the next few days in more detail.'

Evgeniy walked back to the apartment; on his way he called Ivan.

'The goods have arrived.'

'No problem. I am on my way home.'

On entering the apartment Evgeniy found Ludmila asleep in bed. Not wanting to disturb her he set his mobile 'phone alarm for one thirty, removed his jacket, placed a cushion beneath his head and lay on the sofa in the lounge. So far all had been successful. He would talk to Ludmila about the drive from Elounda to Heraklion later and ask if she had encountered any problems.

Upon his return to the hotel Evgeniy found the men in good spirits, clean and rested, but none of them were wearing their shoes.

'They are too wet,' explained Ibrahim. 'If we put them on our socks will become wet and our feet cold.'

Evgeniy frowned. The men would need to wear their shoes if he was to take them to the dining room that evening for a meal. 'You have a hair dryer in a drawer in your room. Collect the dryers and your shoes and you can use them to dry out your shoes whilst we talk.'

Obediently the men returned to their rooms and came back with their shoes and three hair dryers.

'I imagine you would like something more to eat. Have a look at the menu again and choose whatever you wish. Whilst you do that I will collect some more hair dryers so you will have one each.'

Evgeniy walked down to the third floor and using his master key opened the door of a bedroom. It was obviously occupied so he closed the door quickly. He visited five bedrooms before he was able to collect three hair dryers and take them back upstairs to the conference room.

He placed the dryers on a chair which he pushed under the table out of sight, collected the three the men had brought from their rooms and did the same. 'Put your shoes over there under the window as if it is customary to take off your shoes once inside. Have you decided what you would like to eat? Once your food has been delivered you can start to dry your shoes out. You will need them to wear this evening in the dining room even if they are still damp. Once we leave this room you will speak only in English, and it will be general conversation only. There must be no mention of your unorthodox arrival here.'

'Is there anywhere we can do any washing?' asked Salim.

'You can rinse out your underwear and shirts in your bathrooms and hang them inside the shower. Make sure you have a clean white shirt to wear tonight and you will also need to wear a clean shirt tomorrow for your photographs. When you go shopping you can purchase a new one if necessary to wear on your flight. Once you are in England you will find there are plenty of launderettes where you can take your washing.'

'How long are we staying here?' asked Ibrahim.

'You are my private guests attending a trade conference. The photographer will arrive tomorrow morning and will be paid two thousand dollars by each of you. I will bring the money with me. He will return in the evening with your new passports. The following day you will be taken to a travel company by Ludmila. I have already changed some of your money into Euros. You will use your new British passports to book a flight for England as soon as there is one available. Ludmila will be there to assist you if necessary. It is essential that you arrive at Gatwick together. Just follow our instructions and provided all goes well you should not be staying here for more than four days.'

'How much is our stay here going to cost?' asked Ibrahim.

'The cost has been covered by the amount you have already paid. I will not be presenting you with a bill. Do you have any more questions, gentlemen, or are you ready for me to order your meal?'

'Are we expected to pay for that?'

Evgeniy shook his head. 'As I said, all your expenses at the hotel have been covered by the initial amount that you paid.'

Once the men had eaten and Evgeniy had left them Ibrahim grinned at his companions.

'This is obviously a good hotel, but I think we are being over charged.'

'So what do you plan to do about it? If we object and ask for some money back that man could turn us out on the streets.'

'Oh, we have to pay. We have no option, but when we go to the dining room this evening we choose the most expensive meal offered. We may as well get our money's worth. In the meantime we ought to continue trying to dry out our shoes.'

Vasilis entered the hospital and made his way to the room Bordelli shared with three other men who were similarly incapacitated. He stopped short at the door. There was a policeman sitting next to the bed.

'What's wrong?' he asked anxiously.

Panayiotis looked up and smiled. 'There's nothing wrong. I'm just visiting to be a witness to Giuseppe's signature. I am in uniform as I was unsure if I would have time to return home and change before I have to go on duty.'

'Gave me a bit of a shock. I didn't know you were in the police force.'

'No reason why you should know. I'm based in Aghios Nikolaos and happen to live in Elounda.'

Giuseppe shifted himself further up in his bed. 'Because I'm in hospital my lawyer said I needed someone who knew me to confirm that I was in my right mind and not being coerced into something detrimental to my future. Don't see why taking off my legs should affect my mind. I'm no more stupid now than I was before.'

'Do you want to see the photographs of the drains?' asked Vasilis taking out his mobile.

Giuseppe nodded. 'Might as well, although I understand from you that the problem has been dealt with.'

'It was only one section that needed to be replaced. Had it been the complete run and down into the main drainage system in the street I would have had to ask for you to pay for the repair.'

'Good job it was no worse then. You're getting a nice apartment in the centre of Elounda for a bargain price as it is. I wouldn't have wanted to pay for a repair that was of no benefit to me.' Giuseppe returned the 'phone to Vasilis after only a cursory glance.

Vasilis pocketed his mobile and looked at his watch. He knew that the price Giuseppe had asked for the apartment was far more than it was worth, but he was not prepared to argue. By the time he had paid for the necessary renovation he would have paid almost as much again, but the area, being flat and close to the supermarkets, was ideal for Cathy and he did not consider that anything was too expensive if it was for her. He just wished the lawyers would appear and the transaction could be completed.

The six men presented themselves in the conference room, each dressed identically in white shirts and black trousers. Evgeniy had warned them not to remove any moustaches or beards so they looked the same as on their Syrian passports. Evgeniy greeted them cordially, although he had not been amused at the cost of the meal the men had ordered the previous night. He should not have told them that their meals were included in the price they had paid to leave Syria.

He wanted to get rid of them as quickly as possible. If they over stayed it would disrupt his timetable with Nassam and also add to the risk he was running in harbouring them. The conference room was booked for a three day meeting two days after they left and he did not want to cancel the lucrative arrangement. Once the conference room had been cleaned the bedrooms would need to be made ready for the next occupants that arrived from Syria.

Once the photographer arrived Evgeniy left the hotel to take three guests to the airport in the Mercedes. He knew the car was noticeable and a talking point amongst the other drivers who drove saloon cars and he wanted them to accept its arrival at the airport as a regular occurrence. He called in at the apartment where he found Ludmila lounging on the settee watching a film.

'I wish I had the time to sit and do nothing,' he remarked.

Ludmila shrugged. 'I went shopping first thing this morning. There's cold meat and fresh bread if you want some lunch. When I came home I started ordering items for the apartment. I deserve a break.'

'What have you ordered?'

'New bedding and towels, a sandwich maker, a toaster, kettle, some crystal glasses and some decent silver cutlery. I can't bear eating with that cheap stuff they left behind.'

'When will these items arrive?'

'Within the next few days.' Ludmila closed the television and opened her lap top. 'Have a look at this china and tell me which you prefer. I haven't ordered it yet.'

'Why are you looking at Royal Worcester?' asked Evgeniy.

'Why not? You say you are planning to stay here so we should make ourselves as comfortable and happy with our surroundings as possible. We could have Crown Derby if you like the design better.'

'I'm really not fussed. Choose whatever you like best.'

'I'm trying to decide which would look better on the lace table cloth.'

'What lace table cloth?' asked Evgeniy, looking at the polished wooden table.

'I've ordered a hand made lace table cloth from Bruges. That way the table top can be covered and I won't have to be continually polishing it. It will also look good if you want to entertain.'

Evgeniy did not argue with his wife. He had no intention of entertaining in the apartment. Any visitors he needed to show hospitality to would be taken to the hotel to eat and the expense absorbed into the accounts.

'I've come to collect the money for the photographer,' he announced. 'He should be returning this evening with the new passports so he'll want to be paid.'

'The money is in the safe. It's exactly as Panos gave it to me. I haven't touched it.'

Evgeniy opened the bag and placed the mobile 'phones to one side. He spread the money out and began to count out two thousand dollars from each envelope that bore a man's name and placed it inside his wallet. 'It owes me three thousand dollars where I changed their money into Euros,' he muttered. 'I'm going to take that and a further five hundred from each of them to change into sterling.'

'Write a note and leave it in the bag; that way you'll remember what you have had and know what is still owing to you. Don't forget to leave me the Euros for when I take them to book flights and buy new shoes tomorrow. I imagine they'll be quite pleased to know they have some money in their pockets.'

Evgeniy removed the Euro notes from his wallet and handed them to his wife and she placed them inside her bag.

'I'll give five hundred to each man so he can pay for his own flight and shoes. If you leave me the other three thousand dollars and I can call in at some exchange bureaus to convert it into sterling.'

'Make sure each man has fifty for Nassam and enough for the accommodation.'

Ludmila frowned. 'Maybe we should allow another two hundred and fifty for each man. Nassam hasn't said how much the accommodation is going to cost them.'

'Four hundred and fifty pounds should be more than sufficient for a week in a cheap boarding house. They've probably brought some dollars out with them and they'll be able to change dollars or Euros easily enough in England.'

Evgeniy handed his wife the money and made a further note on the piece of paper. Once the men had left Crete they were no longer his responsibility. He had his money and they must fend for themselves in their new country.

As he returned to the hotel and arrived on the fourth floor he could hear the men talking excitedly together in Arabic and frowned. If he could hear them, it was possible that Dimitra and the sewing ladies could hear them also. They must be reminded to talk more quietly.

Monika saw Theo varnishing the wooden door to his taverna and walked across to speak to him.

'Not long now until the season starts,' she remarked.

Theo nodded. 'Thought I ought to get on and have everything

finished. I kept putting things off whilst I went into the countryside and visited friends. This is my last job, then I can have a few days to myself again before we open and the rush begins.'

'Are you planning to go to Rhodes to visit your brother?'

Theo shook his head. 'No, he's working all day. I'll indulge my hobby for a couple of days and then just go out for some drives. I thought your mother might like to join me as I have to go down to Sitia. She would be able to see a different area of Crete.'

Monika swallowed her surprise. She had never thought of Theo as having a hobby. 'I'm sure she would. Have you sufficient staff for the coming season?'

'I expect so. My usual employees are coming back to me. Why? Are you looking for a job?'

'No, but my mother is. She's going back to the bakery for a few weeks, but once their niece finishes school they have said she can work there instead of my mother.'

'It's not always sensible to employ friends. If you are not satisfied with their work you feel embarrassed to tell them to leave.'

'I'm sure you would be satisfied with my mother. She's a hard worker.'

'I was thinking of the bakery employing their niece. Many teenagers are lazy and unreliable.'

'So you would consider having my mother work for you?'

'Maybe. How has your shop been faring throughout the winter months?'

Monika realised Theo was deliberately changing the subject and she was not going to get any offer of employment for her mother from him.

'The library has been moderately successful. I collected some more books from the apartments and hotels when they closed down and Mr Iliopolakis brought me down some boxes of books from Heraklion. Did you know he had sold his hotel up there?'

'I heard he was coming down here to live. Fortunate to have that big house so he can be with his son and Saffron.'

'I understand that he is looking for somewhere in Elounda that is on level ground so Cathy can go out independently.'

'Not much down there for sale. Anyone who has property usually rents it out during the season or has locals living there permanently. Is Vasi going to ask his father to keep "The Imperia" open during the season?'

Monika shook her head. 'I believe Vasi plans to close at the end of the month. Mr Iliopolakis has decided it is time he retired, so I doubt that he would want to take on the responsibility.'

'Yes, retirement is a great thing to look forward to, but he will need something to keep him occupied.'

'I'm sure he has various projects in mind. I'll not hold you up any longer, Theo. You finish varnishing your door and I'll go back to sorting my books.'

Monika waited until she and her mother had finished eating their evening meal. 'I saw Theo today. Apparently he's planning to have some time off before he opens for the season. He says he wants to indulge in his hobby.'

'Oh, no.' Litsa's face fell.

'What's the problem?'

'He likes to shoot rabbits. I've told him I don't approve.'

'It's probably his way of keeping his eye in as a marksman.'

'That's what he says, but I insist that he aims at a bottle or tin can when I'm with him.'

'You've been shooting with him?'

Litsa blushed. 'When we went up to Katharou.'

'Did you shoot?' asked Monika, feeling her heart fluttering with trepidation.

'He showed me how to hold the gun and aim. I enjoyed the experience, but I wasn't very good. It took me a long time before I was actually able to hit the bottle he had stood up.'

Monika shook her head. She was not sure that she approved

of her mother learning how to use a gun. 'Theo said he was going to ask you to drive down to Sitia with him.'

Litsa nodded. 'He's suggested that we drive down to Sitia and then on to Ierapetra and return to Elounda from there.'

'Have you agreed to go? You'll not be able to cover all that distance in one day. Are you planning to stay over night somewhere?'

'I'm sure Theo will have something arranged.'

Monika frowned. What did Theo have in mind for her mother whilst they were away together? 'Just be careful. I understand that part of the road to Sitia can be quite dangerous as it goes through the mountains. We've had a lot of rain and there could be landslides.'

'Of course Theo is aware of that possibility and will drive carefully. You don't need to worry, Monika. I will be quite safe with Theo.'

Litsa smiled happily whilst Monika wondered exactly what the relationship was between them.

March 2015
Week Three

Evgeniy was feeling pleased with the way the arrangements had worked out. There had been no problem booking all six men on the same flight to England and they had been delighted when he returned their mobile 'phones and gave them five hundred English pounds. At the airport they shook his hand and thanked him before waving goodbye as they entered passport control. He waited until he was certain that the men's passports had not been challenged before he drove back to the hotel.

He took the elevator to the fourth floor and checked the rooms the men had used. He needed to ensure there was nothing left behind that belonged to them. Having opened all the drawers and the wardrobe and looked in the bathroom he examined the rubbish bin. The scraps of paper he found he placed in his pocket.

From the conference room he called Mrs Planatakis. 'There is a conference booked for Monday so it will be necessary for the room to be cleaned before then, also the three bedrooms on this floor.'

'The bedrooms? Have they been used?'

'They were used by my private guests. They need to be made ready for whenever they are needed again.'

Mrs Planatakis sounded horrified. 'You should have said, sir. I do apologise. They were not on the cleaning schedule.'

'That was no problem. My guests preferred not to be disturbed.'

'I will speak to the maids and send them up as soon as they have finished the current guests bedrooms.'

'Thank you. I will expect everything to be in order by tomorrow.'

'Of course, sir.' Mrs Planatakis frowned. She had never heard of the bedrooms on that floor being used by Mr Iliopolakis for private guests, but Mr Kuzmichov's arrangements were none of her business. 'There is just one other thing I need to mention to you. The chambermaids on the third floor have reported that three hair dryers are missing from the bedrooms. They must have been stolen by the guests.'

'How annoying. Does this often happen?' Evgeniy was cross with himself. He should have thought to return the hair dryers he had borrowed for the men to dry out their shoes.

'I've never known hair dryers to be taken before, although we do occasionally lose a towel.'

'Oh, well, you will have to purchase three more. Is there any way they can be labelled?'

Mrs Planatakis shook her head. 'I don't think so. We could ask the sewing ladies to stitch tags to each one, but if a guest was determined to take it they would just cut the tag off. Are you happy for me to order three replacements?'

'Yes, go ahead. A hair dryer is considerably cheaper than a bed cover or blanket.' He made his way along to the bedrooms the men had used and checked the drawers again. Instead of the usual one dryer that was placed in a drawer there were two and he had not spotted the second. He now had to remove the three extra dryers before the maids came to clean the rooms and found them.

Evgeniy pulled out his mobile 'phone and called Ludmila. 'I need you to come to the hotel immediately and bring a large shopping bag with you, not a plastic carrier. Come up to the fourth floor and I'll meet you in the conference room.'

'What's the problem?'

'I'll explain later.'

'I'm expecting the delivery of an internet order to arrive.'

'This is more important and you'll only be here for five minutes. Come now.'

Evgeniy waited impatiently for his wife to arrive. He left the door ajar so he would be able to hear the elevator arriving and if it was one of the maids he would intercept her and send her into a bedroom. He wanted the hair dryers removed before they were seen and awkward questions asked of him.. He placed all three on a chair and draped his jacket over them only to have to recover it again to retrieve his mobile from the inside pocket.

'Yes,' he answered tersely.

'All went as planned this end. Let me know when you need me again.'

'Probably in about ten days. I'll call you.' Evgeniy replaced his jacket over the hair dryers.

'What kept you?' he asked of Ludmila irritably when she arrived.

'The delivery came just as I was leaving and I had to check it and sign for it. I'm pleased I was there as it was the bedding and the parcel is larger and heavier than I had expected. I couldn't have carried it back from the depot and there's nowhere there to park.'

'Put these in your shopping bag and take them back to the apartment,' ordered Evgeniy, ignoring Ludmila's excuse.

'Why do we need three hair dryers?'

'I borrowed them from the guest bedrooms for the men to dry out their shoes. Mrs Planatakis now thinks they have been stolen and I had to tell her to order three more.'

'Why didn't you put them back?' asked Ludmila.

'It was too late once the maids reported they were missing. How could I explain their reappearance?'

'So what am I to do with them?'

'Take them home. I'll bring them with me the next time they're needed.'

'When will that be?'

'When Ivan 'phones. I've had a call from Nassam and there were no problems.'

'I ought to buy some more suitcases in readiness. We could go to Rethymnon tomorrow. It's another large town and there are bound to be shops selling suitcases.'

Yannis sat with John and looked at the web site despondently. 'I've only had one order, and that's for an ickythoi.'

'You have to be patient, Uncle. It takes time for word to get around.'

'I was expecting the museums to want some.'

'That is a brilliant idea,' exclaimed John. 'Why didn't I think of that?'

'Think of what?'

'I'll compose an e-mail to the museums saying you are selling your collection of replicas at a bargain price and asking if they would like to purchase them to sell in their shops. I'll quote them the current price the manufacturers are asking compared with your price. They can be offered a discount for quantity and reminded that once the pots are sold there will be no more available. We'll give them the details for the web site and they can see exactly what you have in stock. How does that sound?'

'What kind of discount are you thinking of?' asked Yannis anxiously.

'Let me talk to Nick about that. She has a better head for figures than me. Now, show me which pot has sold. I'll mark it as such on the web site, get it packed up and taken to the post office.'

'What about the payment?'

'Whilst I'm packing it up you need to 'phone your bank and ask if the credit has reached your account. I won't post it until that has been confirmed.'

'Is there any bubble wrap? This pot was one that came from the shelf in the shop but I'm sure I would have saved the packing materials.'

'I'll have a look around. We could always rob another pot of its protective packaging.'

'That's not sensible. Better to leave those that are wrapped as they are.'

'We could do that on this occasion and I could buy a roll of bubble wrap when I go to the post.'

'I suppose so.' Yannis sighed. 'At the moment I seem to be spending money rather than making any.'

John placed the pot, securely wrapped and boxed, into the pannier of his bike. He would call on Dimitris on his way back and collect Skele. As he entered Elounda he saw Cathy and Vasilis sitting at a bar opposite the church and he slowed to speak to them.

'Has the sale of the hotel gone through and have you found anywhere to live yet?' he asked.

'Yes, to both your questions,' smiled Vasilis. 'We'll be staying with Vasi and Saffron for a while yet, but I've bought an apartment a short distance up the road from here. It's going to need a considerable amount of work before it will be ready for us to move in.'

'That's great. It will keep you occupied and stop you from missing the hotel.'

'I do keep waiting for a 'phone call,' admitted Vasilis, 'but I have more than enough to be getting on with. I've also bought a piece of land with the idea of building a house there for Cathy and myself.'

'So why buy the apartment?'

'I have to get the plans drawn up and approved before I can start work on that. I'm reckoning at least a year before it will be ready. Where are you off to?'

'Uncle Yannis has finally agreed to sell his stock of pots and I've made a web site for him. His first sale came today so I'm on the way to the post office.'

'He's selling all of them?'

'That's right. Monika said she needed the space in the shop for her books so he moved most of them into the house. That was fine before Grandma Elena came to stay, then Mum insisted the spare room had to be cleared. We all of us have boxes of pots in our rooms and can't wait to have the space back.'

Cathy looked at Vasilis. 'We'll need some pots.'

'Will we?' he asked in surprise.

Cathy nodded firmly. 'There is the patio at the back of the apartment. They can be used for flowers and we can take them with us when we finally move into the house.'

'If you say so. You'd better give me details of the web site and we'll have a look when we go home to see if any are suitable.'

'I won't mention it to Uncle Yannis. He'll be so disappointed if you don't want any.' John picked up a serviette and scribbled down the details of the site. 'I'm sending e-mails to the museums to see if they want to buy some replicas to sell in their shops. They will be getting a bargain as they are being sold for less than the asking price from the manufacturers.'

'Then we'd certainly better have a look and decide quickly. We wouldn't want them yet, of course.'

'Of course, you'd not have to add on the cost of the transport and I'm sure we could store any you wanted until you were ready to receive them.'

'I thought you were in a hurry to get rid of them?'

'We are, but firm sales to friends could be stored without too much inconvenience. I'd better go. I don't want to find the post office is closed and I have to come back again later.' Feeling pleased with himself John climbed back onto his bike and rode away. He would have to see if any other people he knew would be interested in buying some pots.

'Do we really need pots for the patio?' asked Vasilis of Cathy.

'It's practical. We can get various sizes and they'll be easy for me to look after. I won't need to do any heavy digging or kneeling down to weed. We can have a look at the web site when we get home and if we decide they're not suitable we can just have a quiet word with John and Uncle Yannis will not be upset.'

'You order whatever you think will be suitable,' smiled Vasilis. 'Are you still going to ask Ronnie to help you with the interior decoration?'

'Definitely, provided she is willing. I thought I should wait until it actually belongs to you and I can take her inside to look around.'

'I'm planning to ask the Palamakis boys to start pulling out the kitchen and bathroom next week. She ought to make her visit before that commences. Arrange a day and time that is convenient to both of you and I'll bring you down.'

'You don't think Saffie will be offended if I ask Ronnie, do you?' asked Cathy. 'After all, she advised Vasi on the decoration of the Heraklion apartment.'

'Why don't you ask Saffie to come down with you before you ask Ronnie? You can tell her you're planning to ask Ronnie for advice also. You don't have to accept suggestions from either of them.'

'That's a good idea. I'll ask her as soon as we go back home. She could always bring me down in her car if you're busy.'

Vasilis raised his eyebrows. 'What am I doing that is going to keep me so busy?'

'I thought you planned to sit on a jetty and fish.'

'The weather is not warm enough yet. That is a summer occupation for me.'

Cathy laughed. 'I will be interested to see how long your new hobby lasts.'

Saffron was delighted to be invited to visit the apartment the following morning. 'I'm not sure about any ideas for interior decoration. I only did that with Vasi as a way of keeping myself occupied when I was in Africa for six months. Why don't you ask Ronnie?'

'That's a good idea. Do you think she'd be willing?' Cathy did not mention that she had every intention of asking Ronnie's help. 'Vasilis says he's arranged for the work to start next week. I feel quite excited. When we went to Rethymnon we looked at all the shops that sell tiles and bathroom fittings and I've also looked up on the internet. I don't want to make a mistake and have something done that I regret afterwards. I wouldn't feel able to ask Vasilis to have the work done again, he's spent so much since he sold the hotel.'

'Don't feel too guilty about that. He'll probably be asked for an enormous amount of tax so the more expenditure he can show the better. Have you anything particular in mind?'

'I want the kitchen to look light and airy, but I don't want plain white tiles and certainly not the acid yellow ones that are there now.'

'You could have white and some patterned ones in between, or a frieze at the top or running through them.'

Cathy nodded. Neither idea appealed to her.

'And your bathroom?'

'Vasi says he'll have part of the wall taken out so that it leads straight out from our bedroom and have the door in the hallway blocked up. I have to decide on tiles that don't clash with the bedroom décor or make it look too dark. There's only a small window high up in the wall in the bathroom.'

'We'll have a look tomorrow and see if I can come up with any suitable suggestions.'

Vasilis knocked on Panayiotis's door and waited patiently for the man to open up. He was in his pyjamas with a dressing gown over the top that he was holding closed.

'I do hope I haven't disturbed you. I wanted to tell you that my wife is planning to come down to look at the apartment tomorrow and again later in the week with a friend. She won't have to bother you as I have had some extra keys cut.'

Panayiotis nodded. His sleep need not have been disturbed for that message.

'I also wanted to tell you that my builder is planning to come in next week to make a start on the renovations to the apartment. Giuseppe said you might know of people who would like some of his old furniture.'

'I can ask, but if no one is interested it will have to be disposed of.'

'My builder can do that provided you give him permission. I have asked him to start dismantling the kitchen. It might be a bit noisy as he will be knocking the tiles off the walls.'

'That will be no problem to me next week. I'm back on the two 'til ten shift during the day for the following two weeks. After that I will be out over night and want to sleep during the day. I don't know which is worse, the two in the morning until ten or the six until two during the day. You're always worried that you'll take a cat nap and oversleep. It doesn't do to arrive late and when you get home it's difficult to sleep properly because everyone else is up and around. Even having four days off after the spell of night work is difficult. You no sooner get used to having some time to yourself and you're back at work again.'

Vasilis felt guilty. 'Had I known you were sleeping I would not have disturbed you. You'll have to let me know your work schedule so it doesn't happen again. Let me know your timetable for the next few weeks and I'll ensure that any work that will cause a noise can be done whilst you're out. My builders are pretty amenable.'

'How long is the rubbish going to sit outside? You won't be able to leave it directly outside Giuseppe's or it could obstruct the traffic so it will probably sit outside my windows.'

'It will be removed at the end of each day,' promised Vasilis. 'No one wants to look out at an unsightly heap of rubbish for days on end.'

'I'll appreciate it and I'm sure my neighbours will also.'

Cathy opened the door of the apartment and Saffron walked inside.

'This room is larger than it looks from outside.'

Cathy nodded. 'I'll be able to keep my wheeler over there close to the door and there's still plenty of space for a lounge suite and we can have a dining area at the back.'

'Have you decided on a colour scheme for in here?'

'I will keep the walls and paintwork white, I think, but I'll need to think about floor tiles and the colour of the lounge furniture. There's also the carpet for the winter to be considered. Come and look at the kitchen.'

'I see what you mean about those yellow tiles,' said Saffron. 'Are you having natural wood cupboards?'

'I haven't decided. The appliances will be white, so wood could be suitable.'

'In that case a pale yellow tile could look good.'

'At the moment I am definitely off yellow,' remarked Cathy.

'Just bear it in mind. Are you keeping the patio doors?'

'Definitely. We will want to use the area during the summer.'

'There won't be very much tiling showing once you've had the cupboards fitted.'

'Do you think I should have the same colour floor tiles in here as in the main living area?'

'That would depend upon the colour you finally choose. Why don't you put the wall tiling on hold until you've decided on the floor? That could make a difference to your final decision.'

'Come through to the bedroom.' Cathy opened the door into the hallway and then the bedroom door. 'There's furniture stored in here at the moment and it isn't that large so I think the walls may have to be white again.'

'You can always add colour with your throws, duvets and curtains.'

'Vasilis is planning to have the wall knocked through to the bathroom so it becomes en suite. The door in the hallway will be blocked up and there is a cupboard at the end of the hall. That will be taken away and Mr Palamakis has suggested that a small cloakroom is made there. Visitors would have to pass through our bedroom otherwise, but it's the floor tiles that are worrying me at the moment. Should I have the same colour in the kitchen, lounge and hallway and something different in the bedroom and en suite?'

'What does Vasilis say?'

'He says it is up to me to choose whatever I like, but I want him to be happy with my decisions.'

'How big is the bathroom?' asked Saffron.

'Not very big and there's only a small window in there,' replied Cathy as she opened the door.

'Pretty horrid,' observed Saffron. 'The first thing I would do is ask Mr Palamakis if that window can be enlarged. It would make it much lighter.'

Cathy nodded. 'I have spoken to Vasilis about that. It should be no problem as it looks out onto the patio. He says he will need to check if the people who have the shop will be able to see in from their upper floor windows.'

'You can have a blind so I don't see that as a problem.'

'Vasilis says that would be the solution when we have a shower but if we just come in to use the toilet we don't want to have to think about pulling a blind down each time.'

'Could you have glass with a pattern on it.?'

Cathy sighed. 'That could cut the light out so there would be no point in enlarging the window.'

'Suppose you had the wall knocked down completely and made this part of your bedroom and had the en suite at the other end? Would that solve the problem?'

'I don't know. I'll have to ask Vasilis to discuss it with Mr Palamakis. The drain pipes run under the patio, except for the separate cloakroom we want. I'm not sure how the drain run would be affected. They might have to go beneath our bedroom floor.'

'What are your floors made of? Do you know?'

'Concrete.'

Saffron pulled a face. 'That would mean digging a channel

through and cementing it in afterwards. Not a good idea in case there was a drain problem at a later date and they had to be dug up.'

'I think it could be more practical to leave the bathroom where it is. After all, we are only going to be here for a year or two whilst Vasilis has the house built.'

'What will you do with it then? Sell it?'

'I don't think Vasilis has thought that far ahead. He could sell it or let it out. If he lets it he will be responsible for the maintenance whereas if he sold it would be up to the new owners to keep it in good repair. That's a problem for the future. At the moment I need to decide on the floor tiles.' Cathy felt somewhat dissatisfied. Saffron had not really come up with anything constructive in the way of decoration and she hoped Ronnie would be a more positive help to her.

Ronnie stood and looked around the room.

'Pretend it was going to be yours,' said Cathy. 'What would you do?'

'Have you any definite colours in mind?'

'No, we'll be getting new furniture so I thought if the walls were white we could choose any colour for the suite.'

Ronnie frowned. 'Do you want the walls white?'

'It's practical. It makes it look light and airy.'

'So what colour floor tiles did you have in mind?'

'That's one of my problems. Do I have the same colour throughout or change colour in the hallway and our bedroom?'

'It will make everywhere look larger if you have the same colour tiles everywhere. If I was decorating this room for myself I would have cream coloured floor tiles with just an odd fleck of brown in them.' Ronnie walked through to the kitchen. 'Is everything being pulled out?' she asked.

'Mr Palamakis's grandsons are starting next week.'

'Have you decided how you are going to place your new equipment and work tops?'

'Not really.'

'Right, that can be done later when you know exactly how much space you have, but I would recommend that you have the same tiles through here as in the main room. Are you keeping that door over there?'

'It leads into the hallway and to our bedroom.'

'Decide if it is necessary. If it isn't ask Mr Palamakis if that wall can be taken away. At the moment that hallway is wasted space.'

'There's a cupboard down the end that will be removed and a cloakroom made there. I'm not sure if we would want that opening straight off the lounge area.'

'So keep a half wall but take it back.'

'Then you'll see our bedroom door,' demurred Cathy.

'If you leave the door to the hall you will see that so what is the difference?'

'None, I suppose.'

'Have you thought about colour in there?'

'Not yet. I need to have something that will go with the new bathroom that will be en suite.'

Ronnie opened both doors. 'Difficult to see the dimensions of your bedroom with all that furniture stacked in there.'

'Saffron suggested that the walls were white and I put colour in here with the curtains and bed covers.'

'Would you really like me to work out the decoration for you as if it was going to be my apartment?' asked Ronnie.

Cathy nodded eagerly. She had hoped Ronnie would offer. 'I'd be grateful. I don't want to make mistakes, but do you have the time?'

'I have a stock of paintings that I completed during the winter for Saffron. I've also done some of Kastelli. Give me a few days. I won't be offended if you decide not to use any of my ideas.' Ronnie already knew exactly how she would go about renovating and decorating the apartment, but she wanted to put her ideas and colour schemes on paper before she presented them to Cathy.

Evgeniy examined the accounts that Dimitra gave him and she sat before him nervously. 'That all appears in order,' he declared finally.

'There was one thing that worried me, sir. I understand some visitors used some of the bedrooms and the conference room last week. There is no record of this on the accounts.'

'They were my private guests and as such they were not charged for their stay here. I plan to hold other similar conferences, probably about two or three each month. It is unnecessary for the details to be recorded in the weekly accounts.' Evgeniy was annoyed that the woman had immediately found the omission.

Dimitra gave a sigh of relief. 'I was concerned that there was an error somewhere.' She had spent a considerable amount of time checking the total number of guests in the hotel the previous week and the amount they had paid in case she had made a mistake. Now it occurred to her that Mr Kuzmichov might have refrained from telling her about his guests to test her reliability.

'You do not need to worry. I fund these guests from my other business interests. They will be recorded on those accounts which are entirely separate from the hotel.' He knew the costs would be absorbed into the hotel expenses and it would be money in his pocket. He had gained over forty thousand dollars for very little effort on his part.

'What are you doing?' asked Kyriakos as he looked over Ronnie's shoulder.

'Cathy has asked me to give her some advice about colour schemes in the apartment Vasilis has bought. She told me to pretend it was mine.'

'So you are going to use the same colours there as you have here?'

Ronnie shook her head. 'I'll show you when I've finished. I've had an idea about their bedroom that I hope Vasilis will approve.'

Ronnie took a clean sheet of paper and drew the outlines of the apartment. 'Cathy says Vasilis is planning to have a hole knocked through the wall to make the bathroom en suite, but both rooms are quite small. There is a hallway leading down to a cupboard and she said they planned to have that enlarged and made into a cloakroom. I think it would be a better idea if they took that wall away completely. It would make their bedroom larger and they could also enlarge the bathroom area. What do you think?'

'So what about the cloakroom?'

'That could go next to the patio doors. It would have to encroach into their bedroom but there should still be sufficient space for them to have their bed there, if not they could have a built in wardrobe to square the room off. I'll do two different designs for her. She may not like either of them, of course.'

Kyriakos shook his head. 'If the wall between the bedroom and the hallway is going to be removed why don't you also remove the wall between the bathroom and bedroom and change the rooms around?'

Ronnie frowned and then smiled. 'Actually that's a brilliant idea. There's no reason why the bathroom shouldn't be where the bedroom is now, but it doesn't solve the problem of where to put the cloakroom.'

'There's no reason why the cloakroom should not be on the end of the bathroom and accessed separately from opposite the kitchen.'

'Like this, you mean?' Ronnie took another sheet of paper. 'That makes the bathroom 'L' shaped.'

'Does that matter? You could have the toilet on the outside wall and that should leave sufficient space for a shower between the cloakroom wall and the wall that borders the lounge area.'

'I was thinking of having the entrance to the en suite in the centre of the bedroom wall.'

'You still can.' Kyriakos took the pencil from Ronnie's hand and used it to point to the diagram she had made. 'The cloakroom wall is there with the toilet next to it. The shower is placed down the end with a basin next to it.'

'You should be working as an architect not a taverna owner.'

'And you should be working as an interior designer not a beach artist. Together we could have made a fortune.'

Ronnie laughed. 'I enjoy sitting down in the square and painting pictures. How many people do you know in Elounda who would want the interior of their houses specifically designed?'

'The foreigners who buy property over here.'

Ronnie shook her head. 'I have ideas, but it needs a qualified draughtsman to draw up plans that comply with the building regulations. Mr Palamakis may say my ideas are impractical and he would not get permission to do the work.'

Kyriakos shrugged. 'It is internal work. There should be no problem. Are you going to spend all evening redesigning Cathy's apartment?'

'Why? What did you have in mind?'

'I thought I could cook a meal for us and we could sit in bed and watch a film.'

'I'll draw out a new design for the bathroom, but I can stop painting whenever you say the meal is ready and I don't need to do any more until tomorrow. How does that sound?'

Ronnie raised her eyebrows questioningly and Kyriakos grinned back at her. As far as he was aware the only film that was being shown on the television that evening was one they had already seen and not particularly enjoyed.

March 2015
Week Four

Mr Palamakis arrived with his grandsons and they moved the furniture from the bedroom into the street. The table he wanted he placed to one side. He would have to ask Panayiotis if he could take it. There really was nothing else worth saving, both the couch and the armchair were stained and the wooden chairs were badly scratched. Panayiotis watched them from his window and finally joined Mr Palamakis.

'Would you be willing to drop off a few items at the police station in Aghios Nikolaos?'

'Which ones?'

'The couch and armchair. I know a family who would be grateful. They came here as refugees from Albania. Decent people, but struggling to find permanent employment and make a living.'

Mr Palamakis nodded. 'If you direct me to the address we could off load them at their door.'

'That would be more than helpful. I was expecting to have to borrow the police van and ask my colleagues to help me with them.'

'Anything else? We're going to start removing the white goods from the kitchen. Do you know if they're working?'

'As far as I'm aware, but again the only people I know who are in need are the people I've already mentioned. Would you be able to take them along with the other items? If they don't work I'll be responsible for their disposal.'

'If these people are in as much need as you imply why don't we load up everything and then they can take whatever they want.'

'I feel I'm imposing on you.'

Mr Palamakis shrugged. 'Whatever they take will be less for me to take to the tip. I would like that small table for myself if you're agreeable.'

'Certainly. If there is anything that you would like please help yourself.'

'Only the table, thank you.'

Panayiotis looked at his watch. 'I don't want to be a nuisance, but I have to be on duty at two. Will you be ready to leave by one? I need to be at work on time.'

'Near enough. I'll bring the truck over from the car park and the boys can start loading now. One of them can come with us whilst the other starts removing the cupboards in the kitchen. I'll need him to help me if there is anything weighty to go to the tip.'

Panayiotis led them into a street in Aghios Nikolaos. It looked a decent, affluent area, but according to Panayiotis some of the apartments were occupied by Albanian refugees, having been placed there by the government with just the basic amenities.

'Doesn't look a bad area to live in,' remarked Giorgos who had accompanied his grandfather.

'Panayiotis says they are a decent family, willing to work and better themselves. They've obviously not come to his attention for the wrong reasons.'

'If they're struggling it could be just a matter of time before they turn to burglary or shop lifting.'

'You can hardly blame them if they see their children are starving. We're just delivering rubbish that Panayiotis says they would find useful. We don't have to become friends. Looks as though we've arrived.'

Panayiotis had drawn up outside an apartment block and opened the main door. Once inside the neglect became apparent; the paint was peeling from scuffed walls and bare wires hung where a light bulb should be placed before the flight of stairs that led to the higher floors.

'Who owns this property?' asked Palamakis as he followed Panayiotis through the door.

'Someone in Australia I believe which accounts for the deplorable state the interior is in.'

'So they are paying rent to stay here, not just squatting?'

'The people in this block are refugees and subsidised by the government. They have no choice but to stay and make the best of it.'

'They need to be refurbished.'

'I agree and the government would like to do so, but who is going to pay for that? Also, once they were respectable again those who are living here now would not be able to afford to pay rent. They'd either be out on the streets or living under canvas. This is better than nothing.'

Mr Palamakis waited whilst Panayiotis knocked on a door in the hallway and waited for a man to open it a crack. When he saw who his visitor was he opened the door a little wider.

Panayiotis beckoned to the man to come outside and pointed to the truck load of furniture. 'For you, Blerim.'

The man looked at the items and shook his head. He pulled out his pockets showing they were empty. 'No Euros.'

'Free. Gift. No Euros.'

'No Euros?' repeated Blerim.

'Doesn't he speak Greek?' asked Giorgos.

'A certain amount.'

'Then please explain to him that we want to give all this rubbish to them. I'm not going to be very happy standing here when you leave. At least your uniform is respected.'

Panayiotis nodded and turned to Blerim. 'You take anything you want from the truck. Rubbish – going to the tip. No Euros.'

Blerim was galvanised into action. With a broad smile on his face he lifted a chair from the truck and carried it inside, returning with one that had part of the back missing and placed it to one side.

'So much for getting rid of our rubbish,' muttered Giorgos. 'It looks as if we will be getting rid of his.'

Mr Palamakis and Giorgos lifted the furniture piece by piece from the truck and carried them inside whilst Blerim began to stack damaged furniture into the hallway. When the fridge and washing machine were carried inside by Mr Palamakis and Giorgos there were tears in Blerim's eyes. There was no way he could afford the electricity to run them, but maybe, one day, when his circumstances improved, they could be put to good use. At present they used the minimum of electricity, switching on the low powered bulb in the living room in the evening and using the kettle only when necessary.

Finally Giorgos placed a box containing china, cutlery and pots and pans on the table. Sitting in a corner of the room was a woman wrapped in a blanket, a small child sitting on her lap, her face hidden against her mother's chest. As the furniture had been brought in the woman's eyes had grown wider with amazement.

'Where is Andon?' asked Panayiotis.

'School,' answered Blerim. 'Good boy now.'

'How is Lejla?'

Blerim shrugged. 'We try. No change.'

'Have they got a bed?' asked Mr Palamakis knowing the one from the apartment was destined for the rubbish tip the following day.

Blerim appeared to understand and beckoned them through to the next room where each window was blocked up with cardboard. In the dim light a selection of dirty mattresses on the floor covered by thin blankets could be discerned. He placed his hands together in supplication and Mr Palamakis saw for the first time that the man's hands had been mutilated. Three fingers had been cut off at the first joint and his finger nails were either missing or misshapen.

'Tomorrow we bring a bed and covers. Now we go.'

Giorgos was about to throw the damaged and useless furniture that Blerim had stacked in the hallway into the back of the truck and Blerim stopped him. 'For fire,' he explained.

Giorgos shrugged climbed inside the truck. He was more than ready to leave.

'Well, that saves us a journey to the tip. Are you really bringing them the bed tomorrow, Grandpa?'

'I'll bring the bed and anything else in the apartment that I think they might find useful. Did you see the man's hands? It's my guess that he was tortured at some time before he left Albania. I'll have a word with Panayiotis tomorrow morning.' Mr Palamakis took out his mobile 'phone and called Yiannis. 'How are you getting on in the kitchen?'

'I've finished dismantling the cupboards and I'll move the wood into the front room by the door. Then I'll make a start on removing the tiles.'

Ronnie called Cathy. 'Is it convenient if I come down and show you some preliminary ideas?'

'Yes, I can't wait. Will you stay for lunch?'

'If I may. It will give us time to talk and you can discuss with me anything that you want changed.'

'Do you want Vasilis to be around?'

'Yes, that would be an excellent idea. I've a proposal to make that he might refuse to contemplate.'

'Now I'm really intrigued. See you in about half an hour.'

Ronnie sat at the kitchen table with Cathy and Vasilis. 'These are only my ideas, remember. You might hate them. We talked about the floor tiles being a cream colour with a faint brown marking going through them. I've had a look on the internet so see if you like any of these.'

Ronnie turned her lap top round so they could both see the screen.

'Those are far too dark,' Cathy pointed to one photograph, 'And those you can hardly see that they have any brown in them.'

'You need to see them in the tile shop, this is just to show you the selection on offer. The colours in the photos are never exact. Now, if you choose one of these tiles for the flooring throughout here are my other ideas.' Ronnie opened up a folder of paintings. 'We'll start with the main living area. I would paint the walls a very light lime green.'

'Lime green!' exclaimed Vasilis.

'Don't sound so horrified,' smiled Ronnie. 'You have the floor tiles which are a neutral colour so you can afford to be daring. I looked on the internet and saw some curtains with a white background and quite large pale green, dark green and brown leaves. I think they would be perfect. What do you think?'

Again Ronnie turned her computer round to show the curtains. 'You could have an oatmeal suite and add green or brown cushions.' She slid a painting out from her folder. 'I'll leave it with you to look at and discuss properly later.'

'The kitchen is more of a problem until I know the dimensions. At the moment I am thinking of you having a tall fridge freezer in the corner by the end wall. Coming back from there you have the sink that you will want to keep under the window. The washing machine can go one side and the dish washer the other with a work surface on top. You could end up with a decent sized cupboard at the end for cleaning materials. On the end wall by the freezer I suggest you have a work top with cupboards underneath where you store your pots and pans. You can have a hob on top and also an oven so you do not have to bend down. I am hoping it will leave sufficient space for you to have an area where you can put hot dishes whilst you are serving. On the return wall opposite the sink and the window I've placed a series of drawers where you can keep your cooking utensils and cutlery and then cupboards where you could keep your china and glassware. There will be a work top that you can use when preparing meals or baking.'

Cathy nodded. 'That looks good. I hope the kitchen will be large enough.'

'If the width is a problem the cupboards have to be made

narrower or they are placed up above the work top, but they could be difficult for you to reach. I'll have another look when Mr Palamakis has pulled everything out and take some accurate measurements. You will have to decide upon the colour of your work tops and cupboards.'

'What would you have?' asked Cathy.

'Very light coloured wood and a worktop that is slightly cream with some ripples of brown or fawn in it. I would then try to get some wall tiles that matched the floor tiles.'

'And the bedroom?'

Ronnie smiled. 'This is where I am proposing something drastic. Remove the wall that borders the bedroom and bathroom completely so you have no hallway. That would give you two larger rooms.'

'But no cloakroom,' protested Vasilis.

'The cloakroom would go there.' Ronnie pointed to her sketch. 'The bathroom and bedroom would be swapped round. There should be no problem with the drains as you would only need to tap into the run from the current bathroom. You will have to check with Mr Palamakis if it is possible to remove the hallway wall and the dividing wall between the bedroom and bathroom safely and extend the wall across the current hallway. If that cannot be done then your original plans will have to stay as they are.'

Vasilis picked up the sketch and studied it. 'I like the idea. Where would the doors be?'

'The one for the cloakroom would be down by the patio windows and the one leading to your bedroom would be in an appropriate area in the back wall of the lounge.'

Vasilis nodded. 'I think that could work provided Mr Palamakis says it is feasible. What do you think, Cathy?'

'It could solve the problem you envisage with the current bathroom window being enlarged.'

'But we would want a larger window in the bedroom.'

'So you have curtains or a blind. You only need privacy whilst you are getting dressed or undressed.'

'Even with a larger window the bedroom could be somewhat dark. Have you had any thoughts about décor in there?' asked Cathy.

'It would be practical to paint the walls white, so that the room was lighter. You could have deep turquoise tiles in the bathroom and pick up the colour in your bedroom curtains with maybe a chair and some cushions in the same colour. As I've said, these are only my ideas and I'll not be offended if you don't like them.'

Vasilis picked up the sketch Ronnie had made with the walls removed. 'May I keep this and show it to Palamakis?'

'Certainly. If he says it is impossible then I'll think again and come up with some other proposals.'

Mr Palamakis looked at the pile of broken tiles on the floor of the kitchen and the dismantled wooden cupboards that Yiannis had moved towards the door of the living room.

'Do you want us to start bagging them up?' asked Yiannis.

'Not yet. We need to get the mattress out of that back room along with any other bits and pieces that are still in there. Then we can dismantle the bed. Once that's done we'll call it a day. I want to have a word with Panayiotis tomorrow before we go any further.'

Panayiotis was surprised when Mr Palamakis knocked and asked if he could have a serious talk with him.

'Is there a problem?'

'I'm hoping you can help me solve one. I was horrified when I saw the conditions that family had been enduring. No one should have to live like that. How did you come across them?'

'I happened to see Blerim around the tavernas scavenging in their rubbish sacks. I was a bit suspicious and he conveyed to me that he was looking for food to take back to his family. I then caught the boy stealing fruit and vegetables. I insisted that he took me to his family. I was going to give them a warning. When I

met Blerim I realised the family were genuinely in need. I spoke
to one of the taverna owners and asked if he would leave some
decent left overs in a box that I could collect and deliver to a
destitute family. He was a bit dubious at first, but I promised
him that whenever I caught a fresh squid or octopus he could
have it without having to pay me. My uniform helped persuade
them also.'

'Has Blerim tried to find work?'

'In Albania he was a dentist, but that's impossible for him
now. He has applied to be a refuse collector and a road sweeper
but he was unsuccessful on both counts.'

'Did they give a reason?'

'They did not think he would be able to manage due to the
state of his hands and feet.'

'I saw his hands.'

'His feet are in much the same state. He was tortured which
was why he decided he had to leave Albania. The Greek authorities
gave him refugee status and then moved him from place to place
on the mainland and finally over here.'

'Do you think he could do some manual labour?'

'Probably. What are you thinking?'

'I could give him some work at the moment and possibly
some more later on. My grandsons are willing workers who will
turn their hand to most things, but manual labour is a waste of
their abilities.'

'You'd pay him?'

'Of course. The going rate. Six Euros an hour. I'm delivering
the bed up to him once I've brought the truck round. Would you
be willing to come with me and talk to him?'

'Certainly. I'll just put my uniform on. I find it helps up in that
area. People tend to leave me alone and also avoid the family in
case they complain to me and I take the complaint further.'

'So neighbours won't try to steal anything we've given them?'

'Most unlikely. If they leave anything they don't want outside their door it will be gone in a flash, but no one will try to take any items from inside.'

'I'll let you know when we're ready to go. Giorgos can sit in the back and help unload. You can't be expected to do that in your uniform.'

Blerim was obviously waiting for them to arrive and opened the door immediately with a smile on his face. His wife still sat in the corner, huddled in the blanket with the child on her lap, but there was a small fire in the hearth and a pot sitting at one side. The damaged furniture that had been stacked in the hallway was gone and a large pile of wood sat in the corner of the living room.

'Is the child not well?' asked Palamakis.

'Physically I think she is fit, but she has not recovered from the scenes she witnessed in Albania,' explained Panayiotis. He turned to the woman. 'Andon? School?' and she nodded by way of reply.

Giorgos and Mr Palamakis man-handled the old mattress from the back room, stood the other two mattresses up by the wall and brought in the wooden bed frame from the truck. Once assembled they collected the mattress and placed it on top, along with some blankets and sheets. Blerim began to thank them profusely and Mr Palamakis turned to Panayiotis.

'Ask him if he is willing to do some work. He can come back with me in the truck. He and Giorgos can sit in the back. When we finish for the day I'll bring him back to Aghios Nikolaos and drop him off nearby.'

Blerim understood the word "work" and when Panayiotis spoke to him slowly and then added the word "Euros" Blerim nodded eagerly. He spoke to his wife and then at Palamakis's instruction scrambled up into the bed of the truck with alacrity.

Mr Palamakis introduced him to Yiannis and then handed him a sack and a shovel, pointing to the heap of broken tiles on the kitchen floor. Blerim seemed to understand immediately and began shovelling industriously.

Yiannis and Giorgos returned to the bathroom and could be

heard smashing up the cast iron bath that was in there. At each blow Blerim winced visibly. They carried the heavy pieces of broken bath through to the living room and placed them inside the doorway. Mr Palamakis indicated that the sacks Blerim had filled should also be carried through and stacked there ready to load up the truck and be taken to the tip

'And the wood,' he said, tapping it with his hand.

Blerim looked at him sadly and pointed first to the wood and then to himself. 'I will take,' he said.

'You mean you want it? It's no good for anything.'

'For fire.'

Mr Palamakis shrugged and nodded. It would be less to take to the tip and he could deliver it for Blerim when he took him home.

Whilst Yiannis and Giorgos continued capping off the pipes to the basin and toilet prior to their removal their grandfather put Blerim to dismantling the cupboard in the hallway. Despite his mutilated fingers he seemed able to manipulate a screw driver efficiently.

Before leaving for his duty at the police station Panayiotis appeared with mugs of coffee and a thick sandwich for Blerim. 'I don't expect he has eaten since last night. You can't be expected to share your lunch with him so I thought I could make up something.'

Blerim wolfed the sandwich down as if he was starving and Palamakis eyed him in concern. Whatever food he was able to procure he was obviously giving to his wife and children and going without himself. Tomorrow he would make an extra sandwich for the man to have.

Towards the end of the afternoon Mr Palamakis collected the truck from the car park and the two younger men began to load it with the sacks of tiles and the broken bath. Blerim collected the wood and placed it to one side. He hoped the builder realised he wanted the wood to make a fire and would not insist on taking it to the tip. He also hoped the builder would take him at least part of the way back to Aghios Nikolaos. He had not worked so hard in a long time and was not relishing the relatively long walk home. His loss of some toes meant that he now walked with a slightly rolling gait and after a while his hips began to ache.

Mr Palamakis dug into his pocket and handed Blerim thirty Euros. 'Euros for work,' he said and was taken aback when Blerim threw his arms around him and thanked him profusely in Albanian.

'Tomorrow,' said Mr Palamakis, pointing to Blerim and the apartment, 'I collect you early,' and Blerim nodded eagerly as he scrambled into the back of the truck. Mr Palamakis was not sure what he was going to ask the man to do that would keep him occupied once the bathroom tiles had been knocked off the wall and sacked up. He would need to speak to Mr Iliopolakis for further directions before he could proceed further.

Vasilis looked at the sketches Ronnie had left behind. 'What do you think, Cathy?'

'I'm not certain about the colour schemes she has in mind, but swapping the bathroom and bedroom around and removing the hallway is a good idea.'

'I'll call Mr Palamakis and ask if I can meet him at the apartment tomorrow and discuss it. He may say it isn't possible. We'll probably need to have a visit from a building inspector regarding the new drain runs once they are completed to ensure they work efficiently, and we'd certainly need his approval for another toilet to be constructed.'

'What about lights and electric sockets? Ronnie didn't mention them. Would Dimitris be able to install them?'

'I'm sure he could, but first we need the dimensions of the kitchen so you know where the dish washer and washing machine are definitely going and also your worktops. You don't want to find you have a socket hidden in a cupboard or too high up to reach. You decide how many sockets you would like in the kitchen for the kettle and other appliances and then we can work out the most practical places for them.'

'I'd quite like some wall lights in the living room, and bedside lights.'

Vasilis nodded. 'I'm sure they can all be arranged.'

Vasilis, armed with Ronnie's sketches, met Mr Palamakis shortly after he arrived at the apartment. His grandsons could be heard knocking the tiles off the bathroom wall and Vasilis frowned. It was far too noisy to hold a conversation.

'Come and sit in my car,' he said and Mr Palamakis followed him to where Vasilis had parked his car a short distance down the road.

'How are you getting on?' he asked.

'The kitchen is stripped out, the hall cupboard dismantled and the boys are knocking the tiles off the bathroom walls. That's why it's so noisy in there. Do you want the boys to start plastering the kitchen walls tomorrow?'

'I want to show you this first. Ronnie came down. She had arranged with Cathy to do some sketches suggesting colour schemes. She also suggested removing some walls. I need you to look at it and tell me if it's possible.'

Mr Palamakis looked at the sketches where Ronnie had removed the walls in the bathroom and bedroom area. 'That can be done,' he said at last, annoyed that he had not made the proposal himself. 'I will need to build up the walls so they meet and put up a strengthening steel. It would mean you lose the cloakroom you wanted.'

'Ronnie suggested that the cloakroom was repositioned like this,' Vasilis pointed to a second sketch. 'The rooms would be changed around so that the first room was the bathroom area instead of the bedroom and an entrance door made in the lounge wall. Without the hallway wall the rooms would be considerably larger.'

'I'll need to look at the drain runs. They may have to be renewed. There's no problem removing the old ones that will be disused, but it may not be possible to join new pipes into the ones that are there now.'

'But you can do it? You think this idea is practical?'

'I do, but it will also mean removing the paving slabs in the patio.'

'I've only had a quick look out there, but it probably needs relaying anyway.'

'I'll have to go home and collect my acroprops before I start to knock those walls down. I don't want to find that we have the ceiling landing on our heads. I was going to ask Yiannis to start re-plastering the kitchen walls today but it would be better to wait until the dust has cleared. That could work in well with Panayiotis. He says he does not mind how much noise we create during the day at the moment, but he would appreciate having some peace when he's on nights.'

'Whilst I'm here can you measure the kitchen area for me, please. I don't want Cathy ordering items that are too large to fit in.'

'No problem. You ought to meet Blerim anyway. I've taken him on temporarily to do some of the manual labour. He's an Albanian refugee, but Panayiotis vouched for him.'

Vasilis raised his eyebrows but made no comment. He had never known Mr Palamakis employ anyone except his sons and when they decided that building work was not for them he had employed his grandsons. Mr Palamakis was pleased to be asked to do the extra work. It would certainly add to the amount that he would be charging Mr Iliopolakis and he could continue to employ Blerim for a few more days.

'I'll let you know when the walls have been removed. Until then it's probably best if you keep away unless you want to get covered in dust and dirt.'

Vasilis smiled. 'I know I can leave it up to you, Mr Palamakis.'

Mr Palamakis called a halt to the work in the bathroom and explained that the walls were now going to be removed. 'You come back with me, Giorgos, to collect the acroprops and Blerim can knock some more tiles off; then he can start bagging them up.'

Theo loaded his hunting gun and spare cartridges into the boot of his car. It was the last week that he and other marksmen were legally allowed to hunt rabbits and sell them to the butchers. Although he went up to the Katharou Plateau and practised his shooting skills he only hunted rabbits occasionally just to prove to himself that he could still hit a moving target.

Shortly after midnight he drove to Elounda, across the Causeway and up the road towards the white house. He parked as far along the road as possible before it became a dirt track. There were two other cars already there and he could see the light of four torches as the men climbed up the hill. Theo placed his spare ammunition in his belt, slung the strap from his gun over his shoulder and tucked the gun beneath his arm. Quietly he began to ascend the path that ran through the scrub land, holding the torch steadily before him and listening for any movement in the undergrowth.

He stopped as he heard the crack of another hunter's gun. Moving on again he picked out the shape of a rabbit and swung the torch round. Momentarily dazzled the rabbit froze, but by the time Theo had raised his gun to take aim the rabbit was bounding away. Calculating the distance Theo pulled the trigger and was rewarded by seeing the vegetation stop moving. He walked forward to where the rabbit was lying on the ground and checked that it was dead before he placed it in the bag that hung from his belt. Once he had bagged four he would claim the night had been a success and return home.

By three in the morning he had four dead rabbits in his bag and began to make his descent. The other hunters were still up on the hill; they would have two more hours before daybreak and were planning to take advantage of the last of the darkness. He wanted to be the first hunter at the butcher's shop with his fresh rabbits. As he reached the cart track he switched off his torch and made his way to his car where he placed the rabbits and the gun into the boot and locked it securely.

Unconcerned about noise he started the car and began to drive slowly down towards the bridge that led to the Causeway. As he reached the small beach at the side of the road he saw there was someone sitting on a rock. He drew the car to a halt and walked over.

'Are you alright? Would you like a ride back to Elounda?'

As the person looked at him Theo saw it was a woman, dressed entirely in black.

'Thank you, but I have no problem. I am waiting for my companions.'

Theo nodded, assuming she was waiting for the hunters who were still up on the hillside.

'In that case I will leave you. I hope you will not have to wait too much longer.'

Theo returned to his car and drove on towards the bridge that crossed the canal. As the windmills came in sight he was surprised to see a black Mercedes parked behind the ruined one. The lady who lived in the restored windmill during the summer months never arrived until June and she certainly did not drive a Mercedes. Theo continued on to the bridge and as he did so he could see a dinghy at the far end negotiating the entrance carefully. It must contain the companions the woman had mentioned. They had obviously been fishing, and not hunting as he had assumed, but it was risky to take such a flimsy craft out into the open sea at night and even more foolhardy not to have any lights. A passing fisherman could easily run them down.

Ludmila watched as Theo drove across the Causeway. It was disconcerting to have the man arrive whilst she was waiting for Panos to deliver the men. She hoped he would not be waiting to stop the car after she reached the coast road. She looked alternatively at the sea, waiting for Panos to arrive, and across at the mainland where she could see the lights from the car moving steadily and finally disappearing from view. She gave a sigh of relief and flashed her torch in answer to Panos's signal. Provided all went well she would not tell Evgeniy about the man who had spoken to her.

April 2015

John sat with his Uncle Yannis at the computer. 'I told you it was a good idea to approach the museums,' Yannis said smugly. 'Hersonissos have placed an order for ten pots; one pithoi, three Geometric, three Attic ware and three black figure.'

'Well that's a good start. We'll reduce the overall numbers and put a message on the site to say that the Hersonissos museum has bought them. That could encourage some of the other museums to follow suit.'

'Can you post them?'

John shook his head. 'Not a good idea. It would cost as much to send them to Hersonissos as it would to Chania. We'll pack them up and I'll ask Dad if I can borrow the car tomorrow and deliver them. I'll make a note of the mileage and tell him that you'll pay for the petrol.'

'Shall I come with you?'

'You can if you want; provided you don't change your mind about selling them at the last minute. It will probably be about a three hour journey by the time we've handed them over and the museum has checked that there is no damage.'

Yannis gave a deep sigh. 'I'll be sorry to part with them.'

'If you come with me I don't want any tears,' said John in a stern voice and grinned at the look on his Uncle's face. 'You never worried about selling them to customers in the shop.'

'That was different. I always knew I was going to order some more. Once my current stock has sold that will be it.'

'You know it's sensible, Uncle. At the moment they are all packed away in boxes. You could always keep one of each kind and have them as ornaments in your room so you can look at them. I could build you some shelves to display them.'

Yannis nodded. 'I'd like that.'

'Fine. We can work on that idea later when we've changed the web site and packed the pots that are sold.'

Evgeniy had heard from Ivan that a further six refugees were due to arrive that week.

'The arrangements will be exactly the same as before,' Evgeniy advised Ludmila.

'I have four suitcases. I'll buy another two. Why don't I go to Hersonissos tomorrow and purchase the cases? I could exchange some dollars whilst I'm there. If we continually use the exchange bureaus in Heraklion sooner or later word will get round that someone is exchanging dollars regularly and questions will be asked.'

Evgeniy nodded. 'That makes sense. It could be a good idea to carry dollars with you wherever you go and take advantage of changing them into Euros. I've not banked the money from the previous arrivals so I have plenty of dollars in the safe. I can explain away a certain amount by claiming they were hotel guests from America and requested to pay their bill in dollars, but that is not going to happen two or three times in every month. If I put dollars into my Russian account regularly questions will be asked and I'll be asked for proof of the transaction. I thought I would save them up until I had a sizeable amount, copy an old shipping bill and change the date on it.'

'Are you coming to Hersonissos with me?' asked Ludmila.

'No, I need to speak to the manager tomorrow and ensure there are no conferences booked for the coming week. I also ought to speak to the housekeeper and tell her I have private guests arriving and the rooms will not need servicing whilst they are staying and Dimitra is due to present the end of month accounts to me. I'll need to tell her about the extra guests or she'll be querying why they have not been entered into the accounts.'

'Why don't you refuse all conference bookings until November?'

'I don't want to do that. Sooner or later the organisers would start to look elsewhere. Provided I can fit them in with our arrangements there is no problem and they are profitable.'

'So if there is one booked for the time you are using the rooms what will you do?' queried Ludmila.

'Either tell them that there has been an unfortunate double booking or allow them the use of the other conference room. There's no need for you to be concerned about that.'

John wrapped the pots carefully and loaded them into the car. 'Are you coming with me, Uncle Yannis?'

Yannis gave a deep sigh. 'I suppose so.'

'It's up to you,' replied John. 'I'm quite capable of handing over some pots and waiting for them to be checked.'

'They might ask you some questions about them and you wouldn't know the answers.'

John rolled his eyes. The museum curators should know even more about the pots than his great uncle. 'I'd like to leave within the next five minutes.'

'I'm ready now,' Yannis replied.

Despite a considerable amount of traffic on the main road John arrived at the museum in Hersonissos in under an hour.

'Stay in the car for five minutes, Uncle. I need to go inside to ask where we can park and unload.'

John exited the museum rapidly accompanied by a man who indicated a gate at the side of the parking area and unlocked the padlock. He waved John through and replaced the chain and padlock.

'Sorry about locking you in, but we can't have the general public wandering around and coming in the back way. The store rooms and workshops are accessed from here and we wouldn't want them to damage anything. I'll ask for the assistant curator to come and help you unload. He'll show you where he wants the pots.'

John nodded. 'I'll stay in the car until he arrives.'

'Would I be able to look around the museum whilst you off load?' asked Yannis.

'I expect so, but you'd better ask permission before you go wandering in.'

'Will I be expected to pay? I haven't brought my wallet with me.'

'I have some money with me if necessary,' grinned John. 'I'll explain that you're a penniless old man and I gave you a lift in my car out of the kindness of my heart.'

John worked deliberately slowly with the assistant curator, removing the pots from the car and carrying them safely inside where their protective wrapping was removed. He was not sure if his Uncle Yannis had visited the museum at Hersonissos before and wanted to give him ample time to study the pots that were on display. Finally, accompanied by the assistant curator they went in search of the elderly man.

Yannis was standing before a collection of large clay pots and talking animatedly to a guard and five Greek visitors. He looked at John in surprise.

'Is it time to go? I was just explaining how these pithoi were used for storing cereal and wine, and often valuable items were also stored inside and a seal placed over the opening. I've talked to them about the Attic ware and the black and red designs. We only touched on the geometric briefly and I'd planned to tell them more about the marine designs.'

'I'm sure they have been interested and appreciated your

knowledge, Uncle, but we really should leave now. Your delivery has been checked and all is in order.'

'I should have asked you to print me off some business cards,' grumbled Yannis. 'I could have given these visitors my details and they may have wanted to order something from my collection.'

'Leave it with me.' John raised his voice. 'Thank you for allowing my uncle to talk to you about pottery. He is very knowledgeable and until recently he had his own shop where he sold the museum replicas. Now he has decided to retire and part with his collection. If there is a particular item you like that is not stocked in the museum shop please ask the curator for Yannis Andronicatis's details. He has a web site where you can contact him and view everything he has for sale. Thank you for your time. Enjoy the remainder of your day.'

John took his uncle's elbow and began to steer him towards the door. 'I'm not sure you're supposed to give talks to visitors without having an official guide licence. It's a good job that guard was understanding or you could have been arrested.'

Yannis looked at John in surprise. 'I was only telling them what I knew about the pottery. The guard seemed to know very little and one of them was saying such silly things and making ridiculous suggestions about their usage that I just had to put him right.'

'Not everyone is as knowledgeable as you, Uncle. I've arranged that I can leave the car here for a while and we can go and have a drink. I imagine you need one after all that talking.'

'What has happened to my pots?'

'They have been safely unpacked and checked. They are in the store room and I expect they will be on display and for sale in the museum shop within a week.'

'I'd like to come back and see them.'

'No way. You'd probably end up buying them back. Now, what would you like to drink? I'm having a shandy and I think it should be warm enough for us to sit outside.'

John opened his mobile 'phone and called Nicola. 'Everything went well. We're just having a quick drink then I'll be driving home. Oh, wow!'

'What's wrong? John, what's happened?'

'Nothing. Don't worry. I've just seen a superb black Mercedes pass by and that was just my reaction. I'd love to know who owns it.'

'I doubt they'd be offering you a ride. Don't frighten me like that again. See you in about an hour.'

Mr Palamakis measured the area where the cloakroom would be situated and made a chalk line on the floor; he made another on the wall where he was going to suggest a small window was placed. Having allowed for the wall to be built he measured the area where the shower would be installed. There should be sufficient space for a hand basin to be placed between it and the wall of the new toilet with a cupboard built beneath to hold towels and spare toiletries. Once the toilet and hand basin were in situ he would have to allow the opening from the bedroom to be wide enough and ensure that there would be sufficient floor space for Cathy to enter in a wheelchair at a future date if necessary. He hoped Mr Iliopolakis was not going to ask for a door to the opening or that would present a problem; it would not be possible for a door to open into the bathroom and if it opened into the bedroom it would be inconvenient.

'I will give you the dimensions of the shower area, Mr Iliopolakis. I have calculated that there is sufficient space for the hand basin to be situated next to it, but I need to know where the waste pipe will be situated. Some showers have them in a central position at one side and others at the end. I will need to dig up the floor for the drain runs and water pipes and I don't want to dig up more concrete than necessary.'

'What about our toilet in the bathroom?'

'That is no problem. I will situate it on the outside wall and a hole can be knocked straight through. A separate pipe can come from the mains to fill the cistern. Later the paving slabs will have to be lifted to accommodate the new pipes leading to the main drainage system. It would be better to have all that work completed before Yiannis begins to re-plaster the kitchen.'

'And the windows?'

'You tell me the size you want in the bedroom and I'll get that area of wall removed. The toilet and bathroom windows are no problem as they will be far smaller and the area where they will be is restricted. Provided you are happy with the arrangements as they are at the moment the doorway to the cloakroom can be made a short distance from the patio windows and a door from the lounge to your bedroom.'

'What about the entrance to the en suite?'

'Roughly in the centre of the dividing wall. You'll not want a door, will you?'

Vasilis shook his head. 'There's no need. It will only be Cathy and myself using it,' and Mr Palamakis gave a sigh of relief. 'Can I come down and have a look?'

'Certainly.'

'I ought to bring my wife down to have a look?'

'Better to wait until all the walls are down and the dust has settled. She will be able to get a better idea then and if she wants any changes then is the time to say. Easier to change plans now rather than later.'

Cathy was pleased when Vasilis said Mr Palamakis was willing for her to inspect the apartment two days later now when the last of the walls had been knocked down and the rubble removed.

'We need to decide where the entrance door to our bedroom will be and how large we want the window. He wants to know which shower we have chosen so he knows where to dig up a section of the floor for the drain run. Once that work has been completed and cleared he can start building the wall extensions and the cloakroom,' explained Vasilis.

'Let's have another look at bathroom fittings on the internet.

We can drive into Aghios Nikolaos later and have a look at those we like before making a final decision.'

'We can do that later. At the moment we only have to decide on the shower tray. We should go for the largest that will fit in the area. They are set sizes unless you have one specially moulded to order. It is the panels and door that you have to choose and then whether you want the basin as a pedestal or a vanity. Palamakis has said there should be enough space between the shower and the new toilet wall for a vanity with a cupboard underneath.'

Cathy nodded. 'A vanity is a far better idea than a pedestal. They always manage to collect dirt at the back and are so difficult to clean.'

Blerim could hardly believe it; every day for the past two weeks Mr Palamakis had met him down on the main road in Aghios Nikolaos that led out of the town and on to Elounda and at the end of each day he had given him a substantial sum of Euros for the work he had completed. He had given his wife ten Euros every day to enable her to purchase some decent food, although Panayiotis was still delivering him a box of left over food from the taverna. The remaining Euros he placed in a tin box beneath a floor board in the bedroom.

Although he had never participated in manual labour before he found he was becoming stronger and was not utterly exhausted by the time Mr Palamakis said they were finishing for the day. He also felt a certain amount of satisfaction when he saw the truck loaded up with the rubble from the walls they had dismantled. He did have other problems nagging away at him; once the manual labour had been completed Mr Palamakis would have no further use for him. He hoped Mr Palamakis would tell the refuse company that he was quite capable of doing a day's hard work and they would then offer him a job. He desperately wanted to earn enough money on a regular basis to enable him to move his family to some better accommodation, buy some warm winter clothes for them at the end of the summer and be able to take his young daughter to a doctor.

Lejla had not spoken since witnessing the attack on her father and their subsequent flight from Albania. Blerim sensed that the child was severely traumatised. She would nod or shake her head when asked a question, but refused to participate in verbal communication.

Although Panayiotis had said he would not be troubled by noise from the house next door during the day he would be relieved when the sound of banging and crashing stopped. He was returning to night duty and would need to be able to catch up on his sleep during the day. He saw Mr Palamakis arriving and decided to remind him that he would like to know that he was going to be undisturbed.

'The worst is nearly over,' Mr Palamakis assured him. 'Today will be a bit horrendous as we have to make the new channels in the cement floor for the drain runs. We'll be using a pneumatic drill this morning. I've just collected it from the hire firm. Now Mr Iliopolakis has said where he wants the entrance from the lounge to the bedroom area we will have to knock through and also part of the outside wall has to be removed so there can be a larger window in the bedroom and one made in the cloakroom. That should be the worst of the disruption over. Once the rubble has been cleared away Blerim will be mixing cement and Yiannis will start constructing the new walls whilst Giorgos lays the waste pipes.'

'I'm grateful to you for employing Blerim. He's a decent man.'

'He's also a hard worker; never complains whatever I ask of him. He has no ability for plastering, carpentry or painting unfortunately. When we reach that stage I will have to tell him I can no longer employ him. I can't afford to pay him for doing nothing.'

'I'm sure he will understand. I'll have a word with the refuse department and if you say he has been quite capable of doing all the work you asked of him they may reconsider their decision and employ him.'

Cathy looked around at the two rooms that had now been knocked into one. 'That was a really good idea of Ronnie's. I'm so pleased I asked her advice. It makes the bedroom and bathroom so much more spacious.'

'Are you going with the lime green walls in the lounge?'

'I'm not sure. There's plenty of time to decide. I liked the curtains she showed me. If I decided to have those I might have the lime green by the windows and patio doors and then I could have ceramic wall tiles of the same colour extended into the kitchen. Has Mr Palamakis given you the measurements in there now it has been stripped?'

Vasilis nodded. 'He's allowed for the plastering in his measurements so we can see which appliances will fit in. Do you want the window enlarged?'

'Could it go most of the length of the wall? That would make the kitchen much lighter.'

'I'll ask Mr Palamakis and then I think we should leave him and his men to get on. We can spend the afternoon looking at kitchen appliances. It will make a change from shower trays and bathroom fitments.'

'As we're down here could we drive on to Plaka? I know Saffie was opening today and I expect Monika was also. It would be nice just to pop in and wish them well.'

'What you really mean is that you would like to visit Monika and choose a few books to take home with you. You wished Saffie a successful season before she left this morning.'

'Would you mind?'

'No. Now I'm a retired gentleman of leisure I can do whatever you fancy.'

The drain runs excavated, the window openings made and the new walls built, Blerim approached Mr Palamakis. 'I thank you. Tomorrow no work.'

'Why can't you come tomorrow?' asked Mr Palamakis.

'No work. All done.'

'Not at all. I still have work that you can do. All the paving stones need to be lifted and stacked. Once the new drains are in situ and passed by the building inspector the ground will need to be levelled and the paving slabs put back down.'

Blerim's face lit up. 'Is good. I work more for you.'

Vasilis visited the apartment, pleased with the progress that had been made.

'An extra hand makes all the difference,' smiled Mr Palamakis. 'I've arranged for the building inspector to come tomorrow and provided he passes the drains Blerim can start to fill in the trenches, level the ground and replace the slabs. Have you decided about your electrical fittings? You won't want to start chipping away at new plaster to put wires in.'

'I've spoken to Dimitris. Shall I ask him to come along and discuss the work with you?'

'Have you decided where you want the lights and the power points. He'll need a plan to work from.'

Vasilis nodded. He would talk to Cathy as soon as he returned home.

'The windows should arrive next week and once we have those in and the electric wires run through everywhere we can finish the plastering and think about installing the bathroom fitments.'

'I'll have to remind my wife that she must decided on the tiles she wants. She has a deep turquoise in mind at present.'

'Try to steer her away from the small mosaic effect. The larger the tile the easier and quicker they are to install as there is less cutting needed.'

'I'll bear that in mind,' agreed Vasilis.

'I think Blerim will be capable of doing the grouting, but after that I can't think of anything else he can do that would be useful.'

'Ronnie recommended pale lime green walls in the main living area. Cathy is a bit doubtful. She thinks if the walls beside the entrance and the cloakroom were lime the rest of the room might look better being painted white.'

'Whatever suits you, Mr Iliopolakis. Even if we painted the whole room pale lime it would not be difficult to repaint it in white if you didn't like it. A couple of coats should do it.'

'The bedroom will be white. We have decided it is too small an area to take colour and once we have some built in wardrobes and other furniture around there will be hardly any wall showing anyway.'

Panayiotis passed his report to his Superintendent. Now he could go home. It had been unfortunate that he had been called out to attend the scene of an accident shortly before his evening duty ended. Usually the hours that he spent at the police station in Aghios Nikolaos when his schedule was timed from six in the evening until two in the morning were spent chatting with his two companions or participating in a game of cards. Tonight had been different. He had waited until the injured had been removed from the scene by ambulance and then interviewed the witnesses. It was essential that he had completed his report before he left so the incident could be followed up and thoroughly investigated.

Yawning widely he climbed into his car. He was conscious that he was tired and must drive with care. Joining the traffic that was leaving Aghios Nikolaos he drove steadily, allowing other vehicles to overtake him. As he reached the traffic lights he saw a Mercedes waiting and expected it to continue to Aghios Nikolaos, probably delivering or collecting visitors. Panayiotis wished he had a car of that calibre. On a policeman's salary such a vehicle was beyond his wildest dreams. He was most surprised when the car took the road that led to Elounda.

Panayiotis followed the car along the road expecting it to continue down into the town, instead it took the sharp right turn that led down to the coast road. He frowned; the driver must have lost his way; none of the hotels or self catering establishments along there were open until next week. It was not his concern, he just longed to be in his bed and hoped there would not be any undue noise from the builders next door during the morning so he could catch up on his sleep.

Evgeniy escorted the new arrivals up to the conference room and ordered some food. As they ate he gave them their instructions and then showed them into the bedrooms. He had taken in the three extra hair dryers and insisted they used them to dry out their socks, shoes and trousers.

'I cannot take you down to the dining room looking wet and bedraggled. You are posing as business men attending a conference here.'

The men were tired and subdued, but obviously relieved to be somewhere warm and safe and willing to comply with the instructions the hotel owner had given them.

As Evgeniy left them Dimitra was exiting the lift, a bag in her hand. She flushed with embarrassment.

'I'm sorry, Mr Kuzmichov. Were you looking for me? I had to pop out for something personal.' She looked down at the carpeting. 'I think one of the maids must have spilt some water. I noticed it had happened once before. I'll ask Mrs Planatakis to speak to them and tell them to be more careful.'

Evgeniy frowned 'There's no need to worry Mrs Planatakis. I am sure it will soon dry out. As the lift is here I will use it to go back down to my office.'

Evgeniy looked at the floor of the lift. There were definite wet footprints that he had not noticed when taking the men up. He would check the second lift and then ask one of the maids to clean the floor. This was something he must be aware of in future and find a way to avoid. He would also need to check the interior of the car. If the men had left wet footprints in the lift the carpets in the car would also be wet. He would ask Lanassakis to remove them and make sure they were dried out.

Ludmila listened to her husband's complaint about the wet carpets in the car and the marks in the lift. She shrugged. 'The men do not always jump quite far enough and land at the edge of the sea. It isn't deep but it makes their shoes and the bottom of their trousers wet.'

'The Dimitra woman brought it to my attention. She said she had noticed the wet carpet before and wanted to blame the maids. I told her not to worry about it, but I don't want her to see wet carpet on a regular basis.'

'If you put some carpet in the lift that would absorb some of it. You could tell them to wipe their feet as they enter the hotel and to wipe them again whilst they're in the lifts. That should remove most of the residue.'

'When I looked in the car I found the mats in there were also damp and had some pieces of shingle on them.'

'Then put some plastic covering down and remove it before you ask Lanassakis to clean the interior..'

'Maybe we could find somewhere better for you to park and the men could change their shoes and trousers before they get into the car.'

'They haven't any other shoes with them. They can be told to roll their trouser legs up so they don't become wet.'

Evgeniy sighed. 'I'll give it some thought. We need to overcome the problem. I'll have some carpet placed in the lifts for a start.'

Elena accepted Marianne's offer of a ride into Elounda. 'Call Uncle Andreas and ask if it is convenient for me to take you up to his house. I won't be able to park there, but it will save you the walk up the hill. I need to go into the village for some shopping so it is no trouble if he says a visit is not suitable today I can always bring you back with me.'

'I would like to see his house and I am sure I could manage to walk down the hill easily enough. We could have some lunch somewhere and then I'll catch a taxi back.'

'I wouldn't hear of it. If you spend time with Uncle Andreas you are to 'phone me when you are ready to return home and one of us will come to collect you. I don't want Helena accusing me of neglecting you and making you walk miles or have taxis to get around.'

'You are certainly not neglecting me. I'm enjoying being here with all of you and having company. I'm not exactly lonely in New Orleans, but there are days when I stay in and see no one.'

'Provided that does not happen too often and is your choice it is not a problem. I would relish a day to myself where I could do as I pleased.'

'Are you working too hard?' asked Elena anxiously.

'It isn't hard work. I have to spend some hours on the computer most days dealing with the bookings that come in, but there is no pressure on me to clean the house or get meals. Bryony and Nicola are always willing to help out and the men are not demanding.'

Elena frowned. 'Should you be on the computer now instead of driving me around?'

'I told you I had to come into Elounda. If anything urgent needs to be dealt with they can contact Giovanni and he will tell them I will give it priority when I return. I won't be out for more than an hour. Uncle Yannis is my only concern. He has aged visibly since Ourania died. I'm hoping this idea John has of selling his pots will give him something to occupy his mind.'

'It takes quite a long time to get used to being without your partner. I don't know how I would have coped when your father died if you had not come home and taken charge. Then there was John to keep me occupied.'

Marianne smiled. 'That was where you were such a help to me. I had no experience of babies and he was a bit of a shock.'

'He has turned into a fine young man and has a family to be proud of.'

Marianne nodded agreement. 'I'm just sorry that he was unable to achieve his ambition of being a photographer for National Geographic, but he seems to have accepted that it won't happen now. I'm so pleased he married Nicola and not a local girl whom I didn't know and might not like. On the whole, life has been good to me, thanks to Giovanni and his family.'

Elena duly admired her brother's small house, although she felt he had been foolish to purchase anything that was up such a steep hill. He might be able to manage the walk easily at present but would he be able to do so in a few years time?

Andreas smiled at her concerns. 'The property was cheap as it needed renovating and modernising. I don't plan to stay up here for ever. When I was staying with Giovanni and Marianne Marisa told me about Yannis. I didn't know he was so involved with the resistance during the war.'

'Really? I had no idea.'

'He doesn't talk about it and had probably virtually forgotten as he was just a boy when the Italians were billeted on them. Marisa reminded him and he agreed to tell me how he and his Aunt Anna fooled them on a number of occasions.' Andreas chuckled. 'Apparently he led them on some wild goose chases up into the mountains and Anna took a resistance leader to the hospital in Aghios Nikolaos right under their noses.'

'That all sounds rather exciting,' commented Elena.

'I should imagine it was frightening more than exciting. Had their activities been discovered they would probably have been shot. Anyway, that got me to thinking about the other elderly people who live around here. I've just about exhausted the locals of their memories and I've been visiting Pano and Mavrikiano and talking to the elderly who live there. Once I've decided they have nothing more to tell me I'll put all my notes into order and compile a workable script. I've already made a start by using Yannis's reminiscences and adding additional information from the locals. I've sent my first ideas off to my publisher. He seems quite enthusiastic.'

'If it is successful will you have to return to the States?' asked Elena.

'Very likely, but I'm not sure I would want to return there to live. I'll miss the friends I have made up here. When the hill becomes too much for me to manage I'll probably start to look for somewhere down in Elounda or Plaka, although both areas are so busy during the season.'

'It already seemed very busy when we arrived in Elounda.'

'The tourists are arriving. Everyone is hoping for a good season. They come up here, of course, but it is far quieter than down in the village. Do you want to eat up here with me or would you rather go to a taverna?'

'I'd be happy to stay here and eat with you. You can tell me more about your writing.'

'If you're really interested I can show you a few pages that I have printed off. I could then introduce you to some of my neighbours who have given me the information.'

Elena nodded eagerly. 'I'd enjoy that and there's no reason for me to return to Marianne's until the evening.'

May 2015

The first of the Syrian refugees had arrived in England full of hope for their new lives. They had not been challenged upon entry at Gatwick, their false British passports allowing them to pass through easily without comment. Nassam had been there to meet them and driven them through the outskirts of London, finally depositing them at a cheap lodging house. They had paid the rent for three rooms for the next two weeks from their English money and congregated together to discuss their future plans.

'I think we need to have a look around the area this afternoon and get our bearings. We need to find the hospital and schools so we can apply for work.'

'Why don't we ask the man we met downstairs where they are?' asked Salim.

Ibrahim shook his head. 'I'm not sure that is a good idea. We're supposed to have been living in England so should know details like that.'

'We've relocated and this is a new area for us,' argued Aziz.

'I still think it would be better if we asked someone on the street for directions. We'll need to split up. We'll draw attention to ourselves if we go around in a group.'

'We also need to find one of these launderettes we were told about. My clothes need a proper wash. I can't turn up asking for work wearing dirty clothes,' remarked Salim.

'We ought to go out now and find somewhere to get a meal.'

The men nodded in agreement. They had each bought a sandwich during their flight and paid with some of their remaining Euros and been appalled at the price that was charged.

'We need somewhere cheap. If there's a supermarket nearby we could buy something to make a sandwich.'

'I'd like something more substantial than a sandwich.'

'We can't afford food like we ate at the hotel. We'll look for a cafe, not a restaurant.'

In the days that followed the men walked the streets and found there was a hospital and two schools in the vicinity. Aziz rubbed his shoes over with some toilet tissue to remove as many scuffs as possible and entered the building. He approached the reception area nervously.

'Good morning. Would it be possible to speak to the Principal?'

The woman frowned. 'Do you mean the head teacher? Are you looking to enrol your children here?'

Aziz shook his head. 'No, I am looking for a position on the teaching staff. I have my qualifications with me.' He pulled the envelope containing his certificates from the University in Damascus.

'I'm sorry. We do not accept applications directly. As far as I am aware we have no vacancies for teaching staff at present. When we need a teacher we place an advertisement in the circulars that are sent out to staff and any who wish to change schools have the opportunity to apply. The notice is also sent to the Job Centre and you could enquire there to see if they can help you.'

Feeling disheartened Aziz replaced the envelope into his pocket. 'I'm new to this area. Could you direct me to the Job Centre, please?'

Salim had fared no better in the school he had approached and made his way to the Job Centre where he saw Aziz waiting to be called up to a vacant position at the counter.

Ibrahim walked confidently into the hospital and smiled at the young man who sat behind the reception desk.

'Good morning. I hope you will be able to help me. I need to speak to someone in charge of employment.'

'What kind of employment? '

'I am a qualified heart surgeon. I have my credentials with me.'

The young man looked at Ibrahim doubtfully. 'If you would like to take a seat over there I'll see if I can find someone to help you.'

Ibrahim waited patiently as other people approached the desk and were dealt with quickly. He was beginning to think he had been forgotten when a woman approached him.

'Are you the gentleman who is enquiring about employment?' she asked.

Ibrahim rose to his feet with alacrity. 'Yes, Madam. I am a qualified heart surgeon and looking for a position at a local hospital.'

'I am the Manager, maybe we should go to my office so we can talk.'

Ibrahim followed her eagerly down the passage way and into a room. 'Please have a seat and tell me about yourself.'

Ibrahim thought rapidly. He could not confess that he had entered the country on an illegal passport or claim he had worked in another hospital in England as she would be sure to check and know that his claim was false.

'I left England with my parents at a young age and studied in Syria to gain my medical knowledge. I have my certificates here with me stating my qualifications. Having worked there for some years I decided the time was right for me to return to England and look for a position here.'

'So you have not worked anywhere in England before?'

'No.' Ibrahim passed his papers across to her and she looked at them totally unable to read the Arabic writing.

The woman shook her head. 'I am not doubting your ability, but I would be unable to offer you a place on my staff. I do not read Arabic and your qualifications would have to be verified by someone who is proficient in the language. If they were satisfied you would then have to attend an assessment and possibly a retraining course to ensure that your expertise complied with English standards. Would you like me to ask for the appropriate forms to be sent to you?'

'How long will this procedure take?'

'I cannot say. I can request the forms today and you should receive them tomorrow. You will need to complete and return the forms, along with photocopies of all your papers. I do not know how long it would be before you received a reply with a date for an assessment.'

'Is there no way the procedure could be speeded up? I was told that all the hospitals over here were in need of specialists.'

The woman smiled. 'That is true and we would welcome you with open arms if you had English qualifications. Please, do not be offended, but without being able to verify your papers you could be claiming to be a surgeon without any medical knowledge whatsoever.'

'I understand,' replied Ibrahim miserably.

'Whilst you wait for an assessment date I suggest you visit the Job Centre. They might have something to suit you during the interim.'

Ibrahim sighed. 'Thank you. I will do that.'

She handed Ibrahim back his sheaf of papers. 'If you would just write down your e-mail address for me I will ensure the forms are sent to you. You will be able to reply on line in the first instance.'

'I do not have access to a computer at present.'

'I suggest you visit the local library. They will have computers for public use there.'

Ibrahim shook his head. 'I do not have an e-mail address at present.'

The woman smiled brightly at him. 'I will give you my card. It has my e-mail address at the hospital and you can send me through the details of yours.' She stood up and extended her hand. 'I am sorry I can help you no further.'

Feeling dismissed and dispirited Ibrahim exited the hospital. He had been led to believe that it would be easy to obtain suitable work in England.

The Manager shook her head. The man had been well spoken and polite, but she would have expected a heart surgeon to have access to a computer and also to provide her with an address in a better area of the town.

Now, two months later, all the men were feeling depressed. They had visited the Job Centre and viewed the work that was being offered. They all needed some work before their funds ran out or they would be unable to pay their rent or buy food. They had exchanged the last of their Euros and any dollars they had carried out with them for sterling. In desperation they had accepted menial jobs; Ibrahim and Aziz were working at large supermarkets during the evenings restocking the shelves, Salim had accepted a vacancy for a hotel porter, Mohammed was spending his day sweeping up rubbish in the streets and the other two men were delivering leaflets in the area, returning at the end of the day foot sore and weary. They were dissatisfied and disillusioned, but could see no way out of their dilemma.

They had moved from the boarding house to another across the road where they were able to rent two rooms more cheaply, although with three beds in the room there was little space. Ibrahim and Aziz were able to purchase food at a discount as they worked at the supermarkets, but as they had no cooking facilities their diet consisted mainly of bread, fruit, vegetables and cold meats that had been removed from the shelves as their expiry date had been reached. Two days each week they visited a cafe for a hot meal, but the food on offer was not really to their taste.

They had bought an electric kettle and some mugs so they were able to make a hot drink with the coffee and sugar that Aziz bought each week at the supermarket, but the new life they had envisaged for themselves had not come up to their expectations. It was a miserable existence and they were worse off than they had been in Syria.

Vasilis and Cathy saw less of Vasi and Saffron now the season was well underway. Saffron had insisted that she employed a lady to come to clean the house through twice a week, and refused Cathy's offer of doing the work.

'I'm quite capable,' said Cathy. 'I used to clean the apartment in Heraklion and only asked a window cleaner to come occasionally.'

'I'm sure you are, but this house is considerably larger than the apartment you had in Heraklion and there are four of us living here, not two. I don't think Vasilis would be very amused if he thought you were working here as a cleaner and I certainly do not want you wearing yourself out. You also need to concentrate on the décor for your new apartment.'

Cathy had been forced to concede that Saffron was probably right; she would find cleaning the large house tiring and it would also give a local woman a small income.

Saffron would drive to Plaka and spend the time at her shop, often not arriving home until after Vasilis and Cathy had retired for the night. The days when Bryony worked for her she would arrive home at mid-day and then spend her time on her computer, checking her accounts were up to date and ordering more stock until Vasi arrived home. Vasi visited his hotel in Aghios Nikolaos, spending most of the morning there, before continuing on to his hotel in Elounda where he would spend the afternoon, ensuring he was home by the evening.

The arrangement appeared to work well for them and they had organised that they always had one complete day to themselves during the week when they could relax. Vasilis began to wonder if he had made a mistake in purchasing the apartment in Elounda. Had it not been for Cathy he would have been content to stay up at the house on the hill until the apartment he planned down by the sea had been built.

Cathy was becoming excited about their proposed move. The en suite bathroom had the fitments in place and was in the process of being tiled with the turquoise tiles that she had finally chosen and Blerim was tackling the grouting. Once that was finished the kitchen appliances would be delivered and the worktops and cupboards placed in situ so the tiles could be fitted around them.

Once the floor tiles had been laid she had decided to experiment with Ronnie's idea of painting the walls of the lounge and dining area a pale lime green and having matching tiles in the kitchen. As usual, Ronnie's eye for colour was correct. The dark green granite worktops and light wood would blend perfectly with the small area of tiles that were on show.

She now had to choose the curtains and furniture and was spending a considerable amount of time looking for ideas. Finally she telephoned Ronnie and asked for her further advice.

'May I visit the apartment? I know the curtains I had in mind for the lounge originally, but they may not be right when I actually see the room again.'

'It hasn't been painted yet, but I've decided to go with your idea of the pale lime green.'

'In that case the curtains I showed you would look good in there, but I hadn't actually considered the bedroom. What have you decided for the kitchen?'

'I'll show you. I think you'll approve. When would it be convenient for you to come to look? It will have to be during the day as the electrics have not been connected to the mains as yet so there are no lights.'

'I'd far rather look in natural light. We've moved down to the self catering apartment now so I could come along tomorrow when Kyriakos goes up to the taverna. Would you like me to collect you from the house? It's no trouble and would save Vasilis from having to bring you down and hang around.'

Vasilis was pleased when Cathy told him she was visiting the apartment the following day and Ronnie would be collecting her. He had an appointment with the architect whom he hoped would commence drawing up the plans for his new house. He had not discussed the idea he had for elevating the building so that Cathy would have an unobstructed view across the bay or the lift to allow her easy access. He wanted both to be a surprise for her once the plans had been passed.

Panayiotis was pleased that the apartment was nearing completion. Mr Palamakis had warned him whenever there was to be any noise, but he had found the screech of the tile cutting unacceptable to his ears. As soon as the work commenced he would leave the house and go into the main road and sit in a taverna until it was time for him to go into Aghios Nikolaos for his duty. When he had his free days he had taken his small boat out into the bay and gone fishing, returning later with sufficient small fish for his supper along with two squid that he presented to the taverna owner.

Both Mr Palamakis and Panayiotis were tired of the continual complaints from the man across the road who had accused Vasilis of harassing his mother. As soon as the first noise was heard he would come across and hammer on the door, asking how long they were going to be there and when they would be quiet.

Mr Palamakis explained to him the work they were doing was bound to make a noise, and it would be completed as quickly as possible. In the meantime he could only ask the man to be understanding and explain to his mother. After three days the man accosted Panayiotis and complained again, asking him to do something in his official capacity to stop the men from working.

Panayiotis shook his head. 'I cannot do that. The workmen are not breaking the law. The apartment has been sold and the new owner is making alterations. He is as anxious as you for the work to be completed, but he has told the men they are not to work into the evening. The residents need to able to rely on some peace at that time of the day.'

'My mother needs some peace during the day. All the crashing and banging that she hears distresses her. She lies awake at night worrying.'

Panayiotis spread his hands. 'I'm sorry. Would it help if I came and reassured her that the work should take no longer than a month to complete?'

'A month? She cannot put up with it for that length of time.'

'I'm afraid she has no choice unless she is able to go and stay elsewhere.'

'If you can't stop them I'll contact the building inspectors and get them to come along. They'll have to take notice of him.'

'The workmen are doing nothing wrong,' repeated Panayiotis patiently. 'The building inspector would be most unlikely to stop their work.'

'We'll see about that.' The man had turned and retreated to the house where he lived with his mother.

Panayiotis had warned Mr Palamakis that the man was going to the building inspector and request that the work be stopped. Palamakis had shrugged off the information.

'There is no law that says we cannot make a noise doing building work during the hours of daylight.'

'I have tried to explain to him, but he's a difficult customer.'

'Glad he's not going to be my neighbour, then.'

The man had come across daily and complained to Palamakis, and also to Panayiotis if he was around, but there had been no sign of a building inspector visiting until Palamakis requested that he should come and inspect the drains and pass them. Now most of the tiling was finished the man should have no further cause for complaint.

Ronnie drew up outside the apartment and walked around to help

Cathy out. 'You can't park there,' called the man from across the road. 'You're causing an obstruction.'

Ronnie ignored him and walked into the apartment with Cathy. 'Mr Palamakis, is there anywhere Cathy could sit for a short while? I've been told my car is causing an obstruction so I'll take it to the public car park.'

Mr Palamakis was not sure about Ronnie's message but he understood that he needed to find something for Cathy to sit on. He looked around wildly. There was no furniture anywhere, some unopened packets of tiles and some timbers that were unused along with the men's tool boxes were the only items in the room.

'Blerim,' he called, 'Can we find a seat for the lady?'

Blerim came out from the bathroom, his hands caked in the white grout. He moved two unopened packs of tiles a distance apart and straddled them with two lengths of timber. From the floor he picked up a large piece of discarded cardboard, brushed it down and placed it on the timber.

'Will do?' he asked.

Cathy smiled. 'That will be fine for me to rest on. Thank you.'

Blerim nodded and returned to the bathroom whilst Mr Palamakis hovered close to Cathy hoping Ronnie would return quickly. The improvised seat would soon become uncomfortable.

'Wander through and tell me what you think,' said Cathy when Ronnie returned.

Ronnie looked around the en suite bathroom and Blerim stood to one side whilst she nodded her head in approval. It was compact, but not too small and the archway into the bedroom would make it look larger when a mirror had been placed above the vanity basin. Removing the hallway had made the bedroom considerably larger; she stood and considered. The walls should definitely be white, and then Cathy could have turquoise curtains to pick up the colour of the tiles in the bathroom. She would look on the internet and see if there was anything that she thought would be suitable.

'Superb,' commented Ronnie to Cathy. 'I'll have a quick look in the kitchen and see how that is coming along.'

'See what you think of the tiles I have chosen. I think they will look right, although they won't be exactly the same shade of green as the walls in the lounge.'

'Where are they?' she asked. 'I like the enlarged the window, but I couldn't see the tiles anywhere.'

Cathy frowned. 'They should be there. Ask Mr Palamakis or one of his boys.'

'I don't want to interrupt them. They're plastering ceilings. Mr Palamakis, where are the tiles for the kitchen?'

'Is good?' he asked.

'Yes, very good, but where are the kitchen tiles?'

Mr Palamakis looked puzzled and Ronnie indicated that he should follow her into the kitchen. She pointed to the walls. 'Tiles?' she asked and repeated the word in Greek.

Mr Palamakis smiled. He did not correct her although she had asked where the roof tiles were. He pointed to the containers that Cathy was seated on.

Ronnie laughed. 'If you want me to see the kitchen tiles you'll have to get up, Cathy. You're sitting on them.'

A look of horror crossed Cathy's face. 'I hope I haven't damaged them.' She stood beside Ronnie whilst Mr Palamakis undid the strapping on one of the boxes and opened the cardboard to show the tiles inside.

'They're quite a good match. Provided a tile is not actually next to the painted wall I doubt if anyone will notice the colour difference. I think they'll be more interested in admiring your granite worktops. How are you dressing the window?'

'It's hardly necessary to have anything there. I will want to look out on the patio when it is cleaned up and planted. I thought just a plain white blind would be suitable, just so it doesn't look too bare.' Cathy shifted her weight from one leg to the other and the movement was not lost on Ronnie.

'I'll go and get the car; then you can sit somewhere more comfortable whilst we talk. Perch back on the tiles for a few minutes as I have to go over to the car park.'

As Ronnie drew up outside once more the man from across the road shouted at her. Mr Palamakis shouted back at him.

'Can't you see the lady is disabled? She is being collected. The car is not being parked.' He shook his head. The man was impossible. He would not be pleased when Vasilis and Cathy lived there as Vasilis would have a disabled badge that entitled him to park wherever he wished off the main road.

Vasilis sat in the architect's office and showed him the sketch that Mr Palamakis had made. Mr Kortanakis shook his head.

'It is an outlandish proposition. To attempt to put a building on top of a pile of earth would be most unsafe, natural ground movement would cause subsidence and the earth would wash down in the winter rain. If you are not planning to commence building until you are seven or eight metres above the current ground level you will need to have foundations sufficiently deep to have stilts.'

'I do not want the house on stilts,' said Vasilis firmly.

'They could be clad in stone to form a wall so they would not be noticeable.'

'That would mean a large blank wall that would look ugly.'

'To make a bank is not practical,' declared Mt Kortanakis. 'I suggest that you have a three storey building and you and your wife occupy the top floor. That will give you the view you say you need.'

'I don't want three floors. There must be a solution.'

'Probably,' replied Mr Kortanakis off handedly. 'If the building is going to seven or eight metres above the current ground level you will only be able to have two floors anyway.'

'I only want one. I want all the rooms on the same level so my wife has easy access everywhere.'

Mr Kortanakis ignored Vasilis. 'If you wished to add another floor at a later date you would have to re-apply for permission to build higher and if granted those rooms might need to have lower ceilings.'

'I have no plans at all to add another floor,' said Vasilis firmly. 'My son will obviously have the house at a later date and whatever he wishes to do will be up to him. At present it is essential that my wife has accessibility to all the rooms and also a good view over the bay from the front patio. There must be a lift at the side of the building that takes her up into the main hallway along with a flight of steps that lead down to where I can park my car.'

'How many rooms do you want?'

'A lounge large enough to have a dining area, with the kitchen adjacent. A hallway and at the side of that a bedroom with bathroom en suite and a separate toilet for visitors. Patio doors in the lounge area so we can see the view during the winter and they should also give access to the patio area. The doorways to the bedroom and into the en suite have to be wide enough to accommodate a wheelchair should that be necessary in the future.'

'Is that all?' Mr Kortanakis looked at Vasilis in surprise. 'Suppose you wish to have visitors to stay?'

'That is most unlikely, but I could always ask my son to accommodate them either at his house or the hotel.'

'What about the rest of the land you have available?'

'I haven't really considered any use for that at present.'

'I think you should. If you built down by the road you could build a three storey apartment block at the back. I'm sure you would have no problem letting them.'

'I wouldn't contemplate that and I do not want to build adjacent to the pavement.'

'Then you could set the building further back and have a large garden in the front.'

'If I had a garden it would mean employing a gardener. If we sat out there we would not have the view across the bay,'

Mr Kortanakis sighed in exasperation. 'If the rooms you propose take up all the space available you will have enormous areas that are difficult to heat. You would do better to have more rooms of lesser size.'

'We don't need any extra rooms,' replied Vasilis firmly.

'Think about it, Mr Iliopolakis. It is wasted space. Have you thought how visitors will approach the apartment? I don't think you will want them coming in through the flight of stairs at the back.'

'Of course not. They will use the steps up to a front door and enter into the main living accommodation.'

'If the house is elevated the steps will need to be quite a steep flight.' Mr Kortanakis looked at the man before him. He had more money than sense. He could easily build two apartment blocks on the land available.

'I don't think your idea is practical or feasible. I can only design the building you have in mind provided there are stilts beneath, steel supports and reinforced concrete. That would give you plenty of car parking at ground level.'

'That would look incredibly ugly.'

'The supports could be clad in concrete so they look like pillars.'

Vasilis shook his head. He picked up the sketch that Mr Palamakis had made and placed it in his pocket. 'I'll bear in mind your advice about the bank in the front.'

Vasilis left the architect feeling less than satisfied. He did not want an apartment sitting on stilts, but he could also understand that an earthen bank would soon be damaged by the winter rains. Ronnie had recommended the removal of the hallway in the apartment and also produced a colour scheme that both he and Cathy found acceptable. He would ask her advice about the front elevation and also how she thought the rooms should be laid out. He would impress upon her that his ideas should not be confided to Cathy as he wanted the spectacular view he proposed to make to be a surprise for her.

'So what did Ronnie think of the apartment?' asked Vasilis.

'She was most impressed. She wanted to see the colour of the kitchen tiles and I was sitting on them!' Cathy laughed. 'They were not very comfortable but better than nothing.'

'Sitting on them?'

'The Albanian man who is working there had made me an improvised seat whilst Ronnie parked the car. A man from across the road shouted at her when we first arrived and again when she came to collect me. Mr Palamakis shouted back at him.'

'I'd better have a word with Palamakis and see what it was about. I don't want to fall out with the neighbours before we've even moved in. What was Blerim doing?'

'Grouting the bathroom tiles. Have you seen his hands? I don't see how he manages; they're so damaged.'

'Palamakis has told me he is most impressed by the way the man has worked. It's a shame he can't employ him permanently.'

'Maybe we could find some odd jobs for him to do when we've moved in,' suggested Cathy.

'There shouldn't need to be any jobs outstanding when Palamakis has finished. I suppose we could ask Blerim to come and clean the windows on occasions.'

'That would be better than nothing. How did you get on with the architect?'

'He says he needs the exact measurements of the land before he begins to draw up any plans. I need to do a bit more investigating so I may well be out for a while tomorrow.' Vasilis was not going to tell Cathy that he was planning to call Ronnie and ask if he could meet her.

'That's no problem. I'm hoping I will be able to sit outside in the sun for a while and read. It seemed very pleasant when I was out earlier.'

Vasilis drove to the self catering apartments where Ronnie and Kyriakos lived during the season.

'Isn't Cathy with you?' she asked.

'No, this is just between you and me. I don't want Cathy to know my plans yet.'

'That sounds very mysterious. What can I do for you?'

'When I first looked at the land with Mr Palamakis he suggested that I built up the land so when the apartment was constructed there would be a wonderful view across the bay for Cathy. I showed my architect the sketch Palamakis had done and he seemed very dubious that the idea would work. He wanted to put the apartment up on stilts and then clad all the frontage in stone.'

Ronnie shuddered. 'That would look hideous.'

'I agree. I want to put a bank up in front, but the architect said that was impractical as the earth would get washed away.'

'He's probably right. How far back from the road will the building be?'

'I'm not sure.'

Ronnie took a sheet of drawing paper. She drew a line half way across. 'Let's say that is the level of the building.' She drew another line a short distance further down. 'That is your patio. All this space here is the ground that goes down to the road.' She looked at the rough sketch quizzically. 'You could have steps that stretch across the frontage and lead up to the patio area.'

Vasilis looked at her doubtfully. 'I'm not sure about that.'

'Then what about having terraces and a flight of steps at the side?'

'Terraces?'

Ronnie nodded. 'You would have to build retaining walls in between for the earth, but you could have as many as you wanted.'

'I wouldn't want them to look like steps.'

'Of course not. You will need a wall on the road and the first terrace could be a little lower. Decide how wide you want it and then another wall could be built, possibly about a metre and a half high, and then another terrace. That would not look like steps and you could have the terraces as high and wide as you wished.'

'Do you think that would work?'

'I don't see why not. That way the earth would not get washed away in the winter.'

'It won't look very attractive.'

'Then fill the terraces in with concrete rather than earth and have some artificial grass. That looks good all year round. Whatever system you decide upon you'll need a drainage system underneath or you'll end up with the terraces full of water.'

Vasilis nodded slowly. 'That would probably be cheaper and easier to maintain.'

'All you need to do is decide how high up the apartment is going to be situated and the area of land between the front wall and the building.'

'What about the steps leading up to the front door?'

'If you are having your main entrance to one side then that is where the steps will have to be. You'll need them to be wider than a conventional flight so they are in keeping with the wide frontage. Once you know the height they have to cover you could work out having three or four steps and then a flat area before the next three or four.'

'You mean terrace those as well?'

'Why not?'

'Ronnie, you're a wasted talent as an artist. You should have trained as an architect. If I tell you exactly how I envisage the apartment when it is complete could you draw it up?'

'I expect so, but my plans would not be acceptable. You have to be qualified and have some letters after your name.'

'With your permission I would pass it on to my architect and tell him that was exactly what I wanted.'

'It may not be good enough,' replied Ronnie dubiously.

'I'm sure it will be, but small alterations can always be made later. How much do I owe you for your consultation?'

'Owe me? Nothing.'

'Rubbish. I insist that I pay you. I have taken up your free time or interrupted your painting schedule.' Vasilis laid a fifty Euro note on the table.

'Certainly not. If your architect accepts my plans I'll think about reimbursement then. Advice is free.'

June 2015
Week Two

Ibrahim looked out of the window of the room he shared with Aziz and Salim. He had taken advantage of the sunshine they had during day to sit in the small area they called a park. It was used by people to walk their dogs and there were seats around the perimeter. It was not particularly attractive, but better than sitting in the bedroom all day doing nothing.

As he stood there he saw a large taxi draw up. Six men alighted and were handed their cases from the boot before entering the house where he had once lodged. The taxi driver followed them in and Ibrahim saw it was the same man as had met them upon their arrival at Gatwick. Were these men also from Syria? If he saw them around he would try to get into conversation with them and find out where they had come from.

Vasilis was feeling pleased. The decoration of the apartment was completed. He was not entirely certain that he liked the pale lime green walls in the lounge, but Cathy seemed happy with them and that was the most important thing. The furniture was due to be delivered during the week and that would break up the expanse of colour. Once that was in situ the curtains Ronnie had suggested could be hung at the front and also at the patio doors and he was sure that would make a difference.

The en suite bathroom, although compact, was certainly large enough for their needs, and there was more space in the bedroom now the hallway had been removed. Having had a wardrobe built in on the far wall there was still room for a dressing table and stool where Cathy could sit each morning whilst attending to her hair and make up. Cathy had taken Ronnie's advice regarding the décor and kept the walls and woodwork white. Looking on the internet she had found some curtains that she thought would be suitable, white with turquoise and blue flowers, and planned to have them from floor to ceiling with pulls at each side so they would be easy for her to open and close.

Cathy had declared herself delighted with the kitchen. She had storage cupboards that she could reach easily when sitting on her high stool. The work top opposite the sink gave her an area for food preparation, and had space beneath to push her stool into when she was not using it. The work top at the far end held the hob and an oven that she need not bend down to access. The small, separate cloakroom next to the patio windows and opposite the kitchen area would be useful during the day as she could use that without having to walk back into the lounge, through their bedroom and into the en suite.

There was still the patio to be dealt with. The paving slabs had been taken up, the ground levelled and new ones laid. It looked very bare, but Vasilis knew that once the garden furniture had been installed and Cathy had some pots of flowers around it would look attractive. He just hoped the sun would penetrate the area, but not trap the air so that it became unpleasantly hot during the day.

Vasilis wished his ideas for the apartment down on the coast road were progressing. Mr Kortanakis had raised objections and problems that he had not thought about. If he had the steps leading to the front door to one side and leading into the vestibule the house would not look symmetrical.

'I don't want it to look like a box.' If he moved the steps to a central position the patio area would have to be far smaller than he had envisaged.

'If you insist on having the steps at the side it will make the rooms you have planned for the bedroom and bathroom very small. You could always have them at the back next to the kitchen.'

Vasilis shook his head. 'I certainly do not want them there. That is where I plan to have the lift and the access stairs down to where I will park my car.'

'Then there is the problem of where to place the back up generator for the lift,' continued Mr Kortanakis as if Vasilis had not spoken. 'It would need to be housed so it does not suffer damage from the rain or the Saharan sand that blows across at intervals.'

'There is plenty of land available. Make the apartment wider. That way the steps can still be at the side rather than in the centre.'

Mr Kortanakis pursed his lips. 'That will mean redrawing the plans.'

'Then do so. If you are not capable of putting my requests into place I will find someone else who can.'

'I'm sure we will be able to reach a compromise.'

'I am not prepared to compromise,' declared Vasilis. 'Please give me the plans you have drawn up so far and I will pay you for your time.'

Mr Kortanakis frowned. 'I don't think you will find anyone who can improve upon my ideas. I have followed your instructions.'

'Not to my satisfaction.'

Vasilis left the architect's office in a thoroughly bad humour. He knew how he wanted the apartment to look and Mr Kortanakis seemed to think he knew better. He would speak to Vasi and see if he could recommend an architect who was willing and able to comply with his requests.

Cathy was waiting for Vasilis when he returned. 'Have you any plans for this afternoon?' she asked.

'Nothing,' replied Vasilis despondently.

'Would you be willing to drive me to the apartment and then on to Plaka? I decided which curtains to order for the bedroom this morning, but I need the exact measurements for them to be made up. I then sat and finished my book. I've nothing to read.'

'Which curtains have you chosen?'

'The ones with the turquoise and blue flowers. I thought they would add some colour to the room and also go well with the bathroom tiles.'

Vasilis nodded, his thoughts still on the architect. 'Of course. It should only take a few minutes to measure up for the curtains and then we could have some lunch in Plaka.'

'I'd like that, provided everywhere is not too crowded with tourists.'

'I'm sure a table can be found for us. Locals always get preferential treatment. I'll just have a wash and change my shirt. Give me five minutes.'

Vasilis drew up outside the apartment in Elounda and the man from across the road came out immediately. 'You can't park there,' he shouted.

Vasilis walked across to him. 'I am able to park wherever I wish provided I am off the main road. I have a disabled permit and my wife and I are visiting our apartment. I am not causing an obstruction and we will not be here for very long.'

'We've suffered enough disruption with all that work you've been having done.'

'I'm pleased to say that is now over. Once our furniture has been delivered we will be moving in and we are not noisy people.'

'You'll have to find somewhere else to park your car.'

'I'm sure that will be no problem. Please excuse me. I need to attend to my wife.'

Vasilis walked back to where Cathy still sat in the car. 'That was the man who shouted at Ronnie when I came here with her.'

'He obviously thinks he owns the road. I'll have a word with Panayiotis and see if there is somewhere I can park that does not interfere with the neighbours. I don't want to have to pay to use the public car park every day. Let's get the measurements for the curtains and then we can drive on to Plaka. I've assured him that we will not be here for very long.'

Plaka was busy, but Vasilis helped Cathy over to the wall at the front of the taverna where cushions had been placed for people to use whilst waiting for the bus. The waiter came over to her whilst Vasilis drove down to the car park.

'Are you planning to have lunch here?'

Cathy nodded. 'Do you have a free table?'

'For you, of course. Give me a minute whilst I move some people around to make sufficient space for you.'

'I don't like to disturb others.'

'They have nearly finished and it could encourage them to leave. We do not want them sitting there for the rest of the afternoon or until they know the bus is due.'

He hurried away and by the time Vasilis returned he had organised a table and chairs beside the far wall overlooking the pedestrian area and the shops.

'You are away from the traffic noise and fumes here,' he said as he placed a menu before each of them. 'Something to drink whilst you decide what you would like to eat? We have a special today, mushroom pie.'

'A small beer for me and water for my wife.' Vasilis knew that Cathy would only have a glass of wine during the evening. 'Do you want a selection or a main meal?'

Cathy looked down the menu and shook her head. 'I'd like the mushroom pie.'

They lingered over their meal until Cathy declared that she could eat no more. 'That was delicious, but I should not have eaten any of the nibbles beforehand. I've eaten far too much.'

'Would you like coffee or are you ready to go down to see Monika now?'

'Monika, I think. We can always go across to "The Pines" for coffee afterwards.'

Vasilis helped Cathy down the road to the bookshop where

Monika immediately rose from her chair and gave it to Cathy. 'Is this a social call or are you looking for a book?'

'I'm actually wanting more than one or I'll be asking Vasilis to bring me back again in a few days.'

'Any particular author?'

'Not really. Can you recommend anyone?'

'I'll bring you a selection. If you don't find any you like there I can always bring over some more.'

'Whilst you ladies chat about books I'll go for a wander,' said Vasilis, hoping he would see Ronnie sitting down by the harbour painting.

Ronnie had arrived a short while earlier and already had a small group of people watching her work. Vasilis waited patiently until she had completed a sale, then moved forwards.

'I need to talk to you, Ronnie. This is not the time as you're busy. Could I come up to your apartment tomorrow and discuss the plans for my new apartment?'

'The one you are moving into or the one you are having built?'

'The one I'm building. I have a problem with the architect I was using. He has come up with a number of objections to the sketch you did.'

Ronnie frowned. 'They were only ideas. I did say they might not be acceptable.'

Vasilis nodded. 'I just want to ask your opinion.'

'Are you still keeping your ideas from Cathy?'

'Definitely. Could I come up to the apartment tomorrow?'

'Of course.'

Vasilis smiled. 'I ought to make my way back to Monika's and let you get on with your painting. I left Cathy in there choosing some books and said I was going for a walk around. We called in at the Elounda apartment earlier and measured up for the bedroom curtains. We've had lunch here and she's probably ready to go home now and wanting to sit outside on the patio in the last of the sun and starting a new book.'

Ronnie sat with Vasilis and he spread out the architect's plans on the table in front of her. 'I don't want to have the steps in the centre of the building. They would need walls at each side for safety and that will make the patio smaller. Mr Kortanakis has said that if I stick to my original idea of having them to one side it will make the bedroom and bathroom too small.'

'So enlarge the frontage.'

'How can I? I still need somewhere to park my car and have access to the lift and the stairs up to the main area. He also said that I need a housing for the generator to avoid damage.'

'Can I mark your plans or do you want me to make a new sketch?'

'A new one would be better.'

'You are still planning to have the apartment built at a higher level?'

Vasilis nodded and Ronnie continued. 'So you have an entrance at the side where you park your car and have the lift and stairs. Make a concrete roof over the rear of the parking area. That would mean Cathy could access the lift and you the stairs when it was raining without getting wet and you could then build your bedroom over the parking area. You could still have the stairs to one side, but it would give you more floor space inside. You could also have an area beneath the steps where the generator could be housed.'

Ronnie drew swiftly. 'How does that look? It would mean less floor space in the entrance area as your bedroom wall would be almost next to the door, but you would still walk straight into your lounge and dining area and it would not look cramped.'

Vasilis studied the sketch. 'I think that is the answer. It does make that side of the apartment look a bit flat with just a window.'

'So have a balcony outside. That way you could have patio windows down to the floor and a glass barrier to the balcony so you did not lose any light.'

'Wouldn't that be dangerous?'

'You'd need to have toughened glass and that should be safe enough.'

'You really are a genius, Ronnie. May I take this? I'm actually looking for a new architect as I'm not satisfied with Mr Kortanakis. I'm sure he'd still be able to find reasons why your design was not practical. I'm thinking of going up to Heraklion to a man I know there.'

Ronnie nodded. 'Good idea. He'll be able to look at the design with fresh eyes. Take him the measurements of the ground area as he's bound to want them.'

Vasilis made an appointment with Mr Sfyrakos, an architect that Vasi had recommended, and made an excuse for his journey to Cathy. 'I need to visit my specialist at the hospital for my check up. I know I could probably go to Aghios Nikolaos, but I'd rather see the same man again.'

'Do you want me to come with you?'

'No, there's no need. It's only routine and I could be kept hanging around. I'm sure you could visit Marianne. I could take you there and collect you when I return.'

Cathy accepted the proposal. There really was no need for her to visit the specialist with Vasilis. She would probably not be allowed into the consulting room with him and even if she was she would not understand what was said.

'You will tell me if there is a problem, won't you?'

'I promise,' declared Vasilis, 'But I'm sure all is well with me.'

Mr Sfyrakos examined the sketches that Vasilis placed before him. 'These would have to be drawn up to scale before I could give you my final opinion. May I ask why you wish to have a single storey apartment built at that level?'

'There is a wonderful view across the bay, but if I built at ground level that would not be seen.'

'As far as I can ascertain, taking into account the area of land you have available, there is no reason why you cannot have the apartment elevated on steel supports with reinforced concrete between them to support the weight of the building. I would have to speak to a structural engineer and he would need to work out the number of supports needed for safety. Assuming you are able to go ahead with the building you are going to be left with a large area at the back. Have you had any thoughts about the usage?'

'Not really. Possibly have it paved.'

Mr Sfyrakos nodded. 'Practical, but the ground would have to be supported in the same way as the front or you would have a deep drop to the ground. You could have a flight of steps going down, of course.'

'Out of the question.' replied Vasilis firmly. 'It would mean the area was unusable by my wife. It would have to be on the same level as the building.'

'In that case the area would have to be supported and filled with concrete.'

'I suppose I could have a patio at the rear.'

'No reason why you shouldn't bear that in mind. It would give you an area where you could eat outside in the summer months. You would need to have access to it from the kitchen. I suggest that you have a walkway down the side that leads from the front patio to the rear with a kitchen door either at the side or the far end.'

Vasilis nodded. 'I hadn't really considered access, except for any necessary maintenance. I've concentrated far more on the design of the front of the building and the interior.'

'Do you wish me to proceed? The work involved with the structural engineer will be expensive and my services are not cheap, but my plans are usually passed without question.'

'Provided I can have what I want and as quickly as possible I am willing to pay.'

The meeting had taken far less time that Vasilis had anticipated and he decided he would telephone Dimitra and ask her if she would like to meet him for some lunch. He was curious to know how Mr Kuzmichov was running the hotel, but he was loath to go there where he knew all the staff.

'I would like to meet you, Mr Iliopolakis. I have one or two concerns that I would appreciate discussing with you.'

'Surely you should speak to Mr Kuzmichov if there are any problems.'

'It's not as easy as that. I'll explain when I meet you. I don't want to eat at the hotel. Could we go somewhere quiet?'

'Certainly. I'll be outside in about ten minutes.'

Vasilis sat across the table from Dimitra. 'Aren't you happy working for Mr Kuzmichov?'

Dimitra shrugged. 'I'm not unhappy. He's always very polite and respectful towards me, but I can't say I like him. I'm sure he is doing something odd.'

'Like what?'

'Well, first of all he bought a big black Mercedes car and said it was to transport visitors to and from the airport. He put it through the accounts as an expense. He also charges for the petrol through the accounts, but it appears that he fills up the tank every couple of weeks.'

'I'm not surprised. I expect a Mercedes has a high petrol consumption.'

'He only uses it occasionally. He collects some men from the airport and a few days later he takes them to catch a flight.'

'Maybe they are important visitors.'

Dimitra frowned. 'If they were I would have expected them to be given the best rooms at the hotel. They stay in the bedrooms next to the conference rooms.'

'Possibly that is more convenient for them if they are attending a conference.'

Dimitra shook her head. 'They always arrive very early in the morning and leave wet footprints on the hall carpet. One day the lift floors were very wet as well. I mentioned it to Mr Kuzmichov and then he had the lifts carpeted. Why should their shoes be wet if they have come from the airport?'

'Strange,' commented Vasilis.

'The first time some men arrived I asked Mr Kuzmichov why there was no record of them registering at the hotel and paying for their stay. I thought he may have deliberately omitted the details to see how accurately I checked the accounts. He said they were his private guests and he would deal with the costs incurred himself.'

'And does he?'

'There has never been any payment entered into the accounts that I deal with. They eat down in the restaurant with Mr Kuzmichov in the evening and have room service during the day. According to the receipts I have from the chef those meals are never paid for either. You always kept the accounts meticulously.'

Vasilis frowned. 'I can only assume that Mr Kuzmichov has a private account that he uses for their expenses. I'm sure you have nothing to worry about, Dimitra. Provided you keep the hotel accounts scrupulously whatever else Mr Kuzmichov does is not your concern. Everyone has different business systems. I expect his guests are Russians and have connections with his import and export business.'

'They don't look like Russians and I'm sure it isn't Russian that I have heard them speaking. Sometimes, if they are all together, they do get quite noisy. I just feel there is something not right.'

'What about the other staff? Have they voiced any concerns?'

'Mrs Planatakis isn't happy. When Mr Kuzmichov's guests are staying she is not allowed to let the maids clean their rooms until after they have left and he gives permission.'

'I'm sure they would have complained to Mr Kuzmichov if they were dissatisfied. They may have confidential documents with them and are worried that they will be mislaid or the contents disclosed by the chamber maids.'

'If you say so, Mr Iliopolakis.'

Vasilis shrugged. 'It is the only reason I can think of why they would not wish to have their rooms disturbed. Ignore them, Dimitra. Would you like a baklava with your coffee?'

Vasilis took Dimitra back to "The Central", leaving her a short distance away from the main entrance as she requested. Although he had assured Dimitra that there was nothing to worry about, her conversation niggled away at him. He drove to the rear entrance of the hotel. If he was challenged he would apologise, say that he had been so used to parking there that he had turned in without thinking.

He immediately saw the Mercedes and there was a convenient space next to it where he drew in carefully.

'You can't park there.' Mr Lanassakis hurried across to him. 'Oh, I'm sorry. I didn't realise it was you, Mr Iliopolakis.'

'Hello, Lanassakis. My mistake. I was so used to just driving in that I did so automatically. Of course I'm no longer entitled to park here. Who does that car belong to?' Vasilis indicated the Mercedes.

'Mr Kuzmichov.'

'Very nice. Does he use it often?'

Lanassakis shrugged. 'About twice a week and when it has been used I have to clean it thoroughly. He insists that there is not a mark left inside or out.'

'I don't imagine that it gets very dirty.'

'You'd be surprised. I was having to shampoo the carpets in the back area until Mr Kuzmichov put some rubber mats there.'

'They were that dirty?' exclaimed Vasilis.

Lanassakis nodded. 'Wet and covered with little gritty stones. Now I only have to take them out and brush them off before I hose them.'

'Have you had car maintenance added to your list of jobs?'

'I get paid an extra five Euros a week for looking after the car,' he announced proudly.

'He obviously appreciates your services. I'll go and find somewhere else to park. I don't want to get you into trouble.'

'I'm sure Mr Kuzmichov would not object. Shall I see if I can find him and let him know you are here?'

Vasilis shook his head. 'No, the area I plan to visit is some distance away. It would be more convenient for me to park there.'

'I'll tell Mr Kuzmichov that you were here and ask him if I can allow you to put your car in the car park in future.'

'There's really no need to bother him. I rarely have occasion to come up to the town. It was good to see you, Lanassakis.'

Vasilis drove away. The Mercedes was certainly a car to be admired and respected, but why should it get so wet and dirty if it was only being used on an airport run? He was not sure how seriously he should take the information that Dimitra had imparted to him, but it seemed a coincidence that she had reported wet floors in the lifts and dirty carpets. Could the men be airport workers that Kuzmichov was accommodating? That could account for dirty carpets, but why would he use the Mercedes to bring them to the hotel when they could use the airport bus that would bring them into the centre of the town?

'How did you get on?' asked Cathy when he met her at Marianne's.

'Absolutely fine. No problem at all. It took far less time than I had expected so I phoned Dimitra and asked her if she would like to meet me for lunch.'

Cathy raised her eyebrows. 'Really? What made you do that?'

'Spur of the moment and I was also interested to know what was happening at "The Central".

'It's no longer your concern, Vasilis.'

Vasilis smiled. 'I know, put it down to nosiness on my part.'

'So what did Dimitra have to tell you?'

'Apparently the first thing Mr Kuzmichov did was to buy a large Mercedes.'

'What did he want that for?'

'According to Dimitra he said it was for taking guests to and from the airport.'

'Surely it would be cheaper to offer to pay their taxi fare,' commented Cathy.

Vasilis nodded. 'It's all a bit odd. Dimitra says that a group of men arrive and are brought in by the back entrance and given the bedrooms next to the conference rooms. They stay for a few days and the maids are told not to clean that floor whilst they are there, although Dimitra says there are often very dirty marks on the carpets in the hallway.'

'How does Dimitra know all this?'

'Her office and room are on the same floor. She asked Mr Kuzmichov why there was no record in the accounts of the men's stay. He said they were his private guests.'

'So that must mean that he is paying for them.'

'Probably, but after I left Dimitra I thought I would go and have a look at the Mercedes that she mentioned. Lanassakis was in the car park and he said that he has to ensure that the car is kept spotless, but it often returns quite dirty, both inside and out. He said the floor mats were always damp and had small gritty stones on them.'

Cathy opened her eyes wide. 'Where would that come from at the airport?'

'Maybe he is collecting them from the ferry terminal. That could account for the damp and the shingle.'

'I don't see how. They moor at a concrete jetty not a shingle beach. Are they the same men who keep returning?'

'I have no idea. Dimitra may have seen them if she went down to eat in the restaurant at the same time but she gave me the impression that Kuzmichov was being very secretive about their visits. He won't let the maids clean their rooms whilst they are staying.'

'Do you think they could be Russian spies that he is bringing into the country?' suggested Cathy.

'What on earth would Russian spies find to interest them on Crete? I expect there is some very simple explanation.' Vasilis shook his head at Cathy's improbable idea. 'Have you had a good day?'

'Most enjoyable. I've been telling Marianne all about the apartment and she's longing to see it. I've promised to ask her to come over and bring her mother and Grandma Marisa with her when we've moved in and become a bit organised.'

'Her mother will still be staying with her then?'

Cathy smiled. 'At the moment she does not seem to have any plans to return to America. Marianne says she's no trouble and can stay as long as she wishes.'

'I can see we are going to have to arrange a number of little gatherings. The apartment is not large enough to have everyone at once.'

'Who do you want to invite?'

'Well, Saffron and Vasi, obviously, and I thought Monika and her mother would like to see it. There's also John and Nicola and Bryony and Marcus, of course.'

'What about Uncle Yannis and Uncle Andreas?'

'I'm sure they'll be willing to come when Elena or Marisa are there. We shouldn't have to make a separate occasion for them.'

'Don't forget Ronnie and Kyriakos.'

'I certainly won't,' promised Vasilis. 'Ronnie has been quite invaluable.'

'Will you invite Mr Palamakis and his grandsons?'

'Yes, but not when the family are there. I thought Blerim could come with them and we could ask Panayiotis to come at the same time.'

'That's a good idea. I find Mr Palamakis a little difficult. All he seems to have to say is that it is good. I've only met Blerim the once. His poor hands are in a terrible state. I had to stop myself from shuddering when I saw them.'

Vasilis nodded. He was still thinking about the men Dimitra

said arrived as Kuzmichov's private guests and Lanassakis's need to clean the car after a short trip to the airport.

As Ibrahim walked along the road towards the supermarket where he was working he came face to face with two of the men who had moved into the house where he had lodged originally. He stopped and smiled at them.

'Good afternoon,' he said in Arabic. 'I believe we are neighbours.'

Both men regarded him somewhat suspiciously. 'Where do you live?' asked one.

'Across the road. I happened to see you arrive. My companions and I lived in the same house when we first arrived.'

'Why did you move?'

Ibrahim spread his hands. 'We could no longer afford to pay for three rooms so had to find somewhere cheaper.'

'Aren't you working?'

'I managed to find a job filling shelves in a supermarket. Not what I wanted, but better than nothing.'

'What about your friends?'

'We have all found some form of occupation that brings in sufficient for us to pay the rent and buy some food each week, but it isn't what we had expected.'

The two men exchanged glances. 'How did you go about finding work?'

'We were sent to the Job Centre.'

'We've just come from there. There's nothing suitable for us.'

'What work were you hoping for?'

'We all have professional qualifications, but they don't seem to take those into account.'

Ibrahim nodded understandingly. 'We found the same situation applied to us. We were told that England needed doctors to work in the hospitals, but I was told I would have to have an assessment and be retrained.'

'You're a doctor?'

'A qualified heart surgeon. What about you?'

'Ear, nose and throat specialist. I was told the same thing.'

Ibrahim looked at his watch. 'I have to go or I'll be late. I can't afford to get the sack. Could we meet up some time and talk further? I'd like to hear about the latest conditions in Syria. I'm free during the day.'

The man hesitated and looked at his companion. 'Come over tomorrow.'

'I'd rather we met somewhere away from our lodgings. Do you know the little park around the corner? I usually spend some time sitting there during the afternoon.'

Ibrahim hurried away. He wanted to know more details about the arrival of the men in England. Had they also made a journey by sea and subsequently flown over from Crete?

June 2015
Week Three

Ibrahim sat in the park waiting for the two men he had spoken to the previous day. They sat down beside him, looking weary.

'Are you able to help us at all? We've been to the Job Centre and so far all we have been offered is work at a car wash or road sweeping. Yakob is considering accepting the car wash, but we're not manual workers.'

'What are your professions?'

'I told you, I'm an ear, nose and throat specialist and Ahmed is an anaesthetist. Salihe is a chemist and the other two are teachers. We were told there would be no problem with getting work here.'

'Who told you that?'

'The man who offered to help us to get here.'

'Did you pay him a large sum of money to be taken by boat to an island and stay in a hotel until you had some new passports?'

'We all of us used up most of our savings,' Abdul said despondently.

'I think you were duped the same as we were. We were told that once in possession of British passports it would be easy for us to obtain work in the hospitals and schools. Have you filled in any of the forms that have been sent from the hospital?'

Ahmed shook his head. 'It isn't possible. They want details of where we lived when we were born along with the names and occupations of our parents. How about you? Have you returned yours?'

'No, for the same reason. We were given to understand that no questions would be asked if we had British passports.'

Ahmed and Abdul nodded. 'We were told that. It must have been the same man.'

Ibrahim looked at his companions sympathetically 'Did you sail from Syria with a man called Ivan and get rowed through a canal to a waiting car and on to a hotel?'

'It seemed too good to be true when we stayed in the hotel. The man who took us there talked to us and reassured us that if we did as he said we would be able to enter England without a problem. He arranged for someone to provide us with a false passport and gave us money in the local currency to pay for our flights.'

'No doubt that was your own money that he was giving to you, not his. Do you know if any others have been brought over the same way?'

'I'm not sure. There are so many people around of different nationalities.'

'Keep your ears open. If you hear any of them speaking Arabic ask where they have come from and see if you can find out how they came here. I can't believe that we are the only ones who were taken in.'

'What can we do?' asked Ahmed.

'I don't know, but I'll talk to my friends and see if they have any ideas. Provided it isn't raining I'll be in the park each day. You can always call for me at the lodging house and we can go to a cafe and talk.'

'Why can't we talk in your room?'

'I don't trust the landlord. If he thinks we're holding meetings he could alert the police thinking we were plotting terrorism or inform the immigration authorities.'

'That could mean we were arrested,' said Ahmed in alarm.

'At the very least we would be held in a detention centre until they had investigated and then we would most likely be sent back to Syria.'

'If the fighting stops and the country returns to normal I'd be happy to return,' said Abdul. 'I suppose you could call me a coward, but I didn't want to be trapped between two fighting factions and end up injured or killed. I saw what happened to so many of my friends and colleagues.'

Vasilis thought no more about Kuzmichov and "The Central". He spent three days down at the apartment waiting for the new furniture they had ordered to arrive. The lounge suite and dining room furniture was no problem to him but he was unable to assemble their bed without help and asked Mr Palamakis if Yiannis and Giorgos would be able to assist one morning before they moved on to work elsewhere.

Once Yiannis and Giorgos had completed the frame and placed the mattress on top he then asked them to remove the protective covering from the other furniture and dispose of the plastic for him. He inspected everything carefully for any damage and imperfection before he called Cathy and said he would collect her and she could decide on the placement.

Cathy looked around critically. 'It's fine where you've put everything, but it still looks rather bare.'

'Once the curtains are up and some of our pictures and ornaments are around it will look more like home.'

'I'll ask Ronnie if she would be willing to hang the curtains for me. I know I can't stand on a step ladder and do it. The bedroom curtains should be arriving tomorrow and then all we'll have to do is bring down everything that is stored up at the house and we'll be able to move in.'

Vasilis nodded agreement. 'I don't want you doing too much and over tiring yourself. I can bring some boxes down tomorrow that have kitchen equipment in them and you can tell me where you want things placed in the kitchen cupboards. I can leave their final arrangement up to you whilst you are here with Ronnie and dealing with curtains.'

'We'll need some cushions for the sofa. I know we have the ones we brought with us but I don't think they will look right.'

'Why don't you discuss that with Ronnie? She's bound to have some ideas and they can always be recovered or we can buy some new ones.'

Whilst Cathy was busy with Ronnie in their new apartment Vasilis hoped to visit Mr Sfyrakos and see if he was happy with the new plans the architect had promised to draw up.

Lucy sat on the sofa with her legs drawn up under her whilst Peter listened to the party political broadcast. When the news had started she hoped there would be something that interested her. As usual there was the plea for more doctors and specialists and the only way to attract them would be investing more money in the health service. She nodded her head in agreement, then listened with less interest to the report that there had been a nasty accident in Northumberland, an armed robbery in Manchester and a group of immigrant refugees rescued from the English Channel.

She frowned. 'Do you think some of these refugees are getting through and coming to London?'

'Probably,' answered Peter. 'They'd expect to get lost in the crowds up here and find work more easily than in the smaller towns.'

'Over the previous ten weeks I've been approached on twelve separate occasions by men who claimed to be British but had worked in a hospital in Syria previously. I explained to them the procedure for assessment and retraining, took their addresses and sent on the necessary papers to enable them to apply. The one I entered on my computer today was flagged up showing his address was already in the records.'

'Probably two of them sharing the same lodgings.'

'Quite possible, but they all seem to live in the same area. If they are the specialists that they claim I would expect them to live in a more salubrious area.'

'Would it be the same man who continually returns and is using the addresses of friends?'

Lucy shook her head. 'I don't think so. They have all applied in person and I'm sure I would remember if I'd seen any of them more than once. I spent a long time explaining to each one about retraining and assessment. I've sent out the relevant papers, but none of them have been returned to me.'

'They may have applied to other hospitals and returned their assessment papers there.'

'It's possible, I suppose,' agreed Lucy.

'That's probably the answer. It's not your responsibility to check up on them after you've given them as much help as possible.'

'It just seems a strange coincidence that they should all say they had lived and worked in Syria, claim to have medical qualifications and live in the same area of London.'

'If you're really concerned print off the records that you have and take them to the supervisor. See what he says.'

'I doubt he'll take much notice. He's more interested in trying to keep the hospital costs down so that we are within our budget by the end of the year,' replied Lucy morosely.

'Do you want me to have a word with Barry? Ask his opinion.'

'It's hardly a matter for the police and they all showed me British passports.'

'Then forget it. They're not likely to be refugees that have managed to get to England from France.'

Vasilis was disappointed when he called Mr Sfyrakos to hear that the plans were not yet ready for his inspection, but would be by the end of the week. Mr Sfyrakos offered to send them through on the computer, but Vasilis was not happy with that idea.

'I'm not conversant with the rules and regulations regarding building plans now. I built my original house years ago before all the new safety standards became compulsory. I'd far rather look at them in your office so you can explain to me anything I don't understand. I can also ask you to make immediate alterations if I want to change the layout.'

Mr Sfyrakos sighed. He hoped Mr Iliopolakis was not going to be one of those customers who changed their minds frequently about the design of their property.

'Of course, Mr Iliopolakis. I quite understand. Would Friday be convenient for you? I'm sure they will be ready by then.'

The bedroom curtains for the Elounda apartment arrived two days later than Cathy had expected. Ronnie had visited and finally hung them, along with the curtains in the lounge and at the patio doors whilst Cathy began to fill her kitchen cupboards with china and glass.

'It's beginning to look like home at last,' smiled Cathy. 'I'll ask Vasilis to bring down our bedding tomorrow along with some of the remaining boxes and then we can finally move in. I'll be pleased to have my clothes properly unpacked. Now the weather is getting warmer I'm having to search through our cases to find something lighter to wear.'

'You'll be able to sit outside on your patio and get a sun tan,' remarked Ronnie.

Cathy shook her head. 'We haven't organised any garden furniture yet. I'll have to remind Vasilis. I'm sure there will be a number of other items that we'll need. Now the lounge furniture is in place and I can see how much space is left I'm going to have a bookcase on the back wall. I'll need somewhere to place my father's books and then I have to decide where to hang our photos.'

'You ought to have the bookcase made to measure or you could be left with an ugly gap at each side. You could stand some of your photos on top.'

'I won't want them falling over whenever we go in or out of the door to our bedroom.'

'Provided you don't slam the door that should not be a problem.'

'I'm thinking more of me being clumsy and bumping it as I go past. I can always decide where to put them once we are here permanently.'

Whilst Vasilis returned to the house for more of their possessions Cathy took her walker and negotiated the short stretch of tarmac that led to the main road. It was not difficult to get her walker up the kerb and onto the pavement that led to the supermarket. Vasilis had promised to take her to the large supermarket on the road to Aghios Nikolaos the following day to stock up on basic provisions, but she wanted to buy some meat and vegetables to make a surprise meal for him that evening.

She looked across the busy road. It would be very pleasant to sit down by the waterfront some days and watch the activity that was always taking place there. She would have to find an accessible crossing place or she would have to continually ask Vasilis to accompany her.

She walked up the ramp to the entrance of the supermarket and approached the cashier hoping she would be understood. 'I want to buy a few items, but I cannot manage a basket. I'd like to place my shopping bag on my handles and use that.'

'No problem. If you need help ask me.'

Cathy smiled in relief and began to walk slowly around the shelves. She selected a pack of chicken, more than she needed, but the remainder could go into the freezer. She then remembered that she had not switched the freezer on and must do that as soon as she returned home. The meat would stay fresh in the fridge for a few hours until the freezer was at the right temperature. She picked up two lemons, some potatoes, carrots and broccoli, along with a lettuce, tomatoes, onion, cheese and a dressing. By the time she reached the cashier the bag was too heavy for her to lift onto the desk and was grateful that the assistant lifted it off the handles and placed it on the counter.

Once it had been unpacked and the items rung up on the till

the cashier repacked the bag and hung it back on the handles of Cathy's walker.

'Do you have far to go? Will you be able to manage?'

'We've just moved in around the corner.'

'Wait a minute.' The cashier raised her voice and called to a man who was somewhere at the back of the shop. 'Can you help the lady?'

A man looked out from behind a plastic curtain. 'What does she want?'

'She needs to get down the kerb. Says she only lives around the corner.'

The man took the bag from the handles. 'I'll carry this,' he said.

Cathy walked back along the road with him following her. She manoeuvred the walker down the kerb and waited for the bag to be hung back on the handles.

'I will bring it,' he said and Cathy did not argue.

She walked up the ramp to the front door and the man nodded. 'Bordelli's home.'

'It is our home now.'

He nodded and waited until Cathy had walked inside. She expected him to place the bag on the floor, instead he walked through to the kitchen and deposited it on a work top.

'Very nice,' he said, looking around appraisingly. 'Better than Bordelli's.' With a smile he left her, closing the front door behind him. If this was the kind of service she would receive she would always shop there.

Having remembered to switch on the freezer, Cathy unpacked her bag. She should have thought to buy some coffee and milk whilst she was out, but was loath to return to the supermarket a second time. When Vasilis arrived she would ask him to go round, in the meantime she would have a rest. She wished she had thought to bring her lap top with her that morning as she could have passed her time looking at garden furniture. She had no book with her that she could read and there was nothing to look at outside except the houses and the road. For the first time she wondered if they had made the right decision, although not having a view had never worried her when in Heraklion. Here it was different, knowing that the bustling water front was only a short distance away.

Vasilis returned and deposited three boxes and two suitcases. 'I can go back for some more later on. I'm sure this will be more than enough for you to deal with until later. I've made a sandwich and then we can go round the corner for a meal this evening.'

Cathy nodded. She would not tell him that she had other plans. 'Could you go round to the supermarket and buy some coffee and milk, please. I've been so used to opening Saffie's cupboards and helping myself to whatever I want that it was quite a shock when I went to make myself some coffee and realised I had nothing here.'

'I'll go now, then we can both have a cup of coffee before we eat. We'll need some for tomorrow morning anyway. Would you like me to get some tea bags for you?'

'That would be lovely for later this afternoon. I may have thought of one or two other essentials by then and ask you to go again. I would like you to bring my lap top down for me the next time you go back to the house. That was another thing I realised I did not have. I wanted to look up garden furniture.'

Cathy took advantage of Vasilis's absence that afternoon to prepare the vegetables ready for their evening meal, placed the chicken in the oven and then commenced unpacking the suitcases and hanging their clothes up in the wardrobe. She then made herself a cup of tea to enjoy whilst she was making out a long shopping list for the following morning. Although she planned to patronize the local supermarket she knew it was practical to visit the far larger establishment where there would be a greater variety of items to choose from and at a far cheaper price.

Cathy made herself a cup of tea and turned on the oven to start the chicken cooking, remembering to start the extractor fan so the smell of cooking would not penetrate into the lounge.

Vasilis returned with more boxes and two more suitcases. 'I would never have believed we had so many possessions.'

'We had the extra bedroom whilst we were in Heraklion,' Cathy reminded him. 'I used to put things away in the drawers and wardrobe and tended to forget about them. I'll have to be more disciplined now we are living here.'

'I remembered your lap top.'

'Thank you; I feel lost without it. I think the sun will stay on our patio until quite late each day. We really must order some garden furniture so we can begin to sit outside.'

'Not too much or we won't have the space for the pots you say you want out there.'

'I'll bear that in mind, then we ought to look at Yannis's web site and see what he has available. We don't want silly little ones, but certainly not those great big pithoi.'

'Whatever suits you. Much as I enjoy looking at a well kept garden I have no desire to participate.'

'It's probably too late to do anything now, but I can make plans for next spring. I'm going to unpack another suitcase.'

'The television!' exclaimed Vasilis. 'I was going to say I would watch the news and then I realised it was still up at the house. We haven't decided where it should be situated.'

'I'll leave you to think about that whilst I go and unpack another suitcase. You can always watch the news on your lap top.'

'It's not the same,' complained Vasilis.

Cathy finished placing underwear and jumpers into the drawers and returned to the kitchen to check on her cooking.

'Oh, no. I don't believe it,' she exclaimed..

'What's wrong?' Vasilis immediately joined her.

'The oven isn't working.'

'Let me see.'

'I know the electrics must be installed and connected as I've used the kettle.' Cathy shook her head in puzzlement.. 'I put the fridge and freezer on earlier. Are they working?'

Vasilis opened the doors to both appliances and placed his hand inside. The both felt cold. He switched the oven on and off and then switched on the kitchen light. That worked perfectly.

'I think there must be a fault on the oven. I'll ask Dimitris to come and have a look at it tomorrow. It may be something simple; if not it will have to be returned.'

'I'd planned to cook a surprise meal for you,' said Cathy miserably.

Vasilis squeezed her shoulders. 'I would have appreciated it, but we can have it another night. We'll go round the corner to the taverna tonight as we had planned originally. Do you want me to bring the car?'

'I'm sure I can manage to walk. I went round to the little supermarket this morning without a problem.'

'You should have waited until I was here.'

'Then the meal that I was preparing to surprise you with would not have been a surprise. They were so helpful. The man in there carried my bag back for me and put it in the kitchen. He knew Mr Bordelli used to live here.'

'He probably helped him around with his shopping.'

'I shall certainly use them in future. Once we have done the really big shop tomorrow I should only need fresh items each day. Are we dressing up to go out?'

'I don't think there is any need. We are only going round the corner to the local taverna.'

'I'll just have a wash and freshen up my make up, then. I'll not be long.'

As Vasilis went up to pay their bill he saw Panayiotis standing just outside by the rear door and walked out to join him.

'Have you come here for a meal? I should have asked you to join us.'

Panayiotis shook his head. 'Thank you, but I have only come to collect some food for Blerim.'

The owner appeared and handed Panayiotis a cardboard box which held some wilted lettuce along with other items.

Vasilis frowned. 'Can't they afford to feed themselves?'

'They struggle if Blerim has no work. He's trying hard to save up sufficient to take his daughter to a specialist.'

'What's wrong with her?'

'She witnessed the treatment that was meted out to her father and she was severely traumatised. She refuses to speak.'

'So you buy food for them?'

Panayiotis shook his head.'I have an arrangement with the owner here. He gives me food that is left over from the previous day and he cannot serve to his customers. There's nothing actually wrong with it. In return I give the taverna any squid or octopus that I catch. I enjoy going out fishing at night but I don't enjoy living on fish continually.'

'I had an idea that when we were settled I would sit on the end of a jetty and fish.'

'You won't catch much of interest around the shore. You need to be in deep water for the squid and search the rocks for octopus. Would you like to come out with me and see how it's done?'

Vasilis nodded. 'I'd be interested. Let me know when you're planning to go out.'

'Probably next week when I have my days off.' He lifted the box onto his shoulder and Vasilis returned inside to pay his bill.

'What kept you?' asked Cathy. 'Who were you talking to?'

'Panayiotis. He collects food from here to take up to the Albanian family.'

'Are they that poor?' Cathy felt guilty having just eaten an appetising meal followed by a strawberry ice cream.

'Panayiotis said Blerim is saving up to take his daughter to a therapist. She refuses to speak, due to the events she witnessed.'

'Poor little girl. Therapists are so expensive and it could

take months before it has a beneficial effect. Couldn't we help him?'

'We could be incurring considerable expense for an unlimited amount of time,' warned Vasilis.

'Surely we could afford it?'

Vasilis looked at his wife. It was not surprising that she wanted to help having been severely traumatised herself after her car accident so many years ago that had ruined her modelling career and was the cause of the severe arthritis that she suffered now.

'I'll have a word with Panayiotis. He's asked me to go out fishing with him next week.'

'Isn't he working?'

'He'll have his days off and he's going to show me how to catch squid.'

'I thought you were going to sit on a jetty?'

'Panayiotis says I won't catch very much there. Apparently squid live in deep water.'

'It won't hurt you to have some time to yourself. You've worked so hard organising the apartment and also dealing with the sale of "The Central".'

'That reminds me, I have to go up to Heraklion again on Friday,' announced Vasilis.

'What for? Has the specialist sent for you? Is there a problem?'

Vasilis smiled at his wife's concern. 'Nothing at all to do with the specialist. I was dissatisfied with the architect in Aghios Nikolaos that I had asked to draw up plans for the building down by the beach. Whatever I asked him to do he seemed to think was impossible. I made an appointment to see another up in Heraklion when I was there the other week.' Vasilis knew he was not being strictly truthful, but he did not want to have to explain his ideas for the building to Cathy.

'Will you see Dimitra again?'

Vasilis shrugged 'Possibly, but I'm not that interested in what happens at "The Central". It's no longer my affair.'

'Would you like me to come with you?'

'No, there's no need. You have plenty to get on with here or you could spend the day with Marianne again.'

'Provided I'm not imposing on her.'

'The idea of returning down here to live was so you could visit your friends more easily.'

'I just feel she probably has enough to do now her mother is staying. If it was warmer I'd be able to spend the day on the beach and go for a swim. The pool up at the house will be too cold for at least another month. Such a shame as I would have liked to take advantage of it whilst we were staying there.'

'You can say that you want to look at Yannis's pots and decide which ones would be suitable for the patio.'

'That's a good idea. That would keep Yannis occupied and enable Marianne to get on with her work on the computer.'

'Call her tomorrow.'

'You need to 'phone Dimitris, remember, to sort out the oven. If he can only come on Friday I'll have to be there.'

'I'll call him first, then you can make whatever arrangements suit you and Marianne.'

Dimitris was puzzled when Vasilis called him and said that when Cathy had tried to use the oven it did not work.

'I tested it when I connected everything and it was working perfectly when I left. As soon as John has collected Skele I'll come down and have a look.'

'I'll wait in for you. If there's a fault it will have to be returned.'

'Of course. Are all the other electrical appliances working perfectly?'

'As far as I'm aware. The kettle and toaster are and the fridge feels cold.'

'What about the hob?'

'I don't think Cathy has used that. Shall I go and switch it on?'

'Just turn one hot plate on and let me know if you can feel any heat coming from it.'

Vasilis went into the kitchen and turned on the hob, holding his hand over the ceramic plates. 'I can't feel any heat from it at all.'

Dimitris smiled to himself. He had an idea he knew exactly what the problem was. 'Put your hand beneath the worktop and at the back on the wall you should feel quite a large square box with a switch on it. Make sure the switch is in the down position.'

Vasilis felt around until his fingers located the box that Dimitris had mentioned. 'I think the switch is up, but I can't see unless I get down on my hands and knees.'

'See if you can push it down.'

There was a resounding click. 'I've done that.'

'Now switch on the oven and the hob. Has a light come on to say the oven is working and can you feel any heat from the hob?'

'Yes, there's a red light above the oven controls, and, yes I can feel some heat from the hob.'

'There's nothing wrong with either appliance. I turned the main switch off for safety after I had tested it. I didn't want the hob to be switched on accidentally and something placed on top that would burn. I should have left you a message telling you to turn on the main connector before trying to use it.'

Vasilis smiled in relief. 'I feel a bit stupid, but I'm so pleased I haven't got to ask you to come and disconnect everything so it can be returned. Should we turn that switch off when we're not using it?'

'No, that would be very inconvenient for you. You'd have to constantly remember to put the switch down whenever you wanted to do any cooking. It will be quite safe left on now you are living there. Let me know if you have any more concerns, but I certainly don't need to come up to put a switch down for you.'

Vasilis told Cathy about the switch and that the oven and hob were now working perfectly.

'How foolish of me. I looked in the cupboard above to see if there was a switch there like there was in our old apartment. I didn't think to look underneath the work top, now I'll be able to cook supper for you tonight.'

'And you can make arrangements to visit Marianne on Friday. Have a look at Yannis's web site so you have an idea of the pots you want and how many. I'm sure he'll be pleased to get rid of some more.'

'I'm not sure if he will, but Marianne will certainly be grateful. When I was there last week there were boxes of pots in their lounge.'

Vasilis drove up to Heraklion and looked at the plans Mr Sfyrakos had prepared for him. 'Can you talk me through them? How large are the rooms going to be?'

'Let me start at the beginning. I've spoken to a structural engineer and he is making the necessary calculations. He has suggested that the site be levelled completely and you decide how far back from the road you want the house to be situated. The footings are dug, steel supports are placed in strategic positions throughout the area and a high wall is put in place up to the floor level of your proposed apartment at both the front and back.'

Vasilis shook his head. 'I don't want any large blank walls.'

'Hear me out,' smiled Mr Sfyrakos. 'You can then decide how many terraces you want in front of the wall and we can calculate the measurements.'

'What about at the rear?'

'You could have the same arrangement at the rear. A patio area and terracing or just a large paved area. In the meantime I suggest we concentrate on your ideas for the actual apartment.'

Vasilis nodded. He was far more interested in the facade and the lay out of the rooms than the rear of the building. 'How large can the patio at the front be?'

'As large as you wish. It will be supported by the concrete pillars beneath and the concrete base to the building.'

Vasilis placed his finger on the plans. 'So, if I have a wall at the front on the pavement and then a terrace a metre wide, I could have another wall built at the back of that terrace and have another terrace a metre wide, then another wall at the back and then the patio could extend from the building as far as my neighbour's property?'

'Theoretically, yes. I will need to work out the measurements exactly. The width of each wall will have to be allowed for, which will either mean the patio is a little smaller or the terraces are a little less wide.'

'I'd rather lose some width from the terraces, but I still want them to look in proportion. I've had a further idea for the patio. Am I able to put a swimming pool up there?'

'A swimming pool? Why would you want a pool up there? The sea is only across the road.'

'My wife happened to say that she enjoyed swimming in the pool at my son's house. She would find it difficult to walk on the shingle and get in and out of the sea safely. Can that be done?'

'At this stage we can make allowances for it. There would have to be a recessed area beneath the patio and strengthening done to support the weight of the water. You'll also need an area where the mechanism to empty and refill the pool could be housed, possibly under the terraces.'

Vasilis nodded. 'Let's forget about the terraces for a moment. Build a retaining wall where the patio can be situated and allow for an area below for the pool mechanism. The patio will need to be wide enough to accommodate the pool and a large seating area as well. Once that has been done the width of the terraces can be decided. I'd now like to see what you have in mind for the interior.'

'The bedroom and en suite are restricted in size due to the wall beside the front door, but they should certainly be sufficient for your needs. The bedroom will be approximately twelve metres wide and ten metres long and the en suite eight metres square. If you wanted the bedroom to be any longer the en suite would need to be reduced by the same amount. The toilet can be no larger than three metres square due to the steps that you want leading down to the garage. At a future date you will have to decide which way you want the toilet door to open; inwards or out towards the steps and if you want the steps on view or have a door at the top. Personally I would recommend a door for safety.'

Vasilis nodded. 'I'd really like to have the separate toilet up at the other end near the front door. If I have a door on the steps and a door on the toilet there could be a problem if both doors were opened at once.'

'That would mean that you ended up with a large toilet and a narrow en suite. It would be far better to have the toilet left where it is and have the lift and steps changed round.'

'I'll give it some consideration and let you know my decision. What about the lounge, dining and kitchen area?'

Mr Sfyrakos spread his hands. 'It's a shame that you need to have the stairs and a lift opening off them, but they can be as large as you like. You have the whole area between the front door and the wall of the property next door. I would recommend that you have a walk way down that side leading from the patio to the rear of the building. At present I have designed the lounge and diner to be fifty square metres. That would leave you a walk way at the side of two metres. Those dimensions can be altered however you please. The front wall leading on to the patio will be glass, of course, with just a small retaining wall at each end. The kitchen will be twenty five square metres. That may sound large, but by the time you have had worktops fitted along with the appliances and a central work area the space will be filled. I have allowed for a smaller patio door at the side of the kitchen that will give you access to the walkway and also to the rear of the building. You realise that such a vast area will cost a considerable amount to heat during the winter?'

'If I begin to find it too expensive I can have some walls and doors put in place and divide the areas up'. Vasilis shrugged off the problem.

Mr Sfyrakos sighed. 'Are you happy with the interior plans overall?'

'Perfectly happy. It is just a question of deciding on the position of the toilet and whether to swap the position of the steps and the lift over.'

'And the rear of the property. Have you come to any decision about the area?'

'I'll think about that in more detail later.'

'It would be advisable not to mention the terracing at the moment. Present the plans with a high retaining wall at both the back and front with the patio situated on the top. Once they have been passed you should be able to do as you please with the remaining frontage. Are you are happy for me to make the alterations to these plans that we have discussed?'

Vasilis nodded. 'I think so. Could you e-mail a copy to me? I can then concentrate on them quietly at home and contact you accordingly.'

'You realise that until they are approved you are unable to commence building. Have you a time scale in mind?'

'Not really. We have somewhere to live at present, but if it was completed by this time next year I'd be more than happy.'

Mr Sfyrakos drew a breath of relief.; he did not want to lose Mr Iliopolakis as a customer. 'Provided you are completely satisfied I will have to ask you to visit me again and place your signature on them.'

Vasilis smiled; he understood exactly what Mr Sfyrakos was saying.

July 2015
Week One

Panayiotis knocked on the door of Vasilis's apartment. 'Are you busy? I've come to tell you that Blerim has accepted your offer of help for Lejla gratefully and I've spoken to the hospital.'

'Come in and have a seat. What would you like to drink?'

'A small beer would be very welcome as I'm not on duty today.' Panayiotis settled himself in an armchair and looked around appreciatively. 'You've certainly made this apartment very much more attractive than when Giuseppe lived here.'

'Taking down the hall wall made a lot of difference and then a fresh coat of paint everywhere.'

Panayiotis nodded. He knew the amount of work that had been undertaken by Mr Palamakis and his grandsons.

'So, Blerim is willing to accept some financial help for his daughter?'

'He'll do anything for his family. If it was for him he would probably refuse. He would be too proud. I took him up to the hospital with me and found a woman who could translate from Greek to Albanian. She's a trained therapist specialising in children and being a woman Lejla should feel more comfortable with her than with a man.'

'Won't her mother be with her?'

'Initially, but when the child becomes more confident she will be alone with Thalia. There could be things that she would not want to share with her mother.'

Vasilis raised his eyebrows. 'Like what?'

Panayiotis shrugged. 'I don't know, but she was probably as upset by her mother's reaction as she was to her father's treatment. It could be difficult for her to talk about that with her mother present.'

'How long will this therapy last before it has the desired effect?'

'Impossible to say. It could stretch into some years. Is that going to be a problem?'

'Financially, no. I'll have to apprise my son of the situation so if anything happens to Cathy and myself he knows he must become responsible.'

'You're a good man, Vasilis Iliopolakis. We could do with many more like you around.' Panayiotis drank some of his beer. 'Do you fancy coming out fishing tomorrow night?'

'Tomorrow night?'

Panayiotis nodded. 'Do you have other plans?'

'What time?'

'I usually leave about midnight and trawl up and down the centre of the bay. I'll throw a dead fish over the side and hope the squid will come up to feed. I don't always catch one, of course.'

'Midnight! What time do you return?'

'Depends. If I catch one quickly I'll pass over the area once more. Sometimes there's more than one to be had and then I'll return. Other times I'm out there until it's almost dawn and not see a sign of one.'

'I didn't realise you went out at night. I thought you planned to go during the day.'

'You won't see them when the sun is shining on the water. Is night fishing a problem?'

'I'm not sure about leaving Cathy alone at night. If she fell she would need my help. I wouldn't want to think she was lying on the floor for hours.'

Panayiotis nodded. 'I understand. Forget it, it's not practical for you.'

'I suppose I could ask her if she was willing to spend the night with my son and Saffie. That would put my mind at rest but I wouldn't be able to make it a regular occurrence.'

'You might not enjoy the experience anyway. Speak to your wife and let me know. I will be going out whatever your answer.'

Vasilis waited until they had finished their evening meal before he approached Cathy.

'Panayiotis has asked me to go fishing with him tomorrow night. He says that is when you can catch the squid.'

Cathy frowned. 'At night? Won't that be dangerous?'

'I'm sure Panayiotis doesn't take any risks. He says he just trawls up and down inside the bay. It's not like going out on the open sea and fishing. I'm just concerned about leaving you alone. Would you be willing to go and spend the night with Vasi and Saffron?'

'Why should I have to go and stay with them?'

'I certainly wouldn't go and leave you alone here. If you fell I wouldn't be able to get back to the shore for ages to help you. I'd have to 'phone Vasi and ask him to come down. I'd be much happier to know that you were safely with them. I can't consider going otherwise.'

Cathy looked at her husband doubtfully. At least when it was daylight you could see where the shore was, but that would be impossible in darkness.

'I don't want you sitting up all night wondering if we'll be wrecked.'

'Of course I wouldn't wait up,' smiled Cathy, knowing full well that she would be unable to sleep knowing Vasilis was out fishing. 'I'll want you to promise to call me when you're back on shore, whatever the time. Provided Panayiotis says it's perfectly safe I won't stop you.'

'I won't make it a regular event, but I would like the experience.'

Vasilis climbed gingerly into Panayiotis's small boat.

'Do you want to put a life vest on?' asked Panayiotis.

'Will I need it?'

'Shouldn't do, provided you can swim. It's calm enough.'

'Do you wear one?'

'No, I don't go out if the weather is bad. This is for my pleasure, not my living. I don't need to take a risk. Are you settled?'

Vasilis nodded. The lights around the small harbour made everywhere look safe and inviting, but when he looked out at the black expanse of the sea he felt his stomach lurch.

The outboard motor chugged rythmically as Panayiotis drew out of the harbour and motored down parallel with the coast before turning out into the deeper area of the bay. The boat rocked as he flung a net over the stern, followed by a dead fish and Vasilis clutched at the wooden seat.

'We'll drag that behind us for a while and then bring it up and see if we've been lucky.'

Vasilis nodded. He had expected Panayiotis to produce a fishing rod. Panayiotis motored slowly down the centre of the bay until he was half way to the canal before hauling the net aboard. He threw back the few wriggling and gasping fish and then flung the net overboard again.

Almost at the canal Panayiotis examined the net again and turned to make another run hoping for better luck. After six such runs Vasilis began to feel extremely bored and wondered how many more times they were going to go up and down the bay without catching the elusive squid. Finally, with a sigh of regret, Panayiotis declared they would go down to the canal again and if they were unsuccessful they would try one last time as they returned to the harbour.

As they were a short distance from the canal Vasilis saw a large black car driving across the Causeway and wondered where it was going at that hour of the morning. He tapped Panayiotis on the arm and pointed. Panayiotis frowned and picked up a pair of binoculars, looking through them at the car.

'It's a Mercedes and it's drawn in to park behind the windmill,' Panayiotis said quietly.

'How do you know?'

'Night vision binoculars. Keep your voice down. Sounds travel at night across the water.' Panayiotis motored a little closer to the Causeway, cut the engine and turned off his lights. 'We'll keep an eye on them and see what they're up to. They may be a courting couple or they could be planning to rob the Kanali.'

Vasilis shook his head. Both scenarios seemed unlikely to him. The only person he knew who owned a Mercedes was Kuzmichov. Had he driven down to keep a private assignation with a lady? That could explain why the car needed such a thorough clean by Lanassakis.

'Can I see?'

Panayiotis handed him the binoculars and Vasilis looked at the car. 'I'm sure that's Ludmila,' he exclaimed as someone exited from the driver's seat and pushed the door closed quietly. 'It's far too small for Kuzmichov.'

'What are you talking about? Who's Ludmila?' asked Panayiotis.

'I'll explain later. Can you keep watching her and tell me what she does.'

Panayiotis watched Ludmila walk up the road and around to the small beach area. She was obviously waiting for someone. The gentle splashing of oars could be heard and from the canal entrance emerged a dinghy that was rowed towards the shore and three men jumped out.

'Interesting,' said Panayiotis and handed the binoculars back to Vasilis as the men stood there uncertainly and the dinghy rowed back through the canal. 'I think they're waiting for someone else to arrive.'

It was a further half an hour before the dinghy returned with three more passengers. As soon as they were ashore Ludmila led them up the beach to the road and down to where the car was parked behind the windmill where they were out of sight. A short while later the car nosed gently out and onto the bridge leading to the Causeway.

Panayiotis started the engine and turned his lights back on. 'I can't risk sailing back into the bay without lights. It's against the law and I wouldn't want to be rammed by a boat coming out.'

Vasilis sat there silently. Panayiotis seemed to have forgotten his intention of making another trawl in the hope of catching a squid. 'Keep an eye on that car and let me know where it goes,' he ordered as he opened the throttle and increased their speed.

Bemused, Vasilis watched as the car drove along by the coast and finally up the steep hill leading to the main road. Panayiotis moored and helped Vasilis ashore.

'Not a very successful fishing night, I'm afraid, but I'd like to talk to you about that car. You say you recognised the driver?'

'I think so.'

'So are you able to tell me what was going on?'

Vasilis shook his head. 'I've no idea.'

Panayiotis eyed Vasilis sternly. 'I believe you, but you obviously know something. Come back to my place and we'll discuss it further.'

'I have to 'phone Cathy first.'

'At this time of the morning?'

'I promised her I would call as soon as we arrived back. That was a condition she imposed when she agreed to stay the night with Vasi and Saffron.'

'Do it as we walk home.'

Vasilis opened his mobile and pressed in the number for Cathy. It was answered almost immediately and Vasilis heard her give a sigh of relief.

'We're safely home. You stay at the house and I'll come up to collect you later. I'll probably snatch a few hour's sleep first.'

Panayiotis opened the door to his house and ushered Vasilis inside. 'Have a seat. I'll make some coffee.'

Vasilis looked around the lounge whilst Panayiotis busied himself in the kitchen. There were no ornaments or pictures; a television was fixed to the wall at the far end and on the table was a computer, with books taking up all the other available space.

'You're an avid reader,' remarked Vasilis when Panayiotis reappeared with steaming cups of coffee and glasses of water.

'When I have the time. There are many that I haven't yet read, but I can't resist buying a book if I think it will be of interest to me. I haven't asked you here to talk about books.' Panayiotis looked at Vasilis intently. 'Tell me about that car. How do you know the driver?'

Vasilis hesitated. 'I can't be absolutely certain, but it looks like the car from the hotel.'

'Which hotel?'

'The one I owned in Heraklion. It was bought from me by a Russian.'

'You owned the car?'

'No, I went up to Heraklion the other week and met one of my ex-employees. She told me that Kuzmichov had bought a Mercedes and used it to transport guests to and from the airport and the hotel.'

'I would have thought an arrangement with a taxi company would have been more cost effective,' remarked Panayiotis.

'That was the agreement I had when I was there.'

'So why would the man want a Mercedes?'

'Possibly prestige. I thought she may have made a mistake; and it was just a large car. I went around to the car park later and spoke to the man who was cleaning it. Apparently he has to keep it immaculate and complained that it often returned quite dirty. If it is being driven down here and parked by the windmills that could explain the shingle and dampness inside that he complained about.'

'You thought you recognised the driver. Was that the Russian?'

Vasilis shook his head. 'It looked like his wife, Ludmila. The person who got out was too small for Kuzmichov.'

'Would you happen to know the registration number?'

'I didn't look and even if I had I doubt if I would have remembered it. I could be making a mistake. There might be someone else in the area who has a Mercedes.'

'It's possible. Tell me exactly what the man who cleans it told you.'

Vasilis frowned. 'I've told you. The employee I spoke with said that men arrived on a fairly regular basis and stayed on the top floor of the hotel where the conference rooms are. She said the carpet was often wet by the lift and dirty footmarks were on the carpet down the hallway. Kuzmichov told her they were his private guests and they never stay more than four or five days. A few days later another group arrive. She was concerned that they were not appearing in the accounts she keeps.'

'Interesting.' Panayiotis looked thoughtful. 'Assuming that you are correct that the car we saw is owned by the Russian and it was his wife driving, why was she collecting men from the canal?'

Vasilis shook his head. 'I've no idea.'

'Are you able to contact the employee and ask her if any men have arrived?'

'Yes, but I wouldn't want to compromise her in any way.'

'Could you ask her for the car registration?'

'I wouldn't want to do that. It would mean she had to go to the car park and she has no reason to go out there. I'll be going up to Heraklion again fairly soon and I could check on the registration then.'

'It would be quicker for me to ask one of the local police to make a note of it and send it down to me.'

'Why do you want it?'

'I followed a Mercedes once before when I was returning from duty. It turned down the hill to the coast road and I thought the driver was lost. None of the hotels or self catering establishments were open at that time and had I not been so tired I would have stopped them and told them they were on the wrong road to collect visitors. If I happen to see it again I can check if it is the same vehicle.'

Vasilis yawned and the action was not lost on Panayiotis. 'You need to go and get some sleep. I'm sorry our fishing trip was not successful, but thanks for your help.'

Although Vasilis felt tired he was unable to sleep. He kept going over the events of the night.. Why would men arrive through the canal and then be met by Ludmila? It made no sense to him. The ferries and hydrofoils docked at Heraklion and any visitors destined for the hotel could disembark there. Was Cathy right when she had suggested that they were Russian spies, outlandish though the idea had appeared? He would mention it to Panayiotis, although he expected the man to laugh at him.

Panayiotis did not attempt to go to bed. He opened up his computer and made copious notes of the information that Vasilis had given him. There was certainly something suspicious taking place in the area.

Cathy greeted Vasilis with relief when he drove up to the house to collect her. 'You look very tired,' she remarked.

'I found it difficult to sleep when we arrived back. My body clock was probably awry.'

'Did you catch any squid?'

'Not a sign of them. We saw something else, though.'

'What was that?'

Vasilis proceeded to tell Cathy about the Mercedes arriving and collecting the men who had been landed at the beach. 'Maybe your idea of Russian spies was not so far off the mark.'

'What did Panayiotis say?'

'I haven't told him that. He's finding out the registration of the Mercedes in case it is seen again down here.'

'Why doesn't he ask the police in Heraklion to go and question Kuzmichov?'

'He has no proof that it was his car, and besides, if something underhand is going on he wouldn't want to alert him to the fact that the police were suspicious.'

'So what are you going to do today?'

'Nothing. It's not my concern.'

Cathy smiled. 'I meant how are you going to occupy yourself today?'

'I thought I'd just take it easy and laze around. I might have a siesta this afternoon. Why?'

'I've seen some garden furniture on the internet that I think will be suitable for the patio. I wanted your opinion and if you agree we could order it. John said he would get the pots packed up and deliver them whenever it was convenient.'

'I'll have a look at the furniture when we get back home and then we could have a snack lunch followed by our siesta and go out this evening for a meal. Shall I ask Panayiotis to join us as a way of saying thank you for arranging the therapy for the Albanian girl and taking me fishing?'

'Good idea. You could also ask him if Blerim is working anywhere at the moment.'

'What do you have in mind?'

'When the pots have arrived do you think he would be capable of filling them with compost for me? The sacks are heavy and I can't move them around. If I take a pot to the sack I can't move it once I've filled it.'

'I could do that for you.'

'I know, but I'm thinking of work for Blerim.'

Panayiotis accepted Vasilis's invitation. 'I rarely go to a taverna to eat as I don't enjoy a meal out on my own. Most of my friends are also in the police force and their wives often ask me to join them but due to our shifts it can be quite difficult to get together.'

'I told Cathy about our fishing trip last night.'

Panayiotis nodded. 'What did she say?'

'When I first told her about the Mercedes and Kuzmichov's visitors she suggested that Kuzmichov was hosting Russian spies,' laughed Vasilis.

'I don't think they're spies. I think it more likely they are drug trafficking.'

'Why would they need six men if they were bringing in drugs?'

'Probably each man would go to a different town on the island.'

'That wouldn't explain them staying at "The Central".

Panayiotis looked at Vasilis speculatively. 'I agree. According to you, your acquaintance said the men stayed for four or five days and a few days later some more would arrive. I thought I'd go down at night and watch out for any activity.'

'Surely they'll notice that your boat is there again.'

'I'm not planning on taking the boat. We may not have been noticed last time but I don't want to risk being seen and running into trouble. I wouldn't stand much chance if six thugs decided to set upon me. I'm planning to go down and do some fishing off a jetty in a week or so's time. I can go far enough along the bay to be able to see any movement over on the other shore or around the canal. If the same events are repeated I can take cover behind the bushes or bathing huts when the car leaves so I'm not seen.'

'And then what will you do?'

'Nothing. I put in a report to my senior officer and ask for a few men to be put at my disposal. They would be stationed near the canal and that beach and could see exactly what transpires.'

'Suppose it never happens again?'

'Then I will be in trouble for wasting my colleagues time,' smiled Panayiotis. 'If your information is correct that it is happening on a pretty regular basis it will just be a question of patience on our part.'

'Can I come with you?'

Panayiotis considered the proposal. 'Why do you want to come?'

'Call it curiosity.'

Finally Panayiotis nodded. 'I'm not engaged in official police work so I don't see why not, provided your wife doesn't object.'

'She didn't like the thought of me being out at sea at night. Sitting on a jetty fishing should be safe enough. I could park my car near by and if Cathy needed me I could be back home in no more than ten minutes.'

'I might have to book you for speeding,' observed Panayiotis with a smile. 'It will be good to have company and will be less conspicuous than a man on his own. Just a couple of mates doing some fishing.'

Ludmila waited until Evgeniy returned from settling the latest arrivals into "The Central".

'I think I may have been seen last night. There was a small boat in the bay quite near to the canal and beach. I thought it was the lights reflecting off the water as I drove round. As I drove back over the Causeway a boat put it's lights on and began to motor back to Elounda.'

'No one followed you from Elounda?'

'No, and I wasn't stopped anywhere.'

Evgeniy shrugged. 'It was probably just a local fisherman.'

'Why should he have been sitting there without lights and then left at the same time as me?'

'Coincidence I expect. They probably extinguish their lights so the fish don't swim away. If you see him there on your next trip call me and I'll cancel the drop.'

'One night I was seen waiting on the beach and a man asked me if I wanted a ride back to Elounda. I told him I was waiting for my companions and he drove off.'

'Why didn't you tell me before?'

'It didn't seem important. Panos hadn't arrived so I was there alone. There were some lights high up on the hill that night. I think some men were out hunting as he drove down from further up the road. I've not seen him or the lights since.'

Lucy looked at the man who sat before her. Once again she had explained the details of re-training and assessment before he was accepted for medical work of any kind. This was the second Syrian she had interviewed that week. Maybe it would be a good idea for Peter to have a word with Barry and ask his opinion. He worked for Immigration Control at Heathrow and would have access to the records of those who had been granted asylum over the past few months.

Once the man had left her office she printed off the details of all the Syrians who had applied for work at the hospital over the previous three months and placed them in her bag. She would ask Peter to show them to Barry and if he said they were all legitimate she would shred the papers and no one would be any the wiser.

Peter handed the papers over to his next door neighbour. 'They're not exactly confidential, because they don't have any medical details on them, but Lucy shouldn't really have printed them off and brought them away from the hospital.'

Barry read the notes slowly, continually referring back to an earlier page. 'Lucy's right,' he said finally. 'There is something strange going on here. All the men claim to be British citizens who have been holidaying in Crete and returned through Gatwick. I'll contact the authorities there and see what they have to say. They may all have been thoroughly checked out, of course, but if they presented British passports that is unlikely. They would just have been waved through. May I keep these papers for the time being? My enquiries may take some time.'

'Thanks. It's obviously worrying Lucy. I'll tell her you're looking into it and will let us know when you have found out anything.'

Dimitra answered her mobile, surprised to see that it was Vasilis calling her. 'What can I do for you Mr Iliopolakis?'

'I just have a couple of quick questions for you. Have you had any more men arrive at the hotel?'

Dimitra frowned. 'I believe so. Mr Kuzmichov was up on this floor early this morning. Do you want me to ask him?'

'No, definitely not,' Vasilis swallowed. 'He might think I was trying to interfere with how he runs the hotel. It was just curiosity on my part and not important. My other question was to ask if you would be free for lunch again? I have to come up to Heraklion on business next week.'

Dimitra did not hesitate. 'I would appreciate that, Mr Iliopolakis. I feel quite safe when I am with you.'

'Then I'll call you the day before I need to come up to make sure you are available.'

Cathy ordered the garden furniture that Vasilis had approved and then 'phoned John. 'I'm happy for you to deliver the pots whenever it suits you. I'm going to ask Vasilis to buy some bags of compost and then I can start to get them prepared.'

'Don't tell Uncle Yannis you are going to put earth in them. He'll have a fit. He wasn't pleased when Dad said he was putting flower pots inside those we have.'

'I'll just ask you to place them strategically around the patio and when the furniture has arrived I'll make sure that Uncle Yannis is one of our first visitors. I won't admit that I propose to put plants in the pots later.'

John carried the pots through the apartment, taking great care not to knock the walls or paintwork and removed their protective wrapping. Cathy ran her hands lovingly over one.

'They are beautiful. I feel guilty about proposing to fill them with compost and flowers. If we had sufficient space inside I would have them as ornaments as Vasi has up at the house.'

'I hear that Vasilis is planning to build a house down by the shore. You'll have to insist that it's large enough for you to have some of Uncle Yannis's pots inside.'

'I'm sure it will be,' smiled Cathy. 'Vasilis always has big ideas. I'm surprised he is prepared to live here. The apartment in

Heraklion was larger than this one and he always said that one was too small for his liking. Vasi was reluctant to sell it to him and return to live in the house down here. It is far too large for two people.'

July 2015
Weeks Two and Three

Vasilis reported to Panayiotis that he had spoken to Dimitra and she had confirmed that some more men had arrived at "The Central".

'I've arranged to meet her again this week when I go up to Heraklion to speak to my architect. I'll see what else I can find out.'

'Be careful. You don't want Kuzmichov to know you are interested in his guests.'

'I'll be discreet. Talk about the hotel generally and then ask casually how long the latest arrivals stayed. I won't mention our fishing expedition.'

Vasilis sat with Mr Sfyrakos with the plans spread out before them. 'I've a suggestion for one small alteration and I hope you will approve. If the toilet was left where you propose it could be made a little smaller. You only need a toilet and hand basin in there. That would mean that the entrance was set back and in the event of the door to the steps being opened at the same time as the toilet door neither would cause an obstruction.'

Vasilis nodded. 'I suppose that would be practical. A shame it will ruin the symmetry of the wall.'

'The only way to avoid that would be to make your bedroom and en suite less wide. I don't think you would be happy if they were narrower.'

'That's true,' agreed Vasilis. 'It is essential that the doorway to the toilet is sufficiently wide to accommodate a wheelchair.'

'Bearing that in mind I have increased the width by half a metre. This will mean that either your bedroom or en suite is half a metre smaller. The difference in area could be adjusted between them and would not be noticeable.'

'I have to think of the future. If my wife does eventually become dependent upon a wheelchair I have to ensure that the en suite is large enough for her needs. I think the half metre should reduce the size of our bedroom.'

Mr Sfyrakos nodded. 'The best decision in my opinion. I'll alter the measurements accordingly. How large do you want the balcony you propose?'

Vasilis frowned. 'Sufficiently large for a small table and two comfortable chairs.'

'Then the area used will reduce your bedroom floor space. At present the length of the room is ten metres. If two metres was allowed for the balcony you would still have a very large room. The alternative would be to insert supports that are extended from the wall of the house and the balcony is built out onto them.'

'That would make the balcony project out from the house. I'm not sure that would look right.'

'Think about it, Mr Iliopolakis. You do not have to make a decision today. I have spoken to the structural engineer again and said that you want facilities at ground level for a generator, lift and maintenance room for the pool that you propose. You will need to decide upon the size and depth of the pool that you want. Would you like to look at his design?'

Mr Sfyrakos spread the plan out on the table. 'That is where the lift will be. It will be necessary to excavate a shaft and the cross hatched area underneath is where the housing is situated. It will be encased in concrete. The stairs will rise up at the side and open into the house. There will a room just for the generator and next to that a walkway that gives you access to beneath the pool along with a storage room for any equipment that might be needed. Your car can be garaged in the area and you will have sufficient space to open the doors to their fullest extent.'

Vasilis nodded. 'That all looks and sounds practical.'

'The wall to retain the bank will be approximately there which will give you a patio area thirty metres in width, including the walkway on one side and a flight of steps at the other. The exact position of the pool is up to you, but you will need to confer with the contractor to ensure that the area beneath is in the right place. Once concrete pillars have been made and walls built you do not want to have to start to knock them down.'

'I understand. I'll make an appointment to speak with him provided these plans are passed.'

'Now, we move on to the rear of the property.' Mr Sfyrakos produced another plan. 'Again a retaining wall is built at the far end of the area and another where the rear wall of the house will be situated. He has suggested that the area be concreted with a drainage system installed. You will have to decide if you want soil out there for a garden or just have the whole area tiled as a patio. If you decide to have a garden area then I suggest you have the soil moved round before the construction of the house begins.'

'What difference would that make?'

'Once the side wall of the house has been built there is a limit to the size of vehicle that can have access to the rear. You would certainly not get a tipper lorry down there so it would mean numerous trips with a small truck and men would be needed to shovel the soil into place. Much easier and cheaper to have just two or three lorry loads.'

'No doubt I would still need men to place the soil around evenly.'

'Quite true, but they could come after all the soil has arrived. That way they would not be waiting around and doing nothing between loads.'

Vasilis nodded. That could be a job for Blerim if he decided to have a garden at the rear.

'As soon as I have the figures from the structural engineer and know the number of steel supports that he says are necessary I will visit the planning department and present your plans. You are unlikely to get an immediate decision. Provided they are not rejected out of hand the committee will probably spend some time to look at them in detail. They may also contact me for clarification and it could be necessary for me to check with you regarding your instructions. If that is the case I will call you on your mobile.'

Vasilis sighed. 'It all seemed so easy when I said all I wanted was an apartment built higher up and we could look across the bay.'

'Had you been content with a conventional house it would have been less of a problem. It is the addition of a lift and a swimming pool that could be queried.'

'The lift is essential, but if necessary the swimming pool could be removed from the plan.'

'Not a good idea.' Mr Sfyrakos shook his head. 'If you decided that you did want a pool at a later date you would have to re-apply and stringent checks would have to be made to ensure that the structure below was capable of bearing the weight. Better to have the work done now. If you decide not to have a pool the strengthening and underpinning of the foundations will just give added stability to the building.'

'I'll abide by your decision,' said Vasilis humbly. 'Just ensure that the plans are passed, please.' He passed an envelope across the table to Mr Sfyrakos who smiled and pocketed it. Of course the plans would be passed without question.

Vasilis left the architect with mixed feelings. It would be a disaster if he was not given permission to build as he wished. Had he given him sufficient? He was already hoping that within the next eighteen months he and Cathy would be moving in; already he was finding the apartment where they were now was too small for his liking.

Dimitra was waiting for him a short distance down from the hotel entrance. 'I thought it better not to wait directly outside. If Kuzmichov had arrived he would probably have asked who I was meeting.'

'Does he monitor your movements?'

Dimitra shook her head. 'I don't think so. It would probably just be a polite enquiry as a way of acknowledging me. I really only see him when I present the accounts, but if our paths should cross he is always courteous.'

'Have you met his wife?'

'I've never been introduced to her, but I have seen her occasionally in the hotel. She visits his guests and takes them out sometimes. I expect she takes them sight seeing.'

'Very likely,' agreed Vasilis as he opened the door of the restaurant for Dimitra to enter.

'So what brings you up to Heraklion again, Mr Iliopolakis. Are you looking for another hotel to buy?'

'Certainly not. I had to call on my architect. I'm planning to build a new apartment for my wife and myself down in Elounda.'

'You don't intend to live up at the big house with Mr Vasi permanently, then?'

'We have already moved from there to a small apartment down in the town. It is sufficient for the time being. What about you, Dimitra? Have you thought about moving away from the hotel?'

'I've thought about it, but I'm not sure I'm ready yet. I feel safe in the hotel.'

'How do you spend your free time?' Vasilis could think of nothing worse than spending all day every day in one small room.

'I read and I do cross stitch embroidery. I send for patterns that I have seen on the internet. That keeps me occupied, along with the television, of course. What about you? How do you spend your time now you are retired?'

'Well, we've been busy catching up with our friends, sorting out this new apartment and I went fishing the other day with a neighbour.'

'Fishing?'

'We didn't catch anything and I was rather bored. I doubt I'll bother to go with him again.'

'It doesn't sound very exciting. When you were here you were always meeting new and interesting people.'

'That's true. Do you have any interesting guests at the moment, apart from the friends of Mr Kuzmichov who arrived the other day?'

'They're not interesting. I don't usually see them unless they happen to go down to the dining room with Mr Kuzmichov when I am there eating. Those who arrived last week left this morning.'

'How do you know that?'

'The maids came up to clean the rooms. I expect there will be some more by next week.'

'Mr Kuzmichov must have a lot of business acquaintances or a vast number of friends,' observed Vasilis. 'I understand he has been in the shipping business for years and probably travelled all over the world so that could account for the number of people he knows. Now, what would you like to eat, Dimitra?'

Vasilis felt he had probed sufficiently for details of the men who arrived at the hotel and now he wished to return to Elounda and tell Panayiotis.

Kuzmichov was in the foyer of the hotel when Dimitra returned and looked at her speculatively.

'Was that Mr Iliopolakis that I saw you having lunch with?'

Dimitra blushed to the roots of her hair, 'Yes, sir. I was gone no longer than an hour.'

'What did he want?'

'Want? Nothing.'

'So why was he meeting you?'

'He was in town to meet with his architect.'

Kuzmichov nodded. 'Very courteous of him to invite you to join him for lunch.'

'I appreciated the gesture. Is there anything else, sir, or shall I return to my work now?'

'No, there's nothing more, but I'd rather you did not make a habit of meeting people during the day. The evening is the time for socialising.'

'Yes, sir.' Dimitra hurried towards the lift. She would have to refuse any future invitations from Mr Iliopolakis if he was visiting Heraklion.

Vasilis drove back to Elounda feeling that he had had a successful day. He would tell Panayiotis that Dimitra was sure the men had left and she expected some more to arrive at the beginning of the next week. Although he had said he wanted to join Panayiotis on a jetty he did not relish spending the early hours of each day for an indeterminate amount of time in the hope of seeing activity over by the canal. There was also the question of a viable excuse to Cathy. She would accept one night, maybe two, but she would not be happy for him to participate in fishing with Panayiotis for any longer than that.

'Is Panayiotis around?' asked Vasilis.

'I saw him leave about one thirty. He was wearing his uniform so I expect he was on his way to work. Why do you want him?'

'I was going to ask if he would be willing to come to the garden centre with me tomorrow and help me with the sacks of compost. I could then ask him to speak to Blerim and see if he would come and fill them for you. Once that's done I could take you to the garden centre for you to choose some plants.'

'It could be a little late for planting most things. Geraniums might be suitable. They don't seem to mind it being hot and dry although they'll still need to be watered regularly.'

'I hadn't thought about watering. You can't possibly carry heavy watering cans to and from the kitchen. I'll ask Palamakis to come and install a tap outside so you can have a hose connected.'

'That should be done before we get any compost or I visit the garden centre for plants,' replied Cathy practically. 'I can decide how I want the pots arranged in the meantime.'

'You are not to try to move them yourself. I can do that for you.'

'I couldn't possibly manage the very large ones,' smiled Cathy. 'Even John had quite a problem carrying them through.'

'You are not to struggle with any of them. I'll be here and you just tell me where you want them.'

'We could ask Ronnie for ideas.'

Vasilis shook his head. 'I think we have imposed upon her enough.'

'I'm sure she enjoyed helping to design this apartment and was so pleased when I did everything she had suggested.'

'I'll give it some thought,' said Vasilis, not prepared to admit that he had asked Ronnie to help him with the plans for the house on the shore. 'She's probably busy with her painting now.'

'That's something else I've been thinking about. Do you think she could scale up one of her paintings so we could have it up on that wall? If I measured the space between the wall lights and gave her the dimensions it could fit there.'

'I thought you were planning to place your parents' photographs up there.'

Cathy nodded. 'I was, and then I decided it would be more suitable to hang them above the bookcase when it has been built.'

'Something else I'll need to speak to Mr Palamakis about. I'd forgotten about the bookcase,' admitted Vasilis. 'I've been thinking too much about the building of the new house now we have moved in here.'

'I should have asked,' Cathy said contritely. 'How did your meeting with the architect go?'

'Quite well. He seemed to understand my needs. I met Dimitra for lunch again.'

'I thought you said you were no longer interested in "The Central".'

'I was curious about the men that Panayiotis and I saw and wondered if they had been taken there.'

'And?' asked Cathy.

'She confirmed that some men had arrived earlier in the week and left this morning.'

'So that was really why you wanted to speak to Panayiotis. Bags of compost was just an excuse,' exclaimed Cathy triumphantly.

Vasilis shook his head. 'I was going to ask him to help me.'

John sat in the kitchen with his mother. 'I've had an idea,' he announced.

Marianne raised her eyebrows. 'Then you'd better tell me about it. Are you suggesting that you and Nicola go over to New Orleans to visit her parents leaving the children with us?'

John shook his head. 'No, not yet. We could do that when Grandma decides she is ready to go home. It would save you having to travel to London with her.'

'And leave me with three young children to look after!'

'Bryony would be here to help out, but that's not what I wanted to talk to you about. Dad is going to be sixty in ten days time. I thought we ought to throw a party for him.'

'A party?' Marianne frowned. 'It's almost mid-season; everyone is busy.'

'I'm sure it could be arranged. Saff could close early for once and the rest of us are usually free during the evenings. We just need to choose a day when there isn't an airport run.'

Marianne smiled. 'Actually that is a good idea, John. I'll look at the bookings and see when there is a suitable space.'

'I told Nick you'd agree. It has to be kept a secret from Dad, though. I want it to be a surprise. You give me a suitable date and I'll do the rest.'

'Including the catering?' asked Marianne.

'I'd hate to give everyone food poisoning. That is something far better left to you ladies. I'll let you know how many people are coming well in advance.'

'Who are you thinking of asking?'

'All of us and Uncle Andreas of course. Vasi and Saff, Vasilis and Cathy, along with Ron and Ackers. He may refuse to close the taverna in which case it will just be Ron. Then there's Monika. I thought I ought to ask Theo so that will mean including her mother and I'd certainly ask Dimitris.'

Marianne counted up the numbers quickly. 'That's twenty people.'

John shrugged. 'You know you'll cope. Look how well you catered for Great Grandma's hundredth and there were far more guests then.'

'I also had some outside help.'

'Then arrange some this time, just make sure Dad doesn't get to hear a word about it.'

Panayiotis was interested when Vasilis told him men had arrived at "The Central" and left four days later.

'Dimitra said she expects some more will arrive within a few days.'

'She couldn't be more specific?'

'No, and I took your advice and didn't press her for any more information about them.'

Panayiotis consulted his diary. 'I'm on at two in the afternoon until ten at night next week. I'll go down as soon as I've arrived home and changed and had something to eat.'

'I'll come with you,' said Vasilis with alacrity.

'You don't have to and it could be a complete waste of time,' warned Panayiotis.

'I'll take a chance the first night you plan to go down. I can't leave Cathy every night, but I'll tell her we're going fishing from a jetty on that occasion. I'll drive her along there and show her whereabouts we'll be so she'll see there's nothing to worry about.'

'I understand. Come with me the first evening and if we see nothing I'll go alone after that.'

Cathy looked at her husband suspiciously. 'Why should you want to come this far along? There are jetties much closer.'

'Panayiotis said this was a good location.'

'For fishing or for looking for suspicious activity on the opposite shore? I'm not stupid, Vasilis. Tell me the truth.'

'Both,' admitted Vasilis. 'We're planning to do some fishing and watch the canal to see if anyone arrives.'

'Suppose they see you? They could be dangerous criminals and attack you.'

'Why should they attack a couple of men who are fishing?'

'I don't like it, Vasilis. Could I sit in the car so I could call for help if there is a problem?'

'Be sensible, Cathy. If I thought I was in any danger I would not accompany Panayiotis and I would certainly not involve you. Even if you did call someone for help it would be far too late by the time they arrived to do anything. I've told Panayiotis that I'll go down with him on one occasion. If we see nothing I'll not come down again.'

'And if you do see something?'

'If we see people coming ashore and being driven away in a Mercedes Panayiotis has no intention of challenging them. He says he'll ask for some professional surveillance to be carried out. I couldn't possibly be involved in that as it will be a police matter.'

'You'll only go down with Panayiotis the one night?'

Vasilis nodded. 'I promise, Cathy. I'm very curious to know what they are up to and if Kuzmichov is involved in any way, but I'm also happy to leave the investigation up to the police if Panayiotis feels they should become involved. I'm not going to play detective.'

'Have you heard anything back from Barry?' asked Lucy.

Peter shook his head. 'He said he would contact his colleagues at Gatwick but these things take time and they're sure to be busy. Why?'

'I had two more men come in today. One claimed to be a gastroenterologist and the other a dietician. It seems too much of a coincidence that they all have British passports but gained their qualifications in Syria and have been working there for years.'

'Probably decided that now was the time to leave due to the fighting in the area.'

'If they're all doctors or specialists I would not have expected them to be given permission to leave. They would be needed in the hospitals there.'

'They may have been unable to stop them from leaving as they hold British passports. You've seen how many – a dozen or so? That's very few when you think how many doctors there must be in the country.'

'Fourteen now. There could be others who have applied to different hospitals.'

'Or they could have gone to the Job Centre as you suggested and been offered acceptable work.'

'Is there any way that could be checked out?'

'They will probably say that their records are confidential and you don't know which Job Centre any of them went to.'

Panayiotis knocked quietly on Vasilis's door at one in the morning 'Are you ready?' he asked. 'I've brought a second rod for you.'

'I hadn't thought about that,' admitted Vasilis. 'How much do I owe you?'

'Nothing. It's my old one..'

'Cathy's in bed. I'll just go and check on her, although I expect she's asleep. We'll take my car then if she does need me I can drive home.'

'What's in your bag?' asked Vasilis as they walked towards his car.

'Some bait, binoculars and a flask of coffee, along with a separate bag for any fish that we catch.'

'Will they be large enough to eat? I've only seen some small grey ones around.'

'They grow to a considerable size. You can grill them, provided you have plenty of lemon juice on them they are quite palatable.'

Panayiotis placed the fishing rods between the seats and the bag at his feet. 'Have you ever fished with a rod before?'

'I've never had the opportunity.'

'I'll prepare it for you and show you how to cast and reel in if you get a nibble.'

'Where do you want to stop?' Vasilis drove slowly down the steep hill to the coast road and looked at his plot of land as he passed. Provided Mr Sfyrakos had done as he promised work would be able to start in a few weeks or even earlier if the contractor was available to clear and level the land.

'Drive almost to the Causeway and then you can park up. We'll go to the beach behind the bushes and bathing huts. Let's hope there's no one else around.'

'Is there likely to be?'

'Could be someone else fishing from the same area or a local couple taking advantage of the seclusion. We can always move a little further away. The fisherman won't be happy to see competition but a couple will probably go away.'

Vasilis was relieved to see there was no one else in the vicinity as he carried a rod and followed Panayiotis down onto the beach. Panayiotis opened his bag and took out his binoculars, scanning the opposite shore and the canal.

'No sign of anyone at the moment, but it's early yet.' He hung the binoculars round his neck and removed a tin from the bag. Inside was crawling with maggots and Vasilis took a step back.

'What are they for?'

'Bait. I'll show you how to put one on the hook so it doesn't come off when you cast.'

Vasilis shuddered. 'I can't touch those.'

'They won't hurt you, but if you're squeamish I'll put it on for you.'

Vasilis watched as Panayiotis speared a maggot onto the hook.

'Hold the rod firmly and have the line behind you. Swing it over your head and let the reel run out until it you see the float in the water. Then all you have to do is hold it steady and wait for a fish to bite.'

It seemed all too easy as Panayiotis explained but Vasilis found it difficult to swing the float more than a foot into the sea.

With a grin Panayiotis took the rod from him, checked there was still a maggot on the hook and cast. 'You're keeping the reel too tight. Hold on to this and I'll get mine ready.'

Almost immediately Panayiotis felt a tug on his line and reeled in, unhooking the small fish from the barb and throwing it back. Despite Vasilis's best attempts at casting and Panayiotis continually placing a fresh maggot on the hook for him any fish in the area ignored him. This was no more interesting than when they had trawled up and down the bay hoping to catch a squid and Vasilis was pleased that he had only agreed to come out with his neighbour on the one occasion.

'How long do you plan to stay here?' he asked.

'If there's no sign of anyone in another hour we'll give up. I did say we could be unlucky.'

Vasilis felt his mobile 'phone vibrate in his pocket and he drew it out in alarm. 'What's wrong, Cathy?'

'Nothing. I woke up and found you were still not home so I thought I'd call. Have you caught any fish?'

'None at all, but Panayiotis has. We'll be leaving in about an hour unless we see anything happening. Go back to sleep.'

'Sorry about that,' apologised Vasilis as he slipped his mobile back into his pocket.

Panayiotis nodded. It was just as well there was no activity on the opposite shore that night and Vasilis was not planning to join him again if his wife was going to 'phone at inopportune moments.

Barry called on Lucy and Peter and accepted the glass of whisky he was offered. 'I've received a phone call from Stuart. He's spoken to some of the others who were on duty over the past months. They were not very helpful. Many passengers arrive from various parts of the world with British passports so they don't need to go through the Immigration channel. I mentioned Lucy's concerns and Stuart agreed that there seemed to be more Syrian doctors arriving than one would expect but none of them have been brought to the attention of Immigration.'

'They all seemed to have visited Crete before they came here. Why didn't they fly direct from Syria to Heathrow?' asked Lucy.

'That would seem logical, there are no direct flights out from Syria at present. That may have been the only way they were able to travel.'

'What about the neighbouring countries? There must be direct flights from them.'

'It may have been cheaper if they travelled to Crete and came that way. Stuart says he will contact the air lines and ask them to look at their passenger manifesto.'

'Will they have details of all their passengers?'

'They are obliged to keep them for a certain amount of time. Stuart has taken your concern seriously, Lucy. If illegals of any nationality are getting into the country we need to find out how and stop them. These men may claim they are doctors and have papers to prove it, but can you read Arabic?'

Lucy shook her head. 'Of course not.'

'They were probably hoping their papers would be taken at face value and no questions asked. It was probably a bit of a shock to them when you mentioned retraining and assessment.'

'They've none of them returned any of the forms to me, but they could have sent them to another hospital.'

'It's more likely they were unable to answer some of the questions and thought it better not to return the papers anywhere. May I continue to keep the records you gave me?'

'Yes, although I probably shouldn't have taken the list out of the hospital. All records are supposed to be confidential.'

'It could help Stuart to track them. I'll not say where I obtained the list from and let you know if Stuart turns up anything. Must go, Charlotte said she'd have the supper on the table at seven thirty and then she's going out. It's her Whist evening.' Stuart winked and drained his glass. 'It's really a good excuse for a group of them to get together and gossip.'

Panayiotis went fishing for two more nights before he heard a car travelling along the coast road and saw the Mercedes driving across the Causeway. He trained his binoculars on it and watched as it pulled off the road and parked between the windmills. Patiently he waited until he finally saw someone emerge and begin to walk up the road to the small beach. He strained his ears but was unable to hear the splash of oars. Concentrating on the canal he eventually saw a dinghy appear and three quick flashes of a torch from the beach.

The occupants of the dinghy jumped ashore and the dinghy rowed back through the canal. No one moved and Panayiotis guessed they were waiting for more people to arrive in the dinghy. He was not disappointed when half an hour later the dinghy returned and three more men jumped out onto the small beach. As soon as they had landed the person who had met them began to lead them up to the road and down to the waiting car.

Panayiotis laid down his fishing rod and took up a position behind the sparse bushes that lined the coast road. He heard the car approaching and could see the dimmed headlights intermittently as it crossed the Causeway. He raised his binoculars to his eyes as the car drew nearer but as it passed him by he was unable to see the occupants due to the tinted windows, although he was able to read the number plate. He watched as the car drove steadily along the road and up the hill when he finally lost sight of the lights.

He made a note of the registration number before he packed away his fishing tackle. There was nothing he could do at present, but he would speak to Inspector Antonakis and request that some men be put on surveillance duty in a week's time. Once he had checked that the number plate was the same as the car owned by the Russian at the hotel he would ask for Chief Inspector Solomakis in Heraklion to be informed. He was sure Inspector Antonakis would be able to persuade Solomakis to send a couple of his officers to the hotel and investigate once it was confirmed that some more men had arrived.

July 2015
Week Four

Panayiotis sat in Inspector Antonakis office and the Inspector listened to him patiently.

'How have you obtained this information?' he asked.

'I don't want to mention any names or go into details at this stage, but one of the workers at a hotel in Heraklion was concerned about visitors not being registered and that they did not appear to be paying for their stay at the hotel.'

'Why should this be any of their business?'

'The person is in charge of checking that the accounts agree before passing them on to the owner. She did not want to be accused of inefficiency by not noticing the discrepancy. She mentioned it to the owner and he said the visitors were his private guests.'

'So there is no problem.'

'She was still unhappy and spoke to the previous owner of the establishment.'

'And what did he say?'

'He agreed that it was somewhat unorthodox, but not his concern as he was no longer the owner.'

Inspector Antonakis nodded agreement. 'I don't see that it is any of our business.'

'When he talked to the lady she mentioned that the new owner had bought a large Mercedes to transport guests if necessary. I invited my neighbour, who happens to be the previous owner of the hotel, to go out fishing with me one night. We cruised around and were close to the canal when we saw a Mercedes arrive and park behind the ruined windmill. I cut the lights on my boat and watched through my binoculars.'

'Why should you do that?'

'I thought a robbery might be planned at the Kanali. A woman walked from the car to a small beach and waited there. I then heard some sound coming from the canal and a dinghy was rowed through. Three men jumped ashore at the beach and the dinghy went back through the canal. I expected the group to go to the Kanali, thinking my assumption that a robbery was to take place was correct, but they waited on the beach until the dinghy returned with some more men aboard. Once they were on the shore the woman led them to the Mercedes and they drove back over the Causeway and up the hill.'

Inspector Antonakis frowned. 'I still do not understand why you are telling me.'

'The previous owner had been told that a group of men would arrive approximately every ten days. The men often left wet and dirty marks on the carpeting but these were the men the new owner claimed were his private guests whom he had met at the airport. The man responsible for cleaning the car said that it often returned very dirty, both inside and out, the mats being wet and having shingle embedded in them.'

'So where have these men come from?'

'I don't know, sir. I took it upon myself to undergo surveillance of the area on another occasion and the same events occurred. It could be that drug traffickers are being brought in that way.'

'It's possible, but unlikely that they would be taken to a hotel. More likely to be dropped off at Hersonissos and Malia. Did you follow the car?'

'No sir. The first time I was out in my boat and last night I did not have my car with me.'

'So what are you asking of me?'

'I'd like to request some men put at my disposal to keep a watch on the canal. If they see men transported through and collected by car then the car should be followed. I have the license plate number and it is the vehicle that belongs to the hotel. I checked that out with a colleague in Heraklion.'

'There could be a simple and innocent explanation. We wouldn't want to go into the hotel with accusations only to find that they were staff who had been out for the day and being taken back.'

'If that was so it would be more logical that they would return to Heraklion harbour. I saw a group arrive last night and according to the information that I have been able to glean they stay four or five days at the hotel and then they leave. A few days later a new group arrive. I don't think there would be any benefit in placing men over there until next week.'

'You realise that if something illegal is taking place your informants will be called upon to make statements as witnesses?'

'I'm sure they would be willing to do that if it was necessary.'

'I don't suggest that you undertake any more surveillance on your own. I'll put two officers at your disposal and it will be necessary for you to take them to the area; once during the day and again at night. They will need to be familiar with the area.'

'Thank you, sir. Let me know the names of the officers and I'll speak to them. I think we should be out of uniform so as not to attract attention when I show them the canal and the beach.'

Inspector Antonakis nodded his agreement. 'Let me know when you propose to start the surveillance operation so I can relieve them of their other duties.'

Mr Palamakis had sent Giorgos to install an outside tap so Cathy could attach a hose pipe to water her plants. Whilst there he took the measurements for the bookcase that Vasilis asked for and asked if there were any more jobs that needed doing that morning.

Vasilis was about to say there was nothing when he thought of the compost that Cathy needed. Panayiotis had told him that the car had appeared again and the passengers had arrived through the canal.

'Do you want me to 'phone Dimitra and ask if there are any new arrivals?'

Panayiotis shook his head. 'I've officially handed the matter over to the police so it is far better that you do not contact her. The registration of the car is the same as the one owned by Kuzmichov so we can be reasonably certain that the men were taken to the hotel. Inspector Antonakis is going to allow me two men next week to watch the beach and the windmills.'

'What happens after that?'

'Nothing. The men will send in their reports and if Inspector Antonakis agrees that further investigation is needed he'll arrange surveillance for the following week. In the meantime he'll speak with Chief Inspector Solomakis in Heraklion and suggest that the car is followed. Assuming that the car goes to the hotel the driver and the occupants will be questioned. If they cannot explain their activities to the satisfaction of the police they will be taken to the station for further interrogation.'

'I'll be interested to know the outcome,' said Vasilis eagerly.

'I'll let you know when I know,' replied Panayiotis. 'Now I'm going home to catch up on some of my lost sleep. I'm on six until two as from tomorrow.'

Vasilis did not feel he could ask his neighbour to go to the garden centre with him.

'How many sacks of compost do you want?' asked Giorgos.

Vasilis considered. 'Three, I think, but maybe I should get four.'

'If you don't use it all now it will last until next year and Mrs Iliopolakis will be able to top the pots up with it and buy some more if she has any new plants.'

'Have you seen anything of Blerim?' asked Vasilis.

'Not since we finished your job at the apartment. Why? Did you want him?'

'I just wondered if he was working and also how his daughter was getting on with the therapist at the hospital.'

Giorgos shrugged. 'I don't know the answer to either of those questions. My Grandpa might know.'

'They're not important. Where are you working at the moment?'

'Renewing a floor for a silly woman who let her sink overflow. Luckily for her it was on the ground floor and only damaged the floor and storage area beneath.'

'Easily done,' said Vasilis placatingly.

'Very easily if you put the plug in the sink, turn the tap on and then go out to do your shopping,' replied Giorgos. 'Some people have no sense. The water had seeped down between the floor tiles and she said she only realised she'd left the tap running when she walked back in and had to mop up the mess. Of course the tiles were laid on hardboard and that had rotted so I've had to pull everything up.'

Giorgos continued to complain about the foolish woman and her floor all the way to the garden centre.

'You sound very aggrieved.'

'Of course I am. It's my stupid aunt so I'm expected to do the work for nothing as she's family.'

Vasilis made a mental note to remind Cathy to check that all the taps were turned off before she went out.

'Four more pots are ordered, Uncle Yannis,' announced John.

Yannis looked up with a smile. 'Who wants them?'

'The museum shop in Aghios Nikolaos wants three and the other is to go to Chania.'

'Chania – that's miles away.'

'I know. It will be cheaper to send that one by a courier rather than pay for petrol to drive there and back. I'm not even sure if I'd be able to manage it in one day. By the time it had been unpacked and checked to ensure there was no damage I might have to stay over night.'

'And you'd charge me for that as well no doubt.'

'It would be your pot that I was delivering. I would have to cover my expenses. We worked out how much delivery charges would be when we first set up the web site. The cost of the petrol comes out of that. I should have added in a charge for my time. When I'm doing your deliveries I'm not working for Dad.' John did not mention that his father still paid him the same each week whatever he was doing.

'You could go to the wholesalers in Aghios for your father when you take the pot. That way I wouldn't have to pay you for your time.'

'You're a wily businessman, Uncle. I'll see if Dad needs anything. In the meantime we'll get the pot for Chania packed and I'll arrange a courier collection.'

'Which one do they want?'

'The large pithoi that has a rope decoration on it. That will be a good one to get out of the way.'

'And the other three?'

'Attic ware. I'll need you to help me to ensure I send the right ones. They all look much the same to me.'

'I don't know where anything is now you've moved them all around,' grumbled Yannis.

'Leave it with me. I'll track them down and let you know when I've discovered their hiding place.'

Vasilis was delighted when he received a phone call from Mr Sfyrakos to say that the plans for his house had been passed.

'I haven't mentioned your idea of terracing, but you can probably do that at a later date without asking permission. I suggest you contact Mr Sukiyakis and arrange for him to visit the site and discuss your needs with him. He says he's unable to give you a price until he's seen the amount of work involved.'

Mr Sukiyakis arrived in Elounda the following day and met Vasilis down on the coast road. He eyed the area of land and looked at the plan he had been given.

'I'll need accurate measurements. This is only an approximation; nothing definite. How far back from the road do you want the building and how large do you plan the area at the rear?'

'The back is not important. Whatever land is left over after the building is completed needs to be raised so it is on the same level. Mr Sfyrakos said it would be practical to do that once the retaining wall at the back was erected.'

'And the height of the wall at the front?'

'At least ten metres, so that will probably be the same at the back. The wall bordering the pavement need only be two metres.'

'Well the first thing we will need to do is level the whole area. It's been used as a rubbish dump. I understand that you are planning to have a large patio at the front and want a swimming pool. You need to decide on the measurements for that.'

Vasilis frowned. 'Can you advise me? I don't want to make a mistake that cannot be rectified later.'

Mt Sukiyakis looked at the plans. 'According to these, the living area will spread across the whole width of the land, leaving a walk way at one side. Once the area has been levelled we can mark out the area. Provided you are satisfied with the size of the rooms and the patio area we can place the steel supports into position and make a start on digging down to accommodate them and cementing them into place.'

'There has to be a garage space at the side with a lift and stairs leading up to the apartment.'

'So I understand. There will need to be additional steel supports to take the weight of the floor you plan to have above the garage area. Between the steels you will need reinforced concrete. Leave it with me, Mr Iliopolakis. I'll bring a couple off men down with me along with the necessary machinery tomorrow and we can make a start. You live locally, I understand, so if I have any problems or queries you'd be able to come down to the site?'

'Certainly,' agreed Vasilis. 'I can come down every day.'

'I doubt that will be necessary once we start to make progress. There is just one more thing, Mr Iliopolakis. My men expect to be paid weekly. Is that a problem?'

'Not at all. I can even give you a retainer now if that would suit you.'

Mr Sukiyakis nodded. 'That would certainly be helpful.'

'I've contacted Vasilis and Cathy and also Vasi and Saff and they say they'll be able to attend. Ronnie says she'll definitely come and do her best to persuade Ackers to close that evening. I'll see Dimitris tonight when I take Skele back and go up to Plaka tomorrow and ask Monika.'

'I thought you had to deliver some pots to Aghios today.'

'I'm on parental duty this afternoon. Nick has to take Yiannis to the clinic for his next jab. She gave me the choice, look after the girls or take him. I chose the girls. He screamed the place down last time. I can deliver the pots tomorrow, and drive on to Plaka afterwards. There'll be someone here to attend to the courier when he arrives, won't there?'

'I'm sure there will. Uncle Yannis won't be going anywhere and either Nicola or I will be around.'

'It's probably better that Uncle Yannis doesn't deal with it. I don't trust him not to change his mind at the last minute and say he'll keep the pot. He was terribly reluctant to let Cathy have the pots she wanted for the garden.'

'He doesn't like the thought of them being used as planters. Are you going to call on Uncle Andreas or do you want me to 'phone him?'

'I'd rather leave it until nearer the time. He'd be quite likely to mention it to Grandma Elena and she'll tell Grandma Marisa and before you know it everyone will have heard including Dad and then it will be no surprise for him.'

'I'm hoping we will get an invitation to Vasilis and Cathy now their apartment is completed and they have moved in.'

'I understand there are one or two finishing touches they want to make before they have visitors.'

'How do you know that?' asked Marianne.

'I dropped a few hints when I was speaking to Cathy yesterday. She said she was still finding a home for many of their possessions and a number of items were still packed up in boxes. I'm sure once she is satisfied we'll be invited to a viewing.'

'I would have expected her to want to get the apartment fully organised before she thought about the garden.'

'They probably want to sit out there in the evenings now the weather is good. Where are you proposing to hold Dad's party? Inside or out?'

'I'll arrange a buffet in the kitchen and we can all eat outside. If the sand blows over we can always move into the lounge.'

'Cathy asked if you would like her to bring something.'

Marianne shook her head. 'I know it's customary but she really doesn't need to.'

'That's what I told her, but she'll probably take no notice.'

Ibrahim and Aziz sat in the park and waited. Ibrahim felt pleasantly warm now but when he had first arrived he had been cold the whole time as he only had his roll neck jumper and a windcheater for extra warmth. He wondered just how cold it would become during the winter months as he certainly did not have any spare money to buy a thicker coat. It had been necessary to purchase two new pairs of socks as his others were worn through at the heels and his shoes needed to be mended. The last time it rained he had arrived home with damp feet.

Despite all the men visiting the Job Centre frequently nothing more profitable had been offered to them in the way of work. He considered that he and Aziz were fortunate to have the work at the supermarket. At least they were not out doors in all weather like their companions. It was also a bonus that they were able to purchase food cheaply. He would always examine the containers of food that was out of date and due to be thrown away, removing any that still looked perfectly edible and take it back with him.

Ahmed and Abdul arrived and Salihe was with them.

'I wish we could go back home,' sighed Ahmed. 'At least we would be able to find some decent work.'

'Do you think it would it be safe to return?' asked Ibrahim. 'I certainly don't. From all I've heard the fighting has intensified.'

'I've not taken part in any of the fighting,' declared Salihe. 'Have you?'

Ibrahim shook his head. 'The only time I came into contact with any fighters was in the hospital. If an injured group came in we were all expected to attend to them. You probably saw more of them, Ahmed, as you would have had to give them anaesthetic.'

'They had to be given priority over the other patients,' grumbled Ahmed. 'Even emergency operations for ordinary people had to go to the end of the queue.'

'So what are we going to do?' asked Abdul. 'We can't find decent work and we've no money.'

'If we went to the Immigration authorities do you think they would help us?' asked Aziz.

'Possibly, but we'd be bound to be questioned about our arrival,' frowned Ibrahim. 'We could be prosecuted for entering the country illegally and put in prison.'

'I'd rather be in prison here than in Syria. We wouldn't last long.'

'Probably not,' agreed Abdul.

'I met a man called Jamal last week. I asked him how he had come here and he said I'd never believe him if he told me. I challenged him and he finally admitted that he and his friends came over the same way as we did. Do you think the authorities would believe us?' asked Salihe.

'I was approached originally and told that if I was interested in the proposition my name would be put on the list along with others and I'd have to take my turn,' added Ahmed. 'It sounds as though a number of people were taken in by stories of the good life we could expect over here.'

'So what can we do?' asked Salihe.

Ibrahim shrugged. 'We have the choice of struggling on and hoping things will improve or apply to the Immigration authorities, admit that we arrived illegally and ask for asylum.'

'If we were accepted as refugees would we be able to get proper jobs?' asked Ahmed. 'I really want to work as an anaesthetist again.'

'I don't know,' admitted Ibrahim, 'But at least we'd be able to fill in the forms that offer retraining and reassessment. If we were placed in a detention centre temporarily we would have a roof over our heads and some decent food. By the time they had looked into our cases, even if we were sent back eventually, the fighting could be over by then. If we all went to the authorities together they would have to listen to us. Speak to your friends and ask their opinion. Meet me back here in a week and let me know if they are happy to stay or want to take our chance with Immigration.'

Panayiotis drove the two officers who had been assigned to surveillance duty down to Elounda. He parked in a lay-by half way down the hill and the men looked across the bay.

'It's a fabulous view,' remarked Yiorgo.

'I agree, but we'll not be able to see anything from up here,' said Sotiris.

'Of course not,' smiled Panayiotis. 'I just wanted to show you the general location. There's a road that runs along by the shore leading to the Causeway. There's a bridge across the canal that leads to a taverna and the windmills. That's where I've seen the car parked. The road from there leads around to a small beach and that's where the men who arrive are met. We'll go down to the taverna and have a drink and then wander around to look for somewhere strategic where you will be able to watch whatever happens without being noticed.'

'If anything happens,' said Sotiris doubtfully 'According to Antonakis you couldn't say when the event would happen again.'

Panayiotis nodded. 'I know, but I'm sure it will. It's just a question of patience.' He continued driving down towards the village and took the steep hill leading to the coast road.

'Some nice places along here,' said Sotiris as Panayiotis drove slowly, avoiding the vehicles coming towards him and the pedestrians who wandered into the road.

'Mostly self catering establishments or hotels. Very popular with the tourists.'

'I'm not surprised,' observed Sotiris.. 'Wouldn't mind staying here myself for a week or two.'

'Nothing to stop you.'

'Doubt if I could afford it. I'd have to bring my wife and the children.'

'You could always come here for the day. It's close enough to Aghios Nikolaos.'

'That's possible. I'll suggest it when the children are on school holidays,' agreed Sotiris.

'What do you usually do with them?'

'They amuse themselves with their friends. My wife works and with my irregular hours it's difficult to spend time all together.'

Panayiotis drove across the Causeway and over the bridge. He parked along with the other vehicles that were already there and the men climbed out of the car.

'Although we're officially on duty we're all in plain clothes so we should be able to have a beer,' said Panayiotis as he led the way to the Kanali. 'No official talk. We're just tourists.'

As they sat there a small boat came across from the other side of the water and navigated carefully through the canal.

Panayiotis looked at the waiter. 'Do boats often come through here?'

'All the time.'

'Not at night, surely?'

'One or two of the experienced fishermen might risk it. A short cut back to Elounda.'

'Where does the road lead on to?'

'Up to the white house. They do bed and breakfast and just drinks during the day. There's a turning that leads to two small churches.'

'They could be interesting,' remarked Panayiotis. 'When we've finished our beer we could drive over and have a look.'

'Won't be much to see. They're only open on their Saint's Day.'

'Any decent beaches around there should we decide to have a swim?'

Yiorgo and Sotiris looked at Panayiotis in surprise. He had certainly not told them they might be going swimming.

'Some people go round there. It's pretty rocky and they like to snorkel.'

'Haven't got that kind of equipment with us. We'll have to come back another day. What time do you close at night?'

'We're usually open until midnight. Depends how late the customers stay.'

'Long day,' observed Panayiotis.

'Have to work the hours during the season,' shrugged the waiter. 'We close in October and don't open again until May so we need to make our money whilst we can.' He placed the bill for their drinks into a small glass. 'Would you like the menu?'

'Not at the moment. We're going to have a wander around.'

'The path to the mosaic is up by the side of the taverna.'

Panayiotis nodded. 'We'll certainly have a look at that before we leave.'

'We're tourists, remember,' said Panayiotis in a low voice as they lingered over their beer. 'We don't have to rush.'

Finally Panayiotis placed his empty glass on the table and took a note from his wallet. 'Anyone got a few coins?'

Yiorgo produced two Euros and Panayiotis added it to the money he left in the glass along with the bill.

'Right, we'll go and have a look at the mosaic and then go for a walk up the road.'

Dutifully Yiorgo and Sotiris followed him and tried to look interested when they saw the mosaic.

'Shame they don't cover it in the winter,' observed Panayiotis. 'More is getting washed away each year.'

'Couldn't it be restored?' asked Sotiris.

'Probably, but who is going to pay for it? It's on the Kanali's land so I expect they own it.'

'If I was fortunate enough to have that in my back yard I'd make sure it was well preserved and then charge visitors to have a look,' said Yiorgo.

'Restoration costs money and then they'd have to provide a roof over it. They probably find it more profitable just to run the taverna. Visitors come over to have a look at the mosaic and most people feel obliged to buy a drink as the entrance is free. You certainly need a drink on a hot day when you've walked across the Causeway and they don't all know about the white house.'

'Are we going up there?'

Panayiotis nodded. 'First we have to look around by the windmills. We need a convenient place for one of you to be able to stand and not be noticed.'

The two officers looked at each other dubiously. The ground was open and used as a car park. There was nowhere obvious where they would be able to conceal themselves. If they sat on the rocks down by the canal they would be seen by anyone travelling through and under the bridge.

Panayiotis led the way onto the road where a few sparse trees and bushes grew. A low wall bordered the road and led down to the beach where boulders vied for a place amongst rubbish and weed. He jumped over the wall and stood behind the trees.

'I can see you,' said Yiorgo.

Panayiotis moved a little closer to the canal and sat down on a rock.

'I can still see you.'

Panayiotis sighed and regained the road. 'That place is no good, then. Down by the windmills is useless, it's far too open.'

'There's a bit of a building there.' Yiorgo waved his arm.

'Go over and see if you are able to get behind the wall. Tell me if you see us walk past.'

Panayiotis turned his back on the tumbledown building and walked towards the road when Yiorgo hurried to catch up with them.

'I think it would be ideal, but there's a rusty gate and wire in the entrance. If that could be removed it would be easy enough to stand there unseen.'

'We'll come back tonight after the Kanali is closed with some tools and see what we can do.'

'It might be easier and less noticeable if we removed some stones from the rear wall,' suggested Yiorgo. 'It isn't very high now and if we could take it down half a metre I ought to be able step over.'

'We'll investigate both options,' said Panayiotis. 'That will be your position, Yiorgo.'

They left the car park and walked a short distance further up the road where Panayiotis pointed out the small beach. 'Now we have to find somewhere you can be concealed, Sotiris.'

The landward side of the road had bushes with an entrance to an area of waste ground and Sotiris trod carefully between the rocks and rubbish that had been dumped there to get as close to the bushes as possible.

'I can see you, can you see me?'

'Stay there whilst we go down onto the beach and then let me know if you can still see us.'

Panayiotis looked at the shingle that was amongst the sand. There were footprints down by the water and back up to the road, but they could have been made by tourists who had visited the area. Once they returned to the road he examined the soles of his shoes; there were small stones and sand clinging to them.

'Could you see us?' asked Panayiotis.

Sotiris nodded. 'To have a clear view of anyone I'd need to make a small hole in the hedge. I'm not sure how well I'd see people at night.'

'You don't have to be able to recognise them. Just witness them arriving. Unless we can find anywhere better that will be your position, Sotiris.'

'Where are we going to park our car?' asked Yiorgo. 'It's quite a walk back across the Causeway. If I'm watching down by the windmills a car would tell people there was someone in the area.'

'The car park at the white house should be accessible at night, if not you'll have to drive further up the road and park there.'

'Suppose they drive up the road and see it parked?'

'They have no reason to go up there. Once the men have been met I imagine they want to leave this area as quickly as possible. You are both to hold your positions until the car has driven across the bridge. Yiorgo, you will then move to the windmills and watch the car drive across the Causeway and along the coast road and up the hill. Once it has joined the main road you go up to Sotiris's position and then you can both collect the car and go home. We'll leave now and return later tonight, see if we can remove some stones or unblock the entrance to that building and check that the observation areas we've chosen are suitable.'

'And all we have to do is watch what happens and report back?'

'That's right,' agreed Panayiotis.

'Suppose no one arrives? What do we do then?'

'When you are told that the surveillance will commence you are to be here and take up your positions no later than two thirty. If nothing has occurred by five you can stand down and return home.'

August 2015
Week One

'So are you all organised?' asked John of Marianne.

'As much as we can be. How are you going to keep Dad away until after people have started to arrive?'

'I'm going to ask him to come up the shop and taverna. I'll tell him there's something wrong with the lock and ask him to help me fix it.'

'Is there a problem?'

'Not yet, but when I've added a bit of super glue to the mechanism there certainly will be. Dad will have to spend time fiddling around trying to get it to work. I'll then produce a new one and ask him to fix it for me.'

Marianne regarded John sceptically. 'He'll know you are quite capable of dealing with that.'

'I couldn't possibly do it with my bad hand.'

'What's wrong with your hand?'

'I will have cut it badly whilst trying to deal with the lock myself before I called him. Just make sure Marcus has gone into Elounda to collect Uncle Andreas so he can't ask him to come up to help me.'

'Does Marcus know he's doing that?'

'Not yet. I'll tell him when Dad's not around and also phone Uncle Andreas and tell him the arrangements.'

'Uncle Andreas doesn't know?'

'We agreed not to tell him, remember. I called on him after I had delivered the pot to Aghios Nikolaos and asked him if he would like to come up for a meal this evening. He was happy to accept and I said one of us would collect him and take him home.'

'What about our other guests? I hope they know they are expected this evening.'

'They do, Mum. I told you so last week. The only ones I'm not certain of are Ackers and Theo. I know Ron said she would talk to Ackers, so I expect he will be here and if Litsa is coming Theo will probably come as well.'

John called his mother from the taverna. 'Has Marcus gone to collect Uncle Andreas?'

'He left five minutes ago. I told him to take his time.'

'Fine. I'll call Dad now.'

'What do you mean?' asked Giovanni. 'Why can't you lock the taverna door?'

'I don't know. The key just won't turn.'

'Have you sprayed it with lubrication? It's probably just a bit stiff.'

'I have and I made no difference. Can you come up and replace the lock?'

'Me? Why can't you do that?'

'I cut my hand quite badly when I was trying to get the key to work. I may have sprained my wrist as well. It's too painful for me to use. '

Giovanni gave a deep sigh. 'I suppose I'll have to come. I'll look out a spare lock and bring a screw driver with me.'

John grinned with delight. His father had believed him. He squirted a liberal amount of tomato sauce onto his hand and wrapped it around with the handkerchief he had taken from his pocket. The tomato sauce oozed out and John wiped it away carefully. He did not want his father driving him to the hospital once the lock was fixed.

'Let me look at your hand,' said Giovanni. 'It's bleeding through the bandage you've put on.'

'I'll wrap a tea towel round it. I'm sure it's nothing much. Fix the lock and we'll look at my hand when we get back home.'

Giovanni tried in vain to turn the key and finally agreed that a new lock would need to be fitted. He removed the screws and held the lock up.'

'Someone has put super glue inside,' he exclaimed.

'Really?' John feigned surprise. 'There were some children playing around here earlier whilst their parents were shopping. They must have done it for a joke.'

'Some joke!' grunted Giovanni. 'Make sure you speak to the parents tomorrow. We don't want it happening again. Pass me the new lock and hold it in place until I've got the first holding screw in place.'

John deliberately let the lock slip out of line with the screws on three occasions, apologising for his clumsiness. 'If I kneel down I'll be able to see exactly where to line it up.'

Giovanni sighed. A simple matter of changing a lock was taking far too long and John was not really being much help. Finally he straightened up and turned the key.

'That's working fine now. I'll wash my hands and then we can go.'

'Thanks, Dad. I'll ride back on my scooter and take Skele in to Dimitris.'

'You will not,' replied Giovanni firmly. 'You come back in the car with me. You can walk up and collect your scooter tomorrow.'

'That means Skele will have to come in the car with us. I can't leave him here or let him run by the car. If he became tangled up in the wheels you wouldn't see him.'

Giovanni grimaced. He did not like having the dog in his car, insisting that it made it smell, but there was no alternative. 'Come on then. Your mother will be wondering what has happened to us. I said I should only be about ten minutes.'

Giovanni drove back to the house and was surprised at the number of cars that were parked inside his gateway. He frowned. 'Who has decided to pay us a visit on the same evening?'

'I know Uncle Andreas has been invited for a meal,' replied John innocently.

'That looks like Vasi's car. If Saffron is here with him she could have a look at your hand. I can take you up to the hospital if she thinks it needs stitching or your wrist needs an X-ray.'

'That's a good idea. Go on round to the patio. I'll just remove this makeshift bandage and have a wash before I join you.'

'Won't that make it bleed more?'

'I don't think it will do any harm.' John hurried through to the cloakroom, unwrapped his hand, washed away the tomato sauce and sauntered out to the patio.

His father was standing there with a bemused look on his face. 'What's going on?'

Marianne slipped her arm around his waist. 'It's a party. You have an important birthday this week and we all wanted to celebrate it with you.'

'It isn't for two more days,' he managed to stutter.

'We had to arrange everything when there wasn't an airport run. We didn't want you sitting up in Heraklion whilst we were enjoying ourselves down here.'

'John.' Giovanni turned to his son. 'Who put the super glue in the lock?' he asked sternly.

'I did,' admitted John. 'I'll pay for the new one.'

'And your hand?'

'Good as new now it's had a wash.' John held up his hand.

'So your injury and possible sprained wrist was all lies.'

'Not *real* lies, Pappa. It was subterfuge to keep you away from the house until everyone had arrived. We wanted it to be a complete surprise for you. Can I go and bring Skele round?'

Giovanni shook his head and let out his breath. 'I suppose so.' He looked around the gathering. 'It is a surprise to me. I see you all have a glass in your hand. I'd like one also. I can then say thank you to everyone who is here.'

'And we can drink a toast to you and wish you a happy birthday.'

Vasilis had enjoyed Giovanni's birthday party, adroitly avoiding answering any questions about his building plans. Instead he had conferred with Cathy and arranged a morning when Ronnie and Kyriakos could visit.

'I know I've seen the apartment since it was finished, but some of the ideas came from Kyriakos. He can't afford to close again in an evening so the morning would be ideal for us. I can always catch up on my painting later in the day. I've completed the one you asked for and I'll bring it with me.'

'I've been waiting for the bookcase to be finished and installed,' Cathy confessed to Monika. 'There were books everywhere and it just looked a mess. Now they have been tidied away I feel a good deal happier.'

'I hope the authors are in alphabetical order,' smiled Monika. 'You know how particular I am about that.'

'If you're not satisfied I'll give you a hair cut and you can put them in order for me whilst you're there. Shall we make a time for next week? You could close a bit early and come to supper. Bring your mother with you.'

Cathy turned to her husband. 'I don't want to upset anyone in the family by inviting friends before them. Ask Vasi and Saffron if they would like to come tomorrow. I can easily prepare a meal.'

Vasilis agreed. Entertaining would keep Cathy occupied and she would not be asking for a progress report from the architect. Vasilis had not told her that the plans had been passed and work had already started on the site.

'Get out your diary and arrange a convenient date for everyone. We can't really cope with more than two or three at a time if you are planning to cook for them. There isn't sufficient seating around the table and I don't want you to become exhausted by spending hours preparing food. Just do something simple. Finger food would be sufficient.'

Cathy shook her head. 'You can't invite people for a meal and then just give them finger food. Leave it to me and I'm sure I'll manage something acceptable.'

Sotiris and Yiorgo having been assigned to the surveillance duty found the three nights they had been on duty extremely boring. A few cars had travelled along the coast road, one of them had crossed the Causeway and driven up to the white house and on another occasion a small fishing boat had motored through the canal and across the water to Elounda.

'I suppose we have to be grateful that we only have to spend two and a half hours up here,' grumbled Sotiris. 'If we were expected to stay here for a ten hour stretch I'd complain and refuse to do it.'

'That wouldn't go down well with Antonakis. Be grateful that it isn't cold or raining.'

'I'd rather do surveillance sitting in a car. My feet ache with all this standing and I don't like the rustling I hear in the undergrowth.'

'Probably a mouse.'

'More likely a rat or a snake.'

'You wouldn't hear it if it was a snake.'

Sotiris shuddered. 'I'd rather have a rat run across my foot than a snake slither over it.'

'Unless it decided to go up your trouser leg you probably wouldn't know.'

Sotiris paled visibly. 'I'm going to wear boots tomorrow night. I can tuck my trousers into those.'

Yiorgo chuckled at his companion's discomfiture. 'At least we're being given every day off. We could have been expected to turn up for duty as usual each morning.'

'Panayiotis probably saw some fishermen being dropped off and jumped to conclusions. If nothing happens by the end of this week I'm going to ask to be relieved and someone else can take my place.'

'That doesn't explain the car that met them. Who would be willing to transport smelly fishermen in a Mercedes?'

Ibrahim looked at the men who had gathered to meet him in the park. There were four faces that he did not recognise and Abdul introduced them.

'This is Jamal, Mohamed arrived here with him. Mahmoud and Hamza are other men who came with me.'

Ibrahim nodded. 'Have you considered my suggestion that we apply for asylum?'

'We've spent hours talking about it and I went to the library and looked on the internet for information. Apparently we should have requested refugee status in the first safe country we reached after leaving Syria. That would have been Crete. We don't want to be sent back there. We none of us speak the language. We'd be worse off there than we are here.'

'They might not accept us anyway as we moved on,' remarked Hamza.

This was something that Ibrahim had not considered. 'Surely, if we told them that we had accepted transport to England and only spent four days in Crete where we were not allowed to go out unescorted they would take that into account?'

'Possibly, but it would be taking a risk.'

'We could claim that we considered our lives were in danger and that was why we left Syria.'

'That was certainly true,' confirmed Jamal. 'I was lucky to be at the hospital when my home was bombed or I'd not be here now.'

'They'd want to know why we hadn't confessed to entering the country illegally when we first arrived rather than trying to get work,' added Abdul. 'I can't see them being very sympathetic towards us.'

Ibrahim sighed. The men were obviously unwilling to hand themselves over to the authorities. 'Salim and I have decided to approach Immigration. Is any one of you willing to join us?'

'I am,' said Mohamed, speaking for the first time. 'Whatever happens to us we can't be worse off than we are at present.'

'So when shall we go?' asked Ibrahim.

Mohamed shrugged. 'Whenever it suits you. I'm not working.'

Jamal looked at Ibrahim warily. 'You won't mention us, will you?'

'It might be necessary for me to give the names of the men who arrived with Salim and myself, but there should be no need for me to mention you.'

Mohamed did not answer.

Stuart looked at the three men who sat before him. He found the story they had told him about their journey from Syria and subsequent arrival in England unbelievable. They would have to be kept at a detention centre and be thoroughly investigated. It was more likely that they had made their way overland to Turkey and taken trains to finally end up in France and use the British passports they claimed to have to pay for passage on a cross channel ferry. If these three had arrived in that way how many more had made the same journey?

Stuart sent each man to a separate room where they could be interrogated individually. One of them was sure to confess that their original story was false and tell the truth about their method of arrival in the country. He checked their names against the list that Barry had e-mailed to him; they were all on there along with another eleven. It could be worthwhile asking the police to raid the addresses and pick up any other men who were living there. Having confiscated their passports they had been sent away to prove their authenticity or have forgery confirmed. He could ask the airlines and ferry operators to check if the men's names had appeared on their manifestos over the previous few months.

Sotiris and Yiorgo took up their respective positions behind the shrubbery and the ruined building, prepared to have another boring few hours. It was after three in the morning when the lights from a car could be seen on the coast road and then across the Causeway. Yiorgo stiffened as it drew in and parked behind the ruined windmill. He watched as a woman emerged and closed the door quietly behind her. Dressed entirely in black she was difficult to make out in the darkness.

She took the shortest route to the road, making as little noise as possible as she walked. Once at the bridge she looked along the length off the canal and across the bay, then continued to walk up the road and Yiorgo could no longer see her. He wished he could have arranged a signal of some sort with Sotiris so his colleague would know someone had arrived.

Ludmila walked as far as the small beach and sat on a rock. She continued to look across the bay, relieved that there were no fishermen out in their boats and no cars travelling along the coast road. She picked at the skin around her finger nails, hoping Panos would soon arrive.

Sotiris watched patiently until he finally saw two quick flashes of light from the sea and the woman finally rose and went down to the water's edge. He saw some men jump ashore from the dinghy that had arrived and stand in a silent group beside the woman. The wait seemed interminable until the dinghy returned with more men on board and a package was thrown across to the woman once the men were ashore. She immediately turned and indicated that the men should follow her up the beach to the road.

Sotiris hoped he would not have to stand amongst the bushes for much longer. At every sound in the undergrowth he looked down to ensure there was not a snake moving towards him, although he was wearing his boots and had his trouser legs tucked inside.

Eventually Yiorgo saw the woman arrive back at the car along with six men. She opened the boot and handed a small case to each of them. The men removed a shirt from the carrier bag they were carrying and placed the remainder of their belongings inside a case. Having donned the shirt they climbed into the car, Ludmila closed the boot, pushing it down the last few inches and closed the doors to the car in the same manner to make as little noise as possible before she slid behind the steering wheel.

Yiorgo watched her draw away and drive across the bridge where she was then lost from his sight. Intermittently he caught a glimpse of lights as the car drove along the coast road. He walked up the road to where Sotiris emerged from his hiding place, shaking his boots and examining his trousers to ensure that he did not have leaves or insects clinging to him.

Yiorgo greeted him with a grin. 'Something to report at last.'

Inspector Antonakis listened to the two men as they recounted the events of the previous night. 'Could you see where the men came from? They may have been on the opposite headland and ferried across from there.'

'If they were on the other headland why didn't the car go there to meet them?' asked Yiorgo reasonably.' Many of the hotels have their own moorings. I definitely had the impression that they did not want to be seen which was why they had chosen such a deserted area.'

'Did you hear any conversation between any of them?'

'I certainly didn't hear them say anything. Did you Yiorgo?'

Yiorgo shook his head. 'The driver made a point of closing the doors and the boot as quietly as possible. Once in the car they may have talked to each other, but I didn't hear them say a word.'

Inspector Antonakis looked at his desk calendar. 'Assuming this is a regular occurrence there should be some more men arriving some time next week. You will recommence your surveillance of the area in five days time. I'll discuss this with Chief Inspector Solomakis. You have the remainder of today off, but tomorrow and the next four days you will return to your usual duties. I will let you know the advice I receive from Chief Inspector Solomakis and how he wishes to proceed. On your way out ask Panayiotis to come to my office.'

Panayiotis stood before the Inspector, hoping he was not going to be accused of wasting police time and resources.

'You appear to be correct in your assumption that there is something happening that needs further investigation. Are you certain the number you took of the Mercedes is the same as the one as the car at the hotel in Heraklion?' asked Inspector Antonakis.

'Absolutely certain, sir.'

'I'm putting the men back on surveillance duty in five days time. I want you down there as well. As soon as the car leaves the coast road you will telephone me and I will contact Solomakis. I am going to apprise him of the situation and ask him to have men standing by to intercept the car when it arrives. What was the name of the hotel?'

Panayiotis did not think he had ever mentioned the name. 'Used to belong to Mr Vasilis Iliopolakis. "The Central", sir.'

Inspector Antonakis nodded. 'So I also assume he is your neighbour who imparted the information to you originally?'

'Yes, sir.'

'And the name of the employee who brought it to his attention?'

'I'm sorry, he has never told me her name. He just said she was in charge of checking that the accounts agree.'

'I'm sure Mr Iliopolakis will be able to help me.' Inspector Antonakis smiled. 'Please do not confide in him our intentions. I would not like word to get back to the hotel.'

'I'm confident that Mr Iliopolakis would say nothing, but I'll not mention it to him. He's rather involved with the new house he's planning to build down on the coast road.'

Stuart looked at the passenger lists for the cross channel ferries and discounted them. The names of the three men did not appear anywhere. He turned his attention to the information the various air lines had sent through and began to go examine them methodically. Every other week there were six men with Arabian names listed as having boarded a flight from Heraklion that was destined for Gatwick and three of the names were the same as the men who were being interrogated. He stroked his chin thoughtfully. Maybe their story was not as outlandish as he had first thought.

Armed with the information he telephoned the detention centre at Heathrow where the men had been accommodated temporarily. Although technically they were not under arrest they had been told they must not leave the centre until they had permission.

'I'd like to come over and speak to the men from Syria.'

'They have been individually questioned extensively and all of them describe their exit from Syria and arrival at Gatwick in the same way.'

'I'm beginning to believe them,' said Stuart. 'I also want the other men who arrived with them brought in and questioned as I suspect they are also here illegally. I have their names and addresses. I want to know who is organising this traffic from Syria and put a stop to it.'

Stuart smiled at the nervous man who sat before him. 'Have you been treated well? No complaints?'

Ibrahim shook his head. Was he going to be sent to prison?

'Why did you decide to come to England?'

'We had heard that you were a peaceful country, people were not fighting each other over here like they are in Syria. So many people have died; those that have survived are often badly injured and their only shelter is a bombed building that is unsafe. Water mains are ruptured and there is often insufficient food for the people. It is not a good place to be now. We were also told that you needed professional men, particularly those with medical knowledge and we would be able to find work easily.'

'Surely you were needed in your own country?'

'That's true, but it is impossible to work over there. I was at the hospital in Aleppo. I did my best, but the electricity supply to an area was often interrupted for days at a time. I was removing shrapnel from an old man's chest and the lights went out. The X-ray machine was not working so I had no idea if there were internal injuries. I was in total darkness for a while. By the time the generator gave me some light I saw the man was dead.'

'That was not your fault. You were trying to save him.'

Ibrahim shook his head sadly. 'Had the X-ray machine been working I would have seen that some shrapnel had penetrated close to his heart and he had internal bleeding. I should have treated that injury first; his other wounds were superficial. Two days later the hospital was bombed and all our equipment was destroyed. I moved to Damascus and worked there. That hospital was also bombed. We were doing whatever we could for the injured out in the open.'

Stuart felt sympathy for the man, but he was sure that many other people could tell even more harrowing stories.

'Why did you not cross the border into Jordan as many other refugees have done?'

'We would have been no better off there. We would have been placed in a camp along with hundreds of others and still facing the same problems. We were assured that if we paid we could safely escape to England and be welcomed here.'

'Well, we do need many more people working in health care, but you cannot just enter a country and expect to be given a hospital job when we do not know if you are qualified.'

'I have all my certificates with me.'

'I don't disbelieve you, but under the circumstances we are unable to contact the hospitals in either Aleppo or Damascus and ask for a reference and unfortunately your certificates are in Arabic.'

'They could be translated,' replied Ibrahim eagerly.

'We'll discuss that at a later date. I'd like you to tell me again exactly how you arranged to leave Syria and describe your journey here.'

'I've told you, and the other men who questioned me. I know you don't believe me, but it's the truth.'

'I do believe you,' Stuart assured him. 'I know the flight you arrived on from Crete. I also know you had some other companions on the flight as well as the men we have detained. We already have their names and addresses and we are going to bring them in for questioning. It will make us look more sympathetically at your case if you are co-operative. Now, let's start at the beginning. Who told you they could arrange for you to leave Syria?'

Ibrahim sighed. There was no point in him claiming ignorance if this man already had details of his companions and was going to help him.

'I had made my way to the coast where it appeared to be safer. I was approached by a man and told that if I had sufficient funds to pay him he could provide me with a safe passage to England.'

'How much did he ask for?'

'Twenty thousand dollars.'

Stuart looked at Ibrahim in surprise. 'Did you have that kind of money?'

Ibrahim nodded. 'When the Civil War started I drew out my savings in dollars from the bank. I thought they could collapse at any moment and I would lose everything. I carried the money around with me in a belt. Other people did the same.'

'So you handed over this money without further question?'

'No, I was invited to go onto his boat and he explained the details to me. It seemed quite straight forward and easy. I was given the choice; hand over my money which would guarantee me a place on the boat or walk away. I decided to take the chance and accept.'

'So what happened next?'

'I did as I had been instructed and took some clothes on board.

The following evening I returned and there were five other men there who also wanted to go to England. That night we left the harbour and began to sail down the coast.'

'Rather a dangerous undertaking,' commented Stuart. 'How small was this boat?'

'A reasonable size and it had a motor.'

'How many days were you at sea?'

'I'm not sure. It may have been three, possibly four if you count the nights.'

'What were the conditions like on the boat?'

Ibrahim shrugged. 'We were given plenty of food, had a bathroom and bunks to sleep in. Once we were out of sight of the land we were allowed up on deck.'

'Now, the name of the owner of this boat?'

'It was either Ivan or Panos. They were the only two men aboard apart from us.'

'Which port did you land in? Heraklion?'

Ibrahim shook his head. 'I don't know. We could see the land and when it was dark we sailed in closer to the shore. We then had to climb down into a dinghy and we were rowed ashore. There was a woman with a car waiting for us as we had been promised.'

'It must have been quite a large car to accommodate all of you. Who drove it?'

'The woman and there was plenty of room for six of us.'

'How long did this drive take from where you landed until you reached the hotel?'

'I'm not sure. I think I dozed off until we stopped and the man got in.'

'What man was this?'

'He said he was the hotel owner. He took us up to our rooms and ordered food for us. He told us we had to stay up there and do exactly as he said if we wanted to arrive safely in England.'

Stuart nodded. 'Do you know the name of this hotel?'

Again Ibrahim shook his head. 'It was a big hotel and we were taken in and out by the back entrance.'

'Tell me exactly what happened whilst you were there. How did you spend your time?'

'We were told we had to stay in our rooms unless we were taken down to the dining room in the evenings.'

'Now your passports; how did you come by those?'

'A man came and took our photographs. Our new passports were given to us that evening so we could book our flights.'

'If you were supposed to stay in your rooms how did you book your flights? Was it done over the internet?'

'We were taken to a travel agent by a woman. It may have been the one who drove the car. She did all the talking. We none of us speak Greek. She also took us to a shoe shop so we could buy some proper shoes.'

'Who paid for these shoes and your flights?'

'We did. We were given Euros whilst we were there and also some sterling when we left.'

Stuart frowned. 'How did you get to the airport?'

'We were taken there by car.'

'How long did the journey to the airport from the hotel take?'

'Not very long. Maybe twenty minutes.'

Stuart sat back. 'Right, let's go through these questions again. Your passports are being checked for validity and from the information you have given me they are illegal. You might be able to remember some more details.'

Ibrahim sighed. 'I've told you everything. You won't send me to prison, will you?'

Having finished questioning Ibrahim, Stuart moved first to Salim and then on to Mohamed. Salim confirmed that he had travelled with Ibrahim and the details of their information coincided. Mohamed had arrived in the same fashion but at a later date and with other men.

August 2015
Week Two

Ronnie and Kyriakos enthused over Cathy and Vasilis's apartment.

'Ronnie is so clever knowing exactly the colours that will blend and go together.' Kyriakos smiled at her fondly.

'You were instrumental in suggesting that the hallway be removed. That made so much difference to the proportions of the bedroom,' rejoined Ronnie.

'I think you both deserve our compliments,' smiled Vasilis. 'I will certainly be calling upon your knowledge and expertise in the future, Ronnie.'

'Are you planning to redecorate already?' asked Kyriakos.

'Goodness, no. I am more than happy with the way it looks. I'm thinking of when our new apartment has been built, but that's a long way ahead.' He winked at Ronnie.

'You will have to start charging for your expertise.'

Ronnie shook her head. 'I couldn't possibly charge my friends. What do you think of the painting, Cathy? Is it what you wanted? I can always do another of you're not satisfied.'

'It's perfect. I'm going to have it framed and placed on the wall over there, unless you can think of anywhere more suitable?'

Saffron and Vasi were equally as enthusiastic. 'I know you asked me for suggestions,' smiled Saffron, 'But I would never have come up with the colour schemes that Ronnie suggested. I suppose I am used to white walls everywhere.'

'Maybe we should think about changing them,' suggested Vasi.

Saffron shook her head. 'We don't want to make decisions like that at the moment. If we can find somewhere else suitable to live we could go ahead with turning the house into a self catering establishment next year. White walls would be a lot easier to deal with. Any marks that were made could easily be covered over. If the walls were coloured it could be difficult to get the paint to match and it would mean redecorating a whole room.'

'Do you think that would be practical?' asked Vasilis.

Vasi nodded. 'Both practical and profitable. Unless you are visiting there's just Saffie and myself there. Half of the rooms are never used, but we still have to pay the heating bills during the winter, have the windows washed regularly and employ a cleaner in the season. These expenses would still occur but someone else would be paying for them. If we were living in a smaller house the expenses for us would be halved. We'd have to spend a bit of money in the first instance, some new furniture and bedding, that sort of thing, possibly redecorate, but it would be a good investment.'

Vasilis shook his head sadly. He knew Vasi had never been very happy living up on the hill in such a large house. He wondered what his son would think of the dimensions of the new apartment he was planning to build.

Once the other men on the list in his possession had been detained, along with any other Syrians who were sharing the same lodging rooms Stuart had relieved them of their passports and sent them off to be checked and verified. He now studied the report he had received from the passport authorities. The numbers on the passports that had been confiscated were correct but the names and details differed from the originals that had been issued. In each case the official holder was either confirmed as died or had not renewed their passport once the expiry date was reached due to their age.

Armed with this information he contacted the British Vice Consulate in Heraklion and spent over an hour explaining his concerns.

'Their passports will have been checked by security when they pass through to the departure lounges.'

'I know, but as they are holding passports that purport to be British they are only given a cursory glance and waved through. Are you able to arrange for a more thorough scrutiny to take place? As far as we are aware it is only those of Syrian nationality who are taking advantage of the lax procedure. You might turn up a few more.'

'I suppose that is possible. The airport staff will have to be alerted to the problem. I'll have a word with the Chief Inspector of Police here. It would be helpful if he was willing to provide a few men posing as security. If a discrepancy is found they could detain the suspect immediately and take them for questioning.'

Chief Inspector Solomakis listened carefully to the information Inspector Antonakis imparted to him.

'Are you seriously suggesting that men are being brought into the country illegally and staying at "The Central"? That's a respectable hotel. No one staying there has ever given us any cause for concern.'

'I'm sure none of the usual guests are a problem, but if I thought visitors were being brought to a hotel in Aghios Nikolaos in the way I have described I would certainly want to investigate.'

'So what do you want me to do? Raid the place? If we're wrong and there's an innocent explanation we'll be sued.'

'I am placing my men in the area again this week. I'm arranging for another to be in the vicinity where he can check the number plate of the car as it goes past. There is only the one road and there's not likely to be any other traffic around at that time in the morning so he won't miss it. He will call me with the registration details and I'll pass these on to you. If the car goes to "The Central" allow the occupants to go inside and then take control of the car. If our suspicions are correct there will be evidence inside. Wait fifteen minutes and then send your men inside. According to our information the new arrivals will have been taken up to the fourth floor. We want them all brought in for questioning. Make sure you have a search warrant and it could be a good idea to have one prepared for the hotel owner's private residence as well.'

'Six men, you say?'

'We are expecting six passengers to be in the back of the car. We want the driver so see where they disappear to. They're obviously involved.'

'Any idea who that is?'

'According to our information it will be a woman.'

Chief Inspector Solomakis sighed deeply. 'That's going to mean I have to put extra men on duty. Our resources are stretched as it is. We've been asked to provide extra security at the airport. Some suspicion of travellers with illegal passports.'

Vasilis drove down to his building plot and was pleased to see that Mr Sukiyakis was there with a digger that was removing the top surface of the land along with the rubbish and depositing it into the back of a tip up truck.

'How are you getting on?' asked Vasilis of Mr Sukiyakis.

'Should be ready to start marking out the dimensions tomorrow.' He waved his hand towards some metal stakes with hooks on the end. 'I'll let you know when we've finished and you can come down and have a look. I can walk you around then so you have an idea of the size and location of the rooms. What you see down here will be the same as we mark out higher up. If you want any alterations then would be the time to say. Once you agree the layout down here we can start digging the holes to take the steel uprights. We'll have to hire a crane to take them off the lorry and then to put them in position.'

'Don't you have one?'

'Rarely have the need. It would be sitting around uselessly for most of the year. Cheaper to hire one for a few days.'

The man in charge of the digger switched off his machine and climbed down onto the ground. He looked at the exposed earth suspiciously and kicked at something with his boot.

'Come and have a look at this,' he called

Mr Sukiyakis walked over, Vasilis hesitated and then followed him. Mr Sukiyakis and the digger operator both crouched down and began to examine something that was protruding from the soil. Mr Sukiyakis straightened up and turned to Vasilis.

'That's it, I'm afraid. We can't continue.'

'Why not?' asked Vasilis. 'Do you need me to pay you some more money?'

Mr Sukiyakis shook his head. 'I'll have to notify the police. We've found some bones.'

'Bones? They're probably from a dead sheep or goat.'

Mr Sukiyakis shook his head. 'They look like human bones. By law we have to notify the police and they'll send a forensic team down to look at them. We can't do any more until they give permission. We could be unearthing old bones or someone who has been buried recently. We can't take a chance that we're interfering with a crime scene.'

Vasilis looked at him in disbelief. 'How long is this going to take?'

'No idea. I expect the police will arrive shortly and cordon off the area. They'll leave someone here on duty and no one, not even you, Mr Iliopolakis, will be allowed on the land. You might as well go home.'

'I'll wait for the police to arrive.' Vasilis hoped it might be Panayiotis who came to investigate.

Inspector Antonakis shook his head in despair. His men were used to dealing with traffic accidents and an occasional unexpected, but natural, death. None of them had ever been involved in a possible murder enquiry. He had instructed Achilles to go to the building site as quickly as possible and report his findings, hoping to have it confirmed that the bones belonged to a dead animal not a human. Now, an hour later, Achilles had called to say that he had carefully scraped away some more soil and considered the long bones he had revealed were definitely human.

'Are you going to remove them?' asked Vasilis of Achilles.

Achilles shook his head. 'I can't do that. I've already interfered with them more than I should have done. I wanted to make sure they were human before I asked for forensics to attend. There's nothing more to be done until they've unearthed them properly and examined them.'

Vasilis felt sick. He would have to tell Cathy that there had been a body buried on the land and she might refuse to have their apartment built there.

The whole of the police force had heard about the discovery of the bones down on the beach road. Panayiotis approached Inspector Antonakis.

'I'd like to volunteer for the night duty to ensure no one disturbs the bones. It's an ideal spot. I can sit in the cab of the digger and I'll be able to see the Mercedes if it passes and check the number plate. I'll be in uniform so if anyone comes onto the land I'll have authority to turn them away.'

Inspector Antonakis nodded. It would save having yet another man on a night duty.

Achilles had cordoned off the area and stood at the perimeter to turn away any curious spectators. Two men from the forensic team had arrived at the site and began to unearth and examine the bones.

Vasilis had spoken to Panayiotis who confirmed that no work on the site could progress until the forensic result came through.

'Even then you may have to wait a while longer. If by any chance the person was murdered the whole area will have to be examined, although it is doubtful that anything of any use will be found. The burial must have occurred some years ago as the area was completely overgrown. There's nothing you can do to speed the process up.'

'When will they let me know the outcome?'

Panayiotis shrugged. 'Depends upon what they find.'

'Would you be able to tell me? I don't want to be waiting around for weeks for an official notification. I'd like Mr Sukiyakis to return to the work as soon as possible.'

Vasilis watched from a distance as the bones were placed in plastic bags, marked and then loaded into a cardboard box. It was evident that the remains did not belong to an animal or the men would not be so meticulous. Finally one approached him.

'I understand that you are the owner of the land?'

Vasilis nodded. 'I purchased it earlier this year. I'm having it cleared so I can build here. I have permission and the plans have been agreed. Can the work continue?'

The man shook his head. 'I'm afraid not, sir. In our opinion these bones are old, very old. This could be an important ancient burial site. The whole area will have to be excavated by a team of archaeologists.'

Vasilis looked at him in horror. 'How long is that going to take?'

'I can't say. It would depend upon how many more bodies were found. If it turns out that there is only the one then examination of the site should take no longer than a week. If it turns out to be a complete cemetery it will take an indefinite amount of time. I'm sure they would do their best to complete the excavations by the beginning of November before the weather becomes unpleasant.'

'November! I'd hoped to have the basic building structure up by then.'

'I'm sorry, sir. There's nothing any of us can do. You will just have to be patient.'

Vasilis returned to his car. This was a problem that he had not expected to encounter.

Sotiris and Yiorgo parked their car and walked back down the road both, hoping an arrival would take place that night having spent the previous two hidden in the darkness and seeing no sign of the car or men arriving on the beach.

'Standing behind that hedge gives me the creeps,' shuddered Sotiris. 'Could we change places?'

'Better not to at this late stage. You should have said earlier.'

'You knew I was worried about snakes.'

'Just as likely to be one in amongst the stones of that building where I am. They usually hide away until the sun is up.'

'Panayiotis might be willing to change with me,' suggested Sotiris hopefully.

'He's on bone watch. With luck we'll not have to be here again after tonight.'

'The Superintendent will probably put me on bone watch then,' remarked Sotiris gloomily.

'That wouldn't be so bad. The rubbish and plant growth has all been cleared from the site.'

'I don't want to be sitting there if it's a recent body that's been buried. The murderer could set about me.'

Yiorgo laughed. 'If you had murdered and buried someone would you go back if the bones had been discovered? I certainly wouldn't want to draw attention to myself by showing any interest. I ought to get down to the windmill. I don't want the car to arrive before me.'

'You'd see the lights as they drove across the Causeway,' said Sotiris, still unwilling to leave the safety of the road and go behind the hedge.

'Yes, and then they might see me scuttling to get into position, turn round and drive off. I'll see you later.'

Panayiotis sat in the cab of the digger. This was the most comfortable surveillance he had ever been called upon to undertake. He watched Sotiris and Yiorgo drive along the road and settled back in the seat to wait, hoping the Mercedes would arrive that night.

Now it was August there was more traffic on the road from Heraklion to Aghios Nikolaos and Ludmila had been held up behind two coaches and knew she was arriving later than usual. She would have to leave earlier in future. She hoped Panos had not tried to deliver the men and returned them to the boat as she had not signalled him. She drove swiftly down the road to Elounda, only slowing sufficiently to negotiate the turn down the steep hill. Once on the coast road she increased her speed again and by the time she had driven across the Causeway and parked behind the windmill she was no more than fifteen minutes late. She could hear the splash of oars and hurried across the rough ground and up the road to the beach, arriving as Panos emerged from the canal.

The men jumped ashore and they waited whilst Panos returned to the boat and collected the other three along with the bag of money and their mobile 'phones that he threw across to her. Immediately she led the men to the car and waited impatiently whilst they placed their carrier bags into the cases and pulled on their white shirts.

She drove more steadily back across the Causeway and along the road. If she kept Evgeniy waiting it would be due to the volume of traffic she encountered, although she knew he would not be pleased. He liked to have the men up in their rooms before the other guests began to appear. Had he not been dependent upon Lanassakis to clean the car he would have sacked him; the man was always in the car park when he arrived and watched as the men went into the hotel.

Panayiotis checked that the registration of the Mercedes that passed him was the same as the one he had noted previously and once the car lights had disappeared he took out his mobile 'phone and called the Inspector.

'Panayiotis here. The car has passed me on its return journey. Number plate confirmed.'

He heard Inspector Antonakis yawn. 'I'll contact Heraklion. You stay there until you are relieved.'

Chief Inspector Solomakis did not appreciate having to be in his office by five in the morning. He had become used to arriving at eight, having had a full night's sleep, once he was promoted to Chief Inspector. He went to the canteen where the officers were waiting for him, most having their heads down on the table snatching some sleep.

'On your feet,' he commanded loudly and the men responded with alacrity.

'All of you fully awake and listening?' he asked. 'I don't want to have to repeat myself. You are all to keep out of sight until you have seen the Mercedes drive into the car park. Once the occupants have entered the hotel one of you will watch the car until a transporter arrives. We plan to give it a thorough examination. No one is allowed to touch it for any reason. The rest of you then enter the hotel, one of you stationed at the front entrance, one by the lifts and another on each floor where you can watch both the lift and the stairs. You send anyone trying to go down to the main foyer back to their room with instructions to stay there until they are told they can leave. If anyone refuses you show your badge and threaten arrest. The rest of you make your way to the fourth floor. It is most likely you will find the men up there in one of the rooms. They are all to be brought in for questioning. Any resistance and you cuff them.'

'What time should the car be arriving?' asked Manolis.

'Around six, so get yourselves organised and in position.'

'Heavy traffic,' Ludmila muttered to Evgeniy as she exited the car, taking the bag from beneath the driver's seat with her.

Evgeniy nodded. He would tell her she needed to leave earlier in future. He spoke to the men who were sitting in the back of the car, giving them their instructions for when they arrived at the hotel. As he drew into the car park he saw that Lanassakis was already there. He would have to think of something that would occupy the man elsewhere.

He opened the doors for the men and took out their cases, repeating his instructions that they should take the lifts to the fourth floor. 'Wipe your feet before you enter.' he ordered.

Lanassakis walked over to the car with the intention of commencing cleaning the interior and Manolis hurried over.

'The car must not be touched, sir.'

Lanassakis frowned. 'I have to clean the car. Mr Kuzmichov insists that it is done whenever it returns from the airport.'

'Today it will have to wait. It can't be that dirty.'

'It always comes back wet and dirty in the back. I have to wash the mats, clean the wheels along with the windscreen and lights. I have to do as Mr Kuzmichov says or I could lose my job. He pays me an extra five Euros to clean the car.'

'The car will be removed shortly. It could be relevant to our enquiries. Any problem and we'll explain to him. You just do as I say and no blame will be attached to you.'

Unconvinced and worried Lanassakis turned away. He did not want to lose his job. 'Mr Kuzmichov will not be pleased,' he muttered.

Unconcerned about any noise they made the police began to open the doors to the rooms on the fourth floor. In the conference room they found six frightened men.

'Say nothing,' Kuzmichov ordered them in Arabic. 'Is there a problem?' he asked, trying to smile and appear relaxed. 'I hope there is a good reason for your intrusion.'

'We have orders to take you in for questioning.'

'Questioning? I can answer your question now. I have just collected some guests from the airport.'

'Then you'll be able to prove that and have nothing to worry about.'

'I absolutely refuse to have my guests treated in this manner. Please leave immediately.'

'Do I understand that you are not prepared to accompany me to the station?'

'You are quite correct. There is no reason for any of us to accompany you anywhere.'

'Cuff them,' said the officer curtly and his associates hurriedly obeyed.

'I object to being treated like a criminal,' remonstrated Evgeniy. 'I am a respectable hotelier.'

The policeman shrugged. 'Just following my orders, sir.'

Evgeniy sat sullenly before Chief Inspector Solomakis. His mobile had been removed upon arriving at the police station so he had no way to alert Ludmila. She would probably be asleep anyway and not concerned that he had not arrived back at their apartment until later in the day.

'I think we need to go over your statement again, Mr Kuzmichov. There are a few contradictions that I would like to clear up. You say you collected the men from the airport?'

Evgeniy nodded. He would continue to tell the police officer that he had collected the men from the airport. They were the only people who could contradict him and they were not likely to admit they had entered the country illegally and if they did their story was unlikely to be believed.

'Can you tell me their flight number?'

'I didn't make a note of it.'

'Isn't it usual to check the time of arrival? Their flight could have been delayed and you could have spent a considerable amount of time sitting at the airport.'

Evgeniy shrugged. 'Delays are usually no longer than twenty minutes or so. Better to wait than return to my hotel.'

'And from which airport had their flight come from?'

'I didn't ask. It is none of my business where guests have come from.'

'We understand that your car made an earlier journey down to Elounda. Why would it have done that?'

'Nothing to do with me. Someone must have borrowed it without my permission.'

Solomakis raised his eyebrows. 'Who else has access to your car?'

'Only my wife.'

'So is it likely she would have taken it out in the early hours of the morning without your knowledge?'

'Possibly.'

'Is she in the habit of doing that?'

'She doesn't sleep well. I want to contact my lawyer. I'm allowed a 'phone call.' He would have to call Ludmila and tell her to leave the house and take the contents of the safe with her.

'All in good time, Mr Kuzmichov. The men who were detained with you are being questioned. If they are able to prove that they arrived at the airport then you will be free to leave. In the meantime my men will be bringing in your car for a thorough examination and remain stationed inside your hotel.'

'That's preposterous. A police presence will upset my current guests.'

'I don't think they will be unduly disturbed.'

'I will sue the police. They have no reason to visit my hotel and harass my guests.'

'Mr Kuzmichov your car has been seen on a number of occasions travelling to a deserted area just outside the village of Elounda and returning with men who had been collected from a nearby beach. When you arrived at the hotel this morning you had a number of foreign gentlemen passengers and I do not think you collected them from the airport. We think that is sufficient reason for us to go to your hotel and conduct further investigations unless you are able to give us a convincing explanation.'

Vasilis sat before Cathy miserably. 'I've been told the bones were old. They think the land may have been used as a cemetery at some time.'

'How old?'

'I don't know. They have got to be carefully examined and archaeologists may have to go over the whole site. It could take months before Sukiyakis is given permission to continue.'

'Don't be so depressed. We have an ideal apartment to live in and can stay here as long as we wish. I'm glad the bones are old. I would not have been very happy to know a murder victim had been buried there. I think it could be quite exciting to know that it was a cemetery, particularly if it dates back some hundreds of years. You never know what they might find.'

'It would suit me if they only found the one body,' remarked Vasilis.

'Of course, it could have been used as a burial place for local leprosy sufferers before they were all sent off to Spinalonga. I'm sure John would be fascinated if that were the case.'

'He might be, but I'm not,' declared Vasilis vehemently as he heard the call signal for his mobile 'phone. 'Maybe that's the forensic team saying work can continue,' he said hopefully.

'Mr Iliopolakis, this is terrible.'

'What's wrong, Dimitra?'

'The hotel. It has been closed down.'

'Closed? Calm down, Dimitra. Tell me exactly what has happened. Has there been a fire?'

'No, Mr Kuzmichov has been arrested.'

'Arrested?'

'The police arrived this morning; lots of them, and they came up to this floor and into the conference room. Mr Kuzmichov was there with six men. The police arrested all of them and they said the hotel was closed down with immediate effect.'

'What about the guests who are staying?

'They're all being thoroughly checked and then given permission to stay. A lot of them have been phoning around and have found somewhere else to go, but no new visitors can be accepted. It's been pandemonium here. The managers and reception have been completely overwhelmed.'

'So what has this to do with you, Dimitra?'

'They asked Mrs Planatakis if she had noticed anything unusual about any of the guests. She told them that the maids had been refused access to the rooms on this floor. They came up and questioned me. I had to admit that I had been concerned. This is why I have to go to the police station and make a statement. I'm scared, Mr Iliopolakis. Please can you come up and help?'

If you have enjoyed reading Evgeniy, you will be pleased to know that the next book is planned for publication in December 2019.

Read on for a 'taster' of what is to come......

NEXT BOOK

I have nothing to do with "The Central" any longer, Dimitra. I cannot just walk in as if I still owned it. I'm sure Mr Kuzmichov would be most offended and annoyed.'

'Mr Kuzmichov was taken away in handcuffs. The staff know and trust you and someone is needed here that they can turn to for advice.'

Vasilis sighed. 'When do you have to make a statement, Dimitra?'

'The police told me it was necessary to report to the police station later today and if I did not go they would come and arrest me.'

'I'm sure you would not be arrested. They would simply ask you to accompany them and provided you did so they could not arrest you.'

'Please, Mr Iliopolakis,' Dimitra sounded close to tears. 'Please come up and help me.'

'I'll need to speak to my wife and make some arrangements down here. I cannot just leave her alone. I'll call you back. Just do whatever the police say and you'll not be in any trouble.'

Vasilis turned to Cathy. 'That was Dimitra.'

'I gathered that. What was her problem?'

'Kuzmichov has been arrested and there's chaos at the hotel. She has been told she needs to make a statement and has asked me to go up and be with her and also see if I can be of any help in the hotel.'

'So are you going?'

'I want to have a word with Panyiotis before I make a decision. The hotel is really none of my business. If I have to make a statement about the information that Dimitra gave me originally and seeing Ludmila collect some men from the beach I may have to go up to Heraklion anyway.'

'Couldn't you do that here?' asked Cathy.

'That's why I need to speak to Panayiotis. I certainly I won't consider leaving you here alone if I have to stay over night.'

'I could go and stay with Saffron and Vasi.'

'They're both out most of the time.'

'Marianne, then.'

'She has her mother staying so she hasn't a spare room at the moment. If I do have to go to Heraklion the most practical solution is for you to come with me. I'll see if Panayiotis is home yet. He told me he was on duty down at the building site, guarding the bones. As if anyone would want to walk off with them!'

Panayiotis was in his dressing gown when he answered the door to Vasilis. 'I was just about to go to bed,' he remarked.

'I'm glad I caught you before you had gone to sleep. Can I come in for a minute?'

Panayiotis opened the door wider. 'I was going to call on you later. Some more men landed in the early hours and I understand Chief Inspector Solomakis arranged to visit the hotel.'

Vasilis nodded. 'That was one reason I have come to see you. I've had a call from Dimitra, the woman who mentioned the men to me in the first place, and she said they have arrested Kuzmichov. She has been questioned and asked to go to the station to make a statement. She's in a bit of a panic and has asked me to go up to Heraklion, not only to support her but also to see if I can be of any help at the hotel. Is that permissible?'

'Go up and support the lady if you wish, but bear in mind that you will also have to make a statement. I'm afraid I have had to name you as being the previous owner of the hotel and being out in the boat with me when we first saw the car and men arriving at the beach.'

'Why can't I make a statement here?'

'You can, but it would be sent up to Chief Inspector Solomakis along with our surveillance reports. If your ex-employee has said that she spoke to you regarding her concerns he may well ask you to confirm that. He has the authority to insist that you go up to the station in Heraklion. Could save you a visit at a later date when it's inconvenient.'

'Have you any idea when the forensic pathologists are going to start excavating and how long they will take?'

'No idea. No one had arrived when I handed over to Achilles this morning.'

'So if I did stay up in Heraklion for a few days I wouldn't be able to get on with building?'

'No way. You can be prosecuted if you even set foot on the land, despite the fact that you own it.'

Vasilis sighed. 'I thought all my problems were going to be over when I retired. They seem to be multiplying. There's no way Cathy can stay down here on her own and it isn't convenient at the moment for her to go and stay with either family or friends. She'll have to come with me. A shame Kuzmichov also bought our apartment; she'll have to sit in a hotel most of the time and be bored to tears.'

The knocking on the front door woke Ludmila. Evgeniy must have forgotten his key. She crawled out of bed and stumbled through the hallway. She unlocked the door and turned to go back to her bedroom.

'Excuse me, Madam. We are the police and we need to speak to you.'

Ludmila stopped. 'Has something happened to Evgeniy?'

'Mr Evgeniy Kuzmichov is your husband?'

Ludmila nodded.

'He is helping us with our enquiries and we would like you to get dressed and come to the police station.'

'Are you arresting me?'

'Why should we arrest you, Madam? At the moment we would just like your assistance.'

Ludmila shook her head. 'It is not convenient for me to accompany you. I wish to go back to bed. You woke me up.'

'If you refuse to accompany us voluntarily I will have to arrest you. Please go and get dressed or you will have to leave here in your nightclothes.'

Ludmila gave the officer a venomous look and returned to her bedroom. Had one of the refugees demanded his money back and assaulted Evgeniy? Even if such an event had occurred it was unlikely that Evgeniy would have reported the matter to the police, but he had not returned from the hotel after settling the men into their temporary accommodation. Hastily she donned a pair of jeans and a T-shirt after washing her face and brushing her hair. She certainly did not want to be seen leaving the apartment in handcuffs and wearing only her nightdress. Picking up her handbag and ensuring that she had her mobile 'phone, the keys to the apartment and the safe she returned to where the officer was waiting just inside the doorway.

Vasilis returned to his apartment. 'It appears that I may be asked to corroborate whatever statement Dimitra has made and also give my version of the events that I witnessed when I was out fishing with Panayiotis. Chief Inspector Solomakis is in charge of the enquiry and I know how difficult he can be to deal with. It's better that I approach him before he sends someone to arrest me.'

'Why on earth would he want to arrest you? You have not done anything wrong.'

'I know. I have nothing to worry about. I am only concerned

382

about you. Can you get a case packed? You'll have to come with me and I'll find a hotel where we can stay for a few days.'

'So you are going to offer help at "The Central"?'

'I expect I'll have to ask Solomakis's permission to go there and see what the situation is and if I can help. If he refuses we can come straight back down here, but it's best to be prepared to stay.'

'Couldn't we stay at "The Central"?'

Vasilis shrugged. 'I don't know, but I'd rather know you were safely settled somewhere as I have no idea how long I will be at the police station. I'll call Vasi and tell him we're going up to Heraklion.'

'What's wrong, Pappa?'

'A number of things. Far too complicated for me to go into over the 'phone at the moment. Cathy and I have to go to Heraklion and I'm not sure how long we will be staying. There are problems at "The Central". Nothing really to do with me, but Dimitra has asked me to go up and I need to make a statement to the police. I'm not in any trouble.'

'Well that's a relief. When you mentioned the police I thought you might have gone down to your land last night and dug up all the bones you could find.'

Vasilis sighed. 'I'm not allowed to set foot on the land. There's a police guard down there. All I can do is wait and see what transpires. I'll call you this evening and tell you exactly what the problems at "The Central" are.'

Evgeniy had been escorted to a holding cell and to his disgust had been locked in. 'I am not a common criminal,' he protested. 'I wish to consult my lawyer.'

'All in good time, sir. Once we have finished our enquiries you could well be released and then you will have no need of a lawyer.'

Evgeniy glared at him. 'I will still need to consult my lawyer and ask him to start proceedings against you for unlawful arrest. You have caused distress to my employees at the hotel and also to my guests. What will they have thought seeing me led away in handcuffs?'

Ludmila was escorted to an interview room and her handbag was taken from her. The contents were spread out on the table before her. She wished she knew exactly what was happening so she could have her own version of events ready.

The officer emptied the contents of her purse, finding that it contained only a reasonable quantity of Euros. The numbers stored on her mobile 'phone were scrolled through and the 'phone placed inside an evidence bag. Finally he picked up her bunch of keys.

'These are the keys to your apartment?'

Ludmila nodded.

'And this key?'

'It opens the safe.'

'Thank you. That could save us a good deal of trouble. Mrs Kuzmichov, we have a warrant that enables us to search your apartment and that includes opening the safe and examining the contents. What are we likely to find in there?'

'I have no idea. My husband is the only one who has access.'

'Yet you have a key?'

'That is only for me to use in an emergency. I am not allowed to open the safe.'

'What kind of emergency would that be, Madam?'

Ludmila shrugged. 'The unfortunate demise of my husband. He keeps his business accounts in there and I would need access to those if such an awful event happened.'

'Quite. What business would these papers relate to?'

'I imagine they contain information about the purchase of his hotel.'

The officer smiled thinly. 'Very likely. We will be taking your key to open the safe and ascertain the contents for ourselves.'

Ludmila swallowed nervously. She had placed the envelopes and mobile 'phones from the refugees in the safe before going to bed.